Lindsay McKenna is proud ~~~~~~~~~~~~~~~ in the US Navy as an aerogra~~~~~~~~~~~ known as a weather forecaster. She was a pioneer in the military romance subgenre and loves to combine heart-pounding action with soulful and poignant romance. True to her military roots, she is the originator of the long-running and reader-favourite Morgan's Mercenaries series. She does extensive hands-on research, including flying in aircraft such as a P3-B Orion sub-hunter and a B-52 bomber. She was the first romance writer to sign her books in the Pentagon bookstore. Visit her online at lindsaymckenna.com

Nicole Helm grew up with her nose in a book and the dream of one day becoming a writer. Luckily, after a few failed career choices, she gets to follow that dream—writing down-to-earth contemporary romance and romantic suspense. From farmers to cowboys, Midwest to *the* West, Nicole writes stories about people finding themselves and finding love in the process. She lives in Missouri with her husband and two sons, and dreams of someday owning a barn.

Discover more at millsandboon.co.uk

NO TURNING BACK

LINDSAY McKENNA

COLD CASE INVESTIGATION

NICOLE HELM

MILLS & BOON

First Published in Great Britain 2024
by Mills & Boon, an imprint of HarperCollins*Publishers* Ltd
1 London Bridge Street, London, SE1 9GF

www.harpercollins.co.uk

HarperCollins*Publishers*
Macken House, 39/40 Mayor Street Upper,
Dublin 1, D01 C9W8, Ireland

No Turning Back © 2024 Nauman Living Trust
Cold Case Investigation © 2024 Nicole Helm

ISBN: 978-0-263-32228-6

0524

This book contains FSC™ certified paper and other controlled sources to ensure responsible forest management.

For more information visit: www.harpercollins.co.uk/green

Printed and Bound in the UK using 100% Renewable Electricity at CPI Group (UK) Ltd, Croydon, CR0 4YY

NO TURNING BACK

LINDSAY McKENNA

To the wonderful, courageous people of Ukraine, who are so very brave, resilient and tenacious, who fiercely defend their freedom and their country. Having served in the military, I support your fight for continued democracy. Just know that the people of the USA are behind you 100 percent. We hold the people of Ukraine in our hearts.

Chapter One

November 1, 2021

Captain Ram Kozak was in a quagmire of emotions. On a cold, windy day, he took the steps out of the Ukrainian Army Headquarters in Kyiv. The sky was swollen and pregnant with dark and light gray clouds hanging over the sprawling, beautiful capital. In his hand he clutched a set of orders and that was what made his heart ache. As he climbed concrete steps up to the educational facility part of the massive complex, a shred of hope filtered through him, and the roiling in his gut temporarily subsided.

He was going to see Sergeant Darina Mazur, a US Army Special Forces combat medic on loan to the Ukrainian Army. She was teaching, he'd found out only earlier in the morning, advanced combat field surgery to Ukrainian Army medics. They needed this specialized training because the US Special Forces school was located in the USA and right now, it wasn't feasible for their medics to attend it half a world away. The news that Dare Mazur was the instructor hit him like a powerful emotional earthquake. He did his best to hide the shock as his colonel, who headed up SSO Third Special Purpose Regiment, their ops group known as the Black Wolf Brigade, hurried to meet the Russian threat coming in February 2022. The orders he'd been given were special, that Sgt. Mazur, an experienced field surgeon and combat medic, who had advanced lifesaving skills, would be taken out of the classroom and placed back into his team once more.

He slid his key code card into the slot, and his brown brows fell as he pulled open the thick bulletproof glass door and entered. Well-known for his poker face, Ram was sure his boss saw the shock in his eyes, if only momentarily. Four years earlier, his team had been in Afghanistan, on the front lines, at a top-secret US camp near the Pakistan border. Dare had been their combat medic, going out on every team mission with them, risking her life. She had been assigned to his team because their medic's tour was up and they needed a replacement. Ram wasn't against women in combat. Almost a fifth of the Ukrainian Army consisted of women in every specialty, including combat and some of them being field medics.

At twenty-five, he'd not been prepared for the easy-going, smiling U.S. Special Forces woman. Everyone called her Dare, and in the two years she spent with his team in Afghanistan, she certainly earned her nickname. Whatever hesitancy he had about the American woman dissolved. She might save lives, but she could take them, too, when it came to their mutual enemy, the Taliban and ISIS fighters. She was also cross-trained as a sniper, a backup to the two male snipers who were already on his team.

What he hadn't counted on was his falling in love with her. *That* was a shock to his system. How to remain her commanding officer and never reveal his need to share a personal relationship with her, whether on a mission, at the US camp or aiding her medical efforts to help the Afghan people of the surrounding villages. She was calm under fire. Her specialty, her gift, was her healing abilities, he'd discovered. It didn't matter if it was a camp dog with a bloodied paw, a child with a hurt finger or one of the elderly from nearby villages who needed her medical skills. She was present and accounted for. There was nothing he could dislike about her. Compassion wasn't his thing, but it was hers. Maybe it was her femininity, her softness and gentle nature instead of that testosterone team she was part of, that soothed the inner edges of himself, as well as the rest of his aggressive black ops team. He couldn't really define or quantify it, but Dare's presence was a gift.

Before he'd met her, his gut was always a churning, angry snake in the pit of his stomach when out on an op. He worried about every member of his team. He'd lost his entire family at age eighteen, and he'd adopted his team in the military as his pseudo-family, without consciously thinking about it. The team members were like brothers to him, tightly knit and close. When Dare came into the team, she was immediately absorbed by all of them in the best of ways, but he, as their officer and leader, had to remain remote and unemotional toward her, which was the last thing he wanted to do or be.

Grappling with his memories, he went inside the warm building, the waxed and shining sand-colored tile floor beneath his polished combat boots. He decided to take the stairwell to the third floor, where all the classrooms were located, slowing down, hesitant to meet her once again. The two years they'd been apart, she was given orders to come to Lviv, to teach advanced combat medicine to their Ukrainian Army medics. He thought with time and distance, his ache for her would dissolve. But it had not.

Dare had a minor in botany and loved flowers. The team would purposely keep an eye out for any poor, struggling, thirsty plant when out on an op, and give it to her. She could always identify it and she would smile with delight, her light blue eyes sparkling with joy, as she gently cradled the plant in her hands. She melted his tough outer walls that protected him from the emotions of everyday life. Somehow, she'd gotten through his shield and had gently held his vulnerable inner core that he'd never allowed anyone to get near. But she had. Maybe that's why he fell in love with her. Had she earned his trust? Ram didn't know and savagely stuffed all his fanciful wonderings back deep down inside himself. It had nothing to do with what was about to happen.

He hadn't solved or resolved his lovelorn situation regarding Dare after she received orders to leave his team and Afghanistan. Not wanting to lose touch with her, he continued to take photos with his smartphone during ops of any flowers he saw and later, back at camp, email them to her. Oh, it didn't happen often, but he just couldn't—didn't—want to disappear out of her life. The flower photos kept them in touch with one another every few months and gave hope to his lonely heart, fed his tightly boxed and heavily protected emotions and lifted him, made him feel half-human, but the interactions also continued to stoke the flames of desire for her. Trudging slowly and reluctantly up the steps, he halted at the security door to the third floor, scowling, feeling like a coward. The envelope in his shirt pocket contained her orders. Ram had asked to deliver them personally to her and his boss gave his okay.

Recently, she was transferred to main HQ in Kyiv to continue her teaching duties. Sometimes, she would send him an email, but it would be of Adam Vorona's two young girls, Sofia and Anna, who were six and eight years old. She stayed with them at Adam's home in the village of Bucha, just outside of Kyiv, on weekends. Lera, his wife, would take photos of the three of them painting, drawing or looking at a bunch of plants and flowers spread out on the long wooden table in their kitchen.

He absorbed Dare's smile, the merriment in her eyes, as the girls would spontaneously wrap their small, thin arms around her waist or her neck, adoring her. They called her Auntie Dare. Those photos were priceless to him: water on the desert of his heavily protected and unavailable heart. At times, he would pull out his cell phone that the photos were on and absorb them hungrily, starved for a little humanity. But in his line of work? Emotions could get one killed. Worse, the terror of one of his men getting killed because he'd allowed his emotions to overwhelm his bear-trap mental faculties that kept them all alive haunted him.

For whatever unknown reason, Dare sated his inner emotional thirst, and it was that simple and that complicated, not to mention a complete mystery to him. There were no easy answers for Ram on the silent love he'd carried for Dare over the years. He thought she was still in Lviv, but he'd just found out the Ukraine Army had transferred her to Kyiv six months ago.

His team had been on the move, sent over to the United

States for advanced training in certain weapons, and they'd just gotten back less than a week ago. And now this: orders concerning Dare and his team. They had this odd, out-of-kilter relationship, but there was always a warm trust that simmered just below the surface between them, never spoken about by either of them. After all, he'd never let on how he really felt about her. That was on him.

AFTER HER MORNING CLASS, Dare was finishing up packing the intubation mannequin used to teach her ten Ukrainian medic students how to insert a tube into a human throat. She hauled the bulky piece of luggage to the closet at the back of the large room. The last student from her class had departed ten minutes earlier and she was almost finished with her duties before she left for the day. This was her classroom, with large windows showing the turbulent weather outside. Fondly, she looked around, loving her job, loving being in Ukraine. Since she spoke their language like a local, it was sheer enjoyment for her, as well.

Her students were surprised on the first day of class when she told them she had dual citizenship with the US and Ukraine. Her ability to speak their language was flawless, plus she knew a third language, Russian. She wore her US Army uniform, mottled gray, white and black camouflage fatigues, during the winter season.

Turning, she hauled the huge suitcase to the open closet, sliding it in, pushing it to the rear. There were many other medical cases piled high with apparatuses. Straightening, she was satisfied the case was where it needed to be.

There was a light knock at the door. Frowning, she backed out of the closet, looking toward it. Her lips parted.

Her heart dropped and pounded in her chest as she stared right into the gold-brown eyes of Captain Ram Kozak. She moved from the closet, shutting it and then looking at where he stood in the partially opened door, his gaze as implacable and unreadable as usual.

She grinned. "Well, well, look what the cat dragged in," and she smiled fully, dusting off her hands as she walked toward him. A powerful warmth, much more than casual friendship, sizzled through her unexpectedly. Ram always made her feel feminine in the male world of the military. As CO and officer of his Black Wolf team, he had a powerful draw for her. Dare knew the military would never allow an officer and enlisted person, such as herself, to have a personal relationship with one another. It simply wouldn't happen. Swallowing her disappointment, she smiled in welcome as she drew near to him.

Ram entered the room. "You look well, Dare. Is everything going right in your world?"

She halted a few feet from him, speaking in Ukrainian. "Everything is fine," and then she grimaced. "Well, no, not everything. The Russians are coming," and she sighed. Pointing to a metal desk and chair, she said, "It's good to see you again. Come and sit down? I've been on my feet for three hours and my puppies are howling."

He managed a slight lift of one corner of his mouth, taking a seat at a desk that was opposite of where she sat, a few feet separating them. "You Americans have more strange sayings than I can keep track of, Dare."

She felt her face heating up. She was blushing just getting to sponge in Ram's always unreadable face. But his gold-colored eyes telling her he was happy to see her made her relax. "I know, we love our memes and sayings. How long has it been since we've last seen one another? Two years now since our last face-to-face?"

Nodding, he looked around the light, airy room. "I know you were teaching in Lviv, but I didn't know you had been transferred here to Kyiv six months ago. Seems like so long ago. Does it to you?" He met and held her softening gaze.

"Sometimes it seems like yesterday and sometimes much longer than two years. I missed all of you," she admitted, losing her smile. "I talk to Adam often, and he fills me in on your team who just came back to Kyiv from many months of US training. He said they're awaiting a new assignment being given to you. Is that true?"

"We missed you, too. And yes, we've got a new assignment."

"I never know when you're around, Ram. Every time I tell Adam I should come over and see you, you're gone again. He'd told me you live in a village south of Kyiv."

"My apartment is an hour's drive from the city center. My team just spent twelve weeks in the US," he admitted. "While I was learning tactics and strategy at the Pentagon, the rest of my men went to a couple of other nearby Army bases. There was a group of field-grade officers who went on this training and education program, and I was selected to be one of them." He sighed. "With the Russians going to attack, the US Army offered to train us up on some things we were either rusty on or didn't know about, giving us the latest tactical advantages that they are sharing with us as a country. It was a useful time we spent in the States."

"Adam went with you," she said, nodding. "Lera, his wife, and I would spend weekends with the girls at their home in Bucha. She kept me updated on all of your travels to the US for special, ongoing training."

"Yes, some of my team were learning how to handle a Javelin tank killer that the US has. We received the intel and received the training we needed. It worked out well."

"I haven't spoken to Adam since he got home a few days ago. I'm sure he did well?"

"Yes. All my men passed their field tests. They are the best." He frowned and unbuttoned his shirt pocket, pulling out a folded piece of paper. "You know Adam—he's smart and catches on to new information fast. We have six men in our team who are now qualified to use the Javelin shoulder-carry weapon, and that's a relief to me. Our two snipers refined their skills at another base."

"Everyone thinks Putin will send tanks first into your country."

"In February of 2022. That's what our intel people say as well as what the Pentagon is confirming. Their intel people have been picking up a lot of unprotected cell phone chatter from the Russians," he admitted heavily. "They're coming in the dead of winter so that the soil is frozen and Putin's tanks can roll swiftly across the countryside to get into Ukraine and destroy us. If he tried to do that in January, the ground is still freezing."

"In March," Dare said, "it begins to thaw and his tanks will sink up to their drive sprocket in mud and the treads will come off and they'll be sitting ducks for those Javelins your guys have been trained on."

"Exactly right." He opened the paper and frowned. "I've got some news that may be very upsetting to you, Dare."

She sat up, frowning. "Are those orders?"

"Yes."

"Don't tell me they're sending me back to the States, Ram. I won't go. My place is here. My adopted parents are Ukrainian. I feel this is my homeland, too, and I don't want to be sent away when the going gets tough around here."

He gave her a painful look and handed the paper to her. "I have no say in this. Read?"

She reached for the extended papers, her fingertips brushing his. The ache in her heart for this man, who was incredibly closed up, remained an enigma to her. How badly she wanted to know him on equal emotional footing, having been drawn to him since she met him in Afghanistan so long ago. The officer/enlisted issue always surfaced. She saw his eyes darken and he looked away for a moment, his mouth thinning and tightening.

The orders were written in Ukrainian and she could easily read them. Gasping, she managed in a strangled tone to say, "I'm being ordered back into *your team*? As your combat field medic?" She stared at the orders, reread them several times and then drilled a look into his unhappy looking gaze. "These are legit?" and she waved the papers in his direction. "Seriously, Ram? You're not playing a joke on me, are you?"

"I wish it was a joke," he answered heavily, pushing his fingers through his short, dark hair after taking off his cap. "It's for real, Dare."

"Wow," she uttered, amazed and shocked. "I'm on your team again?"

"Yes. My CO wanted to call you in, but I asked if I could break the news to you myself."

Setting the paper aside on the desk, she muttered, "You don't sound happy about this, Ram. Are *you* okay with this?"

He sat up, pushing his large hands palm down on the thighs of his winter fatigues, holding her gaze. "On a personal level? This is the last place I'd want you to be, Dare. On a professional level, you are fully competent in the field. Everyone knows you are reliable and a strong team member. Everyone trusts you. We wouldn't be breaking in a new field medic, so for the team? I know they'll be happy to have you returning to our fold."

Scowling, she reread the orders. "Did you ask for me?" she demanded, holding his narrowing gaze.

"Hell no! I want you safe. I wanted you out of our country. What's coming early sometime next year are Russians who never take prisoners. You've never seen them in action, and I have." He snapped his mouth shut, a lot of emotions boiling to the surface within him, coloring his tone of voice. He shook his head, giving her an apologetic look for his sudden outburst.

Dare blinked in shock over his unexpected outburst. It was completely out of character for him to become so emotional. It set her spinning and she didn't have time to analyze why. There was anguish in his face for a split second and then it was gone. Feeling like she'd been wrapped in a sudden, violent storm, she dragged in a deep breath, the silence hanging jaggedly between them. "The men and women in my class have been talking about the Russian invasion. I've heard all the war stories, Ram. I understand how brutal they are."

His fist had clenched on the desk and he forced himself to try to relax. "I know firsthand what they are capable of, Dare. I don't want you out in the field with anyone, not even my team. It's not safe…"

Her mouth quirked and she laid the orders aside. "War is never safe and we both know that," she parried gently. "The Taliban and ISIS were just as evil and brutal as the Russians."

He shook his head, his voice dropping to a growl. "No… I can make that comparison, and you can't. I've seen first-hand what they are capable of doing and I don't want you out in the field at all, with anyone, not even my team."

"I suppose you told your CO that?" She saw a tortured expression in his gaze for a fleeting moment before that poker face of his moved back into place.

"I told my CO that I didn't want you in the field." He swallowed hard, looked away and then held her steady gaze. "I lost the argument with him because he knows your ser-vice record and courage. I pleaded with him to let you stay on as an instructor-educator, not to be sent out onto the battlefield." His voice lowered and he shook his head. "Our two years in Afghanistan with you as a member made him adamant that you were going back into the field with us because the higher-ups were desperate for your skills and experience."

"Because we were a good team and got the job done. I know our stats for locating and finding the enemy were consistently high. But it wasn't just me. It was the whole team working as one."

Unhappily he stared at her. "Yes, we were too damned good together, the ten of us. You saved Artur's life, and my CO was very impressed with the field surgery you per-formed on him. I couldn't argue against that. In the end?

He gave me a choice. Either take you on as our field combat medic or find another one to replace you and he'd then assign you to another SSO team." Wearily, he rasped, "Either way, Dare, you were going back out into the battlefield and I told him I wanted you with our team. That I didn't want you assigned to someone else."

She sighed. "Ram, Ukraine is my country, too, my people."

He frowned. "I always wondered why a US Army medic was assigned to Ukraine and to our team."

"You never asked." She grinned a little, seeing humor for a moment skitter across his gaze. "You're a man of few words, Ram. And you weren't exactly personal with any of us."

"Yeah, I know I'm not touchy-feely."

She managed a slight laugh. "Oh, I don't think anyone on your team would *ever* accuse you of being that." And then she gave him a teasing look. "Do you know what I started calling you when we were over in Afghanistan?"

He straightened, scowling. "What?"

"In my head, I called you a teddy bear. You were all grizzly bear outside, but inside, you had a heart, you cared for and loved everyone on your team, you were super protective of them and you were ruthless with yourself when it came to planning an op and having it go off right, not wrong."

His mouth twisted. "Well, you're right about that. I'm the team leader. It's my responsibility to keep you all alive."

"I saw the teddy bear side of you when Artur was badly wounded," she ventured softly. "Up until that time, Ram? I wondered if you had a heart at all…"

Wincing, he avoided her saddened look. "That's *your*

job, Dare, not mine. There is no room on the field of battle for emotions and you know that."

His snapping at her made her sit up a little more. She saw the hurt in his eyes fleetingly when she'd accused him of not having a heart. "I'm sorry," she offered quietly, holding his stare. "I shouldn't have said that. It was wrong. Everyone has a heart." She opened her hands. "It's just that—" she searched for the right words "—you're so unreadable to me…to us…the team. There have been times when all of us have cried out on an op, and that was when Artur was wounded. I cried through my tears as I stitched him up and I prayed to God that he could save him because I wasn't sure he would live. Artur was one of our most favorite guys who always wore his heart on his sleeve…"

Gruffly, he said, "Artur and Adam are like that. Maybe I should pay attention to the fact that both have names that start with an A. Those two were the class clowns on the team, sometimes."

She smiled a little. "They were our comic relief, Ram. They helped all of us climb down off that dangerous cliff we always tread. They helped us laugh when we got back to camp, all in one piece, no one killed. They reminded me of a TV show called *Saturday Night Live*, where fun was poked at politicians and other events and even though they were real and sometimes awful, you watched and you laughed because they found something funny about it. Those two were truly our relief valves. Artur and Adam acted out for all of us, and it was healing."

Ram stared at her. "Yes…they did… I still miss Artur. Although he is now out of the Army, he is alive, his wife and children are happy he is home with them, and he's learning a whole new trade now, creating wood sculptures. Did you know that?"

"Yes, I did. Artur's injuries were too severe for him to ever stay in the military after that wounding, but he's found an outlet for himself and his wood sculptures, according to Adam, and they are now sold to high-end retail stores. He makes a good living for himself and his family. I'm so happy for him. And relieved..."

"I'll never forget when he was wounded," Ram admitted heavily. "We were under constant fire and you risked your life to drag him to safety while we initiated cover fire for both of you. I was so afraid you'd die out there, too..."

She blinked and absorbed his unexpected emotional admittance. And just as quickly, that angst in his expression disappeared. Had she really seen and heard him being emotional? This wasn't the time or place to pursue it, either. "Well," she whispered, "I was scared as hell as I ran out there to drag him to safety. I wasn't sure I'd live to see the next second, but I wasn't going to let him lay out there and bleed to death, either."

"I remember screaming at you not to go," he grunted. "You didn't listen."

She chuckled. "Surely you know a combat medic takes the job without the frills, Ram. It was *my job* to go after Artur. He was exposed. I was to protect and save him. I was the right person for that moment."

He slid her a glance. "I remember it all... That was such a hot mess of an op. Everything that could go wrong did go wrong."

"Except it was Sergeant Kuzma Pavlenko, our comms, who managed to get a US Army Chinook helicopter diverted and to come and get Artur to the base for an emergency operation to save his life. That was something that went right."

"Kuz saved the day," Ram agreed quietly, folding his hands between opened thighs. "Without him..."

"My field surgery made it possible for him to survive for that 'golden hour,'" she admitted, "but without Kuz finding and locating that nearby Chinook, which was already on one mission, diverting instead to help Artur..." She shook her head. "I'm good at what I do, Ram, but I fully admit that without Kuz persuading the pilots to turn and come and help us, I'm positive Artur would not have made it. He had one hour, and that was it."

There was a mixture of emotions in his expression again. Had he changed over the last two years? Was he softening up, as she called it, and showing how he felt? That was good in her estimation. No one liked talking to the ice castle that he'd been with the team when she was on board with them. Dare fully realized every one of them, regardless of gender, had to handle a helluva lot of emotions that could not get in the way when they were out on an op. For her, the trick was how to climb down off that mental cliff afterward.

Like everyone else on the team, at camp, she would sometimes wake up screaming, or a flashback would occur and she'd shout or scream, waking herself up, as well as her teammates who slept in the same plywood building. She wasn't the only one. Every man, with the exception of Ram Kozak, did the same thing. Getting a full night's sleep behind the wire was not guaranteed at all. It was just part of their job. The emotions suppressed during an op came surging up as they slept in the guise of a dream or, worse, a nightmare.

Ram sat up, moving his shoulders to shed the tension out of them. "We were a good team, Dare. That is what stopped Artur from dying."

Nodding, she said, "He's got a decent life now. Adam told me he makes good money for his family off his creativity. Who knew he was such a skilled, artistic sculptor?"

Shaking his head, Ram muttered, "I often wonder who or what I'd have been if my life had turned out differently. Don't you?" He met her serious-looking gaze.

"Oh," she said, rolling her eyes, "don't go there, Ram. My life is more like a patchwork quilt thrown together. If you'd have asked me if I thought my career would be in the military and I'd be a combat medic? In my early teens, I'd have laughed and said that you were wrong." Her grin widened and she opened her arms. "But look at me now. This is who I am. As a child I never dreamed this dream."

He sat back, thoughtful. "You realize we've *never* talked like this with one another before?"

"What do you mean?"

"I mean," and he searched for the right word, "*personally*?"

"From the moment I was assigned to your team in Afghanistan, you instilled in me that it was your way or the highway. Remember? No touchy-feely? No crying? No getting depressed? No having a bad day? We were all supposed to be like automatons, heartless, using only strong mental focus and that was it so the job got accomplished and the team came back in one piece. Oh, I remember those times, all right."

"You're here," he deadpanned, "alive and in one piece. The whole team came home. You can't argue with success, Dare."

A bit of laughter rolled out of her. "Well, I think Artur nearly dying broke everyone."

"It did," he admitted, rubbing his stubbled jaw. "I've changed a little," he admitted wryly. "Artur reminded me of my younger brother, Alex, and I always appreciated his sense of humor, his comedy of errors he always pretended to make in order to give the team a laugh..."

Tilting her head, she studied him in the silence. "I didn't know you had a brother. His name was Alex?" Instantly she saw that hard, expressionless mask drop over his face. Ram became stiff and his gold eyes turned thundercloud dark. Tension flowed through her as she saw him wrestling with some invisible and yet obviously very painful memory to him. She didn't have the courage to ask more, seeing his swift reaction.

Ram jabbed his finger at the orders lying on the desk before her. "Do you really want to go out in the battlefield with us?"

Distraction. Okay, she could understand it. "Of course I do. We're a known quantity to one another. I would think you'd be overjoyed to have nine of the ten original members back together for this coming war."

He nodded. "Sergeant Symon Kravets, who everyone calls Zap, has replaced Artur. He's a satellite and computer expert for our team now. I think you'll like him. He's sharp, fast and obsessed with anything electronic."

She saw him beginning to relax once more...well, as much as Ram *could* relax. To her he was always like an explosive that at any time could blow up. He never had when they were together, but the feeling was still there. Wondering if his family was a sore topic for whatever reason, she realized that sense of tightly controlled emotions was back and it was almost palpable to her. Dare blamed her super sensitivity, her intuition and ability to feel things most men ignored. There had been several times in Afghanistan when she'd sensed danger, where it was located and it had always panned out. In her second year of being with the team, it got so that they relied heavily upon what they called her: the psychic in the group. Dare took it with gracefulness, laughed it off, but still, even Ram listened to her when she picked up or sensed danger nearby. Adam had teased her that she was actually a killer K-9 Belgian Malinois incarnated into a human body in order to save the team's "collective ass," as he called it. Everyone got a huge laugh out of that one. Even Ram, who barely cracked one, grinned over that joke.

"Zap," she laughed softly, "what a great nickname for the new member of the team!"

"You'll like him," Ram said, relaxing a little. "He's young, a twenty-year-old, starry-eyed about being in a black ops unit and all. Said he grew up as a user of combat software games."

"He hasn't been in combat yet to know the difference…"

"No, but he will find out."

"Good thing the rest of team is blooded," she said quietly. "It will help him adjust when the time comes. They'll be support for him as he goes through his own personal shock and trauma. I'm sure he'll realize real war is nothing like his software games."

"Yeah," he muttered, sitting up. "Part of the initiation for becoming black ops. Kill or be killed. It's black or white."

"Is someone taking him under their wing?"

"Kuz is doing it," Ram said. "He's a father by nature, you know that."

She smiled a little. "Well, after all, he has three darling children and a wonderful wife. I'd say he has a lot of good father attributes he can shower on Zap." Most of the men were married, or at least when she left the team in Afghanistan they were. Every once in a while, she'd hear about one of them, usually via voluble comic, Adam, or his wife, Lera, about a team member's personal life, a new baby coming along to be celebrated or someone getting married.

"Kuz has an interest in the computer side of comms, and that's what drew them together. But it's a good thing because Zap is pretty immature." He made a motion with his fingers toward his head. "The kid is green and has all these naive ideas about gaming black ops. I don't think that under ordinary circumstances they'd let someone of his age and idealism into a team like ours, but we're going to need his expertise out in the field like never before. And this is a different war that's going to be waged versus the one we went through in Afghanistan. The Russians will be throwing their best computer hackers at our software programs, trying to mess them up or delete or freeze them so we can't use them."

"I see," she murmured. "Do you feel he'll be a fit?"

Shrugging, Ram said, "That remains to be seen, but I've talked to Kuz privately about my concerns regarding the kid, and he's in agreement with me. Kuz will keep his ass close to his own. And when we enter combat, Zap will have someone who can protect, guide and teach him on the fly. It's as good as it's going to get. Black ops is bloody and murderous, nothing short of that, and Zap has this starry-eyed combat software gamer's idea in his head of what it will be like."

"It's nothing like that," she agreed, sadness in her tone. Once more, she was seeing Ram being more emotional than usual. Clearly, he was worried about Zap being initiated into a live-fire situation where life, death or being taken prisoner was on the line. The kid had nothing to compare real life with the canned software gamer life he'd led before.

"I'm sure you can help him, too," Ram added, giving her a hopeful look. "You were always 'mother' to all of us on the team."

Snorting, Dare grinned wickedly. "You warned me right off the bat not to mother the guys. What's this? All of a sudden looking for a mommy in the group now?"

He had the good grace to manage a twist of his mouth. "You're right, of course. I didn't want you mothering my men."

"And it didn't happen. But obviously, that's a secret fear you held about me? That I'd do that?"

"I guess I was hoping you might let some of that mommy side of you show to Zap. I think the kid is going to need a 'dad' and a 'mom' for a while as he gets rid of his gamer reality and trades it in for the hard-core reality of what war is really like, instead. It's going to throw him and I can't have the kid losing it and forgetting what he's supposed to be doing out in the field working with us."

"It's a delicate balance," Dare agreed, frowning. "I'll do what I can."

He looked at the watch on his wrist. "I must go. Did Adam invite you over to his home in Bucha, yet?"

"Yes, he called me last night. I usually spend weekends with him, Lera and the kids. I act as kind of a babysitter and housekeeper for them."

"And what does that give you?" Ram wondered.

"I get to practice my mothering skills."

He laughed sourly and shook his head, standing. "Touché, you nailed me."

"You're an easy target, Captain."

He placed the hat on his head, lowering the bill. "Well, I sure walked into that one with you, but no one said you were asleep at the switch, either."

"Never will be." She stood, folding the orders and placing them in a ziplock pocket on the left thigh of her fatigues. "When I talked to Adam yesterday he said there was a secret visitor coming for the weekend to stay with them. Is that you?"

"You're good, Dare. Really good. You must have that psychic switch turned on right now."

Grinning wolfishly, she walked up to the desk and retrieved her knapsack, pulling it over her shoulders. "Well, I didn't know until just now. It makes sense that Adam knew because he's second-in-command, and I would be there babysitting this weekend and he wanted to get you out of that combat environment and let you ramp down for a weekend."

"I told him I'd stay tonight and leave on Sunday afternoon."

"Good. You need to be around people who love you."

Chapter Two

By the time Dare got off the bus at her fourteen-story apartment building near the center of Kyiv, her thoughts remained centered on Ram. It was 1300, 1:00 p.m. She had time to change, get a shower, pack a small suitcase and drive out to Bucha, the village where Adam and Lera lived. She liked spending her weekends with them whenever possible.

Ram...the enigma. She'd walked out of his life two years ago and it had been heart-wrenching for her because she'd secretly fallen in love with the hardened warrior who let no one into his inner life. He was all business. Always. Why?

After slipping the code card into the slot of her ground-floor apartment, she pushed the door open with her boot and it closed automatically behind her. Even though it was a rainy, gray day, the three massive floor-to-ceiling windows made her two-bedroom apartment look bright. After placing her briefcase and several other items into the guest bedroom, she went across the hall to climb out of her military gear and slip into a quick, hot shower. That always revived and centered her. She slowly inhaled the rose-scented soap, its delicious fragrance filling her lungs. So, she was going to war—again. The shock still reverberated within her.

Dare was older now, twenty-nine, not a young twenty-five-year-old when she'd been ordered to Ram's black ops unit in Afghanistan. It had been an adventure to her, a challenge she readily accepted, but she soon found out that learning combat medicine in a schoolroom didn't even come close to being out in the field where life and death was a breath away from every member of the team. After two years, she was ready to leave the war-torn fields of Afghanistan, overjoyed at the Lviv, Ukraine, assignment to teach field combat medicine to the medics of this wonderful country.

Ram...

She scrubbed her hair and rinsed beneath the streams of water, trying to tame her powerful feelings of joy intertwined with the shock of him walking back into her life once again.

What was she going to do? What should she do? Was it really orders from higher up that assigned her back to his team? Or did he have something to do with it? Her gut told her someone above him in rank had made that decision because he didn't seem particularly happy to see her back with his unit. Worse, as she stepped out of the shower, grabbing a pale yellow bath towel, starting to dry herself off, she'd seen and felt conflicting emotions around him. Did he not want her on his team again? There had been a crosscurrent within him, but she couldn't suss it out any more than that. Being a sensitive, somewhat psychic individual, she hated that she'd gotten a hit on it but not the whole story.

And usually, that made her impatient and frustrated. Ram Kozak was not the kind of man to let her see what cards he held in his hand and he wasn't about to show them to her now, either.

She hated him being like a Rubik's Cube and she could never figure him out or sense the feelings around him that he'd never given voice to. Yet, as she sat down on the chair and put on a pair of warm, lambswool socks, then pulled on her loose-fitting jeans and a lambswool, long-sleeved pink sweater, she never knew how he really felt or thought. Even Adam, who was close to Ram, like a brother, didn't know his backstory. Where was he born? Where was his family? Where did they live? He never talked about them, and family was everything to the Ukrainian people, so tightly knit and woven together. Adam's parents were dead now, and he lived in the same village and in the same house he'd been born in. She loved that about Ukraine. In the USA, it was vastly different. Extended family didn't necessarily live in the same house or even town.

After combing her short crop of black hair, using her fingers to fluff it up a bit, she tidied up the bathroom, left the door open and headed for the kitchen.

Ram...

As she made herself some coffee, hips resting against the counter, arms across her breasts, she stared down at the colorful tile floor. How shocked, curious and stunned she still felt by today's unexpected event.

She realized Ram had changed from her Afghanistan days with him. He was, well, almost warm toward her, showing a little emotion here and there, which had been completely MIA, missing in action, before. He even cracked a partial smile earlier, which truly stunned her. Their conversation was far more personal, a giving and taking, than it ever had been before. Had he changed because of some incident she didn't know about? He was older now. Or was this the "real" Ram, a man who had a rich tapestry of emotions just like any other human being possessed and was allowing them some airtime? Behind his back, she always thought of him as Ram the Robot. A robot didn't have a heart and possessed no emotions. Just a head full of mental activity and focus was all. This latest version of Ram was far nicer, a tad more open, even a hint of emotion in his gruff voice now and then. All new!

What had changed him, she wondered. Maybe Adam could shed some light on it since he'd been with the team those two years after she'd left. Two years was a long time, she conceded. A lot could have happened. Adam would be the one to talk with and he'd give her the intel. Maybe then she could figure out this new 2.0 version of Ram and understand it and him better. She had to, because she was going out in the field with him again.

The coffee was ready. She put a dab of honey and cream into the mug and went to the living room, sitting down in her rocking chair. Moving it slowly back and forth, the coffee between her hands, she frowned. *Combat. Once again.* She had PTSD, but anyone in black ops got that as entrance to the dark games they played behind the scenes with their enemies. Everyone was on war footing in Ukraine and she could see the worry and strain in everyone's face. They knew what was coming, but she also knew the lion strength of the people's heart to live in a democracy, too. She knew it would rip Ukraine up, but the people were stalwart and fighters. Putin didn't know what he was biting off by trying to steal their land and break their will, trying to make everyone Russian by proxy. That would *never* happen.

Looking up at the ceiling, she sighed. She knew her adopted parents, who lived in Cleveland, Ohio, were worried about it, too. They held dual citizenship, like she did. They had adopted her at three months old after she was left on the steps of an Ohio fire department station. She had no memory of it. Her adopted mother, Maria, and father, Panas Mazur, a world-renowned cardiologist surgeon, had loved her from the moment she was brought to them. They had lived outside the city, in a rural area with a big farmhouse, barn and fifty acres of land. They flew back once a year, to their home, Lviv, Ukraine, near the Polish border, and saw their large, extended family. She had grown up visiting her Ukrainian relatives and always looked forward to seeing them. Half her soul was a part of their beautiful country, and the other half was where she was born in the USA. A foot in two worlds.

Dare preferred the warm, huge, tight Ukrainian family lifestyle. Her parents would stay a month in Lviv and she loved the huge celebratory family gatherings, the women bringing all their favorite dishes, the home smelling of rosemary, basil, garlic and so many other wonderful herbal scents. The Ukrainian people had beautiful ceremonies and dances and she loved the bright costumes, the energy and heart in their songs and movements.

She'd been overjoyed when the US Army had given her a two-year teaching position in Lviv to train Ukrainian Army medics to be even more important in combat than before.

Her mind turned to Adam and Lera, and their two

spunky little daughters, Anna and Sofia. She was so at home with them and even though she had her own apartment in Kyiv, she routinely spent weekends with them, starting on Friday night and driving out to their village, one of the two spare bedrooms hers, the children anxiously awaiting her arrival. Her weekends were so much fun, filled with laughter, giggling and exciting exploration outdoors with the children. Their two red-haired daughters followed her around like happy, wriggling puppies in search of a new adventure. Dare loved exploring with them, the woods nearby offering so much to learn about and such wonderful edible wild mushrooms that one could eat with their evening meals. She was teaching the girls how to identify the edibles from the poisonous ones. Lera had begun to teach them, and show them how to always cook them first, and use them in casseroles, soups and stews. Yes, she eagerly looked forward to spending time with them. Dare considered them her second family, feeling very lucky and enriched by her caring Ukrainian friends.

Finishing off her coffee, she looked over at the top of her TV. There were lots of framed photos, some of her mother and father, Adam's entire family. Her gaze drifted to the last one: Ram Kozak. Dare stared at the warrior, his face set, three-day growth of beard, in black ops gear, staring flatly back at her. She smiled a little, remembering that time. He hated pictures of himself, but she'd caught him off guard one day, lying in wait for him because she knew his habits and routine at the camp, and got the photo. He wasn't very happy about it, but she'd seen a bit of pluckiness about him after she told him she really wanted a photo of him for her family album.

Ram was still a part of her. Much larger than she wanted to admit. Now? Everything had changed in a snap of the cosmic fingers of Fate. They were together again. A unit. A family...

November 2

"COME IN!" LERA SANG, wiping her hands on her apron, smiling at Dare, who had her arms filled with two large paper grocery sacks.

"I'm a little late," she said, breathless, hurrying inside their large village home. It was warm compared with outside, the wind cutting and cold.

"You're never late!" Lera said, taking one of the sacks. "You didn't have to do this, Dare, you know that!" She hurried over to the long kitchen counter with one of the bulging sacks. The area was huge, with a long trestle table with twelve chairs around it. Outside the large bank of windows, the trees were bending with the gusts of rain and wind from the cold front coming through.

"Are we going to have Ram over for dinner?" Dare asked, setting the second sack down on the kitchen counter, unloading all the items to be put into the fridge or the cabinets. She saw Lera's green eyes twinkle. She had her red hair, which was long and could go halfway down her back, twisted into two red braids and then wound up on top of her head. She too wore jeans and a comfy orange sweater that showed off her shining auburn hair.

"Yes! First time ever. Adam had invited him to have dinner and stay overnight with us, but he always turned us down." She grinned. "I think he's invited himself over here because *you* are here."

Snorting, taking the sour cream and other containers across the room to the fridge, Dare said, "I had no idea he was coming until he told me himself earlier today."

"You saw him?" Her eyes went wide with surprise.

Once she placed the items in the fridge, she shut the door and turned. "Yes. Didn't he tell Adam that orders were cut for me to rejoin his team?"

Gasping, her hands flew to her mouth. Lera stared in shock at her. "No! When did this happen?"

Dare patted her small shoulder. Lera was only five feet six inches tall, slender, but a human dynamo who was always in motion. Dare blamed it on her red hair. "It's okay, Lera. I was in shock just seeing him. It has been two years since I've seen him in person. I didn't even know he was in Kyiv. That was six months ago. In the last email I received from him, he said his team was in the US learning new things. And that they just returned a few days ago."

"Adam returned last week ahead of the team," Lera said pertly, quickly disgorging the rest of the contents from the sack to the counter. "You did not know Ram was here in Kyiv, then?"

"Not at all."

"Well, the whole team has been in the USA with the Army training programs on different kinds of weapons," Lera said. "Adam never talked much about it because, as you know, everything in an SSO team is top-secret."

"Sure is," Dare agreed, reaching up to put a box of cornmeal onto a shelf that was hard for Lera to reach without her constant companion, a nearby oak stool.

"Still," Lera persisted, frowning as she folded the sacks and put them away, "Ram has never been over to our home, never asked to come over and share a meal with us. He's always been standoffish and politely turned down Adam's invites to be with us every time."

Dare was familiar with the kitchen and Lera's needs as the chief cook, and she would assist her. "Have you seen Ram at all?"

"No," Lera said. "Why?"

"Well," she murmured, "he's changed somewhat since I last saw him in Afghanistan."

"Oh?" Her red brows arched, interest in her eyes. "How do you mean that?"

"Usually he's like a blank whiteboard. You can't read him at all. I never could tell when I was on his team if he was happy, sad, depressed or whatever about me. This time, when he saw me after my class was over at the institute, he was…" She hesitated, searching for the right word. "Well… He wasn't a whiteboard this time."

Lera walked over to a large glass baking dish where she was fixing a meal for all of them tonight. "You've always said he couldn't be read. Adam says the same thing. He is a very closet-like person, Dare. That hasn't changed, or has it?"

Dare brought over a kitchen knife and saw the cucumbers that needed to be sliced and diced and put in the half-made potato salad. "Don't know. He just…well…seemed more open, but I wouldn't get excited about it. Maybe a crack, not opening the door so you could see what he was feeling and conveying it. Just a hint here and there. That's what changed. And I don't know if that was a one-time thing with him or if he's actually opening up a bit to the rest of the world."

Lera placed the finishing touches on a large pan of chicken Kyiv, a country favorite. The chicken filets had been well pounded, rolled around in butter mixed with fresh dill, and then coated with a mixture of egg and dried bread crumbs. She lifted up the large baking dish and Dare followed, opening the oven door for her. "Thank you," Lera said, grinning and shutting the door. "So? His behavior is finally thawing, perhaps?"

Chuckling, Dare went back to her workstation, finishing off the diced cucumbers and starting on the hard-boiled eggs and dicing them. "*Thaw* is a good word that I was searching for," she told Lera. The woman had a pleased, foxy look in her expression. "What's that look for?" Dare demanded.

"Ohhh, my," Lera trilled, pulling out some cooling garlic bread she'd made. *Pampushky* was wonderful and one of Dare's favorites. It was a dinner bread with a sweet taste, the texture billowy, and the garlic, butter and parsley brushed on it after it had browned filled the air with the mouthwatering scents. "Don't you think it kismet that here you are in town and he's coming back from the USA and has Adam invite him to dinner? Hmm?" She arched one eyebrow, her grin turning positively merry.

Dare knew that feral look. "Don't go there," she warned, slicing the vegetable. "I think he was worried how I'd react to being taken out of the classroom teaching and then summarily dropped back into his team."

Brushing the garlic bread with swift, knowing strokes, it was Lera's turn to snort. "There's more to this! Does he know you are still single and free? No attachments?"

"We didn't discuss anything that personal," Dare said.

"Not that he ever showed an interest in who may or may not be in my life."

"You know that he's still not attached?" Lera said, her smile widening. "Neither of you are. He's thirty years old and you're twenty-nine. You should both be married by now, Dare."

It was Dare's turn to snort. She picked up a large spoon to turn over the potato salad and mix it. "Just haven't met the right person, I guess," she answered a bit defensively.

"You know what I really think?" Lera said, coming over and patting her shoulder.

"You've never held back before and you're on a roll. Why stop now?"

Cackling, Lera gripped her shoulder gently and whispered, "I think he's wanted a relationship with you for a long, long time because that would explain why he's still unattached and why he's invited himself to dinner tonight. And," she shook her finger at Dare, "he's staying over the whole weekend. Did you know *that*?"

Blinking owlishly, Dare stared down at the triumphant, know-it-all look on Lera's thin face that was sprinkled with freckles. She groaned. The spoon in her hand stopped midair. "He did mention he'd be coming to dinner and staying over until Sunday morning. But I honestly do not think it's because I'm here."

"Then, you tell me your idea of why he's invited himself for this weekend. Adam invited him to Friday night dinner. He did not invite him to stay the whole weekend. Now, how did that happen? And why? We do have two guest bedrooms, that's not a problem. I'm sure Adam told him you would be coming over Friday night through Sunday afternoon, living with us for a bit, and perhaps that is why he's coming. *You* will be here!"

She gave Lera a rolled-eye look, forcing herself to pay attention to stirring up the potato salad. "I think you've gone bonkers."

"What does *bonkers* mean?" Lera demanded, her hands now on her hips. "Your American slang drives me to distraction."

"Wild."

Laughing sharply, she shook her head and took the garlic bread, placing it in the warmer above the stove after covering it with a towel. "It's the only good explanation as to why he'll be here shortly. He and Adam are driving back and will be here around five for dinner."

"Occam's razor," Dare muttered sourly, shaking her head.

"You're muttering again. You only do that when you are upset. Who is Occam?"

"He was a fourteenth-century logician and theologian. His name was William of Ockham. His theory states 'the simplest solution is almost always best.'"

Snickering, Lera said triumphantly, "I was right! Mr. Occam agrees with *me*!"

Dare shook her head, giving her a teasing look. "We'll see," she said, "we'll see... Don't forget, he's an officer, and I'm an enlisted person, Lera. We could never have any kind of personal relationship, anyway. The military would not allow it."

"You have always confided in me," Lera reminded her. "You admitted that you were very drawn to Ram, enlisted or otherwise. Yes? Eh?"

"I was… Well, I still am, and that's bonkers, too. The only time I heard from him was an email every couple of months with a photograph of a flower he took while on a mission. He knows I love flowers. I can't read any more into it than that."

Lera couldn't help but allow herself to smile fully. "And why would any man take that kind of time to do something like that for two years after you have been separated? Eh?" Lera poked her finger into Dare's upper arm. "How did it make you feel when he sent you those photos?"

Sighing, Dare put a lid over the potato salad and walked it to the refrigerator. "It always made me happy, Lera."

"Seriously," she opined. "You know? You two remind me of the old Victorian era where a man would court a woman he loved sometimes for years before he would ask for her hand in marriage. No kissing. No touching. No honesty about how each other really felt toward one other…" She snorted and shook her head, throwing her hands up in frustration.

Dare grinned a little. "You're such a firecracker, Lera." She gently hugged the small woman. Releasing her, she said, "It's that red hair of yours on fire again. Okay, in my deepest, dark parts of myself, I felt he cared for me enough to send those flower photos. He knows how much I love botany."

"This is going to become very interesting," Lera said, taking a washcloth and wiping down the counter with quick, knowing strokes.

"Don't you and Adam stare at us over dinner, Lera. We aren't bugs under a collective microscope to be watched for some change in our nonrelationship."

"Oh," she laughed, "we wouldn't do that! What will be interesting," and she looked at her watch, "is how the girls will react to Ram. They've never met him."

"Now, that's something I can agree with you on," Dare laughed.

"You do like him still, don't you?"

"Yes," she admitted quietly.

"And it's serious. Yes?"

She gave Lera disheartened look. "Yes, but it's not going anywhere. If he was really serious about me—and he never showed one iota that he was—don't you think he'd have come clean, been honest with me, if that was so?"

"He's a strange one, I will give you that." Lera slid her arm around Dare's waist. "He's not like everyone else, from what Adam has shared with me. I've never met him, either, so I'm very interested in his reactions to me and the girls, and to you, of course."

It was 4:00 p.m., and Dare saw Adam drive in with the girls in his car. "He's got the kids," she called to Lera.

"Good. Now, we're one happy family again. Ram will be arriving an hour from now!"

RAM HATED LIKE hell to admit it, but he was nervous. That was one emotion that he thought had been crushed and destroyed a long time ago. As he parked his car in the driveway of Adam's home at 5:00 p.m., the sky was darkening with more rain to come. Turning off the engine, he stared at the passenger seat. There was a two-pound box of chocolates for Lera. He'd never met Adam's wife before, and he wanted to make a good impression with her. Adam talked a lot about his fiery red-haired wife and Ram thought he knew enough about her. What put him on edge was Dare. She would be there already, seeing another car in the driveway. He stared over at the mixed bouquet of fresh flowers for her. He knew she would like them.

He sat there for a moment, feeling the terrible past clawing at him. He'd slammed a door so damned tightly on it that he thought it would never visit him again. For whatever twisted, dark reason, the last two years without Dare being with him, he would dream of having a family. And she was his wife. He'd always wake up, of course, breathing hard, sweating, shaking and wanting to sob for the losses he'd suffered. He would sit up in bed, and look around the darkened apartment bedroom, wondering why these silly dreams were happening. Why now?

He would never put anyone through what he experienced. No one. Especially Dare. He cared too much for her. His desire to make her his was sometimes nearly overwhelming. He'd never touched her. Never kissed her. Never spoke of his real feelings he had for her. No, he'd kept a very tight rein on them when she joined their team and lived with them in their plywood quarters at the top-secret camp in Afghanistan.

Trying to put a lid on his past, he looked at the two brightly wrapped gifts next to the flowers and chocolates. These presents were for their two young daughters. He wanted to make a good impression with all of them and he didn't question himself too deeply as to why. Since eighteen, he'd lived his life like a monk in a cave. He wanted no emotional strings attached to anyone at any time except for the safety of his team and trying to keep them alive to go home to their families.

He girded himself internally, placed the gifts and box into a sack and held the bouquet as he climbed out of his car. The wind was gusty and the temperature was dropping. As he closed the door, he wondered if there would be rain or snow to follow. That would be early in the season and the thought nagged him because if the ground grew hard and frozen earlier than usual, it meant the Russians would attack them sooner with their tank columns that were amassing right now near the Ukraine border. Pulling the sheepskin collar of his aviation leather jacket around his neck, he hurried up to the front door.

He barely got the doorbell rung when the door flew open. There were two little redheaded girls, both dressed in jeans and warm, long-sleeved sweaters, their hair in pigtails, waving their arms and smiling up at him, while simultaneously jumping up and down for joy. Adam squeezed between his daughters and pushed the screen door open for him.

"Come on in, Ram. Girls…girls," he pleaded, "let Ram get in the door before you attack him."

Ram smiled a little, shook his head and moved into the warm house filled with many wonderful fragrances of food cooking in the kitchen. It brought back so many happy memories of his family to him.

Adam shut the door, grinning. "They've been very curious who my boss was, and when I told them you were going to have dinner with us? They've been watching for you to drive in so they could greet you first."

"Well," Ram said, eyeing both girls, who now had settled down, their hands clasped in front of them, looking shyly up at him, "that is very nice." He set the sack down, crouched down on the hardwood floor and pulled out two gifts from it. He gave one to each of them. "For you," he said, watching their surprise as they took them.

"You didn't have to do that," Adam said.

Ram straightened. "Best to get off on the right foot?" He saw his second-in-command nod and give him a silly, knowing grin.

"Come on, girls, show Ram to the kitchen, where we'll be eating."

Ram followed as the girls galloped ahead like young wild horses. A pain hit his heart, an old memory from the past striking him squarely in the chest. He'd lost two of his cousins, both young girls about their age, at eighteen. Never to see them grow up. Never to see them fall in love, get married and be happy. Pushing the memories back, he followed Adam into the large, pale yellow kitchen that filled his nostrils with so many good flavors that his mouth watered. It all reminded him of his mother's, grandmother's and aunt's cooking, and again that old grief-stricken pain struck his heart.

"Lera?" Adam called. "Come meet my boss, Captain Ram Kozak…"

Lera smiled and placed the chicken Kyiv on the table. Wiping her hands on her apron, she came over and shook his hand. "We're glad to finally meet you, Captain. You're more than welcome at our home. You're a part of our larger family now."

Ram nodded and shook her thin, small hand. "I brought you something," he said and dug into the sack, producing the chocolates. "Call me Ram? These are for you. Everything you're making smells wonderful. Thank you for all the time it took for you to make it for all of us."

Smiling, Lera said, "You've very kind and thoughtful, Ram. I can see my daughters are eyeballing my box of chocolates already. I think I'm going to have to hide it from them."

Adam laughed and took the box, placing it high on a cabinet where the girls would never be able to reach. They loved chocolate like their mother did.

Ram looked around. "I thought Dare was here? That she was going to have dinner with us?"

"She'll be here in a minute," Lera said. "Those flowers are for her?"

"Yes."

Lera took the bouquet from him. "Adam? Take his coat and hang it up in the hall closet? Ram, you sit at this end of the table," she said and pulled the chair back for him. "What would you like to drink? Some wine, perhaps, an aperitif of bitters before dinner?"

He nodded and handed Adam his coat. "Either one would be fine, Mrs. Vorona." He sat down.

"Call me Lera."

"I can do that."

"Dare is going to love this bouquet!" Lera handed it back to him.

"I hope so."

Lera patted his shoulder. "Don't look so worried. She will."

Ram liked the petite dynamo. Adam dearly loved his wife and he could see why. She was more like a whirling dervish. He smiled inwardly at the image.

"Here she is!" Lera trilled out to him.

Dare halted at the cellar door that led off the kitchen. She had just brought up a bottle of red wine. "Hey, you found their place," she said, smiling at him and closing the door.

Ram stood up, the chair scraping the shining oak floor. "They do live out in the country," he admitted. His heart began to beat harder as he walked over to where she was. Lera took the bottle of wine from her, grinning like a fool, and whirled around and left. He saw a blush creeping up into Dare's high cheekbones as he handed her the bouquet. "After all those email photos of the flowers we happened upon when out on a mission, I thought having real ones would be better. These are for you." He handed the gold-wrapped bouquet to her. Their fingers met and Ram swore he got an electrical shock from their grazing contact. A look of surprise and then pleasure wreathed her smile as she accepted the huge bouquet.

"They're beautiful, Ram. Thank you." She buried her nose in the blooms. There were many lush, pink mallows, several golden sunflowers and small white chamomile daisies with big yellow centers, and many bright blue cornflowers to round out the grouping. The fragrance was exquisite and she inhaled it fully with appreciation.

He stood there, suddenly shy and pleased all at the same time. He'd never seen her blush before and it became her. The sky blue color of her eyes had always intrigued him and he hungrily absorbed her joy over his gift. Mostly, he was relieved she liked them. Relieved that she took them instead of refusing them. But Dare wasn't that kind of person. She'd take muffins from an Afghan horse and collect a gunny sack of them, and then give the manure to a local farmer who thought it was a great gift. He would take it and profusely thank her in Dari. Horse manure was used to help the plants in the field flourish and grow larger and increase the yield of corn or create larger heads of wheat for their family to eat. So, in Afghanistan, it was like receiving a bouquet of flowers.

"I wanted to get the autumn flowers of Ukraine for you," he began awkwardly, seeing how happy she was, her eyes sparkling. "I know how much you love this country and its people."

Dare sniffed and turned away, wiping her eyes with her free hand. She turned back, giving him a watery smile. "You are so thoughtful, Ram. I never expected this. Thank you."

He frowned, felt his heart fly open as he saw tears in her eyes start to gather again. "Flowers make you cry?"

She heard the teasing in his tone and surreptitiously wiped her tears away. "I don't know how you were able to find them at this time of year... That's what impresses me. How many hours did it take for you to locate them? I don't think these would be in florists' shops, do you?"

He had the good grace to manage a partial smile. Sticking his hands in the pockets of his black slacks, he murmured, "Well, my apartment is south of Kyiv, out in a rural farm area. There is a farm wife there who has a small florist business and the flowers come from her garden. Only Ukrainian flowers, by the way. She made up the bouquet for you."

"They are perfect," Dare managed, her voice husky.

"Here," Lera said, holding out a large crystal cut vase

to her. "Let's give them water and set them on the table. They're all beautiful."

Ram took the vase and walked over to the kitchen sink and filled it. He felt a load slip off his shoulders. Earlier, he'd been afraid that Dare wouldn't like the bouquet or refuse it altogether. But she had not. The opposite had happened. And Lord help him, he almost threw his arms around her, wanting to crush her against him and hold her forever. In that moment, she looked vulnerable as never before to him. He realized belatedly that here with Lera and Adam's family, Dare was herself, not the combat medic on a black ops mission, rifle in hand. No, here she was herself and that excited him beyond anything he'd ever expected. That was a miracle of a gift he'd never expected.

How was he going to handle this new situation? He was supposed to stay with Adam's family until Sunday afternoon. How?

Chapter Three

The kitchen was the heart of every Ukraine household and Ram silently reminisced about that as he awkwardly stood aside in the happy beehive of activity. Even Adam was in the mix, helping his wife with the setting of the long trestle table now decked out in a beautiful, crocheted tablecloth that he'd been told had been created by Lera's great-grandmother. It was a wedding gift to them when they'd gotten married. It reminded him of the sacredness of women who made such beautiful objects and then passed them on, generation after generation. There was a deep, heartfelt energy to it that embraced those who were present.

Dare was busy at one end of the counter, Lera on the other, getting the last-minute food preps ready. The girls were thrilled and excited with the gifts he'd given them and they'd run into the living room to check them out more closely. He'd discovered two apps on wildflowers of Ukraine and he knew from speaking to Dare that she was taking them out into the fields to look for and identify them. Dare had peeked at the app he'd given to them on a small computer tablet, and she jumped up and down with the girls, giving him a warm look of thanks for his thoughtfulness. Again, he'd felt heat rush into his face. This time, he didn't have a four-day growth of beard to hide it since he'd shaved, and showered, before his arrival.

"Hey," Adam called, waving to him from the entrance to the living room, "let's get out of the traffic and sit for about half an hour before dinner."

Ram nodded, happy to leave the kitchen area. It just brought back too many painful memories for him.

Adam had placed a small crystal glass of bitters on an antique table between two rocking chairs in the living room and gestured for him to come and sit down. "It's a beehive in there," he joked, smiling and sitting down.

Ram joined him. "Seriously," he agreed. He picked up the glass, sipping the bitters. The taste was tart, musty and he enjoyed it because this was an ancient custom in all of Europe to drink the herbal mixture before dinner so their digestion would be vastly improved, the meal made even more enjoyable as a result.

The girls had run to their bunk bedroom and Ram was sure they were having fun with their new botany flower app.

"Everything smells so good," Ram told his friend.

Inhaling, Adam closed his eyes for a moment and murmured, "I've often told Lera those kitchen smells are like perfume to me."

"Or to your stomach," Ram said, grinning a little.

Opening his eyes, Adam laughed, nodded and sipped from his glass. "Most certainly." He grew somber, passing a look to Ram. "Did you get any more scoop on Russian activity at our border?"

"No, only that they're amassing about one hundred

tanks." His mouth slashed downward. "I'd give my right arm to know where they are going to attack from. There are several major highways into Kyiv from that border area."

Adam scratched his head, his red hair short beneath his long fingers. "That's what worries me, Ram. Bucha is right on the most important highway artery that heads directly into the heart of Kyiv."

"Yes…" Ram noticed the deep worry in the man's blue eyes.

"I don't know what to do to tell Lera of my worries."

"Let's wait until we can get some more chatter traffic from the Russians. Sooner or later, they'll spill where they're going to attack us from because they're foolish and use their cell phones, which American intelligence picks up from their satellite feeds."

"You're right," he sighed, shaking his head. "I hate Putin…"

"I hate him more."

Adam gave him a questioning side-glance but said nothing.

Ram rocked gently, the kitchen cooking scents reminding him of another happy time in his life. Family, feasting and fun. That was how he experienced it growing up. There was nothing stronger among the Ukraine people than their bond with their family, their yearly ceremonies, supporting and caring for their entire village, town or city or the love they held for this largest country in Europe. He purposely blotted out the hatred that ate at him daily regarding Putin. He was a monster unleashed and Ram knew just how violent and heartless he really was. Wrestling with all those crisis emotions he kept to himself, he forced himself to turn to something happy: Dare.

He'd been sent to the USA with his team off and on the last six months after coming out of Afghanistan once and for all. He had kept tabs on Dare's assignment in Lviv, teaching advanced and accelerated combat field medicine techniques to their medics. His own home was in a small village south of Kyiv, a good hour's drive from the center of the city where the military HQ was situated.

He knew Dare lived in the heart of the city, in an apartment in a high-rise a few blocks from the central military buildings. But he never contacted her face-to-face, instead continuing to send her flower emails from time to time. The last six months he'd not been able to, his entire team in the USA and under intense military training with weapons they would use to push back the coming Russian attack. He wanted so much more with her, but now, the war loomed. Just when he'd talked himself into trying to create an opening, a dialogue with her about how he felt personally about her, it was destroyed.

Things had changed within him, however. And maybe… just maybe? He'd gotten the courage to see her in person, and that somehow…and God only knew how…he would let her know how he felt. Ram wasn't sure what her reaction would be because he'd always kept that unscalable wall between them.

Now? All that had changed. Closing his eyes for a moment, leaning his head back on the rocker, he wanted this war to go away, to never happen. He wanted that opening he'd planned on, hoped for, to be the moment he could let her know how much he wanted her personally in his life.

Was he too late? Should he even try? She was back in his team. The last place he wanted her. The last...

"Dinner is ready," Lera sang at the entrance to the living room.

LERA PLACED EVERYONE at the table. Dare wasn't sure she was happy about being next to Ram, but it would have been embarrassing to everyone if she'd said she wanted to sit elsewhere. So, she sat. Giving him a soft smile as she sat down, the pink linen napkin unfolding as she placed it in her lap, she said, to him, "Doesn't this food look good or what?"

He nodded. "Smells as good as I'm sure it will taste, too."

Her spirits lifted a tiny bit. When he'd entered the kitchen with Adam, he looked positively torn up about something, but she could only begin to guess what it might be about. With everyone seated, they all held hands, bowed their heads and Adam gave the family prayer. Ram's fingers were work worn and heavily calloused, and hers, not as much. Her heart leaped with need of him when he gently enfolded her hand into his, holding it lightly. It reminded her of a man gently holding a baby. She knew his strength; he was built tall and solid, but he held her fingers as if she might break at a moment's notice. There had been so few times that they'd actually touched one another, except to settle a pack, hand a clip of ammunition or grasp a loose strap that might make noise and give their position away and tuck it in where it wouldn't make a sound.

THE GIRLS FACED THEM, and Lera and Adam sat at each end of the table. The children were giggling and covering their mouths with their hands, still excited about the tablets that Ram had gifted them. The first course was minestrone soup with Italian sausage. Adam filled the soup dishes and passed them around. The girls, however, had much smaller soup dishes. Ram envied their innocence. In his business and life, there had been very little of that. But he enjoyed the children's reactions and smiled inwardly.

He was acutely aware of Dare at his right arm. The table was long enough to give them ample breathing room, but sometimes his elbow would accidentally brush her left arm. It was Lera and Adam who kept up the table chatter for the most part. His whole world encircled Dare. Was she even attracted to him? His stomach clenched momentarily, afraid of that answer. She had never shown any flirtatious actions toward him, ever. She joked routinely with the other men of his team, but never with him. Why? And yet, the men of his team brutally teased him from time to time, and vice versa. He finished the soup. There would be a salad next, and then the main course, dessert and coffee or tea to follow.

"Eh, Ram," Lera sang, waving her fork in his direction. "Did you put your suitcase in that second bedroom down the hall?"

"Uh," he replied and frowned. "No, it's still in the car."

Adam chuckled. "What? You're afraid if Lera's cooking was bad you'll make your escape tonight? Never to be seen here again?" He laughed heartily. Everyone knew Lera was a fabulous cook. People in their village always begged for her pastries, pies and cakes to be made by her when they held a festival or a ceremony.

"I'll bring it in after dinner," he managed, spooning the

potato salad onto his plate as the bowl was passed to him by Dare. Their fingers met. He hungrily absorbed the momentary contact. And again, her cheeks flushed. Was that a good sign? Or a bad one? If only he could know. "I'll get the suitcase in after dinner," he promised Lera.

November 3

IT WAS DARK and quiet in the household when Ram silently got up, dressed in his pajamas and winter robe and walked down the hall without being heard. Everyone had gone to bed at 2300, 11:00 p.m. The girls had gone earlier. Dare's bedroom was up ahead on the left and he wanted to make sure he didn't make any sounds to awaken her. She had looked beautiful to him throughout dinner and then everyone enjoyed their aperitif wine in the living room afterward.

The girls had crowded around his feet with their new tablets begging him to help them with the software so they could learn how to better navigate the app and they could see all the rest of the flowers. Ram had worked patiently with them, getting each tablet set up, and then the girls oohed and aahed over the colorful photos. They would hurry around the living room showing everyone in a rocker or overstuffed chair. The wood fireplace sent warmth throughout the rooms. Earlier, Adam had put on some quiet classical music in the background and Ram enjoyed the low lighting, the flames of the fire like dancing shadows throughout the room. To his surprise, Dare had chosen to sit with him on a loveseat, but he didn't say anything one way or another.

So when was the right time and place? He felt impatient,

desperately wanting to have a quiet conversation with her. As he stepped from the hall into the living room, his attention was drawn to the kitchen. There was a slight noise, but he wasn't sure what that meant. Keeping his presence unknown as he walked to the entrance, his heart pounded briefly. There was Dare in her fuzzy one-piece flannel pj's with a cream-colored lambswool robe over it.

"Oh!"

"Sorry," he murmured, holding up his hands, giving her an apologetic look.

She pressed her hand against her heart. "You scared me!"

Ram had the good grace to try to smile a little. "I didn't mean to. I'm sorry, Dare. What are you doing up?" It was 0200. Outside, the rain was furiously pelting against the windows. The wind was still coming and going in huge gusts through the trees surrounding the home.

"Couldn't sleep," she muttered, frowning. "I ate too much. I love good food and Lera's is just the best." She touched her tummy. "I was getting another glass of bitters to help with my digestion."

"Go ahead," he urged. "I overate, too. She's a great cook." He sat down at the table, watching her. Every movement since he'd known her was filled with grace. She never made any jerking or jabbing movements and maybe it was a feminine-masculine thing. But he'd seen her under fire on too many missions and she could shoot as good as anyone on his team.

"Do you want a glass of bitters?"

"No. I've had a lifetime of bitterness, I don't need extra."

She hesitated, then gave him a long, momentary look, and then poured the bitters from the crystal glassware into a smaller awaiting glass. "Where did that comment come from?" she asked gently, turning, glass in hand, and sitting at the end of the table where Lera had sat earlier.

He shrugged. "Haven't you seen how some people's lives fall into different categories, Dare? Some lead very happy lives where everything seems to go right for them. They get the breaks, the opportunities. And then there is another class of people who scavenge for every penny, every step in their life. They work hard, much harder than others, and in the end they become very successful, respected people."

"What about this bitter class? How do you see them?"

His mouth twisted and he looked away for a moment. "Oh… They lead bitter lives. They might have had a terrible childhood or a really good one, but then something devastating happens to them and everything turns bitter and it's a dark tunnel that never ends. There's no daylight at the end of it, no hope, and there's no happy ending for those kinds of people."

She studied him in the silence. "So? Which class are you in?"

Ram shrugged, wanting to tell her everything but it was so damned hard to even begin because he had no hope. "What about you?" he parried. "I'll bet you're in the happy-life group." He saw her eyes change and her mouth thinned.

"I'm in the bitter class, Ram."

Shocked, he stared at her. "You?"

Sitting back, Dare felt his powerful emotions and the utter disbelief in his expression. His eyes narrowed. So? He saw her as happy? Or the struggling camp, instead?

"We've never been personal with one another," she began in a low tone, holding his intense gaze. "Do you really want to know who I am? Warts and all? Because for two years, I never felt that you were really interested in me except for my skill levels. Our communication was strictly professional and on an as-needed basis only."

Ram wiped his mouth. He was sweating. He had to drop this damnable shield he lived behind if he was to unveil how he really felt toward her. He felt helpless, a feeling he stopped when his life was murdered and he had to start all over. But he was feeling it now. "I'm not going to lie to you," he began, voice little more than a growl. "I could not be personal with you in Afghanistan."

"Well, that's true," she said, "but there was no camaraderie between us like you had with the men of the team, either, Ram."

He gave a nod, seeing the hurt reflected in her eyes as well as the question: Why? "It was me," he admitted tiredly, wiping his hands on his thighs. "I wanted to. I mean, I really did, but I was afraid."

She settled back in the chair. "Afraid of what? Me?"

"Sounds kind of silly now, doesn't it?" The derision in his voice was aimed at himself, not her. He saw her eyes lighten, her mouth losing some of that tense line as she held his gaze. "I think part of it was your confidence and fearlessness, Dare. You didn't scare at all, no matter if we were in a firefight, or if you were exposing yourself in order to rescue Artur when he was shot, and I was amazed, like the rest of the team, at your raw, fierce courage."

Snorting, she muttered, "Oh, I was scared, Ram. Just as scared as the rest of you. But you have to remember, I'm a combat medic. I know that I'll be the one to crawl toward our wounded teammate under a hail of fire. The likelihood of getting shot was not only real but happens a lot. So far, I've been lucky, but that's just it. My day will come when I won't be so lucky."

Scowling, he growled, "I don't want you to take risks like that...not now, not ever, moving forward."

Relaxing a little, she finished off her bitters and set the crystal on the table. "You don't become a medic for yourself, Ram, you become one for your team, no matter who they are or the danger they are in. You know very well medics will risk their lives every day. And that's not going to change with me when I join your team again."

The silence grew.

Finally, Ram muttered, "I knew you'd say that."

"So why do you think I'm not in the bitter class?"

He was almost relieved by the change of topic. Pushing around in the chair, he said, "Because you don't behave like a person who is."

"I see. What class do you see yourself in, then?"

"Bitter."

"Could you say a little more?"

He managed a twisted smile. "You first?"

Dare nodded, studying him. "I fit your description of bitter, but maybe I'm in more than one class. My mother wrapped me in a blanket and placed me on the steps of a firehouse where a fireman would find me as a newborn baby."

Blinking, he rasped, "You were abandoned?"

"Yes. I have no memory of it, of course. Three months later I was adopted by a Ukrainian couple who had been in the USA for ten years. My adopted father, Panas Mazur, is a world-class cardiologist and had been lured to come do his research and work at the Cleveland Clinic in Cleveland, Ohio. My mother, Maria Mazur, is a high school science teacher in that city. They had dual citizenship with Ukraine and the USA when they adopted me. I never knew I was adopted and I was very much loved and cared for by them. It wasn't until I was fourteen when they sat me down to tell me the rest of my life story."

"That," he struggled, "was almost the worst thing I can think of happening to a person. I'm sorry. It must make you feel very bad sometimes."

"It did at first, but by the time I was eighteen, I'd reconciled myself to the situation, Ram. I didn't let it stop me from doing what I wanted to do with my life. I still don't know who my mother is, but I live with it. The tremendous love Maria and Panas gave me growing up I think did a lot of healing inside me. I didn't feel thrown away or left to die. I've always believed that if you're supposed to live, you'll be protected and able to go on and achieve your dreams."

He sat there, allowing her situation to move through him without slamming the door shut on his emotions regarding it. She was so sure of herself, never questioning who she was, or her dream she wanted to come true. "You're truly an amazing person," he managed, emotions coloring his voice. "I would *never* have guessed you were orphaned."

"It could have turned out to be bitter," she admitted, "but the love lavished upon me by my adopted parents made all the difference, Ram. Love healed me in ways I couldn't even imagine. And they love me fiercely to this day." She smiled softly, lifting her gaze to the ceiling for a moment. "I don't know if it's because they are Ukrainian. Or the tight-knit family, the extended family they have, that has made them this way, but I sure soaked up their love and healed."

"That is an incredible story," he rasped, "and very uplifting, not depressing."

"Oh, I would get depressed sometimes, Ram. I had ups and downs, but that left me early on because my parents would go home to Lviv, Ukraine, where their entire extended family lives, and I absorbed even more of their family's affection for me." She sighed and smiled faintly. "I was the most loved being in the world as far as I was concerned. Later, as I matured, I understood it was the Ukraine family way of living together that was the safety net that helped save me from feeling like I wasn't worth keeping. All the greater family's love was showered upon me like a protective bubble, and as far as I'm concerned, it made the difference."

"I often wondered why you spoke the Ukraine language so fluently," he said more to himself than her. "You have a natural way of speaking it and there are few who would be able to guess that you are an American."

"I grew up with it," she said. "Maria taught me Russian, also." She gave him a wry look. "That might come in handy next year when we're out in the field."

He grunted and nodded. "Russians murder, rape and torture their enemies and they will destroy the civilian populace as fast as they will us in the military. Unless we accidentally listen in on a local Russian radio call or our comms pick up cell phone chatter between themselves. That information could come in handy and we would pass it on to our intel people."

"The Afghan people fought them for years and they won. Russia backed out."

"They've bit off the wrong country, again," was all Ram would say.

She tilted her head. "I like that we're really talking human-to-human with one another. This is a first."

"It is, isn't it?"

"Is it painful?"

He grinned at her teasing. "No. Liberating, maybe…"

"In what way, Ram?"

Shrugging, he said, "I've been wanting to have conversations like this with you ever since I met you, Dare," and he held her shocked expression.

Silence.

"I've never known you to not have a comeback," he teased her gently. She was giving him a strange, confused look.

"Why now?" she choked.

He looked away for a moment, then lifted his chin, holding her bewildered stare. "It wouldn't have been appropriate in Afghanistan."

Nodding, she whispered, "Yes, you're right, of course." Lips flexing, she asked, "Why now?"

"I was waiting for the right opportunity, Dare. I have no say in where our team is sent, but when we came back here, I thought we'd be here awhile, but we weren't. We were sent to America for six months of further training. We got back here the past week. I was still hoping you were here, and you were. I thought you were in Lviv, unaware of your assignment to teach in Kyiv." He held up his scarred hands. "When we came back, my CO gave me your orders to team up with you again and I couldn't believe it. You were here, in Kyiv."

She gave him an amused look. "Why couldn't you believe it?"

Shaking his head, he muttered, "I'm a bitter person, Dare. Nothing ever works out for me. Not the way I want. Not ever. Getting sent back here to Kyiv I thought was my opportunity to try and forge some sort of a personal relationship with you over time. Then, we spent half a year in the USA. And add to this mix, Russia is going to attack our country sometime early next year. Three things to stop me from wanting to have a different...better relationship with you if you wanted one with me."

"And yet," she murmured, "here you are."

"Is this offer one-sided?" Holding his breath, he saw her grow thoughtful, turning the stem of the crystal slowly around between her slender fingers. Fingers that had sewn the injured people back together. She was a lifesaver in so many ways, Ram thought. A lifesaver to him, as well. His stomach clenched as the silence grew heavily between them. Unable to stand it, he uttered, "Look, if you're in a relationship—"

"I'm not."

"Oh."

"And you?"

He raised a brow.

"Hey, what is good for the goose, Kozak, is good for the gander where I come from."

A grin leaked out. "You've always told us how you felt about something. Why stop now?" He saw her blue eyes deepen in color.

"Honesty is the best policy. It's a good ole American saying."

"America has some really interesting slang." He studied her, seeing her arch her back, giving him that demanding look she could give someone. "I am not in a relationship," he admitted. Dare appeared relieved. Could it be true? That perhaps she liked him in a romantic way? Just a little bit? His heart thudded once to underscore that possibility.

"I know absolutely nothing about you, Ram. Only your being our captain and that you're a damned good leader and tactician."

"Have we crossed the Rubicon?" he wondered.

"I don't know. What do you consider a relationship? It has many definitions."

Wariness was in her husky tone and eyes. Ram couldn't blame her. What was he offering her? A bitter person. Who would ever want one of those bad-luck souls around? He sure wouldn't. Why did he hope that she *did* want him around? What could he offer her? What would she think of his past? She'd glibly talked about her past as if it were nothing, but he knew it was monumental. One didn't get thrown away by their mother and not feel the lifelong sting of abandonment. Still, she didn't act like it, always confident in herself and her abilities and skills.

She was not a braggart, nor was she arrogant. Instead, she was quietly skilled at saving lives. He'd always admired and respected her for that. The fact she'd been abandoned, for whatever the mother's reasoning, was a scar she'd carry all her life and Ram was sure it would never disappear. Just as the scars he wore would do the same. There was no escaping that kind of deep, grinding pain that might soften a little over time. He understood he'd die with his, as she would die with hers.

"We have a war staring us in the face," he said heavily. "And we have to work together again in a team where there can be no personal ties to one another."

"And that's why I asked why you would want any kind of relationship. The timing is bad, Ram."

"I learned my lesson the first time with you," he rasped, feeling as if he were going to lose her before he ever had a chance to know her heart, her soul. "I kept putting it off in Afghanistan. I am an officer. You are an enlisted person. The military does not bless such a union. And then, when the US Army hauled you out of my team to assign you to teach in Lviv, I realized all my planning was for nothing."

"Real life intercedes all the time. We know that as black ops. All we can do is expect change, Ram."

"Have you ever had a deep relationship in your life?"

It was an odd question to ask, but she saw how serious he was about it. "A few, back in college. Once I entered the Army and made Special Forces, I knew I couldn't do both. I either focused on one or another." She hitched one shoulder, a wryness to her tone. "I figured if I was able to make it there, to get into their world-class medical combat program, that later I'd have time for a serious relationship down the road."

"And how did that work out for you?"

"It didn't. I was tops in my class and I was one of the few chosen to enter the advanced surgical field combat training, and I jumped at it. I think my dad had a real influence on me regarding it as I grew up. He would show me a stethoscope, an oximeter, and taught me how to take a blood pressure reading with a cuff. He taught me how to stitch a wound closed with an orange and some dental floss. I was hungry to learn anything medical. When I was eight years old, for Christmas, they gave me a child's physician bag, and I was over the moon." She smiled fondly. "I've always loved medicine and helping people. My dad saved so many lives with the skills he had in his hands and with his training. I wanted to do the same thing. When I was twelve, they sent me to a summer camp for children in Switzerland that was all about beginning medical training. It was the best summer I'd had because it was there that I focused on what I really wanted to do in life."

"To join the Army? Become a medic?"

"Yes, to work in the field of medicine in some way."

"BUT WHY THE MILITARY? You had a family that could easily have paid for your premed education at some of the finest medical schools in America. Yes?"

"Yes, my dad wanted me to go to Harvard. But I wanted adventure, Ram. I didn't want to sit in premed classes for four years and pound memorization into my brain. I wanted to be in the field, hands-on, learn on the job and save lives. When I was seventeen, my father talked the local fire chief into allowing me to become an EMT, emergency medical technician. It was a fourteen-week course and I passed it with flying colors. That's when one of the instructors, the assistant chief, who had been a Special Forces combat field medic, told me the stories of the lives he saved in the field. I knew without a doubt that was exactly what I wanted to do. In fact, he contacted a general, talked to him and wrote a wonderful reference letter to get me into their program."

"You're a brave soul, Dare Mazur."

She shrugged. "My poor parents were worried by my decision. There were three of us girls in that class. We all made the cut. One went into communications and the other became a weapons expert."

"And you became the medic?"

"Yep, and I loved it. I really had no time for an affair or ongoing relationship with a guy. All my time was hands-on learning, which I'm very good at. I don't do well learning by book or taking online computer classes. I like being in the thick of things, kinesthetic training, hands-on and then it sticks with me. I remember it."

"I'm sure your parents continue to be very worried for you."

She sighed. "Yes, a lot of worry when I was ordered to go to Afghanistan."

"What about now? They're in America. You are here in Ukraine. The Army now needs us to stay in-country to help us fight for our democracy. They must still be very worried about that."

She became glum, holding the crystal stem between her fingers. "They are beside themselves with worry. I haven't told them about the orders to go into your team, Ram. They were expecting me to come home to the US and be safe."

"Any parent would worry about their child in a situation like this," he agreed. "When are you going to break this news to them?"

She gave him a weary look. "I don't know yet... They realize I'm in the Army and I can't just walk away and go live in Cleveland with them. I just signed back up for another six-year hitch. I thought I'd be in Kyiv teaching during my enlistment...not out on the battlefield again."

Silence fell over them. He roused himself and he sat up, holding her sad gaze. "So where does that leave us? What do you want to do about this?" Again, his stomach clenched. Ram tried to steel himself against the obvious answer that he knew would come from her.

She smiled slightly. "I like the idea of a friendship with you. That is a relationship. What did you have in mind?"

He rubbed his jaw. "I like the idea of a friendship. I want to earn the right to be your friend."

She smiled softly. "That feels good to me. Why not come with us and the girls tomorrow morning? We're going to be hunting for rose hips and Lera is going to teach me how to make jelly out of them."

"Sounds exciting," he deadpanned, a slight lift of the corners of his mouth. "I'd like to go with you." Hope infused him. She hadn't turned him down. She didn't say no. Friendship? It was better than nothing. And perhaps, over time, it could turn into something deeper and more long-lasting.

Chapter Four

November 3

Anna and Sophia were dressed warmly on the cool November morning after the storm had passed. The ground was wet, the grass long, yellowed and tangling around their rubber-booted feet as Dare aimed the happy little group toward a hedgerow of bushes ahead of them. Dare looked up, the sky still filled with low, ragged-looking clouds, the end of the front still coming through, lots of patches of light blue sky here and there. The air was crisp and she inhaled it deeply, loving the scent of the musky earth after the sweet smell of rain had lavished the soil. Most of the trees that ringed the property, a large square of ten acres, were losing their colorful leaves. The wild rosebushes grew between the trees, many of them ten to twelve feet tall. They were very old, well established, and even at this distance, she could see the bright red rose hips that reminded her of red bulb decorations that were hung on a Christmas tree.

Glancing to her right, she saw Ram walking a few feet away from her, looking around, a habit of being in black ops. The cries of ravens erupted suddenly, and she saw a buck and three does running from one area to another.

Right now, it was mating season and she enjoyed seeing the wildlife that were more intent on that than being seen by humans. Smiling, with Anna on her left and Sophia on her right, she said, "Did you see them?" She pointed toward the deer.

"Oh, yes!" Anna cried, "How pretty!"

"They're staring at us!" Sophia said.

"I think they're surprised we're here," Dare agreed. She carried two five-gallon buckets in her hands and Ram carried the other two.

The deer took off, white tails in the air, disappearing once more into the woods.

"Tell me again what we're doing this morning?" Ram asked.

Dare suppressed a smile. He'd overslept this morning and Adam had to rouse him so he could leave on time with them. "Rose hips. Lera's mother was a sixth-generation herbalist. They used the rose hips as a tea or tincture throughout the fall, winter and spring to cure colds and flu."

"I like them!" Anna said, jumping up and down, throwing her arms into the air.

"I do, too!" Sophia said, not wanting to be left out of the commentary.

"What do you like best about them?" Dare asked the six-year-old.

"I like the jelly! I like lots and lots of it on toast with butter!"

"Sounds good," Ram added, smiling a little at the child whose cheeks were a rosy red.

"Rose hip jam and jelly are a forever food here in Ukraine," Dare said to him. "Surely you had it in your family?"

Ram grimaced and said, "Yeah, I suppose we did." He

wasn't going there today. He was trying to learn how to be a friend to Dare. He had no idea how to go about it, however. Men were friends. Women? Well, in his life they were never friends. Lovers? Yes. But a friend? He was having trouble separating sex from friendship, the need to love Dare versus what friends would do instead. He never had this problem before because all his friends were male.

"Did you ever go out with your mother or grandmother and pick them in the late fall like this?"

He squirmed inwardly. "I really don't have such a memory..." he answered, purposefully vague. Feeling guilty more than ever because yesterday early morning Dare had opened up her private life to him, sharing events through her childhood. He'd been a thirsty, hungry wolf for just such information from her because it helped him understand her. He'd always wondered what made her tick and now he knew: her medical doctor father had a powerful influence over her, but in truth, she had an inner love and drive to be in the field of medicine, anyway. It helped explain to him why she was so devoted to her career, why she took risks that all combat medics would take sooner or later—and live to tell about it.

Ram knew he was super protective, like a father with his children, of his team. The responsibility weighed heavily on him, without relief, but he didn't care because he was a Ukrainian patriot and would do anything for his "family" and his country. He saw the questioning in her gaze as they walked with his nonanswer. He didn't like doing that to her, but with two energetic young ones with them, it was not an appropriate place to speak to her on more personal terms. They were approaching one end of a half-mile-long hedgerow of wild rosebushes and he could see the red rose hips everywhere among the leaves.

The girls surged ahead, squealing with excitement, their hands in gloves so that their small fingers wouldn't keep getting poked with the tiny needlelike thorns. The wind was chilly and he'd pulled up the sheepskin collar of his jacket to protect the back of his neck.

Dare was well prepared, a purple knit cap on her short, dark hair. A muffler around her neck, the ends tied at her throat. He remembered when she'd first come to the team, her hair had literally been halfway down her back. It didn't take long for her to figure out that the long strands would get caught in everything and slow her response time, plus cause a lot of other issues when they were getting shot at. He recalled after that mission she'd asked Adam to chop it all off, and his second-in-command looked anguished over doing it. Dare hadn't. She was relieved to get it out of the way. Much to his surprise, she gave the shorn locks to an Afghan woman who weaved it for an older woman who was going bald, and she created a wig of sorts out of it for her.

Afghan women were famous for making something out of nothing. Dare had taken her locks to the village and given them to the weaver, who set to work. Those two years they were there, that particular village always invited them for feasts and ceremonies after that. It had been one of the few positive bright spots in their time in that war-torn, starving country.

"We'll start here," Dare told him, setting the buckets down at the end of the row. "Ram, if the rose hip is green, yellow or orange? It's not ripe, so let it stay on the bush. Just pick the bright red ones."

"There's all colors on this one," he said, looking it up and down.

"A Christmas tree with light bulbs, for sure," she said, smiling over at him.

He felt his heart thud once, privy to that sweet smile of hers that flowed through him. Dare was happy. He could see it in her dancing blue gaze, the tilt of the corners of her soft mouth curving upward. Managing a slight smile, he said, "Strange Christmas tree, but you're right." Right now, she was setting each bucket about two meters apart for the girls, as well as for themselves.

Each child claimed a bucket and swiftly began to collect the ripe rose hips with a blur of tiny hands in motion. She placed the third bucket, hers, between her booted feet, going to work.

Ram said, "I'll go this way," and he pointed to his right. He halted and for a moment watched the little girls as they started at the top, as high as they could reach, and then came down vertically until they were bent over, getting the last of the rose hips at the bottom of the bush they'd been assigned. Then, they'd move a few inches, and start at the top and work their way down another row. He mimicked their way of doing things.

The sun peeked out, warming him and brightening the land around them. He felt a kind of peace descend over him with Dare and the children nearby. It brought back a lot of sweet memories from his early boyhood.

"What are we going to do with all these seeds when we get back to their home?" he wondered.

"Oh, we have a lot to do when we get them home, Ram. It's a process. First, we wash them under running, cold water and take off any thing that doesn't belong on them. We have to make sure there's no bird poop on them, either."

He laughed, and it felt good. "I never really thought about that angle of it." He could see the devilry dancing in her eyes, his smile broadening. "What else? This is really entertaining."

"Every berry is investigated completely, believe me. You don't want to see that rose hip ending up with something white or gray on it, or insect parts sticking out of it, in your jar of jam or jelly."

He chuckled. "Okay, I get your point. What else do you do with them?"

She reached above her head, expertly picking off the ripe seeds, but leaving the rest and not damaging the branch they were found on. "We will freeze all of them over night."

"Why is that?"

"We have to open each one up with a sharp knife the next morning, cutting them in half, and if they're frozen, it's just so much easier to do. We have to be sure to scrape and collect all the seeds inside the hip, and also, each seed has lots of tiny little hairs on it. We have to scrape the inner part of the hip clean so they're all removed. If you don't, those hairs prick you. The inside of your mouth will becoming highly irritated and itch like crazy."

He began plucking the hips, not as fast or as nimbly as Dare, who obviously had lots of experience doing this. Looking down the row, Ram saw the girls going Mach 3 with their red hair on fire, their small hands a blur of speed, the constant drop, drop, drop of the hips into their bucket situated between their feet.

"That's a lot of work." He looked down at his bucket, the

bottom covered. "I must have picked fifty or so already. You three are way ahead of me."

She snorted. "We'll do *thousands* of them before this is all over."

He gave her a teasing, evil look. "Now I see why you wanted me to come this weekend."

"We need every able-bodied person we can find to help us. This is the best time of year to get the rose hips. We aren't the only ones doing it," she said and tilted her head to the right.

Ram saw at least five families of men, women and children coming their way with buckets in hand. "The whole town's coming? What is this? Rose Hip Weekend? Is that why Adam asked me to stay over? He never mentioned *this*."

Snickering, Dare said, "Adam is sneaky, you know that, Ram. Those folks who are coming will be standing two meters apart, just like we're doing. That's your plot or space you pick within. Don't wander into someone else's territory, okay?"

"Wouldn't think of it," he said, lifting a hand in hello at the approaching families. Everyone was merry. There was a lot of laughter and joking as they got to work down the row of rosebushes. "So? Everyone makes jam and jelly out of these rose hips?"

Nodding, Dare dropped a handful into her buckets, glad to have her thick leather gloves on. "The ones that are orange colored will get red in the next several days. Then, you'll see another group of families coming down to pick them when that happens. It's an annual village affair, for sure. Everyone will get enough."

"Adam once said that Lera was an herbalist?"

"Yes. She comes from a long line of women in her family, the information passed down from one generation to the next. She's been helping me to become more aware about herbs since my assignment in Kyiv, and I stay at their home on most weekends. I get to watch her making her herb infusions, decoctions, salves, ointments and teas for the people of the village. There are ten women in the village who are what we call the wise women. They're the ones who know the plants, and they know which ones are medicinal and how to make them so they help a human or animal. I love it because for me, it's a more natural kind of medicine. I like learning about the plants because they can be used out in the field if I don't have anything in my pack."

Nodding, Ram was impressed. "Does Lera have anything for sore knees?"

Dare made a face. "Oh, yeah. Tell me which of our team doesn't have sore joints. In our business, our elbows, knees and hip joints take a beating."

"Your knees, also?"

"Yes." She held up a handful of rose hips. "One of the many medicinal areas these little red seeds help is joint inflammation."

He stared at the innocuous rose hips. "Seriously?"

"Yes. When I came here from Afghanistan I asked Lera for something because my joints were really barking at me. She made a tea out of the rose hips and sent me home with a canister of the powder. I was to make one cup of tea and drink it every day."

"What did it do for you?"

"Within three days, the pain in my knees stopped, the

inflammation and swelling were starting to reduce, which was a huge relief. Two weeks into a cup a day? My knees were like new and the swelling was completely gone. Lera had said that rose hips are very gentle and anyone can drink it as a tea. It's a very active medicinal herb and is superb when used by people like us, or folks who have osteoarthritis or rheumatoid arthritis."

"I think I'd better start giving these red berries a lot more respect," he murmured, looking thoughtfully into his half-filled bucket.

"You can drink a cup of tea daily, or use the jam or jelly on your toast every morning, and it will do the same thing. Lots of different ways to take it. I make up capsules with the powder and will take two of them a day if I don't have time to make the tea on some mornings before I teach classes."

"Who'd have thought a little red seed like this could do so much good for us?"

"Roger that," she said, looking at her bucket, "because medicinal herbs are so important. They can save a life, and if you really want to get technical about it. It was medical herbs since humans arrived here on Earth that saved our species and allowed us to flourish and populate the planet. We were a plant-and-herb-taking population until just recently, the past hundred years or so if you want to think about it. Herbs work. The proof is in the fact there's a huge human population on Earth."

"How else do these unsung seeds help us?"

"If you take four grams a day of the rose hip powder for six weeks it can reduce your cardiovascular risk. It lowers the systolic blood pressure and also lowers your cholesterol levels."

"That's really amazing." He studied the red seed again, impressed.

"And...if that isn't enough? This little seed will take on inflammation anywhere in our body and science is now realizing how deadly that particular condition is for all of us."

"So, the people here in this village drink the tea daily?"

"Yes. The men especially like it because they get sore joints from doing a lot of hard, physical labor."

"Too bad we didn't have this around in Afghanistan," he grumbled. "We sure could have used it."

"Isn't that the truth," she agreed.

"It's kind of a super-medicinal herb?"

"Yes and no. There are a number of medicinal herbs that have a lot of areas of application. Lera knows *all* of them. She's a walking encyclopedia. I keep an herb journal with me, and when I'm here on weekends, we'll sit down at least once or twice and she'll give me information on an herb that grows around Bucha that she uses."

"Do herbs have any vitamin or minerals in them?" he wondered.

"Plants are super good in a nutritional sense." She straightened and opened her gloved hand, ticking off some of the benefits. "Like the rose hips? They have vitamin C, calcium, magnesium, potassium, beta-carotene, quercetin, tocopherols and lycopene. They are a very rich source of so many nutrients that humans need. And people in the USA are severely magnesium deficient because that mineral is no longer found in our soil because of the way the farmers tilled and manage their land hundreds of years earlier.

Magnesium helps us combat stress, and if you're deficient, you may have insomnia, broken sleep and it just gets worse over time." She held up a fat red rose hip. "If you would just take a cup of tea a day? You're helping your body in so many positive ways."

He thought for a moment. "You're right…" He gave her a praising look. She grinned and went back to work.

"Race to fill up my bucket before you do yours…"

"You're on," he growled, and started working a Mach three with his hair on fire.

November 7

DARE HURRIED ACROSS the street and headed toward the military complex building in central Kyiv. She checked her watch. Feeling stressed because she had been late meeting the people in the human resources department, ending her teaching duties at a certain date, had taken more time than she thought.

She reached the top-secret area where she knew Ram's team was going to meet today. Going down a brightly lit, highly waxed hall far underground, she found the conference room and opened the door. Stepping in, she saw Ram standing near the front of the room, the rest of the men seated at the long oval oak table. Each one had a laptop in front of him. Luckily, she had hers in her backpack. She grinned and lifted her hand, saying, "And here I thought I'd never see any of you guys again!"

A roar of welcome went up and every man stood, coming over to slap her back or hug her or grab her hand and shake it in welcome. Dare hadn't expected this kind of reaction, but she was happy to see the team she'd left two years earlier. Off to one side, she saw Ram standing, watching them, face unreadable, although his eyes glittered. A couple of men and Leonid, who was a mechanic and artillery expert, lifted her off her feet, squeezing the breath out of her, a fierce welcome from someone she loved dearly like a long-lost brother, and who had always been super protective of her because she was a woman.

As soon as she was put down, Borysko, a blond-haired, blue-eyed and bearded six-footer, lifted her up and twirled her around, grinning and welcoming her "home" and saying that he'd missed her terribly and was so glad she was back with them.

Blinking back tears, she saw these men as her brothers, most of them around her age. They escorted her to the table, showing her the seat they'd saved for her, a top-secret laptop already open and waiting for her. She noted that Ram would be sitting next to her and that Adam took his seat on the other side of his leader. The table rocked with lots of questions, answers and laughter, not to mention black humor jokes. It was a wonderful welcome. All of them looked older, but she'd been gone for two years from the team, and she knew the stress of constant engagement and combat, which all black ops dealt with. They'd earned every line in their faces, old before their time.

The door opened and suddenly the room quieted. Dare saw two intelligence officers, a man and woman, crisply enter the room. They were majors, so that meant they were bringing a lot of highly classified intel to them. Everyone became seated. Ram sat down and gave her a brief nod of hello. Everyone faced forward toward the intel officers at the front of the long table. Dare pulled out her pen and notebook, something she was never without at these meetings. The laptop in front of her jumped to life and it was connected with the officers' tablets at the front of the room. Feeling like she was settling into an old, well-known groove, she listened to them begin to talk about the coming war with Russia.

The hours had moved swiftly. By the time the intel officers had laid it all out for them, it was 1500, 3:00 p.m. Dare's head swam with consternation. When would she tell her parents that she was a part of Ram's team once more? They knew what that meant. She had put them through two years of anxiety hell, wondering if she would be wounded or killed in action on any given day of the week in Afghanistan.

The last weekend at Adam and Lera's home was 180 degrees different from today. Every face in the room was now grim. She felt Ram's energy, although his back was to her, all his attention on the intelligence briefing. It was comforting to have him close to her right now. This was different. This was their country that would be attacked. He'd always given her that sense of safety even out on missions. She wondered if his men felt the same way, fairly sure that they did.

"Dismissed," the woman major told them, shutting down her tablet and placing it into a brown calf leather briefcase at the end of the conference table.

Everyone stood, little being said until the intel officers had departed. Then, Dare heard the murmuring among the team members. Most of all, she searched Adam's very dire-looking face. He seemed shocked to Dare, but why wouldn't he be? One of the main routes into Kyiv was right through the village of Bucha, where they lived. The intel people left nothing unsaid about Russians and their lack of mercy and never following the Geneva Conventions if they took Ukrainians prisoner. Worse? The woman drilled into them, her dark eyes filled with warning, when she said the Russians would go through a civilian village and they would rape the girls and women and kill the men, and any young man of soldier age would be tortured, shot and buried in an unmarked grave. It turned Dare's stomach and she wrestled with worry over Adam's family.

"Hey," Ram said, approaching her, "you ready to go?"

Shaken, she nodded, saying nothing. She followed him out of the room after saying goodbye to the team. The men would meander out of the room at their own pace. He walked at her shoulder.

"This way," he urged her quietly, opening another door. It led to stairs going up to the surface world above them.

Her feet felt like weighted lead, her shoulders heavy with dread. They climbed three flights and at the emergency door, Ram moved past her and opened it for her.

Blinking, she realized they were out on street level, but not at the main entrance any longer. Weather-wise, it was sunny and beautiful. Cars were whizzing by, and everything looked so peaceful and normal. Easing out onto the sidewalk, Ram scanned the area, always on guard, always aware.

"Let's go to your apartment?" he suggested.

"Y-yes…okay…"

"Or would you rather be alone right now, Dare? I just thought you might like some company."

"I'm really feeling torn up inside, Ram…"

"I think all of us are," he rasped, giving her a patient look. "Your car is parked where?"

She pointed. "Two blocks down on the left."

"Do you want company or not?"

Nodding, she said, "It would be nice to have some private time with you. I have so many worries about this briefing…"

"You're not alone. Let's talk in private."

She heard something new in his low tone as he walked on the outside of her toward the parking lot. It was a beautiful November day, warming up, the sky a dark blue. "It's so peaceful right now…"

"Yes," he murmured. "But not for long."

"I think I need a cup of lemon balm tea. My nerves are screaming," she admitted.

"Make that two cups."

RAM FELT THE emotional storm building in Dare as she changed her clothes and reappeared in the kitchen to make them the tea in her ground-floor apartment. She wore a pair of comfortable brown trousers and a cream-colored angora sweater. How badly he wanted to slide his arms around her shoulders and bring her against him and hold her…just hold her and take away the anxiety he saw in her darkened eyes that normally shined with such life. They were dull looking right now. He wrestled inwardly with his own emotions, mostly for Adam and his family, some for his team as a whole and the rest for Dare. His protectiveness was leaking out and it seemed he didn't have the normal iron-clad control over it he used to.

"Is there anything I can do to help?" he offered, standing, his hips resting against the kitchen counter near where she was working.

"No. I got this…"

"Where do you keep the teacups?"

"Up there," and she pointed to a cabinet.

He needed to do something to help her. "I'll get them," he said.

After finding two beautiful porcelain teacups and saucers, hand-painted pink and red roses on them, he located the flatware drawer, bringing out two teaspoons to go with them. Just the sounds of the copper teakettle being filled with water, something common and daily, was soothing to him. He saw some of her worry ease, her shoulders starting to relax. There was a modicum of peace in the rhythm of everyday life.

"Won't rose hip tea help?" he teased her gently.

She managed a one-sided partial smile. "No, it's not a nervine like lemon balm. Nervine herbs are your stress busters. They soothe the central and parasympathetic nervous systems."

"I see…"

"That was nice of Lera to bag you up some rose hips so that you could have a cup a day after finding out your knees were as bad as mine."

He grinned a little, arms against his chest as he rested against the kitchen counter. She set the copper teakettle on the stove to heat. "It was. And she wouldn't take any money."

"You are family to her, Ram. The whole team is. That is how she and Adam see all of us. Any of the other guys, if they want it for their joints, all they have to do is ask and she'll supply them the rose hip powder. I think if you try it out and get good results, you should share the information with them. Lera would love to give them some. She doesn't like to see people suffer."

"As soon as I find out it works? I'll let them know." Wanting to place his hands on her shoulders as she turned to face him because she was in desperate need of being held, he reminded himself that he had said he wanted her as a friend. Not her lover. "You don't like to see people suffer either, Dare."

"You're right about that. Let's go to the living room, Ram. I'll bring the tea in on a tray and we'll sit on the couch. That okay?"

"Yes, I'd like that." His heart lifted with hope. That word *hope* had been burned out of him at eighteen, but here it was, back again. Ram didn't try to fight or suppress it this time. Instead, he ambled into her living room, the western sun flowing brightly through floor-to-ceiling windows, like a golden waterfall, into the area. Everything about her apartment was neat, clean and welcoming. She liked the color purple, he discovered, the curtains across the huge picture windows filtering the sunlight through light lavender ones. There was a vase of fresh flowers that he'd given her on Sunday, before she left the Voronas' home. He smiled to himself when he saw Dare had mixed into it a few sprigs of rose hips on their twigs, with some bright red maple leaves to top it off.

She came in a few minutes later with a small teak tray bearing the teapot, cups and spoons, plus a jar of honey that Lera had also gifted her with. The ties between Adam's family and her were strong and good. Ram was glad she had a "second family" here in Kyiv because he'd discovered how much she loved her adopted parents, who were safe in the United States. She was a family person. He had been, too, at one time, but that was lost to the sands of time. His life stopped at eighteen. And he'd had to start all over.

Looking back on it, Ram was amazed at that immature age how well he had done despite the traumatic life blow. He could have done a lot of things, turned to addiction to escape his horrifying family history, become a drunkard or done something reckless like take revenge. Having done none of those things, and thanks to the Army he'd joined earlier, they'd helped him through that terrible gauntlet of shock and loss. So, he had himself to thank that he listened and trusted the right people at that seminal moment in his life.

Now? As Dare sat down after placing the tea service on the glass and wood coffee table in front of them, they were all going to be at a similar moment come mid-February of next year. Everyone's life would change drastically for the worse, not the better.

He watched her pour the light-colored brown liquid. It smelled good, a sweet scent and maybe a bit of mint in it? He wasn't sure as he took a dollop of honey. Stirring it, he sat back, a good two feet separating them. He was happy that she'd sat fairly close to him. Did Dare know she needed to be held? Ram wasn't sure because she was such a strong, confident and independent woman. He admired that in her, but then, Ukrainian people had a long history in this part of the world, the ancient people being strong and resilient, too.

She sipped the tea, slowly leaning back on the flowery fabric of the couch. "Mmm, this tastes so good. Try yours?"

He nodded. The delicate porcelain cup and saucer made him feel awkward. His hands were large, square and covered with thick calluses from years of black ops duty. Compared with her hands, her skin soft and fairly unmarred, his were the opposite: white scars here and there along with pink ones, hands deeply tanned, and they weren't pretty looking at all. Sipping the tea, he made a sound in his throat.

"This tastes good, Dare."

"Lemon balm goes down easy. We need to drink the entire cup and then we'll see how we feel after that."

"Anything to come off the cliff we were just pushed over," he growled, nodding, sipping more.

She gave him a warm look, her voice off-key. "Thanks for being here. I don't know how you knew, Ram, but I needed someone...you..."

Those were the sweetest words he never thought he'd hear Dare say.

Chapter Five

Dare poured herself a second steaming cup of lemon balm. She'd seen the surprise flicker momentarily in Ram's gray eyes when she admitted her need of him, his company. His shoulders relaxed and his eyes darkened a little as he studied her. She wasn't sure what that meant.

"I'll be the first to admit that I've never been friends with a woman, so I'm feeling like I'm skating on thin ice, here, with you."

"You have male friends, right?"

"Yes."

"Then regard me like that?"

He managed a slight grimace. "I had many friends who were boys, growing up. Girls were strange to me and I was honestly shooed away from them because I thought they acted and thought differently than boys did."

"Variety is the spice of life, Ram. If we do think and see things differently, that's not a weakness as far as I'm concerned, it's a strength. Instead, I see it as two points of view to be considered is all."

"I think men like to categorize and organize everything into neat little boxes. Nothing complex."

She gave an abrupt laugh. "Women don't fit within those so-called boxes and never will."

"Through the years you were with us, the way you thought and saw things always kept us safer."

Nodding, she sipped her tea. "I can see overall patterns, and we have the ability to zero in on the exact detail that needs to be further studied within that pattern."

"I remember you fixated on a bunch of six-foot-tall bushes near the summit of a hill we were approaching. You saw movement when none of us men did. It saved our lives. It was a trap and the Taliban was setting up to kill all of us."

Nodding, she said, "And that brings me to what's bothering me so much, Ram."

"I felt you freeze behind me at the meeting."

"Yes." She sighed. "Adam's village highway is marked as one of two main routes that the Russian tanks are going to use to destroy Kyiv."

Grimly, he nodded. "Yes... That's not good."

"We need to talk with him and Lera. They need to move out of there, Ram. They can't stay there."

"I was thinking along the same lines." He gave her a reverent look. "I figured you would be considering such an option, too."

She set the emptied cup on the coffee table. "They *have* to move, Ram. And soon. That's all there is to it. They can't stay there. I wish... I wish we could warn the whole village."

"They will be warned by village government officials," he reassured her. "What I worry about is that many of the villagers have nowhere else to go or they may not have the money to make such a move." He frowned. "There's no easy fix on this, especially since it is on such short notice and it is winter."

"I know," she grumbled, scowling. "If they stay... I don't even want to think about it." Turning to him, she set the teacup on the coffee table, hands clasped tight in her lap. "I'm racking my brain trying to figure a way to get them to leave, at least until the war is over. If Lera and the girls could go across the border, into Poland, and stay there—"

"She's tied to Ukraine, Dare. She won't leave this country. They have no relatives in Poland, either."

Pursing her lips, she closed her eyes for a moment and then opened them. "I have plan B."

His shoulders relaxed a little. "Tell me about it."

"I want to try and get them to move into central Kyiv. There's a family apartment right across the hall from me that is up for lease right now. It is large, and they would be so much safer here. I don't believe our troops will allow Russians into Kyiv. I just don't."

"We're in agreement," he said quietly. "So? There's an apartment next door and Lera and her girls could stay there?"

"Yes, and since I'll be with your team, she can also come over with the code card I'll give her, to get whatever she needs from my apartment." She gave him a swift look. "I want them out of Bucha, Ram. I don't care if Lera hates me for forcing this change on her. I'll take her anger or whatever she wants to throw at me if only she'll agree to leave the village for now."

Rubbing his jaw, he sat back on the couch after setting

his cup on the coffee table. "Lera is a levelheaded person. She won't take it out on you."

"I feel you're probably right. Adam, I'm sure, will want her and the girls to leave, too. I believe he will agree with our plan and support it."

Nodding thoughtfully, he said, "It would be best for all of them. Adam will go wild with terror if the Russians capture Bucha. He knows only too well what will happen. I need him focused on our team, on our orders and mission. He won't be any good to me, otherwise."

"I hadn't even thought that far ahead," she whispered, wiping her eyes.

He studied her as the silence cloaked them. "Why tears?" he rasped gently, reaching out, placing his hand over hers momentarily. He squeezed her fingers and they were icy cold. Her fingers curled around his in response. "Dare? You can talk to me. We're going to be friends, right? Don't friends tell each other everything?"

"I—I guess I should," she managed, her voice raspy. The expression on his face was one of caring, something she'd rarely seen. His fingers gently squeezed hers, and fresh tears came to her eyes. She never cried in front of the team. Not ever. Sniffing, she wiped the tears away with her other hand.

He released her fingers and dug into his pocket, producing a white cotton handkerchief. "Here," he said, his voice low, slipping it into her hand, "use this…"

His unexpected compassion broke her. It happened without warning and Dare didn't realize until just then how much anxiety and worry for Adam's family she was carrying. Pressing the cloth to her eyes, she muttered, "I've never cried in front of you."

"I know," he answered, sadness in his tone. "You always went off by yourself, out of sight and earshot, to do it." He reached out, gently massaging her slumped shoulder. "You don't know how many times I wanted to go find you, and be supportive of you, Dare."

Wiping her eyes, she blew her nose, giving him a startled look. "You did?" she croaked.

He nodded, leaving his hand on her shoulder. "It pains me to see you suffering like that. All I wanted to do, I guess, was to hold you, console you, give you my shoulder so you had something to cry on."

Shaken, she clenched the handkerchief between her hands. "I never knew," she whispered brokenly, searching his eyes.

"I was torn about my action, my decision, Dare. My heart wanted to go after you, wanting you to cry on my shoulder, while I held you. I knew how much you were hurting. You're a medic. Medics are all heart. I desperately wanted to be with you, just to give you someone to talk with if you wanted," and he said, patting his shoulder, "to lay your head on me and cry it out." He managed a slight grimace. "I've been holding on to this secret for years. We're more mature now, Dare, and seasoned operators. We know war. It always hurt me to see you walk off, having no one there to hear your cry, or wipe your tears away, to listen to whatever you wanted to share with me…"

The silence fell softly between them. Their gazes met and held. Dare sniffed, her face hot from the tears. "W-why didn't you tell me this before now?" Her voice was wobbly as she was unsure about what she saw, stormy emotions in his eyes, in the way he grimaced and winced when she asked the question.

"Because I was a coward, Dare. That's why."

She straightened, as if slapped, staring at him. "What? No!" The words had come out with fierceness. "You've put yourself on the line so many times for our team. I was afraid for you. You were so brave, as if you knew you were protected by some higher force for good."

"Listen to me," he rasped, choking out the words, "I was a coward for never telling you how much I wanted to care for you. I constantly fought my desire to have a relationship with you, Dare. That was the other war I was fighting within myself."

Gasping, she blinked, her lips, wet with tears, parting. "W-what?"

He dragged in a long breath of air and then released it. "There's too much at stake right now," he said, more to himself than her, his brows scrunching. He held her shocked look and added roughly, emotion nearly overwhelming him, "Dare, somewhere along the way after you joined our team in Afghanistan, I fell deeply and completely for you. I'd seen you with the sick babies in those villages, I saw you treat the women and the aged ones… I've been with you on the battlefield when Artur was gravely wounded and you saved his life…" He shook his head, giving her a look of apology.

"I was a coward for not coming clean with you, not telling you the truth. I was afraid you'd get angry, but what scared me more than anything was that you didn't have the same feelings for me. I sensed it, but neither one of us acted upon it.

"With Russia on our doorstep right now, I made a decision after the briefing today to tell you the truth because it was eating me up alive. I needed to hear how you feel. I don't want to go into battle without knowing if there might be a future for us or if there isn't. And if there isn't? You'll still be our medic and we'll work as a team. I won't hold anything against you if you don't feel reciprocal. Only you and I will know the truth between us and it is ours to keep secret with one another. The team will not know anything. We'll work together, as we always have."

Her heart was pounding furiously and she swallowed hard several times, her tears turning off by the shock of his honesty. Pushing some short strands away from her brow, she sat there digesting everything. She saw the utter suffering in Ram's face, the apology in his eyes and fear that she was going to reject him, reject his love for her.

"You couldn't let me know," she offered quietly, her voice barely above a ragged whisper. "Army regulations. And if that didn't stop you, then what did is your concern for the cohesiveness of our team. Our ability to trust one another with our lives was primary and most important. Am I right, Ram?"

Sighing, he nodded. "Yes, I couldn't see any other way to address my dilemma, Dare. But how do you feel? That's what I need to know."

"I didn't have those feelings...at first."

Nodding, he said, "I understand."

"But something changed between us, Ram. I felt it about three months into our team being together."

"You knew then?"

"I knew something, but I had no idea what it really meant. You were like ice, Ram. No emotion when we were out on the line."

"It kept you alive, didn't it?"

She managed a snort. "Yes, it did. But you were always distant toward me. I could never figure out why. You were warm, smiling, joking and laughing with the men, but you avoided me like I was the bubonic plague."

"I was afraid I couldn't handle my escaping emotions that I held secretly for you, Dare. It wasn't you. I was *my* problem with myself. I'd had my share of relationships, but when you came into my team, you stunned me. I was never the same after meeting you."

She blew out a long breath, giving him a sideward glance. "Well, you treated me like I was off-limits as a human being, never mind someone that you were drawn to. I figured you really didn't want me in your team."

"What?" He sat up, staring in disbelief at her. "Is *that* what you thought?"

"Sure," she snapped, defensive over his sudden, raw emotional disclosure. "Look back on that time, Ram. You ignored me. You never smiled at me. You never joked with me. It was like I was some kind of virulent infection in your team. I could feel this ice coming off you toward me."

Wearily, he shook his head. "Because I wasn't mature enough, Dare. I didn't have what it took to find common ground with you, to help you know that you were wanted. I didn't know how to handle the situation, so I made sure that you would always approach me as the professional you were."

"You were afraid of yourself?"

"Yes." He pushed his fingers through his dark hair in an aggravated motion. "It's different now, of course. I've grown since then. Before, I saw you as beautiful, all heart, a warm smile…" He hesitated. "The way you smile makes my heart open up with such a rush of joy that I have no words for it. I saw you bestow that wonderful smile of yours on the Afghan babies, the children and the elderly. And you were like that with everyone on the team, too. My men loved you like a sister."

"They took me under their wing, Ram. All of them. I felt wanted and they respected me for the skills I was bringing to them in the team."

He managed a grimace and gave her a wry look. "You never piss off the medic on your team. He or she is your best friend who can save your sorry ass and get you back home to your family if you are wounded."

She shook her head. "Medics, in general, are held in esteem by everyone. No medic would refuse to save a team member's life even if they didn't like one another. They aren't built that way."

Silence grew between them. She cast a look in his direction, the suffering clearly in his expression now. "After Artur was carried aboard that Blackhawk helicopter, the paramedic on board and I worked together to keep him stable."

"I'll never forget that day," he rasped wearily. "We all sat on the deck, that helo shaking and shuddering, the noise so high we couldn't hear ourselves think. You two were working all the time on that one-hour flight back to camp. I remember thinking that you looked like an angel among us, your hands were so slender, so graceful, and that each time you touched Artur, who was unconscious on the deck, you were giving him lifesaving energy you held in your heart for him, to keep him alive."

She inhaled deeply. "My whole existence was focused on him and nothing else."

Silence again fell over them.

Ram cleared his throat. "After Artur was taken to the hospital at the camp, you were standing there alone, and we were all whipped, defeated, fearing we'd lost him and that only you had stood between him and his death. We all knew that." He reached out, gripping her hand resting on her thigh, holding her glistening gaze. "I couldn't help myself at that moment. Something old and hard snapped within me and I remember throwing my arms around your shoulders and hauling you against me. I thanked you for saving Artur's life. I lived in a hellish fear of losing any-one on my team. All I wanted to do was to get all of you safely home, out of that sandbox hell, so that you could once more see your family, and the people who loved you.

"I remember that night so clearly, Dare. I'll never forget it as long as I live. We stood there on the helicopter apron, holding on to one another. That was a healing moment for me because I knew I could have lost you that day when you ran into that crossfire and dived for where Artur lay un-conscious, dragging him back, one-handed, behind a huge boulder to safety. You tore open your medical knapsack and went to work on him. Bullets were flying all around you. You saved him that day." His voice lowered. "I cared for you so much in that hour of terror. Your focus, that fierce look on your face as you worked over him… Nothing else mattered to you in that moment. You were so brave…so competent… Since then, I've always seen you as an earth angel who walks among us poor human beings, your touch bringing us life, bringing us hope."

Shaking her head, she muttered, "I don't want to burst your bubble or how you see me, Ram, but trust me, I'm no angel. Not even close…"

He cracked a poor semblance of a smile, filled with pain and memories. "It is the moment of crisis, of life and death, when you find out who you really are, and who the other person is. That day, you were like Michael the Archangel and Gabriel, all wrapped into one. You were intense, you willed your life force back into him. I saw it. The whole team did. Artur should have died, but he didn't. It was you, Dare…you…"

She scrubbed her eyes with her palms. Her heart hurt, but it thudded with joy. "Okay," she whispered unsteadily, "it's time for me to tell you how much of a coward I am, too."

He sat up, blinking as if not hearing her accurately. "What? What are you talking about?"

"You." She raised her gaze to the ceiling and then she slanted her gaze back to him. "I was just as much of an emotional coward as you think you are, Ram."

"Tell me more?"

"You and me. Us." Sitting up, she perched on the edge of the couch and faced him fully. "What you didn't know is that I was drawn personally to you. Don't ask me how it happened, but it did. Maybe it was that day that the team came with me into the Afghan village to take care of babies. I don't know… But when I saw you holding a crying baby in your arms, I saw that icy mask of yours you always wore melt away, and I saw the real you for the first time. It blew me away, Ram. It was then I realized you weren't a robot without a heart…that you were a living, compassionate man and I came to realize what you wanted for your team, was for us to survive this duty. I got why you behaved as you did with us on a daily basis."

His lips compressed and he stared hard at her. "Wait… You were drawn to me?"

"Yes. It was that easy to admit and that hard to carry without telling you or telling anyone else. I figured your iciness was a mask you wore because you cared so much for all of us. You wanted us to live, to get home to our families…and after that realization, it was easy to allow my feelings for you to grow and take root in my heart. I couldn't speak of how I felt toward you. And I wasn't going to confide it to the team members, who were like brothers to me. I was afraid if anyone knew my secret, it could destroy the cohesiveness we had. I understand how, if we had admitted our growing attraction for one another, that it could have hurt the team as a whole and neither of us wanted that. Not ever." She reached over and gripped his hand and squeezed it. "I understood, Ram. I really did."

He cupped her hand within his large, scarred ones. "So? Where are you today? I have to know one way or another, Dare. For so many reasons…"

"When you found out I wasn't in a relationship, you almost gave yourself away to me," she whispered. "I saw the relief in your expression. I couldn't figure out that reaction."

"I almost fainted with joy when you said you weren't in a relationship," he admitted. "Not very mature of me, at all."

Nodding, she absorbed the love shining in his gray eyes

for her alone. "I had lost touch with you except for those emails you'd send maybe once a month or so, of a flower you'd crossed paths with." She touched her heart. "That always gave me hope."

"Hope?"

"That someday…somehow…that we could get together just like this and really sit down and have a heart-to-heart talk with one another without the military lording over us. Just you and me. Two people…"

"Dare—" his voice dropped to a ragged whisper "—are you still drawn to me?"

She smiled a little. "Yes. Is it possible that you're still drawn to me?"

"I never stopped dreaming of you in my life. It has grown stronger and stronger with every passing year. It was eating me up alive. I needed to see you, talk to you and be honest with you…"

"Looks like it happened." She turned her hand over, sliding it into his warm, dry one. "We are in one hell of a box canyon, Ram."

His hand grew firmer around hers. "First, there is us. We've gone four years without ever saying these words, much less doing anything overt about our feelings for one another, Dare. We have a lot of things to sort out between ourselves."

"And this isn't for public consumption, Ram, not to the team, not to Lera or Adam…to no one. No one can know how we feel toward one another."

Nodding heavily, he rasped, "Externally, nothing will change. We are going into a war and we can't upset the team's cohesiveness."

"I agree," she whispered. "Besides, I need time and so do you, just to get used to the fact we want to explore what we might have."

"I was thinking the same thing," Ram agreed. "We need time to absorb all this hidden information we'd kept from one another for so long."

"Not much time left for us. We have to convince Lera and the girls to move into Kyiv."

"That's our first priority," Ram rasped. "This whole coming month is about gearing up for that war. We have orders to be at HQ at 0900, five days a week, to continue our training as a team. So far, we still get weekends off."

"I guess, for us, this is a new kind of hell of sorts?" she suggested, trading a wry look with him.

Giving her a warm look, he said, "I'd like to get to know you, what you want, what your hopes and dreams are. You take the lead. You're fully capable of doing that."

Nodding, she said, "I do need time. We need to understand what we have, what we expect of ourselves and of one another."

He gently placed his hand over hers. "A step at a time, right?"

"The only way."

"Do you have any wine in your fridge?" he wondered, looking toward the kitchen.

"Yes. Do you want to celebrate this aha moment of ours?"

Nodding, he stood. "Don't you think it's about time?"

"Yes," and Dare stood, going to the kitchen. She had some wonderful white Ukrainian wine and poured it into two crystal glasses. Ram joined her and they stood there, touching the lip of each other's glass.

"To us," Ram said, his voice low with feeling.

"To our future, whatever it becomes," she agreed, voice barely a whisper. Dare wasn't sure what that meant right now. As she took a sip, she asked, "What if we really aren't suited for one another, Ram?"

"If it comes to that, I'll respect your decision or vice versa."

"I feel the same."

"What I want for us is that we will be grateful for what we have, respect the other, sit down and talk like adults when problems arise, and I'm sure they will. But we're mature enough, Dare, to climb those hurdles and get over them."

"We aren't really *that* old." She laughed along with him.

He took her hand, leading her back into the living room, sitting down on the couch with her. "This is a dream come true just to do this." He lifted his arm, sliding it around her shoulders, gently drawing her against him, giving her time if she didn't want that kind of closeness to speak up. And if she had resisted, he would have instantly stopped and respected that invisible but very important boundary between them.

Dare rested her cheek against his broad shoulder that carried the responsibility for the whole team, including her. "We have a lot of challenges ahead of us," she whispered. He was so close. Inhaling his scent as a man sent an awakening through her entire body. She felt a pleasant warmth begin deep within her and it sent a craving so sweet with promise, so sharp with need, that for a moment, she was carried on that primal force of him.

"I agree," he said in low tone. "There are two things going for us, Dare. First, we're mature. Secondly, we've had four years together and apart. If we can continue to hold our mutual attraction we've always had for one another, it tells me we have a chance. The bad news is, the war is coming shortly."

"And you'll have to put away your need to want to protect me, Ram. You can't do anything different. The team would know. They are a very smart, intelligent group of seasoned combat soldiers. They miss nothing."

"We'll be discreet, Dare. That I promise you. Our unspoken attraction for one another has already stood the test of four years and they aren't any the wiser."

She turned her face, rubbing her cheek against his shoulder, his scent fueling her raw, physical desire for him, regardless of the world's issues. "I remember my father telling me when I was seventeen that it's better to have loved and lost than never loved at all."

He leaned back on the couch, closing his eyes, savoring her closeness. "It's a good saying, but I don't think it fits what we have with one another. It was as if when I saw you for the first time, Dare, that I already knew you. I felt like you had walked in from the past, back into this time, to be with me once again. It was an overwhelming feeling, an intuition. No woman had ever, before you, affected me like you do."

"Star-crossed lovers, maybe?" she wondered quietly, closing her eyes, feeling the stress of the many days dissolving as she lay against him.

A rumble of a chuckle reverberated through his chest. "Crossed, for sure. But I'm a patient man and I waited."

She barely opened her eyes, thinking how many times she might get a chance to be with him just like this. It felt to her as if she were in a dream, not the cold, hard reality staring back at them presently. "I guess I'm patient, too. I had no interest in having an affair with you. It just never crossed my mind. How I feel about you, Ram, goes so much deeper than that."

"I believe it is the same for both of us."

"There was never anyone else who could stand in your shoes," she admitted.

"But now? As you Americans say? The cat is out of the bag or something like that?"

"You've been around Americans too much," she accused, laughing gently.

He sobered, holding her amused gaze, so close that he wanted to kiss her, but it was too soon…too early. She had to come to him, let him know what she did or did not want from him. The thought was warm, inviting. "I chased you until you caught me, and I will always be yours."

Chapter Six

November 8

As he sat at Adam's dining room table, comforting his sobbing wife, Lera, Ram felt as if his heart were being physically torn out of his chest. They had put the children to bed much earlier, the harsh news broken to Lera by her husband, whose face was stricken with a mix of anger toward the Russians and grief over his wife's sobs. She clung to Adam, face buried against his chest as he held her tightly. They had to leave their home and move into Kyiv for safety's sake. The look of helplessness in Adam's face as he gently smoothed his hand across her hair tore at Ram.

Glancing to his right where Dare sat, he saw she was upset and sensed she wanted to cry right along with Lera, or at least somehow comfort her as a friend. His elbows rested on the table, hands gripped tightly with the swirling energy of shock reverberating through their home. Lera had heatedly fought Adam to remain in Bucha, but in the end, it was he who had persuaded her to move near where Dare lived, and not be taken prisoner by the advancing Russian tanks that would come their way down that main highway that cut right through the middle of their village. She had capitulated because of her daughters, wanting them safe. This house was the only home she'd ever known.

Ram felt Dare's focus on him and lifted his chin, lips tightened as he met her anguished gaze. How badly he wanted to comfort her in that moment, too, just as Adam was comforting his wife. But he couldn't. Sometimes, he didn't want to be a leader of a team, and this was one of them. Asking Lera to move everything of importance to her and the children, out of their home where she and her family had lived for generations, was a big ask.

He tore his gaze from Dare and rubbed the fabric of the thick fleece shirt beneath his opened leather jacket. Nothing helped the pain he was experiencing for Adam's family.

Finally, Lera stopped crying, Dare handing her tissue after tissue from a nearby box, giving her a sad look of silent apology. Adam straightened, rubbing his face savagely, as if to rub away all that was coming their way in February.

"W-what of the other men in your team, Ram?" Lera asked, her voice stricken and hoarse with tears.

"I've talked to all of them. As you know, most of them are married. Those that aren't have extended family around central Kyiv. Few members of my team live in outlying villages around Kyiv, like this one, Lera. I'm urging all of them to either move their immediate family into Kyiv for a while, or to remain where they are unless there is a Russian attack upon them. Those who want to go to Kyiv are starting that process of moving tomorrow."

"Or," Adam rasped, giving his wife a loving look, his arm around her sagging shoulders, "Ram thinks it's best that all the families go to Poland, across the border, because Russia won't attack there since it's a NATO country. If we stay here, even in Kyiv, we will be bombarded. The only safe place for citizens will be the subway system, which is far below ground and safe for people to hide in. Already, the military is stocking food, water, medical supplies and other necessary items all along the subway routes so people have food, water and any other help they need while they are forced to stay underground for days... maybe a week or more at a time..." His voice thinned and he leaned over, kissing Lera's mussed hair as she mopped her face with another tissue.

"I won't go to Poland!" Lera cried out, banging her fist on the table, glaring at Adam and then at Ram. "I don't know anyone there! I don't speak their language!"

"You can stay in Kyiv, near Dare's apartment. I will draw out all our savings and checking from the bank," Adam told her. "You will carry the money on you or keep it in your apartment. My military salary will be electronically sent to your smartphone, Lera, not to the bank. You will always have funds to live, to purchase food and to take care of the children's needs while in Kyiv."

Ram listened to Adam's low, quiet voice soothing his fractious wife, whose expression was one of terror mixed with incredible sadness, frustration and anger. She was being asked to leave everything she ever knew behind. He had no doubt Russians would soften up the village with artillery or missile strikes. And then their tanks would roll in, so close to the jugular point where he and many other black ops teams were being ordered to stop them and halt their forward movement into Kyiv itself. The tanks would shoot to kill. They wouldn't care if there were civilians, women or children murdered.

He knew Russian atrocity up front and close, even though he'd never spoken to anyone about it. They were hardened soldiers, cruel, heartless and without any morals or values. They refused to follow Geneva Conventions. He knew they considered civilians as justified targets to shoot and kill. It made no difference to them. It was so hard for him not to speak of it, to scare Lera enough into leaving with the girls for safety, but he couldn't give Russian inhumanity a voice.

Ram kept his tone low and sincere. "We'll help you, Lera. Adam, my team and I will do the heavy lifting around the house. If you and Dare could pack boxes, suitcases or whatever else you would want for a leased apartment? That would be good." He opened his hands, seeing a sense of helplessness as her eyes once more filled with tears.

"Will they burn our house down, Ram? What will they do?"

It felt like a knife twisting in his gut. Grimly, he rasped, "It could happen, Lera. I'm sorry...so sorry. But think if you and the children were in this house when a missile hit it? Or a tank fired a shot into it? Blowing it up? It would kill or wound all of you. I know that isn't what you want. You have to leave in order to live..."

Dare reached over, her hand gently laying over Lera's lower left arm. "We'll do this together. I'm really good at organizing. We can make a list. I've already talked to the manager at the apartment building, and he says you are welcome to lease that family-sized apartment across the hall from where I live. He's holding it open for lease to you

and Adam. I hope you'll say yes. I will be out in the field
with Ram and the team, and you'll have the code card for
my apartment across the hallway from yours. You can use
it and anything in it you might need while I'm gone. The
manager is a woman and she is very warmhearted. She's
willing to help your family any way she can. You are only
half a block from the entrance to the subway. You will be
able to reach it if Putin starts sending missiles into Kyiv.
That underground subway will save your lives."

Nodding, wiping her eyes, she whispered, "All right…
We'll go and yes, I need all your help…"

"There's a rental company a block away from that apartment building," Ram told her, "and anything you don't want
to take? We can store there, until this war is over."

Jerkily nodding, Lera sniffed, took another tissue from
Dare and blew her nose. "We will go. *But*… I want us to
still have the American Thanksgiving, Dare. You talked
so much about it. I wanted to make it for you, a celebration…"

Smiling a little, Dare choked out, "We'll have Thanksgiving over at the high-rise. That's only weeks away, Lera.
I'll help you make it over there, okay?"

With a nod, Lera turned and looked up at her husband.
"Are you all right with this?"

He kissed her hair. "I am," he rasped. "I think we can
all use a US Thanksgiving at the end of November. I've
never had a turkey dinner, as Dare calls it, but we'll all
work to get the family and goods moved in so we can celebrate it together. It will be a happy time for all of us, especially the girls."

November 9

THE FIRE WAS LOW, mostly coals glowing, sending out sparse light into the living room. Dare sat on the rug in front of the warmth, cozy in her hooded velvet robe, which fell to her feet. It was 3:00 a.m. and she couldn't sleep, so she'd gotten up to make herself some lemon balm tea.

A noise made her sit up.

"Sorry," Ram offered quietly at the opening to the living room. "I didn't know you were out here—"

"We're making a habit of this."

He managed a slight smile. He was dressed in his dark burgundy pajamas and a dark blue robe. His feet were bare. "My mind is going a million miles an hour. I can't close my eyes and sleep it off or make it go away."

She patted the braided rug next to where she sat, her knees drawn up against her body, arms around them. "Come sit by me. Right now, it's nice to have company."

He pushed his hair away from his brow and sat down nearby, but not so near, he hoped, as to make her pull away from him. The last week had been devoted to meetings and more briefings. He saw little of Dare except in a professional capacity. Settling down, he absorbed the low light and warmth coming from the many coals in fireplace, thinking how beautiful and courageous she looked to him. He was still reeling from their open discussion about their love for one another; almost feeling as if it were some kind of dream.

He was afraid of the approaching war. It could be a nightmare that would destroy what they'd just found with the other. The hope in his heart had blossomed. After all these years, their feelings were mutual. It was a dream enclosed by a coming nightmare.

"Do you think Lera and Adam are sleeping? Or are they tossing and turning like we did?" she wondered softly, giving him a long, warm look.

He sat cross-legged, pulling the ends of his robe across his knees and thighs. "I don't know. Adam is a great leader and he knows how to deal with thorny situations well. I believe their love for one another will see them through this chaos and change, but it doesn't hurt that Adam won't let his emotions run away with him and make reckless mistakes, either. He's clearheaded about this. I know he's relieved that Lera and the girls will be in Kyiv, even if he won't say it to her. He doesn't want to see her cry again."

"Just because some women are emotional and cry more openly doesn't mean that we make reckless mistakes. We can behave courageously when things are going terribly wrong. We choose our time to cry, Ram. Just as I suspect you, and the rest of our team, does, also."

He felt a powerful, nearly overwhelming need to coax her into his arms, to have her come and lean against him and hold her. "You're right, of course."

"Women are warriors, don't ever forget that. Sure, I can fire a weapon and I can kill just like any of you can, but that doesn't mean I'm carrying my emotional reactions into the firefight, because I don't."

"The women of Ukraine are fierce wolves at heart. They are patriotic, and their family and our country mean everything to them."

"Just like the Black Wolf badge ID we wear on our fatigues," Dare said, "we are wolves in a pack and it's our duty to protect the civilians of this country. But the women of Ukraine will fight this battle, too. Maybe not like our team does, but they will be on the front lines in so many small, everyday ways, as well."

"Exactly, but I'm afraid, Dare, that most of the people of Bucha will stay, and not leave. I know the government agencies are desperately trying to persuade them to leave now. But you know how adamant we are about our home, our family and the generations that have been in that same house or farm for a hundred years or more. It's hard for them to move under those circumstances."

"Many won't leave," Dare agreed softly, frowning. "You are a people of the land. You are tied to it. Your roots are deep and forever, I know that. And I understand it." Shaking her head, she whispered sadly, "This is one time they need to leave…"

"There's talk of about two million of our people, mostly grandparents, wives with children, will be leaving for Poland. I was talking with our Polish diplomat today before we left after the last briefing. He said Poland is doing everything in their power to arrange help, housing, food, medicine and prepping their schools to handle Ukrainian children."

"It's a horrifying mess for everyone," she muttered fiercely, frowning. "Damn the Kremlin."

"I live to see every last one of them in hell."

"Well, we're going to get our chance to rip them a new one, Ram. We're at the point of the spear on this one. The government is counting on the black-ops-trained troops to stop the tanks in their tracks, no matter which direction they come from. They will keep Kyiv safe from this enemy tank brigade…and fight for the country as a whole. Ukraine will survive this."

He felt his heart tearing, not even wanting to think of what would happen if she was killed in combat. The helplessness that flowed through him was bitter and slicing. "Yes," he managed, "my dream is to protect the country. But I fear the worst…"

November 12

AS DARE DROVE her car into an aboveground parking lot next to her apartment building, it was well past midnight. Ram's truck was also parked nearby. "You have an hour-long drive to your house," she said, pulling in and turning off the engine and lights. They'd just finished a late-night briefing. There was another early morning meeting for Ram.

Yawning, he managed, "Nothing new…"

The streetlights of Kyiv shed shadows and brightness into her vehicle. "You know I have a spare bedroom?"

"Yes." He slanted a look in her direction and saw that gleam in her eyes. That always meant trouble, but not necessarily bad trouble. She compressed her lips and turned, her one arm hooked over the steering wheel, staring at him.

"Stay with me tonight? Don't try to make that drive home. You have to be as emotionally blasted by that last briefing as the rest of us were. You'd have an hour's drive back into Kyiv tomorrow morning to make that 0700 meeting. If you stay with me? That is two extra hours you can get some badly needed sleep."

He stilled the surprise and didn't allow it to translate to his face. "Yes, I'll take you up on your guest bedroom." He drew a long breath and said, "We used the day for moving

Adam and his family and then, this unexpected call from HQ and emergency briefing tonight. Since we've started moving them into that apartment, they are protecting their daughters from a lot of the truth of why they're doing it."

"Lera is making it a fun move for them, getting them excited about a new place to live. They don't have a grasp of their generations of family history in that house or the sadness Lera and Adam feel about moving out of it. I feel so badly for all them…helpless…"

He reached out, sliding his hand that rested on her thigh. "And the girls are overjoyed that Auntie Dare is right across the hall from them. I've seen that as we moved their boxes and furniture into their apartment, that you take them into your apartment and keep them distracted. I know Lera and Adam are grateful for your help.

"We're making good progress in the move, despite all these briefings we're having to attend, to get them here in Kyiv," Ram continued. "Every day, Lera looks less upset. She does like the new apartment and it's looking almost lived in, now. I think another week, and they will be settled in and the worst will be over for them."

"I agree," she whispered, turning her hand over, lacing her fingers between his. "Until then? I want to play, take care of and be with the girls whenever I can. I know Lera is overwhelmed in getting the apartment livable, as well as cooking for her family. I'm going to continue to cook for them when I have a chance." She hesitated and said, "Look, I think we need to circle the wagons here, Ram. Tactically, from here on out, you should stay in my apartment until we are ordered to the front lines. Adam isn't going to be able to help Lera much because of his duties to the team that he's responsible for as the number two in command. If you stay with me, you're close to everything and you can give your support as you can." She tilted her head. "How do you feel about this idea?"

He rubbed his jaw and rasped, "Tactically? It works. Lera is emotionally exhausted. She'll no longer have her part-time job, either. The girls will need to be placed into new schools. There's a lot to juggle right now. I like your idea. Are you comfortable with me in the same apartment with you?"

"I trust you, Ram." Her voice lowered. "I'm hoping it will allow us a little more personal time together, time to talk with one another. There just isn't that much time left to us before the Russians are on our doorstep."

"Our trust in one another is solid," he agreed, his tone serious. "I'd like nothing better than to juggle my workload with helping Lera and Adam." He saw relief in her expression.

"I'm as emotionally torn up as you are, Ram. It would be nice if you were closer. You always steadied me out in tight situations when we were out in the field in Afghanistan."

His brows moved up. "I did?" He saw her give him a rolled-eyed look. "What?"

"I still haven't figured out whether you're symbolic of the fool's card from the tarot deck, the young man stepping off the cliff, into space, not a care in the world, faith that even though he was walking on nothing but air he will not fall to his death, or if you're clueless."

"Can I choose to take the cliff walker?" he teased gently, seeing the darkness beneath her eyes, the fatigue in her gaze. He absorbed the length of her fingers, how warm they were, and although she was strong in combat, right now she appeared comforted by his nearness. It made him feel good, love for her rising within him. Dare trusted him in the most important of ways.

She gave an abrupt laugh over his mild teasing. "You've got a bear trap mind, Ram."

"I really made you feel better out in the field?" It was hard to believe because her aura was one of sheer, rock-solid confidence. The men of his team utterly trusted her and would give their lives for her, if necessary, but she would do the same for them, too. They were like brothers with a big sister among them.

"You have no idea." Giving him a searching look, she whispered, "There's so much I want to share with you."

"But not tonight, Dare. Your game plan is solid and I'll stay here with you. Later this week, I'll drive out to my apartment and get my clothes and gear and bring them into the spare bedroom. Right now? We need to sleep. And from here on out? We're either going to be up to our neck in helping Adam's family adjust, or being ordered to more and more briefings before we receive our orders. At some point? They'll send us out in the field."

"I know…" She squeezed his hand, pulled her fingers free and climbed out of the car.

As Ram egressed from the car, as always checking the area out, he remained slightly to the right of Dare's shoulder and a step behind her. It was a protective guard position. The night was chilly, the wind blowing sporadically. All up and down the empty sidewalk, the trees grew along it, bare and naked in the harsh streetlights, making the shadows look like skinny monsters in his imagination, just waiting to ambush someone. He followed her through the outer door that opened with her card. There was a second entrance and she punched in the key code.

Once inside her apartment, he glanced around, well aware that she was heading down the hall. He followed her as she had opened up a closet and handed him two sheets and pillowcases.

"You have to make the bed. The folded blankets are at the end of it. Each room has a full bathroom." She shut the door and turned, looking up at him. "I'll see you in the morning, Ram. Good night." She stretched upward and kissed him gently on his mouth.

Caught off guard, his arms loaded with linens, the warmth of her lips against his stunned him. It was a quick kiss, and she stepped away, giving him a look that raced through his entire being. In that moment, there was such love shining in her eyes that he'd never seen before, it left him mute with surprise.

"Sleep well," he managed, watching her walk down the hall, turn left and disappear.

Progress. Yes, it was progress. She had kissed him! Out of the blue. Completely unexpected! He behaved like a teenager, in total shock. Shaking his head, he stood there in the semidarkness of the hall, alone, but inwardly celebrating their first kiss. The imprint of her full lips against his filtered through him, melting the hard walls he'd erected inside himself long ago so he didn't have to feel the eviscerating pain of loss. Miraculously, as those walls dissolved, he felt joy...real joy, for the first time since his childhood. She completed him and he knew it. He turned, walking quietly toward the spare room. Dare trusted him in her home. As tired as she was? He was even more tired. The emotional ups and downs with Adam and Lera were stressful because he was a person who instituted changes to get things done, but this was different. This wasn't a tactical or strategy situation. These were two people he loved, wrestling with the nightmare that was about to overtake their country. As would it be for all Ukrainians. It was a sobering reality and he opened the door to the second bedroom.

Still… Despite it, Dare had the courage, the need for him, to kiss him just now. How many times had he wanted to take her into his arms and kiss her? Too many times to count. Ram had always reined in his need for Dare, giving her the space she needed. Now, he knew without a doubt that his decision to allow her to lead had been correct. He felt such peace that it seemed unreal. *One kiss. Her kiss.* When she'd leaned upward, pressing her mouth to his, he inhaled her sweet scent. She loved the Hawaiian plumeria scent and tonight he'd inhaled it like life itself into his terribly broken inner world. The kiss had awakened his other emotions, good ones, that had been packed away in cold storage within himself because they had nowhere else to survive. *Until now. Right now.* She had breathed her life into him. And for the first time since he was eighteen, he felt real hope. Real love.

Standing in the large room, a queen-size bed in the middle of it, he placed the linens on the mattress and got undressed. A good hot shower was a welcome friend and first up on his agenda. Tomorrow was another day. They had it off and he would be able to help Adam and Lera get settled into their apartment. In his heart, he felt light and happy. Right now, that was all this was: a dream. Real life intruded and surrounded them. He ached to hold Dare in his arms, to feel her warm, supple body next to his. More than anything, he wanted time, quality time, with her, alone…

November 20

SNOW WAS FALLING outside the large floor-to-ceiling windows of Dare's apartment. It was late afternoon and she'd gotten some time alone. Adam and Lera's household had settled into their new apartment. She missed Ram. He'd been on a three-day undercover assignment, top secret, and he could tell no one about it. Last night, she'd dreamed once more of kissing him. What would it be like to have their lips meet again? He'd changed in subtle but wonderful ways since her bold kiss with him in the hallway. She felt achy between her thighs, wanting him in every way. Through no fault of their own, life around them was speeding up, intensifying, and so many others needed emotional support and help right now. There were families leaving Kyiv and taking the trains to Poland now by the thousands. Some were leaving the beautiful city and Dare didn't blame them. Adam and Lera's children were now in their new school, and Lera was settling in well. It was a time of quiet chaos and she ached to see Ram.

Sitting down in an upholstered rocker, her favorite because it showed Kyiv outside the massive windows that she loved so much, she yearned to have Ram here with her. Each had to attend meetings. After a mind-bending briefing earlier, her head ached and so did her emotions. Briefings were literal and gutting, no fluff, no hiding the bare truth.

Dare closed her eyes after placing her feet on a padded stool in front of the rocker. She moved it slowly back and forth. It always reminded her of a mother rocking her child. At some point, she fell asleep, the snow falling in big, fat flakes, twirling silently from the light gray sky surrounding the city.

RAM OPENED THE door to the apartment as silently as he could. It was 1800, 6:00 p.m., and he slipped inside, quietly shutting the door. Near the front of the windows, Dare had fallen asleep in her favorite rocker. He smiled a little, walking in a way that he couldn't be heard across the oak floor that shined a deep blond color even in the winter twilight. Dare was still in her camo uniform, her polished black boots resting on the stool cushions, her hands in her lap, head tipped back, revealing the beauty of her slender throat. There were still slight shadows beneath her eyes and he knew why. The drumbeat of war coming closer every day, putting a daily stressor on her and his team.

After placing everything he carried on the kitchen table, he shucked out of his camo coat and dark green knit cap and placed them quietly over a chair. The night would be short-lived for him, another 0700 briefing tomorrow morning. It felt so good to be alone with her, to finally get a chance to be with her, talk with her, listen to her and continue to discover and mend their past with one another. More than anything, he wanted to share a second kiss with her, this time initiated by him. Since the first one, he'd had nothing but wonderful, happy dreams at night, which was completely unlike him. He knew it was because of Dare. She completed him.

Above all, he knew how tired she was and he left everything in the kitchen, went to her bedroom and found a spare blanket. Being careful, he placed it over her, absorbing the light moving across her thick lashes against her cheeks, the softness of her skin, the way it curved, showing the strength of who she was. Forcing himself to leave, he quietly retrieved a sandwich from the refrigerator and remained in the living room, near her.

There was something peaceful about Dare that he couldn't put his finger on. It was a feeling, not an idea or thought. Frowning, he sat there after eating, his elbows on his open thighs, staring off into the darkness of the cold, snowy night. There were few people on the sidewalks now, the lamplight glowing pale yellow to a deep gold, creating dark and interesting shadows along the broad sidewalks on either side of the six lanes of highway.

He got up, washing his hands in the sink, careful to keep the noise down, wiping them on a nearby hand towel. Dare had to attend a daylong medical combat briefing in another part of the same building where he and Adam were also located, getting another kind but equally important report. Moving quietly back into the living room, the warmth making him take off his green sweater, which he hung over one arm of the sofa, he sat down, simply absorbing Dare sleeping.

He closed his own eyes and promptly fell asleep, peacefulness stealing into every part of his being because, for the first time in his life, he was with the woman he'd so deeply fallen for so long ago. Even better? There was mutual attraction between them that was genuine. His last thoughts were that the world might be spinning out of control, but the soft impression of Dare's lips pressed to his in that surprise good-night kiss dissolved all his worry and anxiety. For tonight? Everything was right in his world.

Chapter Seven

November 21

Ram was the first to enter Dare's empty apartment. It was near 1600 and he knew she had a meeting with the medical corps and wouldn't be home until 1700, according to their schedules for the day. He'd gone across the hall, checked in on Adam and his family. They were settling in fine. Let this time, he thought, be special for the family. Soon enough, his team would be out in the freezing weather once the Russians attacked their country.

He'd brought precooked meals home with him, setting them out on the kitchen counter, wanting to prepare them a hearty meal. Knowing Dare would be tired when she got home, he had no contact with her all day due to their separate military demands upon them. He wondered if Dare felt as starved for him as he was for her, wanting to close that four-year gap that had kept them away from one another. He placed the foil-wrapped dinners into the oven at a low temperature, put the lush salad in the refrigerator, found a couple of crystal wineglasses and opened an expensive bottle of burgundy wine to let it sit and air. Glancing at his watch, he saw it was 1715. Soon, Dare would be home.

Home. The word struck him so deeply, as it always did. Tonight he needed to come clean with her, as never before. She had to know the rest of his story, why he was the way he was. More than anything, he knew Dare's huge, compassionate heart would understand why he was so closed up, why he never talked about his family, his parents or their wheat farm. Ram would time it. He didn't want it to be a wet blanket and ruin their evening meal together. Dare was just as starved as he was to be together. She didn't need his explanation, but it was a driving fist in his heart to tell her the whole truth of who he was.

He heard the front door to the apartment open and walked toward it. Dare was in her winter uniform, gray, white and black camos. She set her briefcase inside the door and shut it.

"Hey," she said, smiling, "I smell something good."

He approached her, opening his arms, and drowned in the glistening love shining in her eyes for him alone. "Dinner is warming up in the oven," he told her, pulling her tightly against him, her arms going around his shoulders, her entire body pressed hungrily against his. Dare left no question about what she wanted from him, kissing him deeply and then pulling away, looking up at him, smiling.

"I think you want dessert first?"

He grinned. "Do you?"

She pouted. "No, I'm starving, Ram. I missed lunch today."

He eased her out of his arms and said, "Go get changed. I'll set the table for us." Nothing felt so good as to give her small gifts of love in so many different ways as he saw her entire expression soften.

"That sounds so good," she whispered, kissing his cheek and releasing his hand. "I'm going to get a quick shower and then I'll be ready to eat."

"Go," he said, giving her rear a gentle pat. "Take care of yourself, first." Because he knew Dare all too well on this one. How many times, when out at an Afghan village, she would work tirelessly from dawn to dusk, even into the night, with one of the team members holding a flashlight in a hut, to care for a sick infant or woman, and he had to order her to come back to the camp. She was always deeply touched by the health needs of the children, mothers and the elderly, wanting to help them and relieve their suffering.

Turning, he went back to the kitchen. Ram's heart soared with such incredible happiness he could barely think. That was how Dare affected him, but now, he could allow those sweeping emotional feelings to tunnel through him with rapture and joy instead of suppressing them. She was his. She loved him and he loved her.

"MMM," DARE HUMMED SOFTLY, leaning over, kissing Ram's cheek, "that was a delicious meal and dessert." She saw the color of his eyes change and that was something she noticed last night when they'd lingered and kissed. And kissed again and again…until she wanted more. It was then they wisely stepped away from one another, knowing sleep was so important, that they had a long day ahead of them. His eyes had turned an antique gold color again. They sat on the sofa, him in the corner, his arm around her shoulders as she leaned against him. How thirsty she was for his closeness, the gentleness that existed within him. She'd seen a remarkable difference, a good one, and it made her whisper, "Why are you so different now?"

He tipped his head, meeting her question. "I'm not different. Am I?"

She sat up, her knee against his thigh. "I've never seen this side to you before, Ram. I like it…love it, actually. It's a wonderful surprise. Are you like this when you aren't responsible for the team?"

Frowning, he moved his palm gently up and down her thigh next to his. "Probably." He took a deep breath, released it and said, "There's something else I need to share with you, Dare. I couldn't talk about it until just now." He shook his head. "It's about me, my past… It haunts me and you need to know about it because it affects my life whether I want it to or not. I don't want you walking into a serious relationship with me and not know who I am, warts and all."

Her smile subsided and she heard and felt a heaviness in his voice, his eyes growing dark as he looked away for a moment. Whatever it was, it was serious.

"I know we haven't had time, space or place to know about all our warts," she offered, hoping to lift some of the darkness she felt cloaking him. "You know about my past. And you're right—when you're adopted as I was, it always leaves questions that probably will never be answered. It will affect me for the rest of my life. I try not to allow it to swallow me. I look at how fortunate I was to be adopted, instead. To be loved…"

"You had a lot of courage telling me about your past," he said, turning and gently brushing her cheek. "Now? I need to tell you about mine. It's time. There is no good way to tell it, but I want it out in the open between us so that you understand the private, inner hell I live with. There are nights when I can't sleep because of it. I still have nightmares and flashbacks, Dare. I don't want to scare you if I have one again."

She frowned. "Like PTSD kind of flashbacks or nightmares? We all get those. You know that. We can't be in a war situation and not be wounded by it one way or another. The entire team has them. It's just part and parcel of what happens to us in combat."

He gripped her hand that rested on his knee. "No argument about that, and no, it's a different kind of war that happened to me and that's what I need to share with you." He saw the worry in her expression, her fingers feeling warm and comforting to him as he allowed all of that grief, rage and darkness to flow unchecked through him.

"Have you told anyone else about it?"

Shaking his head, he gave her a rueful look. "I couldn't, Dare. It scares me to go back to that time, what I saw, what I lost. And I'm never sure if I can control my emotions. So far, I have…"

"Then you should share it with me. You have been in my heart since I met you. I truly believe love is the greatest healer on the face of our Earth. And whatever it is? We can handle it together."

He managed a partial smile. "You convinced me a long time ago that women are far stronger, more resilient in times of life-and-death stress than we men are. We're brittle in comparison. I've seen you in every imaginable stress situation and it's as if you are able to absorb the moment and still keep your full focus on what's going on. I've always respected and admired that about you." Giving her what he hoped was a look of love despite the roiling storm gathering more intensely within him, he said, "Let me start from the beginning. When I'm done, you ask me your questions, Dare. Okay?"

"Okay," she whispered, "I won't interrupt." She adjusted how she sat and took his hand in hers, resting it on her thigh, facing him.

Drawing in a ragged breath, he began, his voice low and unsteady. "I was born in the Donetsk Province, in Crimea of Ukraine. In 2014, Russia stole Crimea away from Ukraine. They were sending in special units of Spetsnaz troops into that region, for decades, long before Putin attacked in 2014." His hand grew sweaty and he released hers, wiping it on his other thigh to get rid of the perspiration. Looking up, he saw how concerned she was over his reaction to his story thus far but said nothing.

"Four generations of my family had a large wheat farm on that land. I grew up with members of my extended family, my grandparents, aunts, uncles and many cousins. There were ten homes in the central area of our large farm, plus my brothers, Symon and Vasyl, who were two years younger than me. We were like a small village with our family. I had told my father that I wanted to be in Ukraine's Black Wolf regiment, in black ops, and not be a farmer. He was, of course, discouraged by my choice, but Vasyl eagerly stepped up and told him he would stay at the farm and run it after my mother and father wanted to retire. I was relieved and grateful to Vasyl for his choice." Shrugging, he muttered, "I guess I was like Marco Polo. I wanted to see the world, I wanted to fight for Ukraine's freedom.

So at eighteen, I left the farm and went into Army boot camp. Of course, I stayed in close touch with all my family. I missed them, I missed their love, their laughter, the good times we always had together. Everyone worked on the farm, we had five hundred hectares, or roughly twelve hundred acres of wheat that we grew every year, and it took everyone to harvest it, bring it to the nearby village's granary and then have it trucked to the coast to be put on tanker ships that would go around world, delivering it to other countries.

"I was training for the Black Wolf regiment," he began heavily, his brow deeply wrinkled, "when I received an unexpected call from my commanding officer. I hurried over to the main office area and—" his voice lowered to a bare whisper, edged with grief "—and he told me that Russia had suddenly attacked Crimea, to take it away from the Ukraine. He told me that my family's farm had been attacked by Russian Spetsnaz troops. That they had murdered everyone, and then burned nine of the ten houses to the ground."

Gasping, Dare pressed her hand to her mouth to stop from crying out. Her eyes widened as she considered what he'd just said.

As he rubbed his face wearily, Ram's voice grew hard. "They flew me to Donbas, and I arrived with a Black Wolf team because they weren't sure where the Russians might still be in that area. They had moved on, so we were able to land the military helicopter to see it for ourselves…to see if there were any survivors. I couldn't believe my eyes. There were so many ambulances there, body bags…my God, so many body bags laying out to be taken to Kyiv and the morgue…all of my family. Their homes were destroyed. The farm's mechanic's shed remained and the Russians didn't touch the equipment or the barns with the animals in them. We'd seen this happen before in the Donbas, years earlier. The Russians would sneak in and would kill everyone who lived on that parcel of land, and then set up a Russian puppet owner to take over everything, the land, the wheat…everything. They did the same thing with my family. They murdered every one. I saw the blood on the ground here and there, the houses charred skeletons, still smoking from the fires."

Dare moved forward, sliding her arms around his broken, slumped shoulders, the look of bleakness and the soul-deep grief etched in his expression. She wanted to hold him. He roughly murmured her name, slid his arms around her shoulders, drawing her hard against him, burying his face against her neck. He was trembling. And she could feel how hard he was struggling not to allow his emotions to overwhelm him. Intuitively, she realized Ram needed to cry, to finally relieve himself once and for all of the toxic, lethal shock he'd carried alone for so long. She held him and wondered if he'd ever cried over the loss of his beloved family and extended family.

There were no words she could say to him to make him feel better. The adopted part of her, the part of her abandoned by her real mother, understood all too clearly what it meant not to have family. Ram's situation was so much worse than hers. No wonder he had been bottled up and unavailable in a human sense with his team. He'd been all business, his only priority to keep his team together and come through the war alive and able to go home to their families. Now, she knew why it was his priority, the reason behind it.

Hot tears spilled down her cheeks and Dare didn't care if Ram wanted to see them or not. What a terrible loss he'd endured for so long, by himself. Was that why he was never seen with a woman? Adam had sometimes spoken to her about his loner lifestyle, worried about Ram because he couldn't figure out why he didn't have a relationship with someone, get married, have children and raise a family. Yet, as their leader, he'd always been fair with his team, never raising his voice, but that deadly calm of his that kept everyone in control of their own emotions was always there, embracing and steadying them. Sometimes, she'd thought he was a robot without a heart, but how wrong she'd been! Dare would never tell him that. He was hurt and scarred for life, to the core by the loss of his entire family. Ram was the keeper of intense, deep and dark secrets. What internal strength he had to be able to tightly control them, not allow them into the light of day or to affect his performance as a leader.

She'd promised not to speak until he was finished and now it was so hard not to say something to him. He held her so tightly that she could barely take in half a breath of air into her lungs, the feeling around him as if he were going to explode into a million grieving pieces. How could he have gone so long without unburdening himself? That defied description in her world. She became aware of her shoulder feeling damp where he'd buried his head, and it finally dawned upon her that he was silently crying. It was the best thing in the world for him; a release of so many years of grief held internally and never given voice. Until now. With her.

  She pressed a kiss to his hair, and with her other hand, she began to slowly move her palm across his tight, tense shoulders, trying to soothe away some of his pain and loss he carried so long. Her heart bled for him. He'd been all alone in the world in ways she'd never had to deal with. No more birthdays to celebrate, never another child welcomed into the family's world, or to become an uncle, or never to be able to speak with his brother, Vasyl, or take part in wonderful yearly family ceremonies. Most of all, she wanted to cry over the loss of his parents… More tears fell and she clung to him as tightly as he did to her. Grief laid a person open and it was devoid of safety. The person was at their most vulnerable and unable to protect or defend themselves from the wound. If only she could somehow…somehow ease that terrible loneliness and heavy burden he carried.

WHAT TIME WAS IT? Ram was entrapped in grief, confused and unsure of where he was. He vaguely remembered sobbing until it felt like his guts were being torn out of him. And through it all, Dare had held him, her touch healing as she moved her hand across his drawn-up shoulders and slowly up and down his back. With every pass of her hand upon him, a little more of his grief dissolved and he felt more relief, a lessening of the weight he'd carried as a result. She was magical. He'd always known that about her, and now, he was on the reciprocating end of it, just like the children and elderly Afghans who stood patiently in line for an hour or more just to be seen by her. The gentleness of Dare's calming voice, her meeting the person or child's fearful gaze, very gently touching them in a loving, caring way, and watching their face glow with hope, and watching the fear dissolving in its wake… Dare gave everyone hope and optimism in this toxic, dangerous world they all lived within.

Slowly, his groggy, clouded mind realized he was lying across half the couch. Dare was sleeping against him, her arm wrapped around his torso and cheek resting on his shoulder. He knew they were both beyond fatigue and this proved it. Wanting his head to clear more, he concentrated on her slow breathing, how good it felt to him to have her arm around him, as if to hold him safe during the storm of his grueling release. Looking up, he could see the clock on the fireplace mantel, and that it was well past midnight.

The weight of his grief made him raw as never before. What would Dare think of him now that he'd sobbed openly, without pause, and couldn't control what had been eating him alive internally for so long? Yet, just the way her arm curved around him produced solace and comfort. Miraculously, he felt lighter, not heavier. He had hatred and rage toward Russians that inhabited him from the day his family had been murdered. It had lessened enormously.

Could one person do this much for another person? Lift him out of the cauldron and not feel it eating away at his soul as it always did? He lay there, couch pillows against his back, supporting both of them, looking up at the shadowy ceiling, feeling the shock that something transformative had occurred deep within him. Something healing. He inhaled the scent of her hair, and it was like smelling a fragrant flower, drawing it deep into his lungs, feeling the scent move within him, healing him, too, in another unexpected way.

It was love, he finally realized. How much Dare loved him. It was beyond him to understand all that had just transpired. There was no science to measure the openness of a kind heart like Dare's, but look at the result. He felt so much cleaner within himself that it shocked him all over again as he absorbed the weight of her body curved against his own. They fit so well together, complementing and supporting one another. Closing his eyes, his arms around her, he felt like a starving thief for stealing her warmth, her care, the faint moisture of each breath she took against his neck. *Life.* She was life. She was *his life.* A powerful emotion, startling and yet fierce, flowed through his entire being like a tsunami. This time, it purified, freeing him in ways he wouldn't have ever imagined possible. It was as if his tears had transformed him from a dead man walking into a newly born human being with raw pulsing hope through him, an incredible rainbow of feelings that were gently and quietly swirling throughout him, washing him free of so much of the darkness he had carried.

Closing his eyes, he held her as she slept. Imprinting this night, this moment into his mind and his opening heart, he drifted off to sleep again. Only this time, it was a sleep of peace and dreams, good dreams of a future with her.

November 22

IT WAS NEAR 0600 when Dare slowly awoke. She found herself in her bed, still dressed but covered with a warm blanket. She heard the door open and forced herself to sit up. Blinking, trying to wipe the grogginess away, she noticed

Ram standing in the doorway, looking properly apologetic with two cups of coffee in hand. He had changed and she could see that he'd taken a shower and shaved.

"I must have really been tired last night," she said as she sat up, bringing her legs over the edge of the mattress, reaching for the cup he offered her.

Ram went to sit in a rocker nearby. "It was a rough night for both of us. How are you feeling this morning?"

She sipped the hot brew and looked over the cup at him. "Barely awake…and you're right, last night was hard on you. I should ask how *you* are doing."

He sat back, holding her drowsy blue gaze. "Much better. I felt like some kind of magical miracle happened to me last night, thanks to you, thanks to your care."

She smiled a little. "Because you finally gave up your terrible secret and the awful grief you carried for so long by yourself, Ram. It always helps to talk it out with someone else, to dispel it. Is this the first time you've told anyone about what happened?"

Nodding, he rasped, "You're the only one, Dare. I've never cried over their loss, either. Before, I was filled with revenge, hatred and rage. I had no room left for tears."

She closed her eyes for a moment. "I don't know how you were able to hold all that inside you for so long without breaking."

"Hate is a powerful emotion, Dare. I don't urge anyone to carry it around like I've been doing. All I wanted to do was get back at the Russians for taking generations of my family away from me, the land, their homes… And I will wreak my vengeance on them. That is coming."

Sipping the coffee, she whispered, "No one can blame you for how you feel. I don't."

"But you're right—holding it in has hurt me," he offered, shaking his head. "Last night, I realized that I carried all that hatred within me for so many years."

"I can compare my adoption experience along a similar line," she whispered, pushing fingers through her unruly hair, moving a strand behind her ear. "For so long, I hated my unknown mother. I hated her because she threw me away. I realized when I was older that my rage and anger toward her was misguided. My adopted mother worked with me on that issue. I was eighteen when I finally released my hate toward her and instead started seeing her as a confused, scared, immature young woman who didn't know what else to do with an unwanted pregnancy. Or? Perhaps she'd been raped?" Shaking her head, she whispered, "I would *never* want to carry a child of rape. I couldn't do it, either, if that is what happened to her." She sighed and smiled brokenly. "And I'll never know what caused her to give me away, but I have a far more mature view of it now than when I was a lot younger."

Ram sighed. "And she gave you to a fire department she knew would take you in, feed you and take care of you. She put you in the safest possible place, so I'm sure she loved you enough to do that."

"All those things." She gave him a thoughtful look. "We all have to wrestle with bad things that happen to us, and it takes whatever amount of time to work through it."

"You've helped me so much," he began in a halting, roughened tone. "I laid awake last night for a little while, with you in my arms on the couch while you slept against me, and I could literally feel that ugly hatred dissolving within me, Dare." There was awe in his tone. "You are my gift. I hope you know that…"

She smiled softly and set the cup on the nightstand. "I believe it's the love we've held for so long in our hearts for one another, Ram. Don't you?"

"I believe that now. But I wasn't there until last night. This morning, I feel so much lighter, cleaner inside, thanks to you…"

"Oh, no," she said, "you were ready to release your grief and hatred, Ram. It was your time to make that change on every level, and you trusted yourself this time, and did just that. I'm so happy for you. For us."

He sat there for a long time, thinking, the silence falling softly between them. Finally, he managed, "I believe the love I have for you gave me the trust I needed in order to start the long process of dealing with all this darkness that has lived inside me."

"I agree," she whispered gently. "We had four years, off and on, with one another, Ram, and we both held our love for one another at bay. We couldn't have released it due to the circumstances we were in. We were both mature beyond our years in knowing why it had to be kept a deep secret and we silently, without the other person knowing about it, carry within each of us."

His brows fell and he rested the cup on his thigh. "We'll still have to keep our secret going forward, Dare."

Nodding, she said, "At least we'll carry it together, and for me, that means the world. I feel infused with such happiness that I can barely stand it."

"We're good secret holders," he agreed, his tone becoming more hopeful sounding. "Maybe too good? If command gets wind of our relationship, they'll yank you out of my team in a heartbeat. They won't allow it to get in the way of combat and mission priorities."

She slid off the bed, set the cup on the nightstand and walked across the rug, sitting down, facing him, her hands resting on his thighs. "I know that. If we can do it for two years of combat in Afghanistan, then two more years apart, we have the ability to hide it going forward, too."

Reaching out, he smoothed her hair, relishing being able to touch her. "You're right. Not even Adam can know. We have to pretend I'm staying here only because of that one-hour drive to my home in the village. That we're still the same people as before."

"Roger that. For sure."

He placed the cup on the small table nearby. Leaning over, he kissed the top of her head and then he cupped her face. "But we will know. We're in tune with one another." He eased her chin upward as his mouth descended upon hers, tasting her, giving her the love he held so deeply for her for so long.

FOR ONCE, Dare did not want to put on her winter fatigues and pull on her polished black combat boots and get ready for another long day with the medical unit training. Ram was out in the kitchen, loading the dishwasher. At least she would be near Ram because he and the leaders of the Black Wolf ops teams would be deep into strategy and tactics sessions with their commanders, learning the ins and outs of how to go about attacking the Russians. First, she was glad her job was medical, and secondly, that she was an expert on setting up field hospitals. She glanced out the living room windows, the day dawning at 0700. The November sky was a light blue, and she could see sunlight touching the very tops of some of the tallest apartment buildings in downtown Kyiv.

Pulling on her boots and then tying them, she got up and went out to the kitchen, where she could smell some wonderful scents of food calling to her. She was starved. Last night was such a powerful, emotional moment for both of them. Ram looked amazingly better this morning. She would swear even the color of his skin had lightened from unloading all that emotional trauma from within himself.

Dare willingly became the receptacle of his grief and loss, and intuitively her empathetic instincts, which had been finely honed by combat over the years, knew that she was the right person for him to trust and share it with. Love blossomed in her heart and it felt like a wonderful, warm blanket flowing across her chest, making her feel as if walking on air and not on the floor. Almost giddy with joy, she met and held his intense gaze that radiated his love for her. It took her breath away. She smiled, feeling like ten thousand suns were radiating from her heart toward his. They had loved one another for so long…so long…and now, it was here. Right now. She walked into the kitchen.

Reaching upward, sliding her arms around his shoulders, she met his mouth, cherishing his lips, his moist breath flowing across her cheek. Closing her eyes, she drowned in his masculinity and strength, which he held in check, sharing only his tender, loving side with her to absorb and glory within. That outer strength that was always like a powerful shield was still present, but now, it embraced both of them. She wanted to share so much more with him, but time wasn't on their side, and she deepened the kiss, infusing him with so much of her love that she held for him alone. Slowly, they separated and they opened their eyes. Dare moved her fingers through his dark hair, giving him a trembling smile.

"I could do this all day with you," she whispered, their noses almost touching.

"Me, too," he growled. Raising his head, he rasped, "But not right now. We have to be at our respective meetings."

Groaning, she nodded, wanting to keep her hands around him, feeling the thick muscles in his back tighten. He wrapped his arm around her waist, bringing her against him, pressing a kiss into her tousled hair. "Tonight?"

She reached up, caressing his cheek. "Tonight."

"We need some fuel for today."

"I'm hungry," she admitted, stopping a few feet away from him.

"Breakfast will be ready shortly," he promised, giving her a swift, hard kiss and then releasing her.

Chapter Eight

December 1

Dare gave Ram an apologetic look as she entered her apartment. She'd spent an hour across the hallway with Adam's family. She hadn't been sure when Ram would arrive home. The word *home* sounded so sweet, so reassuring to her. Darkness had long since fallen over Kyiv, and she had another full day of training with field hospitals. He was padding across the living room, a towel across his naked shoulders and another wrapped around his waist, having just come from a shower, his flesh gleaming.

"Sorry I'm late," she offered. Despite her lateness, she could appreciate that he was eye candy of the best kind.

He halted and nodded. "I just got home myself. Chaotic days now."

Shutting the door, she made a face. "Things are heating up, for sure," she said, walking toward him. "I've waited all day for this moment." She dropped her canvas medical bag on the floor and placed her arms around his broad shoulders. The glitter in his eyes made her smile as he pulled her possessively against him. "You look like you're on the hunt," she teased, absorbing his long fingers moving gently across her shoulders, chasing the tension in them away.

"Let's shut out the real world for a while," he growled, leaning down, kissing her, pressing her fully against him.

Making a humming sound of agreement, she relaxed in his grip. With their schedules, which never agreed, the ten-to-sixteen-hour days, they were usually exhausted by the time they arrived at her apartment. But tonight, it was different. She met his mouth with equal relish, her arms tightening around his shoulders. Hunger for him surged through her. His hand running down the length of her spine, cupping her hips, bringing her solidly against him left no question he wanted her. Gradually, they parted and she studied his narrowed gaze upon her.

"Let me take a shower? I'm hungry, but not for food right now. How about you?"

He eased her away from him, giving her a rueful grin. "Is tonight the night? Finally?"

She laughed a little. "I can't stand it anymore," she admitted.

"Same here," he said, releasing her. "Get your shower. I'll see you in the bedroom. I'm not sleeping alone anymore, Dare. You okay with that?"

"More than okay with it. It's just our schedules, Ram, that's all. I'll see you in about thirty minutes…" And she made her way down the hall to the bathroom.

Turning, he padded across the room, locking the front door. The drapes were already drawn closed across the bank of windows that faced the highway. He wasn't sure who was more starved for the other: Dare or himself.

Ram had held off sleeping with her because he knew

how precious sleep was right now for both of them. They'd agreed to wait until a more opportune time, a less demanding time so that they could have some private moments together.

He was waiting in her bed when she came in, a towel wrapped around her. With only one small light on, she appeared out of the darkness of the hall, more magic than real to him. "Feel better?"

She sat on the edge of the bed, removing the towel, naked. "I feel cleaner, for sure. Today was brutal. When I got home earlier, Lera caught me coming in and said Anna had slipped and fallen on a patch of ice coming home from the school bus stop. Could I come over and look at her swollen ankle? She had sprained it. I'm sorry I wasn't here when you got home."

He gazed up at her lean, tightly muscled body, appreciating her beauty, the soft light emphasizing her rounding curves that were naturally hers. Reaching out, he caressed her waist and hip. "You did the right thing. I just figured you were running late as usual."

"I wanted tonight to be ours, Ram. I really did. But real life happens."

"Is Anna okay now?"

"Yes. I wrapped her ankle in an Ace bandage and Lera will soak it in arnica-herbed warm water a couple of times tonight before she goes to bed. That will help reduce the swelling. It hurts her a lot tonight, but in a week or two, she'll be good as new."

"I'm glad you were there for them." He looked up at her as she finished drying her damp hair. "You are always there for so many people, Dare."

She placed the towel on the nearby rocking chair and turned, moving to where he lay in the center of the bed, leaning down and kissing him. "I want to be there for you... for us..."

He nodded, seeing the frustration in her expression. "Tonight? This is special for us, Dare," he rasped, getting her settled next to him, parallel to where he lay. He slid his fingers through her damp strands, smoothing them away from her face. "Tonight is ours...no matter what lies ahead for all of us." He held her luminous gaze. "Do you know how many years I've dreamed of this? How many dreams I've had of kissing you? Making love with you?"

She barely shook her head, lost in the warmth of his burning gaze, his utter vulnerability being openly shared with her. Her heart mushroomed with so much joy.

Leaning over, he coaxed her lips open so that he could fully curve and fit his mouth against hers. Ram felt Dare sigh, as if she'd waited a lifetime for this moment. He slipped his arm around her, anchoring her more securely against him, and moved his other hand beneath her neck and head, angling her more surely so he could take full advantage of her pliant willingness. As he moved his tongue to first one corner of her mouth and then the other, he felt her react, arching innocently against him. A quiver of pleasure thrummed through her and he felt utter satisfaction, allowing her to set their pace. He settled her beneath him.

Ram knew Dare was wet. She was more than ready. It was torture to not engage more with her. She pressed against him, breasts teasing his taut chest, her fingers digging deep into the muscles of his bunched shoulders, signaling she wanted a lot more than just his kiss.

Damp strands of hair clung to her temple where he followed her hairline with tender kisses. She nuzzled beneath his jaw, caressing his chest as he kept most of his weight off her. Ram was reverent toward Dare, kissing her brow, her nose, her flushed cheek and, finally, her lips once more. There was such unparalleled love within Dare as she met his mouth, kissing him deeply and sharing their uneven breaths with one another.

Ram's mind was melting. He rolled on a condom. He ached like fire itself, his body begging for release. Dare's mouth was beguiling, her kisses sensual and filled with knowing. Ram knew she was lost in the heat of their contact. Hell, he wanted to be, too, but one of them had to keep their brain online at least for a little while longer. As her lips hungrily met his, more demanding, needy, Ram groaned. The tempo changed because her mouth was wreaking sizzling heat straight down to his lower body. In agony of another sort, Ram shifted his weight to both his elbows on either side of her head and lifted his hands, gently framing her face once more.

Sharing a fiery, molten kiss with one another.

After easing beside her, he brushed his tongue against the peaks of her nipples, and he heard her whimper, thrusting her pelvis against him. Ram slid his hand down across it, following the taut, satin curve of her thigh, and slowly opened her to him. He heard Dare moan, as if anticipating his coming caresses. It was a good sign, and he began to lick and kiss his way down across her soft, rounded belly. Moving over her, their bodies seated with one another, he opened her more, nudging with his knee, wanting to thrust into her sweet, warm body.

He placed his forearms as a frame around her head and rasped, "Look at me…" Her eyes opened and he saw the hunger and need for him in them. "I'm going to go easy, Dare. I don't want to hurt you…"

She nodded. "I want you, Ram…all of you. Don't be afraid. I need you…this…so badly…"

Kissing her parted lips, he whispered, "This moment is for both of us, sweetheart…" He took his time, feeling her wetness, the urgency in calling out his name, and pulling him into her. He allowed her to set the pace and with every slow thrust, it felt as if his mind were melting to the point where he could barely hold on, barely think.

He engaged that swollen knot at her entrance. She was so ripe, so ready. They both had a lot of stored sexual energy and he was going to relieve her first. Ram leaned over, feeling her close to coming, and caught one of her nipples between his teeth and gently squeezed.

A hoarse cry tore from her as he moved more deeply inside her. The explosive power of the orgasm tore through her so swiftly that she nearly lost consciousness as he prolonged the pleasure for her, milking her willing, hungry body. Dare went utterly limp, her breathing chaotic, her lips parted, eyes tightly shut, off in another world of heat and raw, continuous and gratifying sensations.

After each rush of pleasure, he continued to caress and love her with his kisses, moving teasingly to give her more. His ironclad will had kept him in check, but finally, mercifully, he felt that lightning-like bolt of heat plunge down his spinal column and that raw heat bursting out of him, making him growl with utter satisfaction. He held her tight, frozen with the gift his own body was giving him for having the patience to bring her to the same point of utter bliss.

Afterward, he eased out of her and moved to her side, holding her tightly, inhaling her wonderful fragrance, feeling her arms weakly embracing him, face buried against his sweaty neck. Everything was perfect, each feeling heady, light and semiconscious from the deep pleasure they both gave and enjoyed with one another.

Love overwhelmed him and he threaded his long, scarred fingers through her drying hair, kissing her brow, her cheek, wanting to love her like this for the rest of his life. As he held her against him, her breathing slowed down, and so did his. After the raw release and pleasure came the drowsiness and Ram knew just how tired they really were. Dare had fallen asleep in his arms, her breath now soft and slow. Very soon, closing his eyes, with her tucked up against him, feeling so very protective of her, Ram sank into an abyss of darkness that felt as if both of them were in a nest of sorts, alive, safe and happy.

December 2

RAM WAS THE first to awake. He saw sunlight squeezing between the curtains and the window here and there. Losing track of time, he relaxed because this was a rare day off for both of them. Dare was still sleeping and he understood just how brutally exhausted she had become, and how much she had pushed herself in the last three weeks. She wasn't a machine. She was a human, and he knew from rich experience that they might get away with a hard, extreme push every once in a while, but their bodies would buckle under the weight of the strain and they would sleep twelve hours a day for several days in a row.

He moved his hand lightly down her back, her arm across his torso. Her head rested against his shoulder and neck, and he hungrily absorbed the warmth that was her. Lifting his hand, he made sure the blankets and sheet were well in place to keep her warm. He didn't want to get up. He wanted to memorize this night, and this morning after, as no other.

Ram knew what was coming and he didn't fool himself that they would get any time alone, much less to love one another, once the war began. It was going to be a brutal campaign with no relief, no downtime, no going back to the rear for a rest, much less R & R. Right now, every civilian Ukrainian man and woman was preparing to help those who would be on the front lines.

Dare stirred, muttering incoherently. He couldn't make out what she'd said, feeling her remove her arm from around his waist. He noticed how her thick lashes quivered, coming awake. She was a gift to his heart. He slid his arm beneath her neck and eased her onto her back, positioning himself on her left side, his one leg across hers.

"I want to wake up just like this every morning with you," he rasped, claiming her lips, kissing her gently, feeling her return reaction, her arm gliding over his shoulder and around the thick column of his neck.

"Mmm, so do I." She smiled up into his intense, narrowed eyes. "What time is it?" She lifted her head, trying to see the clock on the dresser opposite their bed.

Twisting his head, he said, "0830. We slept a good, long time." Leaning down, he kissed her wrinkled brow. "Now," he warned gruffly, "we've nowhere to go today, no meetings, no field exercises, no nothing. It's our day off and I want to spend it with you."

Nodding, she licked her lips and blinked several times. "I agree... I really slept hard..."

"We both did," he agreed. Frowning, he asked, "How are you feeling about now?"

She smiled. "Never better."

Relieved, he took a deep breath. "Tell me what you want to do today."

"Can I get some coffee into my bloodstream first?" She laughed softly.

He slowly rose and tucked her back into the blankets. "Stay put," he murmured, "I'll make us some..."

DARE SIPPED HER third cup of coffee in the living room, her legs tucked beneath her, leaning into one corner of the couch. Ram had made coffee, gotten a hot shower, dressed and went to work in the kitchen to make them breakfast. She finally got up, showered, dressed and joined him at the kitchen table. How luxurious it was to have that third cup of coffee with him in the living room. He was like a large male lion in the other corner of the sofa, drinking his coffee, the soft silence of happiness surrounding them. Earlier, he'd drawn back the curtains and snow was once more falling silently from the gray sky. Many people were out and about because it was the Christmas season, some carrying packages and admiring the decorations in the store windows.

"I'm stuffed," Dare admitted, touching her tummy beneath her pink chenille sweater. She had curled up, thick pink socks up to just below her knees, choosing a velvet lavender pair of loose pants.

"Makes two of us. We were pretty starved."

She smiled over the rim of her cup. "Sex starved."

He shook his head. "No...love starved. We loved one another last night. It was a dream come true for both of us."

She nodded. "You're right."

"Are you hungry again?" he teased, grinning.

"No...not yet... I'm completely satisfied, thanks to you."

Quiet fell over them. Ram studied her. She had brushed her hair and allowed it to be loose. In civilian clothes, she looked not only at peace, but happiness was radiating from her, as well. "I was thinking..."

"Uh-oh."

He gave her a partial grin. "The day is ours. What would you like to do with it?"

Sighing, she whispered, "Absolutely nothing, but I love walking in the snow, hearing the crunch of our boots in it...and the churches around the area with their bells pealing. I guess I'm nostalgic about the Christmas season."

"Those sounds always make me feel at peace, too."

She gave him a sad look. "Have you ever celebrated Christmas after your family was killed?"

Shaking his head, he muttered, "I couldn't. It brought back so many happy memories, Dare. I avoided those memories like the plague." He looked up at the ceiling and then held her gaze. "But this time? This year? With you? I want to have Christmas again because you're the greatest gift I've ever had besides my family. You make me feel whole, when I know I'm not. Just getting to hold you, loving you, fulfills me. Last night made me want to cry. A good cry of happiness. You were in my arms, and I was able to love you the way I had dreamed of doing so many times in the past… In some ways, I felt like I was in a Christmas fable and so were you. And we were deliriously happy because we were with one another." He sat up, resting his elbows on his knees, gazing at her. "I never realized the depth of my love for you until last night. I felt turned inside out in the best of ways. I never thought I'd be happy again, but with you in my arms? I felt such an incredible, ongoing joy that flooded me, driving out my darkness, my rage, hatred and grief… It all dissolved. After loving you, I had never felt so light, so damned happy from the inside out that I didn't know what to do with myself."

She studied him, tears swimming in her eyes. "I have to come clean, too, Ram. I feel like we're in a snow globe, in this fairy-tale happy romance and everything is right with the world. I know it's not, but that's how I feel right now. Like you? Loving you, having you within me, us becoming one, sent an incredible ribbon of utter joy through me. I was hoping you could feel it because I wanted to share that with you."

"You did in your own way," he reassured her, his voice thick with emotion. Shaking his head, giving her a rueful look, he added, "We had to wait four years for this moment. Four years…"

"I don't regret it. Look what has happened as a result of it. There's a side to me, Ram, that is the dreamer and the idealist. I didn't know you had fallen in love with me. You never gave me a hint. I thought," and she shrugged, "that it was all me, that it was one-sided."

"I felt the same way, but our military mission stopped it cold."

"What makes you think it won't now?" she asked in a whisper, frowning.

"We're more mature," he said. "We know how to function in combat for the team. We're a unit. We're one. But no one will know what we know."

Rolling her eyes, she managed in a strangled tone, "Our future is so uncertain, Ram…"

"And it wasn't over in Afghanistan?"

She shrugged. "You're the pragmatist. Remember? I'm the dreamer and idealist."

His mouth quirked. "I dream, too, sweetheart. Often. I just didn't let you know about it was all."

"It's nice to know now, Ram," she admitted, wiping the corners of her eyes with her fingers.

"Look, we know life isn't easy, Dare. You were given up by your mother. My entire family was murdered. Is it any wonder that we joined the military and went into another kind of war? That our lives have always been about combat in one sort of mode or another in order to survive?"

Nodding, she whispered, "I've often thought along the same track as you—we've always been in combat one way or another. It's as if our life was written for this…for what's to come early next year."

"We survived Afghanistan," he growled. "Sometime in the future, we will settle down and have a real life together."

"I dream of that." She uncurled herself, set the emptied cup on the coffee table and moved to where he sat. He handed her the cup and she placed it next to hers. She folded one leg beneath her, faced Ram and picked up his hands in hers. "Okay," she said in a low tone, "What if we survive this coming war with Russia? What then? What do you want? How do you see your life afterward with me?"

Ram squeezed her long, beautiful fingers gently. "I will always see it with you," he murmured, holding her worried gaze.

"But…what does that mean, Ram? Do we build or buy a house? What if the Donbas region goes under Russian rule when it's all over? You can never go home. You can never reclaim your family farm or the land. Do you want children? Or not? I need to know these things because it's going to help me get through this war."

He held her hand a little tighter. "After my family was gone, I had no dream of a future until I met you in Afghanistan. Then, I dared to dream. I saw us married, having a home and two children. All I wanted for you, Dare, is for you to pursue what made you happy. If it isn't children? I can live without them. I want to live with you. I want to share my life with you until the day we die."

"You're serious about children?"

"Yes. And you?" He held her gaze.

"I'm twenty-nine now, Ram. If I'm to have children, I'd like to have two by the time I'm thirty-five. I don't want any more than that because it's so expensive to have them." She looked up toward the windows in thought for a moment and then turned back to him. "I'm not even sure we'll survive this war, Ram. One or both of us could be badly injured or killed and we both know that."

"Yes, it could happen. But we go into combat to keep our country a democracy for everyone's family and children, for our future dreams. Without people like us, it wouldn't happen. But it can destroy our dreams we have for one another, too, if we get wounded or killed. It's the last thing I want, but in war, there are no idealists and dreamers, only realists. If you get injured, I will take care of you. I love you, whether you are whole or not. Whether you can have children or not. Love cannot be destroyed, Dare. My love, my loyalty, is to you."

She dragged in a deep breath and pulled her hands from his, wiping her eyes. "I feel the same about you. If you get wounded? I will be there to support and care for you. You have been a part of my life since Afghanistan and I don't want it any other way. We're both seeing the future the same way."

Reaching out, he caressed her pale cheek. "Sweetheart, I love you. And maybe what I'm going to say will sound idealistic, but I believe we will both survive this coming war in one piece, together. We survived Afghanistan. This will be different in some respects, but in other ways, it will be the same. We have passed our trial by fire and not only have we survived, but we've thrived because of it. Ukraine counts heavily on the Black Wolf regimental teams because we are all blooded and experienced. If anyone has a chance to survive this? It is us, so keep your dreams in your heart, as I will mine. We want the same thing—a home and a family. Nothing is ever more important to us Ukrainians than that…"

"There are no idealists in a fox hole," she reminded him quietly. "Right now, today? I'd like to take this time to have serious, searching and detailed talks with you about us, about what we want in our future and how we see it playing out. I know war is fickle and you can't assume anything with it, that it is constantly changing, and abruptly. But," and she placed her hand over heart, "I need to hear, to share that dream, Ram, with you. I want to hear the details of how much you have dreamed for us that I don't know about yet."

He leaned forward, kissing her gently, hands coming to rest on her shoulders. "I promise you, I have four years of dreams and thoughts and possibilities for us, Dare. Yes, let's take this day to look at everything. We have to. I've already had my will changed to give everything I have or own to you, in case I'm killed in combat."

She gave him a shaken look. "I—I hadn't even thought along those lines yet."

"We're going to hammer out plans for our future now," he rasped, kissing her cheek and releasing her. "It will help us get through whatever the Russians are going to throw at us. It will strengthen us, making our resolve unbreakable, and help us keep our focus so we can help our nation survive it all. By laying out our plans? It gives us hope, sweetheart. Hope for a better future, and a peaceful one. Together. My dream of loving you held me together for four years. Think about that. If I can do that, I can keep my dreams alive within my heart."

Silence blanketed them. Finally, Dare whispered, "I like using today to plan. I like knowing you want a home and a family. I have, for the longest time, wanted my own babies... I've helped birth so many in my career as a medic."

"We'll have them, I promise," Ram said gruffly. "I want you happy. We are a team of equals, Dare. We have always worked off one another's strengths, not our weaknesses, and that is one of our main assets that has allowed us to come up to this moment to admit our love and act upon it. We are a team."

Chapter Nine

December 25

It was near 10:00 p.m. when Ram and Dare left the Vorona family activities for the day. They had dinner and gone to church together, come home and eaten some more before everyone got to open their Christmas gifts. Dare was the one with the iPhone camera, taking lots of photos of the girls, of Lera, Adam and Ram. She had been thrilled that everyone loved their Christmas gifts that they had gotten for the family from the Sophia Plaza Christmas Market days earlier.

The flakes were once again falling and everything from the large windows in her apartment showed the snow piling up alongside the wide, massive six-lane avenue. Streets were clean and passable. Kyiv acted like a good Swiss watch: always on time, neat as a pin and clean.

"Oh!" she said, flopping down on the huge sofa, "I'm tired! Are you, Ram?"

He chuckled and removed his sweater, the T-shirt beneath showing off his broad, well-muscled shoulders and chest. "It was a good day," he agreed, guiding her over to the end of the sofa, his arm coming around her shoulders. "The children loved it."

Sighing happily, she nuzzled against his neck and jaw. "It was so hard to keep my hands off of you, to keep my distance over there with Adam and his family."

"I know," he said, a tinge of regret in his tone. "But," he said, sitting up, "maybe this will make you feel less tired?"

She watched as he stood and walked over to a small drawer in the side table next to her rocking chair. What he pulled out looked like a magazine. "What's that?"

He sat down next to her, giving her a pleased look. "Your Christmas present. Didn't you miss getting something from me when we were over there?"

"Well," she said, sitting up, eyeing the folder beneath his large hand in his lap, "yes, but gosh, we got so many gifts from Adam and Lera."

"I didn't want to spring this one on you at the time and you'll see why. I wasn't trying to be sneaky." He grinned.

She laughed with him. "May I have my present now? Curiosity is killing me."

"Go ahead. Merry Christmas, sweetheart." He handed the present to her.

Frowning, she opened up the folder. Looking at it for a long minute in silence, she finally gasped. "No! You didn't!"

Chuckling, he said, "What?" teasingly, his smile widening as she quickly flipped though the glossy tourist brochure's many pages.

"How did you know this about me?" She gave him a shocked look of disbelief.

"I did a little reconnoitering," he answered slyly. "I asked

Lera what was your most ardent dream vacation and she told me that you'd always wanted to go to Forest Castle Spa in the Carpathian Mountains, in southwest Ukraine, near the border with Moldova, to their spa, and to ski, because you loved skiing. I didn't know you skied until she told me just before we moved them from Bucha down here to Kyiv."

Making a happy sound, she stared at him, lips parting. "This says a two-week hotel stay, with spa and skiing all-inclusive! How did you manage to get us two weeks of R & R, Ram? I kept hearing that no one was being granted leave right now."

"I wanted to spend some serious time with you, Dare. I talked to our commander and he relented and gave us the leave. He didn't ask why and I wouldn't have answered him even if he had asked me. Lera told me how much you wished you could get a massage, that it helped your shoulders and back. When she added that you were an avid skier? I began to put a plan together. I know how much you love the mountains. And you know what? I like to ski, too. My other brother, Symon, and I were major skiers growing up."

"There's so much I don't know about you," she whispered, deeply touched as she looked at the lavish five-star hotel room where they would be staying. The place was pricey. And it was at the foot of the beautiful Carpathian Mountains that she loved so much.

"This is another way we can share with one another," he added. "The train tickets and hotel reservation are attached at the end of the brochure. We take the train from Kyiv to Bukovel tomorrow night at 1600. We'll have dinner in their dining car, and there is a reservation for a sleeper car because it's nearly thirteen hours from Kyiv to Lviv, and then from Lviv, down to the resort. We can then have breakfast in the dining car and we'll arrive just in time to start our day together."

She sat back, shaking her head. "I—I didn't expect something like this, Ram." Worried, she muttered, "Two weeks? That's a *lot* of money."

"Don't worry about that," he urged. "I've been saving for a long, long time and it's easy to spend it on you because I have it, and secondly, I *wanted* something special for you, Dare. I want our short time together to mean something... something we can hold on to after this war starts."

"What a beautiful gift you've given to both of us," she whispered, moving through the pages slowly. "I don't know if I'll ever leave the spa. They have twenty different types of massage!" She sighed. "I'll be in heaven..."

He sat back, enjoying her response to his gift. "You can try every one of them. You can have as many types of massage as often as you want."

Giving him a dreamy look, she said, "You really know how to amaze me."

"I hope so," he said, matching her grin. "Lera said you were wishing for a salt peel, whatever that means."

"Oh! It's a lovely way to scrape off the dead skin! It makes your body glow afterward."

"If it makes you happy? I'm all for it."

She peered down at the brochure. "Ohhh, and they have mud baths! Finnish sauna, which I love! That hot and cold water is so good for a person's health and body!"

"She also said you like the hot tub, the Jacuzzi?"

Rolling her eyes, she said, "Yes, I do. All of this is so

wonderful." And then she laughed and shook her head. "Aren't you interested in these? Don't you love massages?"

Shrugging, he said, "I've never had a massage, Dare."

"They have partner massages. I'll get an appointment for us. You'll love it!"

"I love you," he murmured, becoming more serious.

She reached over, kissing his cheek. "This is just the best gift you could ever have given me under the circumstances, Ram. Thank you."

"I'm just wondering if I'm going to get you on a pair of skis or not," and he laughed.

"You will…but first, the massages. How good a skier are you, anyway?"

"Well," he deadpanned, "I don't take off on a sheer cliff or a steep run. I'm more of an intermediate cross-country or moderate downhill skier. Besides, I don't want to run into a tree and kill myself by accident before this war starts."

They both laughed, nodding and understanding his sardonic comment.

She reached out, sliding her hand into his. "Thank you for this wonderful, unexpected gift…" The moment was bittersweet because Dare was already counting the days to when their secret life would end and real life and real-world events would take over instead. Shaking herself internally, she made Ram a silent promise that these next two weeks would be memorable for both of them, in the best of ways. She looked at the train tickets on the last page. Tomorrow, near dark, they would climb aboard one of the fastest, most modern trains in Europe at the main train station in downtown Kyiv. "I feel like Alice in Wonderland," she confided, grinning. "Without the rabbit or the Cheshire cat."

"We don't need craziness," he agreed, pulling her into his embrace, settling her against his body, her head resting on his shoulder, her gaze upon his. "These next fourteen days will probably look and feel like we've stepped into another dimension and into a different world, and left this one with all its problems behind."

"Truly," she said, closing the brochure and setting it on the cushion next to her. Slipping her arm around his torso, she kissed his roughened cheek and inhaled his scent that was more of an aphrodisiac than anything else, stirring her lower body to life. "We're entering a dream world, Ram."

"I'll be your prince if you will be my princess. We'll rule our land together," he teased gently, kissing her hair.

Closing her eyes, she whispered, "I like how you see us..."

December 26

DARE TRIED TO absorb everything all at once. She was completely out of her soldier's duties and now turned into a wide-eyed adult as she looked at the U-shaped, five-story hotel rising above them. They exited a taxi gotten at the train station, baggage taken by handlers after they found out which hotel room they were going to be living in for the next two weeks. Above her, the sky was a bright dark blue with a few errant, fluffy white clouds over the Carpathian mountain range. At 9:00 a.m., the sun was bright and she was glad to be wearing her sunglasses, same as Ram. There were so many groups of people from all over the world coming to this vaunted resort. Ram had told her that the Eastern Carpathian Mountains area was a huge worldwide draw to people who loved the great outdoors, hiking, fishing or, in the winter, skiing, ice-skating and other snow sports.

Inside, they were taken to a special area where they could check in. The huge alcove was richly appointed, expensive and grand looking to Dare. What a change from her life in the military! Ram was dressed in a casual pair of jeans, a white velour long-sleeved shirt that was mostly hidden beneath his black leather jacket he wore over it. She saw the hardness he once wore as a team leader completely dissolve. In its place was the man she discovered on the train ride down here, who was very different, and began to realize how relaxed he was becoming within such a short period. Yes, they both needed this serious break in their lives. Holding his hand, they followed the bellhop to a highly polished brass elevator that was set apart from the other banks. They were taken up to the fifth floor, to the very top of the hotel. As the doors opened, and she stepped into what looked like a very expensive penthouse, she gave Ram a startled look. He said nothing, easing her to one side as the bellhop brought in their luggage, placed it in the bedroom and then left.

"Ram," she breathed, looking around at the designer penthouse, "you didn't say we were staying *here*." Giving him a confused look, she knew the design and well-appointed place was for the rich and famous. They were neither.

"I wanted the best for us," he explained, catching her hand, leading her deeper into the huge apartment. Rows of windows allowed sunlight to cascade in, with light gray and maroon curtains that could be pulled shut or opened at a press of a remote button that sat on a glass coffee table in the middle of the living room area. There were huge, colorful bouquets of flowers here and there in very pricey-looking vases. The floor was made of a rich golden-colored hardwood, polished, with a number of well-placed area rugs.

There was a huge kitchen with everything they could ever need or want. Looking into the refrigerator, she saw it was stocked with food, wine, beer and snacks. They would want for nothing. Dare counted at least four large flat-screen TVs in the penthouse. Mentally, she estimated it was at least twenty-five hundred square feet of room. There were two bedrooms, both with king-size beds, each one with a plush white carpet and two master bathrooms to complete them. The shower could easily hold two people at once. The bathtubs were not only large but had Jacuzzi jets so that it would be like receiving a mini-massage. The place was immaculate, beautiful, and she turned to him. "You weren't kidding when you said this was going to be like Alice in Wonderland."

He chuckled, leading down toward the other end. "It has everything," he promised. Stopping, he opened the wooden door. It was a dry sauna. There were thick Turkish towels sitting on the benches just outside the door, just waiting to be utilized.

"When Lera told me how much you loved saunas, I knew that I would get you the penthouse. It is the only room that has one. There are a number of them down in the spa area, but here, you can step into it any time you want."

"And I can take a cold shower afterwards." Dare nodded, smiling up at him. "You've thought of everything."

She saw him become pensive and serious. "What are you thinking about, Ram?"

"Us. Like we're stepping out of hell and into heaven for a little while." He squeezed her hand. "I wish I could give this to you as a wedding present. That we could live here forever."

Sliding her arm around his waist, she leaned her head against his shoulder. "I wish that, too, but we know different."

Nodding, he held her close, giving her a squeeze and a kiss on top of her head. "Well, for two weeks, we will pretend, and we will enjoy our time together." Turning, he said, "Did you see the champagne in the bucket? The two glasses beside it?"

"Yes, I saw it. I've never tasted champagne. Have you?"

"No. I'm a beer kind of guy."

Giggling, she reached up, kissing his cheek.

Looking out of the bank of windows toward the snow-covered Carpathian Mountains, he asked, "What would you like to do first?"

"See the spa?" She grinned. "I really need two or three days of being pampered first. It will help me ramp down."

Nodding, he led her back to the living room, where there was a personal elevator exclusively for the penthouse. "The spa is underground. Let's go reconnoiter. Shall we?"

December 30

THE AIR WAS FRIGID, about thirty degrees, as Dare took off on a ski trail, with Ram not far behind for a day of cross-country skiing. It was ten o'clock in the morning and there were numerous trails all over the highest mountain, nearly six thousand feet, for them to explore at their own leisure. Ram enjoyed cross-country skiing so today the red knapsack he wore on his back contained two thermoses of hot chocolate, along with a lunch, for when they chose to stop and eat at a mineral and hot springs chalet halfway up the mountain. It was quite a climb to get to it, traversing a gentle two-thousand-foot slope and, sometimes, challenging cliff areas that were to be avoided at all costs. Staying on the trail, according to the map of the area, was very necessary.

Many of the groves of evergreens were Scotch pine. Several thousand feet on the slope below were oak, beech, hornbeam and ash trees, all deciduous and barren looking for the winter. Fir trees grew in thick, richly colored green copses here and there, mostly replaced by spruce. There were fifteen types of coniferous trees and Dare couldn't begin to identify all of them. Ram knew most by name, and she was impressed with his botany knowledge. The forests took up one-third of the country. Dare knew there was a thriving timber export business within Ukraine, as well.

Many other people were out this morning on other, intersecting trails that ranged from beginner to easy, moderate and challenging. Ram would stop with Dare when they were going to climb a particularly risky area where the lava cliff faces were located close to the main track.

Cross-country skiing was very popular, Dare was discovering. Whole families would pass by them. Children that were seven or eight years old had skis on and were sliding along with older members of the family. The crisp air invigorated her as she rhythmically moved on her skis.

There was no wind at this altitude so far, the day clear and the sky an azure blue in the morning light.

The deep shadows of the Scotch and spruce evergreens brought moments of cooler air as they passed by the thick groves, but then they would pop out onto a slope filled with sunshine and warm up again. The concierge at their hotel had been deeply knowledgeable of the trail systems and Ram had sat with him to map out the day's events with him earlier. After getting the information, they packed their lunch, the thermoses and several bottles of the famous Carpathian mineral water that welled up through the mountain fissures, plus protein bars. The water was well-known and desired by people who visited the spa, the spring unpolluted and coming from the depths of the basalt that had created these mountains millions of years earlier.

Ahead was a steeper slope and Dare saw a family of three disappearing over the top of it. Ram had warned her that there was a steep drop-off on the other side of the coming hill, that it could be dangerous. It was a cliff area, a two-hundred-foot drop composed of black lava, covered with ice and snow very near the trail. And if someone got off the trail, they might not see the dangerous drop beneath the snowpack, and they could go over that cliff without even realizing it was there. Ram had pointed it out on the well-prepared cross-country skiing map he had gotten the evening before.

Looking over her shoulder, she called, "Hey, we're almost halfway there!" They had another thousand feet to go. The springs and heated thermal pools were located at the top of this mountain along with a chalet restaurant. Dare strengthened her stride, in a hurry to get there. It would be a dreamy noontime destination and a well-earned five-star lunch!

Just as she crested the hill, she heard a woman down below it, screaming. Her attention was to the left, near that cliff. She saw a young boy, perhaps nine years old, on his cross-country skis going over the edge of it. The father was halfway to the boy, slipping, falling, arms outstretched, nearly touching his son's black nylon jacket, but missing him by inches.

Too late!

Dare gasped and yelled over her shoulder, "Ram! A boy has just fallen over that cliff!"

Instantly, he reacted, swiftly moving forward on his skis.

The mother was screaming hysterically, her hands against her mouth, watching her husband sliding down the slope toward the cliff where his son had already disappeared over the lip of it.

No!

Ram leaped to her left, skiing hard to stop the father from going over the cliff.

Dare halted, watching in horror, a cry jammed in her throat.

Ram was able to grab onto one of the long skis, landing hard on his side, his own skis going upward as he rolled onto his back, his gloved hand gripping the end of the man's right ski.

Terrorized, Dare watched as Ram's incredible strength stopped the skier from going over the edge, snow flying in all directions, some of the dangerous black-lava-sharpened rocks revealed.

Gasping, Dare halted, leaned down and released the

clamps around her boots, freeing her skis. Leaping forward, sinking halfway up her lower leg, she grabbed at Ram's other hand, hauling back with all her strength to stop both of them from inching toward the edge. Landing with an "omph" on her butt, she halted the men. Once stopped, she released Ram's glove, leaped up and lunged past him, gripping the stranger's flailing gloved hand. He looked like a turtle on his back, unable to flip over, the cross-country skis jammed and not allowing him to move at all. Ram continued to keep his grip on the one ski to ensure he didn't slip over the cliff.

Her breath came in huge spurts as she awkwardly made her way to him, speaking in Ukrainian. The man couldn't be more than in his late twenties or early thirties, terrified, asking her for help. She managed to get his boots released from his skis and then she turned him around as he grabbed both her hands and she hauled him to his feet and away from the cliff face. She saw Ram turn over, releasing his skis as well, and quickly getting to his booted feet.

"Dare!" Ram called, taking the man's other arm. "Slide on your belly toward the edge of the cliff! See if you can spot the boy."

Nodding, she instantly lay down on her belly, hauling herself forward, her gloves in contact with the snow and the basalt beneath it. What she didn't want to do was go over the edge, keeping the toes of her sturdy boots dug downward so she didn't slide forward unless she wanted to. The snow wasn't that deep here, her boots acting as brakes as she inched toward the edge of the cliff hidden by the snow. Below, she saw the boy lying unconscious on a small snow-covered ledge of black basalt rock. Below that was at least a 150-foot drop to the snow-clad hill below it.

Her combat senses took over. It was automatic for her to push her emotional reaction downward in order to study the situation through a medic's eyes as she breathed hard, white wisps jetting out of her opened mouth. Behind her, she heard the woman screaming, "Tymur! Tymur!" and she knew it must be the name of their son.

Ram was speaking to them, so she focused on the unmoving boy. Twenty feet down on the cliff face, she saw a large, thick bush, now barren of leaves, sticking out of it. Cursing softly, she saw the boy had clipped it as he fell. A limb the size of her wrist had snapped off. Her gaze moved to the son. Had the limb gone through him? She didn't see the whereabouts of it anywhere in the pristine snow patches on that ledge. Either it had snapped off and missed the ledge, plunging straight down to the bottom, or the limb was partly hidden somewhere beneath the boy's body.

Blood. She saw it begin to stain the white snow on his left leg just above his knee. The boy's position made it impossible to see more of his leg from where she lay.

She got to her hands and knees, jerking a look up the hill. Ram stood with the couple, his gaze intently upon her. "Ram! I need that rope from your pack!"

He shrugged out of his pack, swiftly opening it.

To her relief, Dare saw that he had also taken out the satellite phone that was with him everywhere he went because he was a Black Wolf team leader. Out came the rope. He slogged his way down the slope toward her.

"What's the condition of the boy?"

"Blood on his lower right thigh. Might be a femoral artery injury. He clipped a bush on the way down. And a possible head injury. He's unconscious." She grabbed one end of the rope. "Can you call for help?"

"Doing it now." He tapped in some numbers, holding the sat phone to his ear.

Dare saw the couple, both crying, stressed, holding on to one another, nearly hysterical with terror. She was sure that Ram ordered them to stay right where they were and not come any closer to the edge of this cliff. Turning, she crawled back to the rim, pulling the nylon two-inch rope and hurling it over the edge. Urgency thrummed through her as she saw the faint sign of blood growing marginally larger around the child's leg. Now, she was sure it was a femoral injury. The boy, depending upon how bad the artery had been torn open, could bleed to death in a minute or less. If she was lucky, the artery got punctured but not fully torn open. He'd bleed out, just not as fast, if that was true. It might give her the time to get down there and save his life. Her heart pounding, she saw that there was ten feet of the rope to spare.

Ram came to her side, on his hands and knees after making the call for emergency help.

"I called hotel Rescue. They have a helicopter. I told them what happened." He looked around. "There's nowhere to land around here and I told them to bring a basket that they could wench down from the helo and lower it to the boy."

Rapidly, Dare pulled the rope up. "How soon?" she demanded, handing it to him. She moved back and grabbed her medical pack, placing it on her shoulders and strapping it on.

"Ten to fifteen minutes," he answered, scowling. "The weather is cooperating. There's not a lot of wind today. That works in our favor."

"Roger that. Lower me down there, Ram? That kid isn't going to make it without a tourniquet around his thigh."

Ram understood and looped one end of the rope around her waist, knotting it well so it could not come loose on her descent. He brought the other end up. Dare had been trained for mountain-climbing skills after she joined his team in Afghanistan. They wasted no words, each knowing what the other must do. There was a large pine tree nearby and he looped the other end of the rope around it, snugging and tightening it so that it could not loosen as Dare made her way down the cliff. He went to the edge, gripping the rope. "Ready?"

"Yes."

They were now in complete combat mode. Ram sat down in the snow, using a large, rounded rock to rest his boots against so he could use his weight and leverage to help her get down the cliff safely. Dare was over the cliff, boots against the black lava rock, knees slightly bent while some of the brittle face broke off beneath the weight, falling past her. Gloves around the rope, her focus on the cliff and where she could place her boots, as well as watching the inert child to her left and below her, she made quick work of it. Once on the ledge, testing it, she kept tension on the rope above, unsure if the rock would carry both her and the boy's weight. It seemed to be stable. With the snow on it, she could not tell if there were deep cracks across it or not. That would mean it was unstable. Keeping the rope around her, she shrugged out of the knapsack, dropping it next to the boy, who was pale and lifeless looking.

With a quick check of his vitals, she knew he was unconscious but breathing. Swiftly she checked his legs and saw the red blood staining his left leg just above his knee. There were no broken bones, but his pants had been ripped open and so was his flesh. She saw the leak of blood, a thin spurt with every beat of his heart. Standing, she opened her jacket and jerked off her web belt. She always wore the military belt because it was two inches wide and flat, perfect for a tourniquet. With knowing swiftness, she slid it beneath his upper thigh and began to tighten it.

The child moaned but did not become conscious as she tightened it with precision.

Dare peered down at the gash in his leg, using scissors to slice open the fabric. It was a deep wound. The spurting had slowed considerably due to the application of the tourniquet. Breathing a sigh of relief, she clipped the buckle so that it would stay in that place, cutting off blood supply to that leg. She knew that every ten minutes she'd have to untighten it, allow some blood flow into the leg, or it could create an even worse condition called gangrene, where the boy would lose part or most of his leg as a result. Taking sterile, nonstick gauze from her medical bag, she packed it into the gash until it was filled with it, and then quickly took an Ace bandage from her kit, tightening it around his thin leg so that the pressure of the gauze against the tear in the artery would also act as a wall to block the continued loss of blood. She was aware of nothing else for that moment. Getting the wound wrapped, she grabbed her stethoscope and blood pressure cuff from her knapsack once more. The boy was unmoving and she used one of her gloves beneath his neck to be sure to keep his airway open so he could breathe normally.

She noted that his blood pressure wasn't good, but it had stabilized. He'd lost a lot more blood than she'd first realized. Every second counted now. Dropping the equipment back into the pack, she looked up to see Ram at the edge, silently watching her.

"How long now for the helo?" she yelled, cupping her hands to her mouth.

Ram stood, making another call to Rescue.

Urgency thrummed through Dare. She placed a space blanket around the boy, tightening it so that it wouldn't fall off him and would keep him warm. She glanced at Ram, whose expression was stony. She hurriedly shrugged her medic knapsack over her shoulders and buckled it up.

"Five minutes," he called.

Looking around, she yelled back, "Can that basket be lowered down to here?"

Ram nodded. "Yes, only one tree around. They will have room to maneuver that helo so it shouldn't be a problem getting the basket to that ledge."

That one pine tree kept her tethered and they needed it more than ever now.

The ledge cracked ominously beneath her where she knelt in the snow. Freezing for a moment, she grabbed Tymur, plastering him hard against the front of her body. She yelled to Ram. Too late!

The shelf suddenly gave way.

The rope sang and then jerked.

The air whooshed out of Dare's lungs as she held the

boy in a clenching motion tightly against her pendulum-swinging body. She slammed into the cliff, her back taking the bruising force of impact.

She tried to protect her head as her body swung outward once more. Below her, beneath her boots, she wasn't sure she would survive this or not. The child was like a puppet full of sawdust in her arms, unconscious. He couldn't have weighed more than seventy pounds, but it was enough.

"Are you all right?" Ram yelled, cupping his hands to his mouth, watching helplessly as she swung back and forth into the cliff again and again.

"Yes!"

He straightened, calling the helicopter copilot directly on the sat phone. He saw the bright red-and-white helicopter with RESCUE on its side a thousand feet below them, climbing rapidly toward their position. Once in touch with the copilot, he told the woman what had happened. It would matter because there were three people in that craft. The technician on the crane and the wench assembly positioned out the open door would be responsible for getting the large, rectangular metal basket on a steel cable out of the helicopter and down to where Dare was swinging. He went back to the tree to ensure the knot was in place. It was.

The helicopter climbed up and over them, and then slowly came down in altitude, the whapping of the blades becoming thunderous. The blades were whirling at over a hundred miles an hour, the snow blasting off the trees and around the cliff area. Ram remained kneeling, hand on the rope, on the edge of the cliff and watching as the basket began to descend. Would it get entangled with the rope? He watched as it swung slowly around and around, the man at the door, one gloved hand on the wench button, the other on the lip of the bird's open door, looking down, assessing the situation second by second. He could see the technician talking with the pilot as they descended it more. The basket swung side to side. Part of the problem was the blades were sucking up the air and the cliff face was stopping the flow it needed to keep the helo steady and unmoving. It was called "hover out of ground effect," meaning there wasn't enough air around the immediate area to create the lift that the bird needed in order to stay in the air, much less remain in a fixed position. Ram was all too familiar with that issue. If the helo couldn't maintain its altitude integrity? The pilot would have to abandon the basket rescue. Because if he didn't the bird would sink like a rock, striking the nearby cliff and crashing, probably killing everyone on board, not to mention Dare and the unconscious child in her arms.

His heart was in his throat, pulsing and pounding as the basket came nearer and nearer. Dare had stopped swinging and, with one hand around the child's waist, she fumbled and reached for the bottom of the basket as it swung by, trying to stop and stabilize it. He knelt there, frozen, watching and being badly buffeted by the blades whirling fifty feet above him. The roar of the helo and the wind whipped up huge chunks of wet snow. Small to medium tree branches snapped off and slammed into him, nearly knocking him over. He kept his hand on the rope, watching as the basket moved three more feet, some slack in the steel cable. Once there, Dare struggled and maneuvered the best she could to put the child in the basket safely. Ram knew the strength it took to do something like that. Dare made it look easy.

Next, she had to climb in. Moving the basket around to the other side, she threw her long leg up and over the smooth, rounded edge of it, wriggling and hauling herself upward on sheer, brute strength into it. After rolling over, the first thing she did was release the knot in the rope around her waist, throwing it away from the basket.

Ram quickly grabbed the rope that was flying around in the hurricane-force wind. He flattened on the snow once again, watching as the helicopter started to slowly move upward, the basket barely swinging beneath its belly. The pilot eased the bird away from the cliff, desperate to get more air. Ram saw the technician on the wench begin to draw the basket upward on the metal arm that extended outside the door. He watched until, to his utter relief, the man pulled the basket inside to the deck of the helo. He was never so grateful as of this moment.

Grabbing the sat phone, he called the copilot to find out where they were going. There was a hospital not more than five miles from their resort, she told him. She added that three snowmobiles from Rescue were about half a mile away from their position right now, coming fast, to take the three of them down to the parking lot where their cars were at so they could drive to the hospital. Ram thanked the copilot, more than grateful for their swift response and recovery. He hadn't thought about the three of them being left behind and how they were going to get down the hill. He untied the rope from around the pine tree and made his way up to the couple.

"Your son is alive. The woman who cared for him is a combat field surgeon and medic. She's stopped the bleeding on his inner left thigh and they're taking Tymur directly to the closest hospital for treatment. Once we're down in the parking lot, the hospital is only five miles away from there."

The sound of the noisy snowmobiles filled the air. The couple cried with utter relief and joy, seeing them come over the hill toward them. They hugged Ram, thanking him profusely between their tears. Ram hugged them in return and stepped away, putting the sat phone in his pack, along with the lifesaving rope. More than anything else, Dare and the boy were alive. She was probably bruised as hell getting slapped against that cliff again and again, but she would live. And God help him, he loved her even more than ever before. He could have lost her today…but he hadn't. The crisis had been so unexpected, so close…

Chapter Ten

December 30

Dare waited impatiently out in the visitors' lobby of the emergency room area of the hospital. The Moroz family, husband and wife, were on the other side of the automatic doors, with their son, Tymur. She ignored how much her back ached, looking out the large picture windows toward the entrance/exit door to the busy hospital. Her heart skipped with joy as she saw Ram pull into the parking lot. How badly she wanted to see him!

The noonday sunlight was bright and everything looked perfect for a winter day. She smiled as he came through the doors. His face expressed his worry as his gaze locked with hers. Automatically, she stepped forward, opening her arms. In moments, they held one another, and she felt his warmth, the strength and tenderness that Ram shared with her. Pulling back, holding her shoulders, he said, "How is the boy? How are you?"

She managed a slight smile. "The Moroz family is together with a doctor in ER. He's assessing Tymur's condition right now. I'm not family, so I can't go in there and be with them. But I did give the doctor my medical assessment and what I did to help him, and he was grateful for that information."

Nodding, he devoted his attention to her. "What about you? How are you?" He slid his hand from her shoulder down her back, worry in his tone.

Flinching, Dare pulled away, grimacing.

"You're injured?" he demanded.

"It's nothing. I just slammed into that cliff face three times while holding Tymur. I'm going to have some colorful bruises all over my back for the next week, is all. Come on, let's sit down. The husband said he'd let us know the diagnosis on their son. He'll come out and tell us when he knows more."

Hesitating, Ram studied her. "I saw you hit that cliff hard, Dare. You're right—at the very least, you're badly bruised."

She sat down, not resting against the back of the plastic chair. "I'll survive. Come on, sit next to me?"

He sat, picking up her hand and rested it on his thigh. "Did Tymur ever become conscious?"

"Yes, once we were inside the helo. He was scared, didn't know where he was and I wasn't his mother or father. I checked his eyes with a penlight. Both pupils were equal and responsive, which is a good sign. He's suffered a third-class concussion, but the fact his pupils dilated to the light, both of them, tells me that it's a mild one, not severe and not causing a brain bleed. They'll probably scan his brain, just in case. We'll see..."

Dare had worn her dark green heavy winter jacket that hung over her hips. Ram looked at it and saw jagged tears of the fabric all across the back of it. He knew the cutting edge of basalt was as sharp as a skinning knife. Looking at the fabric, he murmured, "Your coat is chewed up but good."

"I'm not surprised, but it did its work. It protected my back from the worst that could have happened. If I hadn't been wearing it, my skin would have been sliced open, or worse, even cut into the muscles of my back."

Ram knew better than to place his hand against her back. "Are you sure you don't want to be checked out by a doctor while we're here?"

"No. What I want…need, is you and I want to climb into that hot tub up in our suite."

"You took heavy physical stress holding Tymur," he rasped, smoothing away some strands of her hair from her temple. "I don't know how you did it. I was scared for you, Dare. When that ledge gave way?" His voice trailed off and he choked up, wrestling with a lot of emotions, unable to speak.

"I'm okay," she whispered, seeing the pain and anxiety in his gaze. "Bruised as hell, but if I get into the hot tub, that water will increase the circulation on my back and actually help reduce the swelling and pain in those areas."

He looked toward the ER doors. "Here's what we're going to do," he said, standing. "I'll go through those doors, find the Moroz family, find out how their son is and then we're going back to the hotel. They can call us and let us know how their son is. I'll leave our phone number with them. Right now? We need to take care of you, too."

RAM WAS HAVING one hell of a time wrestling with updrafts and downdrafts of anxiety and his emotions as he walked

Dare into their hotel. She could have died. When the ledge unexpectedly broke beneath her feet, he felt like a knife had ripped out his heart. Despite that, her whole focus had been on grabbing Tymur and holding on to him. He had to keep reminding himself that combat medics in the military think nothing of themselves. Rather, their whole life focus is on their patient, the one they are trying to save from dying. This crisis was no different for her, even though it wasn't a wartime situation. Dare was bred to the bone to serve, to save and, if necessary, give up her life so that the other lived to see their family once again. How close he'd come to losing her today...

Taking the personal penthouse elevator, he saw how strained she'd become. "Is your back bothering you more?" he asked as the doors opened to the penthouse suite.

"A little," she murmured. "It's stiff and cranky is all."

Ram knew it was what she called a "white lie." Her American slang and vernacular had been a two-year education for him when they served in Afghanistan. She would treat herself last, not first. And always, she minimized her own wounds. Only when they would get picked up and flown back to the camp would he find out how bad her injury was. It was no different this time.

The hot tub sat at one end of the large, rectangular master bedroom. He helped her undress and when he saw the extent of the bruising, his stomach clenched.

"Your back looks like a war zone," he muttered unhappily, helping her up the steps and into the tub.

"It feels like a major battle going on right now," she said, managing a one-sided grin. Releasing his steadying hand, she sank into the 104-degree water. Wincing at the water deluging her back, she sighed and closed her eyes. She sat down and was covered up to her shoulders with the swirling, clear mineral spring water. At least the pain should begin to recede because the water contained large amounts of magnesium in it, a natural painkiller.

"Ohhh, this feels so good, Ram."

He stood there, worried. "You've got black, blue, red and purple colors all over your back, Dare."

"Is any of the skin broken?"

He looked closely and shook his head. "No."

"Thank goodness," she said, absorbing the healing heat and water.

"I always carry that salve I shared with you when we were in Afghanistan. It's for bruises and sprains. Do you think it will help your back if I smear some of it on after you get out?" he asked.

"Yes," she murmured, opening her eyes. Reaching out, she touched his arm briefly. "I'm okay, Ram. Don't be upset. Bruises heal fast when they get this kind of attention. And that salve you always carried with you has arnica in it. Remember? It was made by Lera and she always sent the team each a large tin of it about every two months. It's a fabulous herbal salve to treat exactly what I've got."

"It will reduce the swelling, then," he said. "You're lucky you didn't crack or bust a rib the way you two slammed into that cliff face over and over again."

She smiled a little, sluicing water over her face and exposed neck. "That's because Tymur was at least seventy pounds. He was heavy."

"He was over one-third of your weight," he grumbled, scowling. Picking up a white Turkish towel that was thick and fluffy, he placed it on the edge of the hot tub so she could reach it when she was ready to climb out.

"My normal medical pack I carried is fifty pounds. The one I had today was about twenty pounds," she reminded him. "Tymur wasn't the only thing weighting me down."

His cell phone rang and he pulled it out of his back pocket, answering it.

Dare listened. It was Mr. Moroz calling. Ram's dark face lit up, and he actually smiled. When he finished the call, he said, "That was the father. Tymur is in surgery for the torn femoral artery. He said to tell you that the surgeon said you did a good job of stopping the hemorrhaging, that you saved his life. They've stitched up the tear in that artery. You were right, he has a level three concussion, and they ran him through a scan and there is no brain bleed, no fracture of his skull, either. He said they'll keep Tymur in the hospital under observation for three days due to his artery needing to mend after surgery. They want to make sure it's on the way to healing before they release him."

"That's all good news," Dare said, grinning. "Do you know where his parents will stay?"

"They are here at this hotel, but they have been given a family room at the hospital. Once Tymur is out of surgery, they will all be taken there. That way, their son will have his parents nearby and the doctor said it lowers the child's stress levels, and that will help him heal faster and better."

Her smile grew. "That's wonderful. Do they live around here?"

"Kyiv," he said. "A rabbit ran in front of Tymur and he chased it on his cross-country skis and that's how he fell over the cliff. It happened so fast his parents couldn't react in time to grab him and stop him from chasing it."

Shaking her head, she sluiced more water on her face and neck. "He's just a child. He probably thought the rabbit was playing with him and he had absolutely no awareness of that cliff or how treacherous it really was."

"That's what his father just told me. They feel guilty that they let him fall over it."

"They shouldn't. Kids move faster than the speed of light. Plus, they had long skis on and you know how awkward they are to make quick turns with. It's impossible."

"The father said they were not aware of that particular trail and had no information about the trails before they decided to cross-country ski on it. He feels very guilty about it now."

"And that's why they probably weren't more on guard at the time they crested that particular hill," she said, nodding. Brightening, she whispered, "At least this has a happy ending."

Ram nodded, sitting on the side of the hot tub, his feet on the stairs. "I didn't think we would get a happy ending out of this…"

"I saw the terror in your face, Ram. I was scared, too." She took the cloth he handed her. "Those two years with you dissolved my fear. Like you and the rest of the team, I can put my emotions in a box and leave them there. That's what got me and Tymur through that incident."

He nodded, saying nothing, but thinking one helluva lot. This was how it was going to be every day when they had to go to war and stop the Russians from taking Ukraine. He loved her like nothing else in his life. Rubbing his chest, he scowled down at the floor. The awful realization that he was going to struggle much more to not be familiar with Dare in front of the team loomed before him. He knew from experience that Dare lived up to her name: she dared death every day when they were out on a mission. So did the rest of them, but now, admitting his love for her had changed everything. How would he stuff it back into that box deep within himself so it wouldn't end up hurting her or his team?

The common-sense part of him, if this hadn't happened to him but to one of his other team members who had fallen in love with her, would assign Dare to another team. That way, neither of them would be distracted or emotionally color a dangerous situation. Then, they could focus 100 percent on their duties. Distraction caused death. It was that simple.

Afraid that he was the weak link in this conundrum, he intuitively felt Dare could avoid being distracted in her work. But he knew damn well, after today's event, there was no way he could stop the surge of emotions that shattered through him when that ledge dropped out from beneath her and the boy. She hadn't heard him scream her name as he lunged forward to somehow save her, either. And, of course, he couldn't save her, but the drive to do just that overrode his experience and knowledge for a few moments. Love, he decided, had sharp edges to it, and that wasn't always a good thing. Today's unexpected event showed him many things, especially the way he reacted and how Dare was cool, calm, focused and not flummoxed by a bunch of other emotions that might have distracted her. He was the weak link.

That didn't set well with him and he simply had to keep digesting his actions and reactions to those awful moments when he thought she and the boy were going to die. Was there a way out of this? If so, Ram didn't see it. At least... not yet. His chest still roiled with forbidden emotions of losing her, and he rubbed the area of his heart, his scowl deepening. What to do?

DARE MADE A soft sound as she lay naked and stretched out on the massive bed. Ram had drawn up the covers to her waist, sat down next to her hip and began to gently apply the arnica salve over her welts and brightly colored bruises. The hot tub had helped a lot; much of the pain reduced. She shunned taking anything, saying that the arnica would further reduce the swelling by increasing circulation in the area. He was careful to apply it lightly but even then, the reddish-purple areas, in particular, were very sensitive, where deeper impact occurred when she hit that cliff. With each light stroke, he watched her eyelids flutter and, finally, close. Her arms were beneath the pillow that she lay upon. Even though it was midafternoon, Ram knew the whole event had taken a lot out of her. She needed to rest.

After finishing, he could tell that she had dozed off. Shock always made a person sleepy after the initial adrenaline phase of it was over. Leaning down, he brought the sheet and a light blanket up across her shoulders. She didn't stir and that meant she was diving deep into slumber. That was good. How many times after a mission did they all crash and burn back at the camp? After placing the jar of arnica on the bathroom marble ledge next to the washbasin, he washed off his hands. He was tired, too. Even though he wanted to hold her, he knew it wasn't a wise idea right now. What he could do was lie on the bed nearby and that would satisfy his yearning heart and his need to protect her. She'd almost died out there today along with that child. Shaking his head, he dried his hands on a towel and left the bathroom.

As he walked without a sound across the tile floor, his gaze upon her as she slept deeply, he wanted to touch her hair but refrained. Ram knew how necessary deep sleep was to a person, and of the great healing mechanisms used by a body during that phase. And frankly, he knew he needed to do the same thing. First, he would take a shower and then quietly slip into the bed and join her in sleeping off the day's shock and emotional upset.

Just as he was ready to get into bed, his cell phone vibrated. Scowling, he walked away and shut the bedroom door to take the call.

December 31

MORNING LIGHT PEEKED into the bedroom as Dare slowly became awake. She was warm and lay on her stomach, the pillow gathered around her arms and pressed to her chest. Hearing an odd noise, she turned over and slowly sat up. Her back felt immensely better than it did before. Flicking on a small lamp, she turned to see that the other side of the bed hadn't been slept in. What time was it? Looking at the clock, it was 0800. She'd slept a long time, and, obviously, the shock was responsible for this.

Once she slid off the bed, she eased into a white, fluffy robe that fell to her knees and then slipped into a nearby set of slippers. Rubbing her face, she opened the door. More noise. It sounded like zippers. Curious, she heard it from the other bedroom down the hall. Padding that direction, she saw the door was open. Halting, she noticed their luggage cases lay on the bed and Ram was packing all of them.

"What's going on?" she called, stepping in, her voice rusty.

Looking up, he stopped packing. "I got a call from HQ yesterday evening. Our leave is canceled and they want us back to Kyiv as soon as possible." He walked over to her, studying her intently.

Her heart skipped a beat as he leaned down, kissing her cheek. "There are no trains until 1000 to Lviv and then to Kyiv and I told my CO that."

"What's going on, Ram? Did something happen?" Her voice was low and fraught with worry.

"He wouldn't say."

"But…that's *your* CO, right? Not mine?"

"He's the general over the entire group, Dare. And he said he needed to see both of us as soon as possible." Shrugging, he said, "I'm sorry. I was hoping our time together wouldn't be like this."

She nodded and wrapped her arms around his waist, holding him. "We're on the edge of war. Why should we not expect something like this?"

"You're right," he growled unhappily, kissing her hair. "We have two hours before the train leaves. Why don't you get a shower and change. I'll make us some breakfast."

Releasing him, she nodded. "Okay…"

Ram stood there after she left, feeling terror. He had wanted to use this morning, whenever Dare woke up, to spill out the truth of how he felt about her going to war with him and his team. But it was too late. The terse orders from the general's adjutant last night kept him nearly sleepless and he didn't want to awaken Dare. She'd needed a good sleep to start her own healing process, so he slept alone, in the other bedroom. He had tossed and turned, wondering if the Russians were already infiltrating their country and their advanced intelligence, thanks to the NATO countries, including the US, were feeding them real-time info along with satellite intel, in order to help them save their country. Had something happened on the ground already?

After finishing the packing, he brought the two pieces of luggage out to the living room. He'd order up some breakfast and have it waiting for Dare when she emerged from her shower. It felt as if the weight and terror of the last twenty-four hours had combined. His shoulders ached with tension. What else could go wrong? They would spend the next thirteen hours on the train, the new year coming in without celebration, but he hadn't been looking forward to it, anyway. They would celebrate New Year's Day by going to Army headquarters and seeing the adjutant, Major Zhuk. So many scenarios crowded into his mind, all bad ones. He'd just found Dare once again, and like a wonderful storybook tale, it was filled with light, joy and love. Now? He felt nothing but internalized anxiety and terror. What was the major going to tell them?

January 1, 2022

AT 1500, Ram and Dare were dressed in their camo uniforms and entering the outer office of Major Zhuk, who appeared to be in his early forties. He was a man with a frown on his broad brow, sitting at his large metal desk, strewn with files across the surface of it. Once they had come to attention, he told them, "At ease," and to sit down at the two chairs that had been placed in front of the desk. They did so.

Zhuk opened up a red file, and he devoted his attention to Dare.

"Sergeant Mazur," he began crisply, "the US Army is giving you a field promotion to captain." He handed the paper across the desk to her.

Dare swallowed a gasp, taking the paper. "Sir? What? Why me? I'm a sergeant."

"No longer, Captain Mazur," he said. "As you both know, Ukraine's military forces are working hand in hand with all the NATO countries. I had a brief talk with the head of Medical in your US Army HQ. They said it was necessary to change your designation, but in order for you to take over the coming orders, you had to become an officer. They realized this was quite unusual, but we are in unusual times. Later, when possible, you will be going through the Officer Candidate School in your country, but that won't be very soon. We, the Ukrainian military, are very aware of your important medical and field surgery status and your work with us in Afghanistan. You have spent two years here, in our country, training our medics for field combat duties with brilliant results. We asked your medical branch of the Army to allow us to absorb you temporarily into our Army, to help us with a very specific and immediate task." He handed her another set of papers. "Here are your new orders."

Frowning, Dare took the papers. She bit back a gasp, looked at Ram, and then the major. "You're assigning me here, to HQ in Kyiv, and I'm to take over Logistics on incoming US field hospitals that will be flown here to Ukraine right now? To provide the support they need to get them up and running?"

"Yes," the major said with a crisp nod. "Look at it this way, Captain—you are on loan to us for as long as the war with the Russians last. You are the hub of a very important wheel. Without field hospitals being set up in AOs, areas of operation, close to the battlefields, to direct the assignment of them, we lack the expertise of the equipment and other supplies coming in from the U.S. We needed an American with Ukrainian language skills to oversee it and you are the perfect person for that important position. You are familiar with field hospitals setup because you are a combat medic. You know about them, how they function and, most important, you know the supplies and what they need. You will be the point person, heading up this very vital area. We want our soldiers to have the best medical field care possible. They deserve this, and your country has been more than willing to provide everything except someone to oversee it. You were the perfect person to stand in that position. Questions?"

Stunned, she held the papers in her lap. "I…well… This means I'm no longer in Captain Kozak's Black Wolf team, then? That I can't be in it or be their team's medic?" She felt her heart tearing open and gave Ram an anxious look. She was unsettled when he looked at her. There was utter relief in his expression. Why relief?

"We've already got a replacement combat medic for his team," the major said briskly. "That aside, do you have any other questions right now? You will be meeting in," he looked at his watch, "one hour with the chief medical officer for the Ukraine Army. I think you will be spending a long night with him. There's a lot of logistics to assimilate. I'm sure you will give him vital information that will help him make the best decisions on field hospitals. You will be his adjutant."

Stunned, she whispered, "No, sir, no other questions." Her throat went dry and she felt as if someone had gutpunched her, the wind out of her lungs temporarily.

Ram scowled and stared at the major. He knew he had to sit and be silent. The major closed Dare's file, placing it in his out-basket. He picked up a blue file with his name on it.

"Captain Kozak, you are being reassigned," the major said. "You will no longer run the team you have. You are being ordered back here, to HQ, to be assigned to the Tactics and Strategy section. You will receive a promotion to major." He handed him a piece of paper. "Congratulations, Major. Further, you will be part of Colonel Marchuk's advanced strategy team and supplying him from your extensive field experience, which is considerable. You will be working here, in HQ, but in another nearby building where our intel people work. Here are your orders." He handed him the set of papers.

Ram took them, stunned speechless as he opened and slowly read them. He'd heard Dare gasp, her hand flying to her lips, her eyes huge with shock. That was how he felt. "Then, sir," he rasped, "you're taking my team away from me? I've been with them since Afghanistan."

"I understand that, Major Kozak. Your team has per-formed brilliantly and that was due to your remarkable leadership. You are now being rewarded because of it."

"But who is taking over my team?" Ram demanded harshly.

"Your second-in-command, Adam Vorona. He will be receiving a field command and commission to lieutenant, and I will be seeing him in person in an hour. He will assume responsibility for the team. We believe that you had great trust in this man's abilities, is that true?"

Stunned, Ram said, "Yes, sir, I do."

"And, if you were no longer leading your team, that Lieutenant Vorona would be whom you would choose for such a trusted position?"

"Yes, sir, I would. He's as good as I am. The men trust him with their lives. He won't disappoint you or Command."

"Good, we thought the same. Then we are in agreement?"

"Yes, sir," he responded.

"Your familiarity with the US military, their customs, their mindset, as well as working directly with them for the last four years, has led us to conclude that your cross-training and experience is going to help us stop the Russians and win this war that is coming. The US president is fully behind us and they are in the midst of getting us whatever we need to win it. You have a deep understanding and experience with US Army infantrymen, with their black ops groups, which will be your focus here at HQ with Colonel Marchuk's group. You will still be instrumental to the Black Wolf Brigade, Major. Only you will be strategizing with the colonel and his team to keep them at the point of the spear, active and being the first to encounter, engage and stop the Russian tanks."

"Yes, sir, I'm glad I'll still be in the mix with the Black Wolf Brigade."

"You are the right officer to put in this very critical position, Major Kozak. You are to leave here as soon as we are done and go to meet with Colonel Marchuk and his group at his office. My assistant in the other office will give you info on how to get over there."

"Yes, sir. Thank you, sir."

"Questions?" The major looked at both of them. "Your clearances will be above top secret and badges denoting that on your uniforms will be given to you shortly."

Shock rolled through Dare. She had top-secret clearance, but there was another one above that. And few people were given that status.

"My assistant has a set of officer's insignias to put on both your uniforms, Captain Mazur. She'll also get you an officer's clothing allowance, credentials to go to our uniform and supplies depot, and get the rest of whatever you need. That set of papers will get you into the Officer's Store to make the purchases you must have. Even though you are a US citizen, you're also a citizen of Ukraine. You will be wearing Ukrainian uniforms at all times when on duty."

"Yes, sir," she said faintly.

"Major Kozak? Your job starts immediately and they are waiting for you right now. Captain Mazur? You will start your new job tomorrow at 0900, here, in this building. My assistant will have an information packet ready for you once we're finished here. Questions?"

Dare and Ram stood, coming to attention, saying simultaneously, "No, sir," did an about-face and left his office for a brand-new world that had just been handed to them.

January 2

IT WAS 0100 when Ram finally made it back to Dare's apartment. He'd called her two different times, letting her know that he was up to his hocks in a strategic plan that he couldn't leave or discuss, and that it was going to be a long night. Entering the ground-floor apartment, he found Dare in her flannel pajamas and fuzzy, long bathrobe. Her legs were tucked beneath her and he saw she was working on a lot of papers that were spread out around her rocker. She looked up when he entered.

"You're home," she said, setting her papers aside and meeting him halfway across the living room. She placed her arms around his shoulders, and he carefully pulled her to him and they kissed. He smelled of cold, fresh winter air, and she pulled away enough to see the tabs with the major insignia on his shoulders. "Are you in shock? I know I am." She released him and they walked to the couch.

Running his hand through his short hair after dropping his cap on the lamp table, he said, "I didn't see this coming at all."

"Neither did I," she whispered, sitting down next to him. "I'm assuming you were in a serious planning session."

"Yes, and it's top secret." He turned to her, worry in his eyes. "How are you? Your back? Those bruises?"

"I know they're there," she said, smiling slightly. "I think some more arnica on them after you get a shower is in order. Otherwise, I'm fine. I'm just in general shock over this turn of events, Ram."

He sighed and shook his head. "Makes two of us." Holding her warm gaze, he said, "You know what this means, don't you?"

"I think I do, or at least I hope I do." She reached out, sliding her fingers into his. "We are safe, in a manner of speaking. That doesn't mean the Russians aren't going to try and take Kyiv, or that we're safe here because I know we're not. But we're not out on the front lines, either."

He lifted her hand, kissing the back of it. "To tell you the truth, Dare? I'm glad this happened. I was torn up inside by the fact you and I, and our love for one another, must be a secret. Hiding it or pretending it didn't exist in the team bothered the hell out of me. I didn't know what to do," he rasped, holding her gaze. "After what happened with that boy the other day? And how I felt when I thought you were going to fall to your death? I came out of that event realizing that I couldn't put my emotions away when it came to you. I didn't know that until that accident happened."

She compressed her lips and nodded. "We haven't had a chance to really sit down and discuss all of what happened on that day. I was thinking what if that had been you with the boy? That the ledge gave way and I was the one up above, watching it happen and me thinking you were going to fall to your death." She placed her other hand over his. "Ram, you and I came to the same understanding that we couldn't stop our emotions, our worry and anxiety for one another out in the field."

"I didn't know what to do," he admitted again gruffly.

"I was going to come back here and ask my commanding officer to take me out of your team and put me in another one," she said in a low, emotional tone. "I didn't know what else to do, except remove myself from the team. I didn't want to do that, but I couldn't see any other way out of our dilemma."

"Well," he said, drawing in a deep breath, "command did it for us." He managed a sour grin. "What I like about it is that you and I can live here, we can get married now because we're both officers and we're not working together. We can have a home, Dare. A life together. I know it isn't a hundred percent safe here in Kyiv, but it's a lot better than being the tip of the spear in a black ops team."

"I've been thinking about all of that, Ram. The thought of having you safe, probably squirreled away in a basement-level concrete-like bunker with intel people, you are very safe even if missiles or bombs start falling."

Nodding, he said, "You're right. We're three stories be-lowground and with plenty of escape routes if we do take a hit." He released her hand and drew her gently against him, holding her. "I want you safe. And I know that when a field hospital is set up, it's usually behind the lines, but you're still not that safe."

"I know," she said, sliding her hand across his upper chest. "But I'll be careful. And it's part of my job as I see it to be out where these field hospitals are going up, to en-sure correct and proper procedures are being followed."

"It's a lot safer than being with a team," he agreed. "I have to tell you, I'm so relieved you are not going to be on the front lines."

"I saw that in your face the instant the major told me my orders. I could almost read how grateful you were for the sudden twists and turns in our lives."

Turning, he kissed her lips, taking in the honey of who

she was, her taste, that fragrance signature that was only her. "I love you," he whispered against her wet lips, looking into her partly opened eyes, seeing her love for him mirrored in them. "Be my wife. Marry me soon? We don't have to hide that we're in love or that we want a life together anymore."

Nodding and lifting her hand, her fingers against his unshaven cheeks, she whispered, "Let's go to a jeweler and we'll pick out the ring soon."

"I'll make sure it happens."

"We can live here, in this apartment. I'm happy to do that because Lera will need help when Adam leaves with the team. I want to be near Lera and the girls. I can be of help and support to them."

"Yes, to all of that." He eased away. "I'm going to get a shower. Meet me in the bedroom and I'll put the arnica on your bruises for you."

"And then," she said, smiling into his darkening eyes, "I want to celebrate this moment with you, with the turn of our luck and being able to live together as wife and husband. This is the best secret Christmas gift we'll ever receive."

He kissed her gently. "Roger that, sweetheart. We have a war to fight and we're going to win it. It won't be easy, but just knowing that I'm coming home to you every night is a priceless gift that will keep on giving. I love you…"

* * * * *

COLD CASE
INVESTIGATION

NICOLE HELM

For all the heroes I've denied.

Chapter One

Anna Hudson was no stranger to mistakes. She was an act first, think later type of person. Because more often than not, that worked out for her.

And if she was being bracingly honest with herself—which her current situation seemed to call for—it tended to work out because she had five overbearing, determined and with-it older siblings to help her clean up her messes.

The fact that she'd spent most of her adult life—which wasn't a huge amount of time considering she was only twenty-five—trying to create some distance, some independence from her family was something she'd been proud of. She certainly didn't *want* someone always sweeping in and cleaning up her messes. She wanted to prove to the people who'd raised her from the time she was eight and her parents had disappeared that she could take care of herself.

Too bad she'd finally gotten herself into a jam no one could save her from. She took a deep breath of the cold, invigorating air. Winter held the Hudson Ranch in its grips and for the first time in her life Anna wasn't wishing for spring. Or summer.

Especially not summer.

She closed her eyes, willing the nausea away. Her doctor—not her *normal* doctor, because even doctor-patient confidentiality wasn't safe in Sunrise, Wyoming, but the doctor she'd found the county over—had told her "morning" sickness could hit at any time and last possibly her whole pregnancy.

Three months in was definitely enough for Anna, but her baby didn't seem to be getting the memo.

So far, she'd been able to keep everything on the down-low, but the more unpredictable the nausea and food aversion got, the harder it was to hide.

She couldn't conceal it forever. Realistically, she understood that. In practice? She'd given herself three months. She considered that fair. Lots of women waited to announce their pregnancy until they were into their second trimester.

The problem was her secret was getting harder and harder to keep. She lived with too many people, had too many friends. And the three-month mark had come and gone.

Surely she could wait until she started to show? That seemed fair. Her family would be upset, but...

"You okay?"

Anna jerked. She hadn't heard Cash approach. She turned to face him and forced herself to smile. She couldn't throw up in front of him. That would be too much. Someone would insist she see a doctor, and then...

"You aren't...pregnant, are you?" he asked very, *very* carefully, and out of nowhere to Anna's estimation.

Of all the people she'd expected to call her out on it, her brothers had been at the bottom of her list. Particularly Cash, who didn't even live at the main house and kept his

nose out of her business the most out of any Hudson—
though that was still pretty nosy. Still, Cash didn't butt in,
for the most part. He had his own daughter to raise.

She supposed it made sense, though. Since he *was* a dad.
Izzy was eleven, and her mom hadn't stuck around for long,
but once upon a time, Cash had been the attentive husband
to his pregnant wife. So of all the people in her life, he'd
been the closest to the signs of pregnancy the most recently.

"Hell in a handbasket, Anna," he muttered when she
didn't answer.

She swallowed down all that wanted to come up. "I don't
see what business it is of yours." Bravado was often the
best response to her overbearing siblings. Or had been.

Cash rolled his eyes. "You wouldn't." He adjusted his hat
on his head. "Who knows about this? Certainly not Jack
or we'd have had a shotgun wedding by now." His frown
deepened. "You're not even dating anyone."

She smiled at her brother, because an off-putting offense
was always the best defense. "I know you're a monk and
all, but there is this thing called a *one-night stand*."

He swore again, taking off his hat and raking his hand
through his hair. "Who is it?" he demanded, all furious
and older-brotherly.

Anna didn't shrink in on herself, though she kind of
wanted to. Pregnancy was making her weak. She sniffed
and lifted her chin instead. "None of your business."

"Why not?"

Anna had always considered Cash the most reasonable of
her brothers. Jack and Grant were the upstanding stick-in-
the-muds, Palmer was more like her—or had been before
he'd decided to go fall in love with her best friend—and

Cash was…the reasonable one. The single dad who kept an even keel no matter what went wrong. His typical response to anything was to hunker down.

But the look on his face was decidedly unreasonable and bloodthirsty.

"I don't need you wading in to fix my problems, Cash. I can handle this."

Cash's expression changed. She realized he might be the calm one, but he was also the worst one to find out about this. Because he'd been in an accidental pregnancy situation himself. As the father of the baby.

"You told the guy, right?" he said. Very carefully. All cool and detached while his eyes were hot with his own issues.

Anna decided silence was her best weapon. But that only made Cash swear even more.

"Anna, you gotta tell the guy."

She shrugged jerkily, because anyone telling her what she had to do grated. Especially when they were right. "Why?"

"Because it's his kid, too."

There was no argument to be had here. First, Cash wasn't the audience. Second, she knew she had to tell the father. Every night she told herself tomorrow would be the day.

And every morning, she chickened out. Not her usual MO, but Hawk Steele was a *problem*.

"He isn't local."

"So take a trip," Cash replied. Firmly.

And she had to blame it on pregnancy hormones. Because she was not a soft woman. She'd learned to be hard. She'd lost her parents at eight, and though her sister had tried to fill in as a kind of maternal influence, Mary was only two years older than she was. So Anna had learned how to be tough, how to be a Hudson.

She'd done the rodeo. She was a licensed private investigator. She'd fought people, shot people, been shot at.

She didn't cry.

But there were tears in her eyes now, even if she managed to blink them away. "Cash, I can do this on my own. Well, not my *own*. But I have you guys. We'll be all right."

Cash inhaled, then pulled her into a hug. Because he had a little girl, and he was a good dad, and he knew how to comfort better than any of them. "We will be, Anna. No matter what." He pulled back, fixed her with a stare that made her wonder if her parents would just despair of her if they were still around. "But he has to know. You've got to give him a chance to be all right, too."

"I know. I do. I just…" Well, bottom line was she just didn't want to. She had always handled guys easily. She had four older brothers, plenty of family trauma. Guys had never scared her, never gotten the upper hand on her. She enjoyed the ones she wanted, then discarded. And had lived that way quite happily and carefully…

Until she'd met Hawk Steele's dark blue gaze across the room at a bar. She'd been handling a private investigation case, away from Sunrise and away from her family, and he had…

She'd *never* felt that way. And as tough girl as she liked to pretend, she'd never had a one-night stand before. They hadn't even exchanged last names at the time. There'd just been something elemental. *Necessary.*

And she'd been foolish enough to forget all her rules. To

forget *everything*. Until she'd woken up in his bed, wrapped up in him, knowing she had to get the hell out before... something.

She hadn't been surprised when he'd shown up in her life a little while later. Because of course she'd looked him up after that night. It wasn't hard to track down a guy named Hawk in Bent County, Wyoming. Especially when, it turned out, he *worked* for Bent County as a fire investigator.

So when her friend Louisa's family home burned down before Christmas, Anna had figured she'd end up running into Hawk Steele. She'd practiced her casual, flirty smile. Her unwavering *I don't care about you* bravado. And it had worked. When they'd run into each other, she'd been calm and cool.

He had been shocked. For a second. But a second of shock on Hawk Steele *was* something.

"I can come with you," Cash offered, bringing her back to the present.

It was a sweet offer. She wouldn't take it, but for the time being, she'd let him believe she might. "Thanks. I'll... He kind of travels around, so I'll see if I can pin him down for a meeting." She pulled back from Cash's hug, flashed him a smile. "Promise."

"Look, if you need me to, I can cover your chores. Izzy can help out a little more with the dogs. Then I can—"

"No. I'm good."

"You don't want to overdo it."

"I know. I listen to all my doctor's many instructions." She looked up at the gray winter sky. The Hudson Ranch had been in their family for generations. Though all of them worked on their pet project—Hudson Sibling Solutions, solving cold cases for people like them who didn't have answers—the ranch was their foundation. The six of them worked together to keep it going.

Because her parents had. And her grandparents. And so on.

"Mom handled all this stuff when she was pregnant with me, right?" Anna said, waving her hand around the stables and the cows and the mountains that made up her life, her roots. "That's the memory. Supermom doing ranch work and taking care of all of us and… I bet she never…" Anna couldn't finish the sentence. She rarely thought of her mother, only remembered odd flashes of a strong, warm woman who'd always made her feel safe.

Until she and Dad had just been…gone one day.

"She was supermom," Cash agreed. "But, first of all, we were kids and she was an adult, so we don't really know what she had going on or didn't. Second, and take it from someone who spent a lot of years trying to be Dad, you don't have to be the parents ours were. You just have to be the one that's best for your kid."

Kid. She still really didn't quite think of whatever was growing inside her as a *kid*. Or herself as a parent. Maybe that was just another thing she was putting off.

"I've got chores to do. Then I'm heading out of town for a few days," Anna said firmly. Because she'd already decided that, and she wasn't changing any plans just because Cash had found her out. "And before you lecture me, it's just research. Nothing dangerous."

Cash's frown was epic, but she was used to big-brother admonitions over her side job.

"I don't think you should keep doing your private investigation work."

"And I don't recall asking your opinion. I told my boss I'm taking a break from the bounties and stuff like that for a while, and that I didn't want to travel as much. This is a simple gathering of some adultery evidence over in Wilde. Take some pictures. Hand them over to the PI office. The end."

"I don't like it."

"Didn't ask you to."

Cash blew out a breath. "Fine, but for the love of God, tell Jack about this before you go. I do not want to be the secret keeper."

"But you're so good at it!"

He groaned as she walked away, laughing. Because... Well, Hawk was a multilevel problem, sure, but Cash was right. She'd be okay. She always was.

ANNA DIDN'T LIKE to admit that pregnancy had an effect on her body. But after a day of driving around trying to catch some salesman cozying up with his pretty lawyer, and coming up empty, Anna was exhausted. And since Wilde was too small to have even a nearby B and B, she'd had to drive over to Fairmont to find a place to stay.

Since she was going under the radar, she stayed at a run-down little motel a few miles outside of Fairmont. Not her first choice, but it was one night and she could sleep one night anywhere, especially as exhausted as she was.

She thought dimly about calling up Hawk. She didn't have his cell or personal number, but she had his work number. After watching him handle Louisa's fire case, she knew he was enough of a workaholic to probably answer even after hours.

But she was too tired. Maybe she'd wake up early and call him.

She crawled into the dingy bed, not even bothering to shower. She'd handle it all in the morning. She was always a good sleeper, so it was no shock when she fell into an almost immediate sleep.

She woke up to a coughing fit. When she blinked her eyes open, they started to sting. It was dark, but something was wrong. Her throat burned. It was too warm. And…it smelled like fire.

She leaped out of the bed in the same motion she swept the phone on the nightstand into her hand. She didn't know where the fire was coming from, but there was one. She ran for the door, grabbed the handle and pushed, thinking it would give, because of course it would. But it didn't, so she just rammed right into it. She twisted the dead bolt, then tried again, but nothing happened. The door was stuck.

The knob wasn't hot, though, so the fire was coming from…somewhere inside. Smoke was filling the room, so she crouched, trying to find some better air to breathe.

She didn't panic. Couldn't. She dialed 911 on her phone while still turning the lock and knob. There was no window in this room. There was one in the bathroom, but she was afraid that was the source of the smoke.

Someone picked up, but before she could even get out a word, something hit her head. Hard. So hard she only had a moment to try to brace her fall before the world went dark.

When she woke up, she was in a hospital bed.

She blinked at all the blinding white. Everything was fuzzy. Groggy. Had the fire been a dream? Was *this* a dream?

She didn't know how long she existed in this odd in-between state before it felt like she was really with it. Before she understood and started to remember.

Panic slammed into her. The fire. Her baby. She put her hands on her stomach, but she didn't know if it was any different. She didn't know...

She looked wildly around the room, expecting to see the familiar face of one of her siblings or at least a doctor.

Instead, standing at the foot of her bed was the one person she didn't want to see.

Chapter Two

Hawk Steele considered himself a man who rolled with the punches. After all, life had been nothing but a series of them. He liked to think he'd come out pretty well, all things considered.

Then Anna Hudson had entered his life. She was more of a gut punch. Or maybe a knee right to the balls. Had been since he'd seen her across the room at Rightful Claim all those months ago. He'd stopped at the saloon in Bent, Wyoming, after a particularly difficult case, looking for a few drinks and maybe a pretty woman to take his mind off it.

He'd found both, but of course, Anna Hudson was no simple pretty woman. The fierce, immediate attraction had blown him off his axis. He'd been relieved when he'd woken up the next morning to find her gone.

Uncharacteristically floored when he'd run into her in Sunrise a while later when he'd been investigating a case that had involved her friend and her brother.

But that flooring had *nothing* on this one. Because he'd heard her brother out there. Very clearly mentioning that Anna was *pregnant*.

Pregnant.

He wanted to believe that this was a coincidence. Sure, he'd had an ill-advised one-night stand a few months ago with the smart-mouthed beauty, not knowing his life would ever connect with hers again. But that didn't mean *he* had to be the father. Maybe she'd had quite a few careless nights with quite a few men over the course of the past few months.

But the way she looked at him now was answer enough.

And Hawk did not know how to deal with that very hard and unexpected punch. Except rely on the one thing that got him through it all. Stoicism.

"So, Blondie, sounds like we have a lot to catch up on."

She hadn't moved, but now she very slowly—and clearly attempting to make it look casual—took her hands off her stomach. "What are you doing here? Where's my family? I need to…" She swallowed. "Talk to a doctor."

"Doctor will be in soon enough. Family is in the waiting room, wreaking their usual havoc. The nurses said you'd be coming out of the sedative and I wanted to be able to ask you some questions right away."

"But…" Her eyebrows drew together. "There was a fire."

"Yes."

"You want to ask me questions about the fire." She looked around the room one more time, shifting in the bed. He tried not to notice how pale she was. Tried not to think about what might have caused that bandage on her head.

She met his gaze, though it flickered with none of her usual confidence. "I'm having a hard time believing Jack let you in here alone."

"He was in here, but then he got a call about the case and stepped out so as not to interrupt your sleep."

"Ah."

Hawk knew he didn't have much time left. He wasn't sure he believed in divine intervention, but if he did, he supposed this was it. "Were you going to tell me?" he asked. When he should probably ask a million other things, but he needed to know this one first. He just did.

She swallowed, and he saw a million answers flash in her hazel eyes. But he didn't know how to believe any of them as the truth.

"I was working on it," she said, her voice hoarse.

Hawk said nothing to that. He'd been standing here watching her sleep for something close to an hour, trying to convince himself this wouldn't be personal. It would be an arson investigation—because it had clearly been arson. A fire started specifically in the room Anna had rented for the night.

But she'd been so still, so lifeless, in this bed. The bandage on her head where someone had hit her over the head and left her to die in a fire. It had taken him almost the entire hour just to deal with his rage over that.

He still couldn't fully grasp the whole *baby* thing.

And he didn't have to. Because the door opened and Jack Hudson strode in, looking thunderous. He was wearing his Sunrise Sheriff's Department uniform, slightly more casual than a county deputy, but Jack Hudson made it look like military whites.

He was a man who seemed to demand respect wherever he went. Under normal circumstances, Hawk would have respected it.

But sheriff or no, he was Anna's older brother. And Hawk didn't do the whole family thing. The Hudsons were a big messy mix of personalities and demands, and he'd had quite enough of them just dealing with the O'Brien fire and subsequent issues last month.

They were like a *circus*. Hawk had built a life of order.

Anna Hudson his one and only deviation. One that was supposed to have been temporary.

Anna looked at Jack. Her expression was heartbreakingly young-looking. None of her usual bravado when she spoke to her brother.

"Is…? Am I okay?" Her hands crept over her belly again. Her stomach. Where *his* child grew.

Child.

That had definitely not been in the plans, ever. Someone didn't get abandoned by their own father as a fetus to repeat the cycle. At least he didn't.

If that was his baby, then Anna Hudson was no temporary problem. She was his. For life.

"THE DOCTOR WILL be in in a few," Jack said. He had his cop face on and Anna knew it was for Hawk's benefit. She also knew him well enough to know that little tic in his jaw was a clear sign he was *very* much not okay. "He'll go over the specifics with you, but luckily most of the reason you were hospitalized is the head injury."

"Head…" She reached up, but Jack crossed too quickly and took her hand in his. He gave her a reassuring squeeze. "We'll get to the bottom of it. Investigator Steele is going to lead the arson case," Jack said, nodding at Hawk. "Bent

County will work with him on the assault angle, and Sunrise will offer whatever manpower we can."

Anna wasn't sure she cared about all that. Not until the doctor came in. Not until she knew… "Jack?"

"The baby's fine," he said. Stiffly. Quietly. As if he was embarrassed, because Anna was *sure* he had to feel that way. Embarrassed and disappointed and ashamed, and not wanting a stranger to the family to know.

Little did Jack know that stranger had something to do with it.

"Can I just answer his questions and then…?" Anna slid a glance at Hawk.

Hawk raised an eyebrow. No doubt knowing what she'd meant to say. *And then he can go and leave me alone.* Because she was hurt and confused and fuzzy, and she didn't know how to keep up her walls when it came to him.

She needed space until she did.

Jack turned to Hawk. "Why don't you give us a few minutes? Until after the doctor checks her out."

"If I recall, we agreed I could be in here so I could ask questions right away. So we get everything as fresh as possible." Because of course a man like Hawk wouldn't give her space or time.

"Well, what have you been doing?" Jack demanded.

Hawk chose not to answer that question and fixed those midnight blue eyes on her. "Take me through what you remember about last night."

"I had a job in Wilde. I didn't get anything, so I was spending the night at the motel so I could head back out tomorrow. Had to go to Fairmont to find a place." Anna walked him through everything she remembered, but she got to the motel in her memory and then everything kind of went hazy and blank. "I remember waking up to smoke, but that's it." She furrowed her brow, trying to find something in all that haze. "That's it," she repeated, feeling like a failure.

Hawk nodded and was clearly not thrilled with those answers, but he surprised her by not pressing her with further questions. "All right. Well, you all have my information if you think of anything else or if you remember any other details." He turned to Jack. "I'll keep you updated on the investigation as necessary." Then his gaze returned to her in the hospital bed. There was the tiniest flash where his gaze drifted to her stomach, so tiny she almost missed it.

"I'll be in touch," he said darkly. Definitely more threat than promise.

But Anna felt like she could breathe once he was gone. She knew it wasn't over. So many parts of this weren't over, but so many things now had happened at once and she had to untangle them. Piece by piece.

Starting with Jack. Who was standing there, a few paces away, looking ominous. He was ten years older than her. He'd been a father figure to her longer than her father had been. He was their…leader, as much as Anna hated to be led.

And she knew, she *knew* he would not be happy about this. How could he not be disappointed in her keeping this secret? His disapproval she could weather, but his disappointment was too much to bear.

"So," he said, finally breaking the silence. "You thought it would be a good idea to tell Cash and no one else."

Jack did always know how to twist the knife when he wanted to. "If it makes you feel better, I didn't *tell* Cash. He figured it out. Besides, the father didn't exactly know before today either."

"What do you mean, didn't…?" Jack looked back at the door. Then a wave of pain crossed his face. "Him?"

Anna didn't bother to answer.

"Anna. Damn it all to hell." He shook his head. But he was Jack, so… "What's the plan, then?"

"The plan?"

"Are you going to get married?"

Anna burst out laughing, which maybe wasn't the right response, but it was the only one she had. "Hi, I'd like to introduce you to the twenty-first century."

"I think it's a fair question. And it was a question, not an assumption or demand."

"But you'd like to demand it."

"I'd like to know that…" He inhaled sharply. "That you're okay, and that you have a plan."

"I don't need a plan to be okay."

His mouth firmed. Disapprovingly. Which was hardly a first. Usually she kind of lived to earn his disapproval. But there was something about this moment, or the cascade of them, or the whole hormone thing and fire thing, that coalesced and it just felt awful.

Unbearable. So that the tears started and wouldn't stop.

She hated that she was crying, but each of her siblings played a role in her life. Oh, she loved to torture Jack in any way she could, because he was wound so tight and all. But he was also her safe place. Her parents had disappeared when she'd been eight, and Jack had stepped into that hole. He'd never once faltered. Not for her.

So if she was going to lose it—those damn pregnancy hormones, she was sure—it was going to be with Jack. Not anyone else.

"Would they hate me?"

He looked as taken aback by that question as he was by her tears. "Would *who* hate you?"

"Our parents. They'd be disappointed, right? They'd think I did it all wrong and—"

He was across the room and crouched next to her bed, eye to eye, so fast she didn't even have time to finish her sentence.

"Listen to me," he said fiercely. "Our parents weren't perfect. I… I tend to remember them that way because that's the nature of things, but they were normal people with flaws and mistakes. But I know… The one thing I'm damn sure of is that whatever concern or upset they might have felt, and that's a big *might*, you'd never have known, Anna. Because they would have supported you. They would have been there for you, no matter what. Just like we will be."

Which of course only made her cry harder. Because it was so ridiculous she hadn't told anyone. She knew that her family was always there for her. No matter what.

"Annie." And she only ever let Jack call her Annie. Just like Mom had done. Only when it mattered. "Someone locked you in that room. Someone bashed you in the head.

Someone set that fire in the room *you* rented. This was no accident. No mistake. Someone wants you dead. So there's got to be a plan. To make sure you're safe."

Chapter Three

Hawk studied the remnants of the burned-down motel room. He'd already been through it once, but it was always good to go through an arson scene a few times, just to make sure you didn't miss anything.

The elements had done their number, but it didn't matter. The more he could get a picture of it in his head, the better chance he had to get to the bottom of it.

But that was part of the problem, too. He had to picture it. That was his job. But usually he could picture a faceless, nameless victim. A mannequin stand-in to keep him from feeling anything.

But all he could see was Anna with her blond hair, sprawled out on the ground, while a fire crept toward her. Only a well-timed 911 call and a trackable phone had kept her from being burned alive.

Purposefully.

Because that fire had been started in room 104. Anna's door lock had been tampered with. Someone had used a lamp to knock her out.

And left her to die.

Hawk saw a lot of bad things in his line of work. He

was excellent at keeping up that wall between fury over the terrible things people were capable of and doing what needed to be done.

It didn't surprise him in the least to be struggling with that when it came to Anna Hudson. Her entire existence seemed hell-bent on making sure everything involving her screwed with who he usually was, what he usually did. *All* his plans.

Because he was going to be a father. And he was very well aware that was as much his own fault as hers, but who else would he have made such a mistake with?

Except he wasn't going to think about this situation as a *mistake*. Maybe it was unplanned, but not a *mistake*. No doubt he had a father out there somewhere who'd viewed him that way. Who'd gotten the hell out before he'd had to deal with the consequences. At best, Hawk had a sperm donor.

And these thirty-two years later, it still bothered him. He'd had the best mom in the world, by his estimation, but even she hadn't been able to fill that hole. He'd known he was missing something, always. Especially when she'd gotten sick and he'd had to pick up the slack.

His child wouldn't have one second of that. Not if he could help it.

"Steele."

Hawk looked up at the man who walked toward him, very nearly catching him off guard. Hawk let his hand slide off the butt of his gun in a casual move as the Bent County sheriff's detective approached. He'd worked with Thomas Hart a few times and was glad to see a familiar face. "Hart."

"Unfortunately, there's no video footage of the parking lot or the rooms, just the main office. Clerk claims she didn't see anything."

"I was afraid of that." He'd already talked to the clerk himself and gotten a similar story. He had the sneaking suspicion that the clerk had been drunk or high on something and truthfully didn't remember or notice anything that happened. Maybe ever.

"I'm heading over to Ms. Hudson's employer's office. Fool's Gold Private Investigations. I figured you'd be headed there too, so we might as well team up."

"Yeah, that was my next stop." He should have left a good twenty minutes ago, instead of brooding over an arson scene.

"I've already talked to Ms. Hudson's boss there. She's expecting us."

"I'll follow you."

Hart nodded and Hawk pulled himself away from the remains. He had the lab running some tests on a few pieces of evidence he'd found, but it would take time. So he needed to pound the pavement while everything was still fresh. There was no rest until he got to the bottom of this.

Because this wasn't his average investigation—and not just because he tended to deal with fraud or onetime fire starters, and this was clearly a targeted assault. It was because it was Anna and his baby.

And the threat was still out there until they figured out who had done it and why.

Hawk followed the Bent County cruiser down the highway to the small town of Wilde. Wilde was even tinier than Bent *and* Sunrise. It didn't have much other than a few churches and a convenience store, and—in an old brick building—the fairly newly minted Fool's Gold Private Investigations.

Hawk parallel parked behind Hart, and they got out of their cars at the same time and met in front of the building.

"You're from around here, right?" he asked Deputy Hart, who nodded. "You know anything about them?" Hawk gestured at the building.

"In a complicated sort of way," Hart replied, pulling the door open. "The lady that runs it is my cousin's husband's brother's girlfriend." Hart shrugged. "You know, that sort of thing."

Hawk decidedly did *not* know that sort of thing. The minute his mother had died when he'd been fourteen, he'd been without family. A thing very few people around these parts seemed capable of grasping.

The building was nice. It looked almost like it had once been a bank with the tiled floors and old-fashioned counters with windows. A young woman got up and skirted the counters. She was dressed casually, wore no jewelry and had a very tough demeanor. She walked with the hint of a limp.

"Quinn Peterson." She gave Hawk a firm shake with her hand, then fisted it on her hip. "Obviously I've heard the rumbles, and I know Anna was hurt. I'm ticked as hell about it. Whatever I can do to help the investigation, I will. Particularly if it ends up relating to one of the cases she's taken for us."

"Thanks," Hawk replied. "We're looking into anyone who might have had motivation to hurt Ms. Hudson." *The mother of my future child.* He had to push that thought away and focus. "So one of the leads is—"

"Any case she worked on that might have gone sour or made her a target. I get it. And I'd love to hand over all my files for you, or have a clear-cut answer, but unfortunately, I don't. We're a private investigation company for women, by women." Quinn shrugged, unbothered. There was something slightly off about her, but not...wrong, per se. Just different. "Sometimes a woman just feels more comfortable getting help from a woman. I don't like to turn people away, so I've got a couple of people who do part-time work for me since I can't be everywhere at once. Anna Hudson is one of them. She's a hell of an investigator, and what's more, I like her as a person."

"Then we'd like to look at those files," Hawk replied. So far, Quinn Peterson played everything just right, but that didn't mean Hawk would let his guard down. He understood privacy, understood why she'd want to keep those files to herself, but it couldn't happen.

"I want to help you get to the bottom of this as much as anybody, but I have to protect my clients, so I can't just hand over my files. What I can do is give you a list of anyone who might have been upset by work Anna did for us and offer my help to investigate them in any way that might help you guys."

Hawk knew he'd get that answer, but he didn't have to like it. It would take him days to potentially get a search warrant, and even that would only fly if he could get a lead to prove the need for one. "Would Anna have her own files?"

"We keep professional files here, but anyone can keep their own personal files, and if she wanted to hand those over to you guys, that'd be her choice." Quinn crossed her arms over her chest as if to punctuate the fact that he wasn't getting her files.

Hawk didn't see much point trying to change Quinn's mind. She didn't strike him as the kind of woman bowled over by charm *or* authority. She was running a *private* investigation company, after all.

He handed Quinn his card. "Email me that list when you've got it."

"Me too," Hart added.

Hawk didn't scowl, though he wanted to. He'd prefer to handle this case all on his own, but there was an assault and he knew he needed to work with the police as he so often did.

Quinn took the card and nodded. "I'll get right on it." She looked up at Hawk. "I do want to help, even if it's not in the way you'd like."

Hawk didn't sigh despite the urge. He kept it professional. "Thanks."

It felt a bit like a waste of a trip. He could have done all that over the phone, but it was good to get a sense of people. He didn't have any bad feelings about Quinn, but he'd see what kind of list she came up with.

He walked back outside with Hart.

"Quinn's legit," Hart said, pausing at his car and slipping on some sunglasses. "I know you've got to look into her, and she'd expect you to. So it's no big deal. But I wouldn't spend too much time on a dead end."

Hawk agreed, but he didn't acknowledge that. "You're leaning more toward someone she investigated that maybe got the bad end of it?"

"That'd be the most straightforward, wouldn't it? Any-

time one of us cops gets threats, we start by looking at people we arrested. This situation is about the same."

About the same. Except Anna was pregnant with his
child.

Would he ever be able to set that aside and get his job
done?

"I'm going to head back to the station. My partner's on
maternity leave, so I've got to juggle some things around.
But the minute Quinn's email comes in, I'll start looking."

"Okay." Hawk squinted at the sky, thinking. He knew
Hart was waiting for him to explain what he was going to
do. It grated, but eventually he relented.

"I'm going to get her personal files." If he had to steal
them out of the Hudsons' house, he would.

ANNA WAS BACK HOME, THANKFULLY. The doctor had said
the baby was doing A-OK, and while Anna needed to take
it easy because she'd suffered a concussion—not her first,
thanks to a few years in the rodeo—and because of the
smoke inhalation, she was also in decent shape considering everything she'd gone through.

Of course, her family was now treating her like she was
made of fragile glass. Mary had arranged her on the couch
with enough pillows and blankets to suffocate a grizzly.
She'd been given water and snacks and Mary had even insisted they all eat dinner in the living room on tray tables
so she didn't have to sit at the dinner table or eat alone.

No one brought up the fire, her injuries or the whole
baby situation point-blank. She appreciated it at first, but
then it started to feel like this odd weight on her chest. An
elephant in the room that reminded her way too much of

those early days after her parents' disappearance when there had been hushed whispers and awkward silences and no one wanting to say what was going on.

So after dessert, but before everyone scattered as they often did this time of night, Anna decided to go ahead and wade right in.

"Well." She surveyed her family. Now not just her four brothers and one sister and one niece, but Grant's girlfriend, Dahlia, and Anna's best friend from childhood, Louisa, who was somehow hooked up with Palmer. There were dogs everywhere, because Cash raised and trained them and one of them had just had puppies two months ago.

"I'm due in June," she said, trying not to look too closely at anyone's reaction. She'd already had her little meltdown in front of Jack, so this wasn't going to be a repeat. Just facts. Just…the truth. "I don't quite have all the plans made yet, of course, but… You know, there's time to deal with that. So…"

She didn't want to mention Hawk. No doubt everyone knew now, and had opinions about it, but if she didn't mention it…

"I can't believe you're having a baby with Hawk Steele," Palmer muttered.

Which earned him an elbow in the side from Louisa. Louisa glared disapprovingly at Palmer. "Hawk turned out to be very helpful with our case."

"Yeah, after he investigated *me* for the fire at your folks' place," Palmer returned. "And he hasn't apologized," Palmer noted.

"He does not seem like the kind of guy who apologizes readily," Louisa said, chewing on her bottom lip. But she smiled encouragingly at Anna. "It doesn't matter. Because it's Anna and Hawk's business. *Not* ours."

It was nice to have her friend support her, proving that having your best friend date your brother wasn't *all* bad if she took your side in family arguments.

"It's because he's so handsome."

Everyone turned to look at Izzy, who had two puppies on her lap, and had dropped that little truth bomb very casually.

"What did you just say?" Cash demanded.

She looked up at her father. Clearly confused by his tone. "What? He's handsome. Like Levi Jones."

"Who the hell is Levi Jones?"

Izzy rolled her eyes dramatically. "Oh my *God*, Dad. Do you pay attention to music at *all*?"

"Your dad's more the Willie Nelson type," Palmer said with a laugh, enjoying his niece's impatience with her father.

"Besides, Hawk is way better-looking than Levi Jones," Mary said primly. Which earned her a glare from all four brothers. Mary only shrugged in return.

"What is wrong with you?" Cash asked.

"Nothing is wrong with her," Dahlia returned in her quiet way. "I quite agree."

"Like way hotter," Louisa piped up, sending Anna a wink so Anna would know she was purposefully riling up the menfolk. Usually Anna's job. "Hawk Steele is distressingly hot."

It was Palmer's turn to look offended, there with his arm around Louisa's shoulders. "Excuse me?"

Louisa grinned up at him. "I love you, honey, but that doesn't mean I've gone blind. Don't worry. You're hot, too."

Anna appreciated how uncomfortable her brothers were with this line of conversation, how Louisa was attempting to entertain her, but as she was trying very hard *not* to think about how good Hawk looked, she needed to nip this conversation in the bud. "Hawk Steele is—"

"Right here."

Anna whirled her head around to look over her shoulder. Hawk stood next to Grant, who'd apparently left the room and let him inside at some point during the conversation.

Anna was not easily embarrassed. She usually found situations like this pretty funny. But...not right now. This was just embarrassing.

Mary stood. "Are you hungry, Mr. Steele? We've got plenty of leftovers. Still warm. It'd be no trouble to make you a plate."

"I'm fine, thanks. I just needed to discuss some things with Anna."

"Of course. We'll give you your privacy." Mary sent everyone in the living room a pointed look that clearly told them to leave.

"We will?" Palmer and Jack said in unison, which would have been more annoying if Palmer didn't look quite so horrified he'd said the same thing as Jack. But Mary could play drill sergeant when she wanted to. She marshaled everyone out of the living room, eventually leaving Hawk and her alone.

Aside from the puppy Izzy had dropped on Anna's lap on her way out.

Hawk stared at the puppy, an unreadable expression on his face.

"I talked to Quinn Peterson today. She refused to give me files of the cases you've worked on."

"Of course she did," Anna returned, trying to not be surprised he'd come to talk about the case. About *business*. Of course that was all he was here for. What else mattered in the moment? "Those people don't need to get dragged into this."

"'This' being an attempted murder investigation? *Your* attempted murder."

She rolled her eyes at him. "Yeah, that. I'll give you a list of people I might have ticked off by exposing their bad behavior, but Quinn's not going to give you her files. I won't ask her to, and even if I would, she'd say no. It's a matter of privacy and integrity."

His mouth firmed, clearly not pleased with that answer. "I'm already getting that list from Quinn, but comparing and contrasting wouldn't be bad. Nevertheless, list or no, you'll give me your personal files."

Anna stared at him for a beat, waiting. When he didn't continue, she scratched the puppy's belly and raised an eyebrow at him. "Or what?"

"What do you mean, or what? That's it. You'll give me your files."

"Because you said so?" she asked, her voice deceptively mild as she cradled the puppy to her chest. Honestly, puppies were smarter than men sometimes.

"Yeah, because I said so," he replied, then frowned deeply at the puppy in her arms as she got to her feet.

"Well, Hawk." She crossed to him, handed him the

puppy. She knew he didn't want it, but he took it because he didn't know what else to do. Or because she had been hurt and that gave her just enough of an edge for him to do things she wanted him to do.

She smiled up at him, though she assumed it looked as unpleasant as she felt.

"Go to hell." Then she turned and walked out of the room.

Chapter Four

Hawk could admit when he'd handled a situation badly. Maybe he didn't know Anna well, but he knew enough not to order her around. He didn't know too many women who reacted well to bossiness, but Anna Hudson was *really, clearly* never going to respond well to *anyone* trying to tell her what to do.

Now he was standing in an empty living room holding a puppy, wondering how everything had gotten so derailed.

But she'd been all wrapped up in blankets and pillows, family and friends all waiting on her and cheering her up—clearly that whole conversation on his attractiveness had been a kind of bit to rile up her brothers. And it had worked. They'd been riled and Anna had been laughing and her friend had been grinning and...

He'd known he didn't belong here. Interrupting. Being the father of anyone's child.

But he was. Whether he *belonged* or not. It wasn't about his comfort or his belonging. It was about facts—and the fact was, Anna was having *his* child. He and Anna needed to discuss what that was going to mean.

And she needed to hand over her files so he could keep her safe.

He needed to get back on his normal footing first. Get in the right headspace. He couldn't keep making these mistakes when it came to her. *Why* did she bring them out in him?

He could go home and regroup or he could just follow her to wherever she'd gone. Sure, it wasn't his house, but he was trying to figure out who was trying to *kill* her. He could take some liberties.

He turned, determined to do just that, but stopped short.

Anna's sister stood there, with that bland, pleasant hostess smile on her face. He supposed Mary and Anna resembled each other, though Mary had darker features, and was a bit taller and willowier, but there was something in the shape of the eyes and nose that clearly signaled they were related.

As far as Hawk could tell, that was about the only similarities the women shared. Mary was always the consummate hostess. Every time he'd come to the Hudson Ranch—and it was almost always without warning regarding a case—Mary was always soft-spoken and carefully, femininely dressed. She always offered a drink or a snack and nothing but kind words.

But there was something about the way Mary stood in his way that had him feeling oddly…uneasy. And like the sisters might be more alike than they appeared.

"Oh, are you going to adopt him?" she asked hopefully.

"What now?"

"We are *drowning* in puppies. Cash can only keep and train so many, so we're looking for a few good people to take the extras." Mary beamed at him. "This one seems to have taken a shine to you."

Hawk looked down at the black-and-brown animal who was currently trying to chew at his coat's zipper. Take the puppy? Was she insane? "No, I…"

"Why don't you take him for a trial run? I'm sure you're a busy man, so if *really* you can't fit him into your life, you can always bring him back. But he's got all his shots and he's halfway to potty-trained. You never know until you try. Right?"

"Halfway?"

"He's a smart cookie, aren't you?" she cooed, scratching the puppy's ears. Mary looked up at him, pleasant smile firmly in place. "And I'm sure you are, too. If Jack trusts you to run this arson investigation, you must be."

"Well, I—"

"Then you're just the person to take him," Mary said with a firm nod. "As far as I know, he doesn't have a name, because no one can agree on what to call him. You can call him whatever you like."

"No, I…" But he was being maneuvered. Away from the living room and the hallway Anna had disappeared down. Mary was herding him toward the front door.

She ushered him right to it. The puppy wriggling in his arms. He turned to firmly tell her he was not taking this dog. To put the dog down on the ground. Mary could get rid of Hawk if she really wanted to, but he was not going to wind up with this dog.

"Besides," she continued, opening the door and then stepping so close to him he had no choice but to retreat. Out into the cold. "A puppy is sort of like a *start* toward learning how to take care of a baby. Don't you think?"

He opened his mouth but no sound came out. She closed the door firmly in his face.

Before he could say or do something, the door reopened. He almost felt relief—this was some kind of prank. Giving him a hard time because of the whole Anna-being-pregnant thing. He could take a prank. He could handle a little ribbing.

But Mary was holding a big plastic bin and she placed it firmly in front of him on the porch. "Can't forget the supplies!" she offered cheerfully.

The door slammed this time and the dead bolt clicked firmly and loudly into place. No prank. No joke.

The puppy in his arms whimpered. Then proceeded to pee on his coat.

"Fantastic," Hawk muttered, with no earthly clue what to do. Except drive home with a pee-covered coat...and a puppy.

ANNA WAS TUCKED into her bed, and Mary was lying next to her like they'd done a million times as kids, relaying the story of the look on Hawk's face when she compared the puppy to a baby. Mary was laughing and it made Anna feel warm and fuzzy.

Her whole life had been a strange dichotomy of loss and so much luck and love it made her head spin. She'd lost her parents at a young age, and there'd been a lot of suffering because of that. But her siblings had always been there for her. No matter what. She had an amazing family, and it was part of why even though the pregnancy had been a surprise, she'd always known she wanted to keep the baby.

"Have you thought about names?" Mary asked, rolling onto her side to study Anna.

Anna stared at the ceiling. Thinking about names meant thinking about reality, and she'd rather think about Mary insisting Hawk keep the puppy. "I've barely even thought about what I'm going to eat for breakfast tomorrow, Mary."

"Well, I'm going with you to your next appointment. Unless..."

"Unless what?" Anna asked, tugging at her sheet in an effort not to look at Mary.

"Well, maybe Hawk will want to go."

Anna glanced over at her sister, who was now examining the comforter. "I don't exactly get strong daddy vibes from the guy." He'd come out all this way and not even *mentioned* the baby. Just her case files.

The jerk.

Mary raised an eyebrow. "Oh, really? I got *very* strong daddy vibes." Then she waggled her eyebrows, shocking a laugh out of Anna, because usually Mary was very prim and proper and above those kinds of jokes Anna and Louisa enjoyed.

But she was trying to make Anna laugh, Anna understood. Because Mary was the mother of the family, no matter her age or place in it. She wanted to make Anna feel better, and she knew all the tricks to do it.

Anna would say Mary should be the one who was pregnant, but Mary would never be so irresponsible as to start something without a plan. To catch the eye of a stranger across the bar and lose herself in a night of...

Well, *that* did not do thinking about.

"I'll let you get some sleep. But you come get me if you need anything."

"It was a bump, Mary," Anna said, touching the bandage on her head. "I'm fine. Doctor said so."

Mary slid off the bed and she tried to smile, but Anna knew her sister too well. She didn't say anything, but she didn't have to.

Until they figured out who'd hurt her, Mary would worry. Mary said good-night and Anna did her best to force a smile.

She was going to need to take control of this situation. The whole attempted-murder thing. The whole...baby thing.

She slid her hand over her stomach. It was still hard to believe. Even when she heard the little *womp, womp, womp* of the heartbeat at the doctor's office, or watched the little wriggle of lumps on the ultrasound screen.

She'd been living in denial, more or less, and she couldn't anymore. Because her family didn't need to be worrying over her. Because growing a baby was important, but so was surviving whoever wanted to hurt her.

So, in the morning, she got dressed and ate breakfast with everyone, and then, even though she hadn't expressly told anyone she was leaving, and okay, maybe *sneaked* off the ranch making sure no one saw her, she drove over to Hawk's place in Bent.

He had a cute little house on Main Street, that much she knew. Of course, she'd only seen both inside and outside in the dark, and she'd been a little...occupied on the inside.

Today, she noted a leash tied to the porch, though no puppy on the end. The sun was just beginning its trudge up in the sky, fighting off January gray. It was early, so she hoped he hadn't gone into work yet, but who knew what an arson investigator's hours were.

Maybe she should just go back home. He was either sleeping or busy or—

Stop being a coward, Anna.

She forced her feet to move. They had a lot to deal with and now they were going to deal with it. On *her* terms. Not his directives. She had a plan in place. A list of things to discuss and talk about.

Mostly about the case, because as far as she was concerned, they still had five months to deal with…the rest.

She knocked on the door, maybe harder than necessary. Immediately the sharp yips of a puppy sounded from inside. Then a crash. Then the door slammed open.

He was shirtless, disheveled, and looked like he hadn't shaved in a day or two with a dark shadow of whiskers doing nothing to hide the sharp jaw. His blue eyes were hotly furious, and he definitely looked like he hadn't slept much. The puppy was running in circles, creating a mess of shredded toilet paper as he yapped and jumped and ran behind Hawk.

Hawk glared. "I blame *you* for this nightmare."

Her mouth was too dry to speak. How…*how* could a man be such a mess and look so damn hot? He was lean but mus-cled. *Rangy*, she supposed, was the word. She knew this. She'd seen him naked, but maybe she'd tried to convince herself her memory was flawed. No man could be that hot.

He had a little tattoo, right over his heart. A hawk, of all things.

She wanted to kiss it.

When she managed to pull her gaze up to meet his, his eyes changed, that dark blue deepening. Just like it had done that first night. Across the bar. Before they'd ever said anything to each other. Just *bam*. Instant, destructive *lust*.

Her breathing had gone shallow. Every nerve ending seemed to braid itself underneath her skin. Just like then.

It would be foolish to follow that same path. Wrong, with everything they had to deal with. She was in danger, so there were *far* more important things at hand than scratching an itch she'd already once scratched.

But… "You know, I'm already pregnant," she managed, though her throat was tight. Her heart echoing loudly in her ears. Loud enough to drown out rational thought, clearly. Her body pulsing with all that sudden need she'd only ever felt so sharply, so *out of nowhere* with him.

"I do know that. Now."

"So, whatever we did…or didn't do, here, in this moment, wouldn't have the consequences it once did. They've already…*consequenced*."

He raised an eyebrow, that dark blue gaze raking over her like a touch. *Please go ahead and touch.*

"That an invitation?" he asked, and she hoped she wasn't hallucinating that there was a new edge to his voice that hadn't been there before.

"Maybe."

He jerked her to him, just like he had the first night. It wasn't rough so much as the tipping point. Something about being alone, something about *them* ignited. She dived her fingers into his hair, curling and holding on as he devoured her mouth with his. He kicked the door shut, then lifted her, and she wrapped her legs around him as he moved her deeper into the house.

Into the bedroom, onto his bed. The puppy yipped excitedly from somewhere behind them, but Anna could not have cared less in the moment. He laid her down on the bed, then paused and just looked at her.

"I don't know what the hell this is," he said, but he was pulling off her boots. Her jeans. Everything in quick, efficient movements.

She pulled off her own shirt since his was already off. "That makes two of us."

"Well, at least there's that." He unclasped her bra, ran his big, rough hands down her body, and then he was on top of her, inside her.

And it was just like the last time. All heat, all combustion. A crazy need she didn't understand. Mutual and encompassing. So it was like what they created between them was its own world and only the two of them knew about it, understood it.

Like this connection had been planted in them long ago, before they'd laid eyes on each other. Hell, maybe before the earth had taken its first rotation around the sun. It felt that big, that weighty.

That right.

And it was that thought that settled into her as he took her over the edge and followed.

Chapter Five

Hawk had long ago forged himself into a person who didn't make mistakes. When his mom had been sick, when he'd done everything to keep her going that he could think of, he'd determined he'd only make the *right* choices. For her.

And even after she'd died, he'd kept that promise to himself, because what else had there been to do? Either keep the promise or just…give up. Giving up felt like too much of a betrayal of everything she'd given him, so he'd worked hard and done the right thing. So that in whatever thing happened after death, she was proud of him.

Then Anna Hudson had come along. Damn, she was beautiful. All spread out in his bed, self-satisfied smirk on her face and nothing else. And he couldn't categorize her as a mistake, exactly. She seemed too…inevitable. Something ignited between them, and maybe it didn't make any sense, but it was…there. Real.

And would likely have him making a few mistakes before all was said and done. Still, it seemed a good time to make it clear he had plans. Naked. Happy. Relaxed.

"I think we should get married," he said idly, toying with the ends of her silky hair as he contemplated his ceiling.

"What?" It came out like a screech.

He glanced over at her. "You heard me."

She leveraged up on her elbows and glared at him, though, truth be told, he had a hard time looking at her eyes. "You do not want to get *married*," she said.

"I believe I said I did."

"Hawk, that's…insane. You do not seem like a draconian, knuckle-dragging, backward-thinking chauvinist."

"You don't know me, Anna." Not that he was any of those things, but he just wanted to make sure to point out that she didn't have him pegged. Couldn't. When they'd spent all of a handful of hours together.

"No, I don't. Which is why I won't be *marrying* you. My *God*. You're as bad as Jack."

"So Jack would agree with me?" He could use the older-brother angle if he had to.

"Jack agrees with the primordial ooze, and this has nothing to do with my brother." She slid out of bed and began to hunt for her clothes, putting them on as she found them. He just watched her move around his room…the puppy chasing her and nipping at every item of clothing she picked up.

"So what does it have to do with?" Hawk asked casually. He wasn't going to make the same kind of mistakes he'd made last night. No demanding. No getting caught off guard with families and puppies. Just calm, rational propositions.

"Sanity?" Anna replied. Sadly, she was dressed now, and she picked up the wriggling, yipping beast he'd been saddled with, who had already trashed his house and somehow had ended up sleeping on his pillow last night.

"Have you fed him?"

"I've done every damn thing I can think of with that creature, but he is a spawn of Satan bent on destruction." They'd even gone on a walk up and down Main Street last night. He'd bought a dog toy at the general store and tried to teach him to play fetch.

He'd bought him *treats*, since Mary's bin of junk had come with food and a leash and a few other necessities but nothing else.

Anna cuddled the puppy close, and he licked her chin as she tsked Hawk. He sat up in the bed. She'd looked so clean and fresh when she'd shown up at his doorstep. Now she was flushed and rumpled.

He really didn't have time for a round two.

But it was tempting.

Still, it was best to press his case when she was still here. Softened by the puppy and good sex. "I grew up without a father because he bailed. I'm not repeating the cycle."

She didn't have anything to say to that for a good few seconds. But she regrouped quickly. "Okay, but that doesn't mean we have to be *married*."

"I happen to think it does. No custody BS. You and me and the kid, Blondie. We'll make it work."

"How?"

"By deciding to."

She stared at him for a very long time, then shook her head. "Hawk, this isn't happening."

He pointed at the spot she'd vacated on his bed. "The sex is good."

"The sex is great. That's not a reason to get married."

He didn't preen at her calling it great, but he didn't hate it either. "I imagine people get married for less." He slid out of bed, didn't miss the way she watched him. And maybe he took his sweet time crossing to his dresser and grabbing a new pair of boxers for her benefit.

"I came here to talk about the case," she said, sounding like she had at the door. A little strangled, a little breathless.

"That is *not* what it seemed like."

"Well, you were all shirtless and disheveled. So sue me for taking a detour. Why do you have a hawk tattoo? Is Hawk even your real name?"

He tried not to tense. "Yeah, it's my real name."

"And you felt the need to get the pictorial form of your own name tattooed over your heart?"

"I did." He pulled on a pair of sweatpants. He'd need to run through the shower before his first meeting of the day, but he had some phone calls to make to the lab first. He glanced at his clock. It'd open in about fifteen minutes. So if he could get her to agree with him and shoo her out of here by then...

"You expect me to marry you, not knowing a thing about you, while you also act completely unwilling to *let* me know anything about you?"

It was a fair point. He didn't like it, but it was fair. So he turned to face her. Shrugged casually. "My mom liked hawks. She was into all this spiritual junk, thought they were her spirit guides or something. That's why she named me Hawk." He didn't pause, because it would give too much space for...emotions. "I got the tattoo when she died."

Anna's eyes softened. That was the thing about her. She acted all tough, brash and like she didn't have a care in the world. After that first night, and the fact she'd been the one to sneak out afterward, he would have been sure she truly didn't.

But he'd watched her with her siblings since. He'd seen her comfort her best friend when Louisa O'Brien's family home had burned down. There was a sweet heart underneath all that barbed wire.

Maybe it was wrong to focus on that, but he'd use it to get what he wanted. What was *necessary*.

"How old were you?" she asked, petting the puppy thoughtfully.

"Fourteen." He'd gleaned enough information about the Hudsons to know the parents weren't around. "You?"

"I'm not sure. My parents disappeared when I was eight. Don't know if they died or what. Hence the whole Hudson Sibling Solutions thing we do."

"Hell."

"Yeah, it was. But I had my siblings." She studied him for a long time. "You have anybody?"

He could lie. Evade. But he thought the truth was pretty clear. "Nah."

She nodded. "I was never planning on, like, keeping you out of it." She didn't quite meet his gaze. "I was just being a coward about the whole thing. So I'm sorry about that."

He shrugged. He'd never seen much use for apologies. They didn't change a damn thing. "No harm done, I guess."

She stepped forward so they were closer, but her eyes were soft and imploring. "But that doesn't mean we should get married. Marriage is about…loving somebody," she said earnestly.

He didn't know about that. He couldn't say he'd ever

been around a happily married couple for very long. But he did know one thing. "Aren't we going to love the kid?"

ANNA KNEW THERE had to be a good response to that question. One that reaffirmed how absolutely ridiculous it was to think they could get married just because they'd created a child, when they were virtual strangers.

Because *of course* they'd love their kid, but a marriage "for the kid" looked different than a marriage because you fell in love with someone.

Didn't it?

"Look—" But she didn't have a chance to say anything else, because something on his face changed and he held up his hand. She might have argued with him—no one held up their hand to her to stop her from talking—but it was something about the way he narrowed his eyes, reached over into the same drawer he'd pulled boxers out of and produced a gun.

"Get in the bathroom," he said, pointing to a door off to the side. "The only window in there is small."

"Hawk—"

"Take the dog with you," he said sharply. Then he disappeared out of his room.

She was not good at doing what she was told, but she was a private investigator, sister to a cop. She knew something about how people reacted to danger and threats, and maybe she hadn't sensed one.

But Hawk had. She trusted that he had, but she didn't like being relegated to bathroom hider. He was a fire investigator. Lived here alone. If he had a gun in his dresser, he likely had other ones.

She looked around the room. The dresser was too far from the bed for that to be the only weapon he had in here. If he was worried about threats, he had to have one within reach from where he slept. She went over to the night-stand, pulled open the drawer. There was an assortment of things—a bottle of aspirin, some sort of medal she'd be interested to inspect later, some cords, and an old-looking, pocket-size book with no title on the cover. Another thing she wanted to inspect, but now was not the time, because behind all that was a small gun.

She shifted the puppy into the crook of one arm, pulled out the gun and checked it. Loaded. "He's going to have to learn some gun safety if he wants to have a kid around here," she muttered to keep her nerves from vibrating out of control.

She moved to the room door, peeking out to survey the living area. The front door was wide open and she didn't see anyone, so she moved into the room. She'd almost made it to the door when Hawk strode in.

He didn't even chastise her for not listening or ask where she'd gotten the gun. "Call 911 from my landline," he said, pointing to an old-fashioned phone on the wall. "Your truck's on fire." He grabbed a fire extinguisher from a cabinet in the kitchen.

"Hawk, you can't... That's a small, indoor extinguisher. What's it going to do?" But she was dialing 911 on the phone.

"Not much, but I know fire. I've got to stop it before it spreads. Stay put. Keep him put, too."

She tightened her grip on the puppy, then relayed all the information she knew to the 911 operator. Once the operator had everything she needed, Anna left the gun on the counter and hurried back to the front door to see how Hawk was faring.

He'd clearly gone through the entire extinguisher, but her truck was still in flames. Some neighbors had come out and Hawk was ordering them all around. Buckets and hoses appeared.

She took one step—just *one* out onto the front porch— and Hawk immediately lifted his gaze to hers. "Do not come out here. Stay out of the smoke."

It was only because of the baby, and because she'd just inhaled too much smoke a few nights ago, that she listened. She closed the door and watched from the window as a cop car appeared, and then a fire truck.

It took time, but they finally got the fire out. Hawk stayed outside talking to neighbors, firefighters, a cop who looked to be about the same age as him and she thought maybe she recognized from her work. When Hawk finally got rid of everyone and came inside, he was sweating and dirty. His eyes were red, and he had a bandage around one hand.

"Oh, you hurt yourself!" She reached forward, as if she was going to do what? Someone had already bandaged it and she wasn't going to kiss and make it better. She dropped her hand and looked up at him.

He had an odd expression, but it quickly smoothed out into that professional I'm-Mister-Arson-Investigator-And-Smartest-Man-In-All-The-Land blankness. "Someone torched your truck. On purpose."

"Yeah, I picked up on that."

He wiped his sweaty forehead on his forearm. But it just smeared soot everywhere. "I called your brother."

She didn't groan, though she desperately wanted to. "You shouldn't have done that."

He shook his head. "Don't be stubborn, Anna. Someone is after you."

"They had to know I wasn't *in* my truck, so they were hardly trying to burn me alive."

"This time. *This* time. Because it's the *second* time, Anna. The first time they did clearly want you dead. So it doesn't matter this time whether they wanted you dead, hurt or scared—it isn't *good*."

She tried to ignore the jitter of fear that went through her at the harsh way he said it. "Sure, but we're...figuring out who."

"Not we, Anna. You'll leave this to the professionals."

The man was truly a piece of work. "I *am* a professional, Hawk."

He scraped his fingers through his hair. He needed a shower. Breakfast. And not to be such a jerk. She figured it wouldn't do to tell him what he needed, so she kept it to herself.

"You know what I mean."

"No, I don't."

"I'm not arguing with you about this."

"Well, if you think you're going to bundle me up and send me home with my brother, you inhaled more smoke than I thought."

"No, I don't think you should go home."

"You think I should stay here?" she asked incredulously. It was one thing if it was about sex, but this was about... protecting her? No, protecting the baby.

"No, I think you should hide."

Anna recoiled. *Hide.* "Hudsons don't hide."

"Well, maybe pregnant ones should."

They were squaring off in his living room. He was all sooty and sweaty, and she was perfectly fine, except for the rising tide of nausea she was desperately trying to ignore.

And worse, so much worse, the little wiggle of softness at the idea that he wanted to protect her. Even as she convinced herself he was only wanting to protect the current vessel of his child, she felt that warmth.

You are a fool, Anna Hudson.

A fool who usually preferred a fight. To wear down her opponent until she got her way. Because she always won. Always got her way.

She had the very frightening thought that Hawk might not wear down as easily as her siblings. She swallowed. "Go take a shower. I'll make us something to eat."

"Listen—"

"It's either that or I lose whatever's left in my stomach from yesterday all over this hideous carpet right here."

His mouth firmed. "We'll eat first. I'm not letting you out of my sight until your brother gets here. You might not like it. Hell, I don't like it for you, but you cannot be alone until we figure out who did this. And before you lecture me about your skills and accomplishments and strengths and blah, blah, blah, I don't care. I would recommend anyone in the same situation—you know, the one where someone tried to *kill you*—not to be alone."

Then he turned on a heel and marched into the kitchen. "Now, what would settle your stomach?"

Chapter Six

Anna decided on scrambled eggs and a piece of plain toast. Hawk insisted she sit while he made it, then made himself some coffee since he hadn't had any this morning. He watched Anna as she ate, making sure she did indeed put something in her stomach.

As for himself, he still wasn't ready to eat, so he sneaked little bites of toast to the puppy under the table.

"Have you named him yet?" Anna asked. She'd gotten a little green there for a few minutes but was looking steadier now.

"Yeah. I think I'll call him Pita."

"Like the bread?" she asked in confusion.

"No, like *pain in the*—"

"Hawk," she admonished. "You cannot name him that."

"If your family is forcing me to take a dog I don't want, I can in fact name him that."

She looked at him for a very long time, so long and so serious, he had the very unfamiliar need to fidget in his chair.

"I think we both know no one could *force you* to do anything."

Something twisted in his chest, a kind of premonition

type feeling his mother would have called spirit guidance or divine intuition or something equally out there. Hawk figured it was just enough experience to know such statements were usually challenges to the universe to prove a person wrong.

He'd like the universe to stay off his back, thank you very much.

Anna cleared her throat and looked away. "That's a terrible habit to teach him, you know," Anna said, pointing to where he'd just slipped another piece of bread to the dog. "And breakfast is the most important meal of the day. *You* should be eating it."

"I've been taking care of myself since I was fourteen, Blondie. I can handle it."

Before she could say anything to that, the doorbell rang, followed by an insistent knocking. "I'm assuming that's your brother."

She sighed. "You really shouldn't have called him." She pushed back from the table the same time he did. Which meant they were facing each other, with his little kitchen table between them. He didn't turn to exit the kitchen like he should have. Something about that hazel gaze was like getting skewered, hooked, *something* painful and tangled.

She batted her eyelashes. "Thinking about me naked?"

He couldn't stop himself from grinning, even as the pounding on the door increased. "You're something else, Blondie." But he sobered, because…she *was* carrying his child. And even if she wasn't… Maybe they didn't know each other, but there was *something* between them. Whatever that was that sparked to life every time they made eye contact. Maybe it was just lust, but lust didn't happen with everyone.

"I'm going to do whatever I think needs to be done to keep you safe. I don't need you to like it."

Her flirtatious smile faded, not to the scowl he expected. Disapproving, sure, but softer. She opened her mouth to say something, but Hawk was pretty sure her brother was going to break down his front door if he didn't go answer it. He moved past her and into the living room, the puppy at his heels.

She followed but stopped in the middle of the room, which he realized she must have tidied when he'd been outside fighting the fire because the evidence of the puppy's war with toilet paper was gone.

"I...thought you'd call Jack," Anna said softly as she caught sight of her brother in the sidelight.

"Figured you'd prefer to deal with this one." He opened the door and Palmer stepped in without waiting for an invitation.

"What the *hell* is going on?" Palmer demanded. He looked at Hawk, then Anna. He pointed his finger at her. "You sneaked out this morning."

"I hardly sneaked."

"I have cameras on the property, Anna. You *sneaked*. *And* turned off your phone."

Hawk gave her a sharp look, but she only shrugged. Leave it to the woman in danger to be a hardheaded problem.

And carrying your child.

"I don't like this," Palmer said, crossing his arms over his chest. Echoing Hawk's thoughts exactly.

"Join the club," Hawk muttered.

Pita took up an unholy racket, trying to bark intimidatingly at Palmer. Who only reached down and scooped up the puppy and patted his rump. The fearsome guard dog whimpered happily and snuggled in.

"She's being targeted, and it's going to take some time to investigate. I called you over here, not just because her truck is totaled, but because I'm recommending you all tuck her away somewhere safe until we have even one clue as to what's happening and why." Hawk would have preferred to be the one tucking her away, but he was going to be too busy investigating to keep her under lock and key.

God knew she needed twenty-four-hour supervision or she'd end up doing something reckless.

Palmer studied Hawk, then Anna. "Great in theory, but have you met her?"

Anna smirked.

But before Hawk could deal with that, Palmer turned a heavy stare on him. "You sure this doesn't have anything to do with you?"

It took Hawk a few seconds to fully understand what Palmer was getting at, it was so insane. "Me? I wasn't anywhere near that motel. Who would target me through her?"

Palmer shrugged in that lazy way Hawk figured was as much an act as anything. "I don't know, but fire seems right up your alley."

ANNA WAS STILL marveling over the fact that Hawk had called Palmer—who was indeed the brother she'd rather deal with if she was being forced to deal with one. Palmer was overprotective and obnoxious in his own way, but he could at least take a joke. Make light of things now and again. He didn't get all bent out of shape when she poked at him.

He'd been the one to convince Jack to let her go to the rodeo. He understood her better than the other three.

But she didn't like him trying to turn the blame toward Hawk. "I think I make far more sense as a target, as the only way anyone would have connected me with Hawk was to know we hooked up one night three months ago."

Palmer made a face, no doubt at the words *hooked up*, which had *maybe* been Anna's intention.

"I'd also like to note to both you pig heads, pregnancy doesn't make me incapable of taking care of myself."

"Then explain the other night," Hawk and Palmer said in unison.

It was Anna's turn to pull a face. "For the love of God, don't start sounding like each other." She shuddered. Then she straightened her shoulders and faced them both down.

"I can be reasonable. Especially since I imagine it's a little rough to try to shoot while puking your guts out, which still happens on occasion. But I don't want anyone talking around me like you have to wrap me up in Bubble Wrap or send me away like some ancient damsel in distress. I'm also an investigator, and I'm damn well going to investigate who's after me."

Both men opened their mouths, no doubt to argue with her, but she knew how to deal with men.

Or at least her brother.

"But, because of the pregnancy, I will make one concession. I won't do anything alone. Someone can be by my side at all times. But not you," she said, pointing at Palmer.

"You want Jack or Grant?" Palmer returned incredulously, Cash obviously off the table since he had a daughter to take care of. And Mary didn't handle any of their cold case investigations and preferred to stay on the administrative side of things and avoid guns and blood when she could.

"No." She jutted her chin toward Hawk. "This guy here says he wants to marry me."

Palmer's jaw nearly dropped to the floor, which entertained the hell out of Anna.

"I happen to think it's a terrible plan," Anna continued, undeterred by Hawk's intimidating scowl. "So we'll be all cozy together while we investigate this little problem, and at the end of things, we'll either prove a partnership like marriage is a good plan—" she flashed him a grin "—or we'll all agree it's a *terrible* one and get on with our lives."

"You're not tagging along on an official investigation," Hawk said.

"That's cute you think you could stop me."

His eyes narrowed and, much like when they'd been back in his bedroom, darkened.

Why was he *so* hot? It was really distracting when she was trying to one-up him and irritate him at the same time.

"You should probably go take a shower while Palmer's here to babysit me," Anna offered, trying to arrange her features to look innocent and angelic.

She watched him fight with the desire to say something or be Mr. Taciturn. The latter won and he turned without saying anything and disappeared into the hallway to his bedroom.

"Anna, you've sure gotten yourself into a mess," Palmer muttered, scratching the puppy in his arms behind the ears. Pita's tongue lolled out in ecstasy.

"Yeah." And it wasn't just the whole someone wanting her dead thing either.

"You're not seriously going to consider marrying the guy, even if this investigation *does* go well."

She knew she should say "absolutely not." She knew she should feel that. But all she could think about was the way he'd stared at the wall when she'd asked him if he had anyone and he'd said *nah*. She looked at her brother. "He doesn't have anyone, Palmer. He's all alone."

"Maybe that's because he's a jerk. You can't just…marry him because you feel sorry for him."

"No. I'm pretty sure at the end of this he'll realize the last thing he wants is to be saddled with *me* as a wife."

Palmer was quiet for a minute, then reached over and gave her hair a little tug like he'd done back when they were rodeoing together and she'd lost spectacularly. "You're not such a bad prize."

She wasn't so sure about that, but there was no point arguing it. She was going to make sure Hawk didn't want to marry her anymore and would be convinced it was his idea all in one fell swoop. "It'll be good." She nodded firmly, as if to convince herself. "We'll figure out who's after me and he'll realize there are better ways to deal with this whole baby thing."

Chapter Seven

Hawk took his time in the shower, even though it was strange to know there were people out there in his house. There were *never* people in his house. He didn't bring women here—Anna being the one and only exception. If he did things with friends, he never invited anyone back here.

He'd never given much thought to why that was. It just seemed natural. To keep to himself. To be…isolated. He *preferred* being alone. He preferred his privacy, not having near-strangers—even if one was the mother of his future child—tromping about his house.

But he needed to weigh his options in some kind of silence and privacy, and Anna needed someone to keep an eye on her. She was acting like she might be reasonable, but Hawk didn't trust her just yet.

It was unimaginable to have Anna tagging along on his actual, professional, by-the-law investigation. He couldn't let her, for a wide variety of reasons that weren't even all personal.

But she was, in fairness, a licensed private investigator. It was about five hundred different conflicts of interest since she was the victim in the case, *and* the mother of his unborn child, but she had experience.

Frustrated with not being certain of the next right move to make, Hawk wrenched off the shower faucet. He had meetings, calls to make and now *two* arsons to investigate. Not to mention deal with Bent County Sheriff's Department on the assault angle. He didn't have time to let Anna tag along and keep his eye on her.

He also didn't have time to argue with her hard head. But he could leave that up to her siblings. No doubt they were experts.

He toweled off, ignoring the odd ache in his chest. He didn't know what that was like. Siblings. Family. Big messy feelings and complications.

Thank God he didn't know what it was like. Losing his mother had been excruciating enough. Why would he want more possibilities for that? He stepped out of the bathroom and into his bedroom.

The puppy was waiting for him in a compliant sitting position, which didn't suit the ornery little minion at all.

He stared at the dog. He did not want it, but the puppy wagged his little tail and looked up at him with dark brown eyes, and what the hell was Hawk supposed to do? Tell Mary to take him back?

"Your name *is* Pita," he muttered as he crossed to his closet and began to get dressed for his meetings and consider his approach to Anna and her brother.

He'd throw her a bone, certainly. He'd allow her to help with some elements of the investigation. She had the best insight into who might be after her, so it made sense, and it would make her feel like she had a say. Feeling like you had a say was always important.

But he needed to make sure she agreed to a situation where she was never alone. He considered having her move in here, but then he'd have to take her with him wherever he went and that wouldn't fly for when he was interviewing people he didn't want her around.

The ideal situation would be her tucked away somewhere secret, with one of her siblings standing guard. In his experience, the people in these far-flung western towns *always* knew someone with a tiny, off-the-grid cabin to hide away at.

But again, the guard was an issue. No doubt her brothers would protect her, but Anna had a lifetime of learning how to outsmart them. Hawk wouldn't be able to relax in that situation.

Still mulling over his options, he returned to the living room. He had an appointment to make, so this would have to wait.

But before he could say anything to Palmer or Anna, she fixed him with a bright, wide smile he didn't trust at all.

"We've come to a bit of a compromise."

"That so," Hawk returned, eyeing the puppy, who had trotted over to the couch and was sniffing the leg.

"You'll come stay at the ranch," she said. "Cash can help you train Pita. I can work with you on the case, and someone will always be around to keep an eye on the knocked-up target."

Before he could say anything, Palmer started talking. Clearly, they were ganging up on him.

"We've got good security all around the ranch, and I can beef it up. It might have been Anna's truck that was targeted, but it *was* in your driveway. Which means someone might be connecting you to this. You both under one roof, with lots of eyes and security. It makes sense."

Hawk hated to admit that it did, that it wasn't the worst plan. And he could tell they really didn't expect him to go for it. Which made him perversely eager to agree.

He wanted nothing to do with the Hudson circus, but this also accomplished a few goals. He'd have Anna constantly underfoot to work on her about the whole getting-married thing. He'd always be able to leave her behind and know someone was watching out for her, even if he brought her into a few investigative things. Plus, he liked the idea of security. Not so much for his own safety, but because any lead—including someone trying to target him—would bring them closer to answers.

He'd prefer her farther away, somewhere secret and isolated, but this was indeed a compromise.

"Okay," he agreed. Easily and without one argument. He had to bite back a smile at the look of shock on their faces. "I've got some meetings, so you can take Anna on back to the ranch. After I get my work done, I'll pack up and be on over to the ranch this evening."

"I should go with you," Anna said, frowning.

Hawk moved past her and picked up Pita's leash. He affixed it to the puppy's collar. "No." He pushed the door open and took the puppy out to do his business, Anna following behind him.

"I *am* going to be part of this investigation, Hawk." She didn't look at the burned remnants of her truck, but then again, neither did he. It felt better to ignore it, and a lot of things, in this moment.

"You should go home, Anna. Make me that list of people who might want to hurt you. *That* will help me with my investigation and make you a part of it." Pita did a little squat, right on the concrete. Hawk scowled. Couldn't even pee in the grass like a normal dog.

"An investigation you've told me nothing about."

He raised an eyebrow at her. "You didn't exactly give me a chance to this morning," he returned. Pointedly. Pointedly enough Palmer groaned behind Anna. "Besides, you didn't give me your files."

"And I won't," she returned mulishly, crossing her arms over her chest. "It's an invasion of privacy. But I'll get you a list."

"Fantastic. So you have your job today, and I'll go do mine. In perfect agreement." He smiled at her. "I'll see you tonight at the ranch."

She narrowed her eyes, scowling, and he was a smart man, so he knew better than to believe her silent exit was going to be *good* for him. Palmer's low whistle and pat on the back as he passed to follow her to his truck only sank that dread further.

"You've got a lot to learn, pal," Palmer muttered.

Hawk watched them get in Palmer's truck and leave. A lot to learn. He supposed about Anna and figuring out how to be a dad, he did.

But when it came to investigating arson, he was the best. And that was the most important thing to focus on today. He glanced at the puppy, who was currently sitting at his feet and chewing on the laces of his shoes.

"Well, Pita. Looks like you're my partner today."

BACK HOME AT the ranch, Anna put together her list. People she'd investigated or bounty hunted who might want to target her and were out of jail or alive enough to do so. She created little dossiers on all of them, ranking them from smartest to dumbest, violent to not even knowing which end of a gun the bullet came out of, and in the end ranked them from most likely to least likely.

Then she emailed it to Hawk *and* the Bent County detective. "Take that, hotshot investigator."

Once she'd done all that work, she wasn't sure if she was more hungry or exhausted. Growing a baby was *hard*.

She yawned. She'd just crawl under her covers for like five minutes and then go get some food. Then she'd go find Hawk. Trail him through his investigation. She could probably figure out everyone he was talking to today.

But when she blinked her eyes back open, the room was dark.

And, just like when she'd woken up at the hospital, a man was standing at the end of her bed.

"Your sister said you were in charge of determining where I'd sleep."

"Oh." Anna tried to get her brain to engage. Tried to think past the way he looked in a suit, his tie loosened as though it had been a hard day. "Well, there's room here." She patted the space on the bed next to her and smiled at him.

Hawk's eyes narrowed and darkened, even in the dim light. Quite the lethal combination. Did the people he interrogated find themselves unreasonably turned on?

"I might not know anything about family dynamics, but I'm not sleeping in the same room with you under your brother's roof," he said.

Poking at her temper, whether he meant to or not, Anna wasn't sure. "It's my roof too, buddy."

"Be that as it may, not happening."

She considered. She didn't want to put him in the guest room. It was far away from hers, and she wouldn't get her whole point across. It needed to feel like they were on top of each other. He needed to be around her constantly enough to be annoyed by her. "I thought you wanted to get married."

"Well, unless we're heading over to the courthouse tomorrow, that's a moot point."

"Not for me. I could hardly marry someone I haven't lived with. This is actually perfect. It doesn't have to be messy with joint leases and copies of keys. It's like a trial run." She smirked up at him. "If I can stand to share a room with you in this big house, maybe, just maybe, I could entertain the thought of marrying you." *Or make you run screaming in the opposite direction.*

He didn't immediately argue, though he did look at her with a heap of suspicion. "I'm not having sex with you with your entire family all around."

She grinned at him, because *sure*. "Mind in the gutter, Hawk. I just need to know if you're a cover hog. What time is it, anyway?" She glanced at her nightstand clock. "Time for dinner. Good—I'm starved." She got out of bed and grabbed his arm as she passed him.

"I already ate," he said, standing firm when she tried to tug him along with her.

She laughed. "Like that matters. Staying under the Hudson roof means you are required to attend Hudson dinner. It's the law." She tugged harder this time, and he reluctantly moved with her out of the room and down the hallway.

"I never agreed to follow Hudson law."

"It doesn't require your agreement. That's the beauty of it." She let him go but hooked her arm with his as they descended the stairs. "So. Get any leads today?"

There was a slight hesitation, no more than a fraction of a second, but she was investigator and woman enough to know he'd considered lying to her. But in the end, he told her the truth, and she had to be *not* warmed by that. Because he'd thought about lying to her, and that should matter.

But it didn't right now.

"No. But I cross-referenced your list with Quinn Peterson's. Almost identical. First few weren't immediate possibilities, so we'll go down the line. Shouldn't take more than a day or two to get initial impressions, and by that time I should have some of my lab reports back from the crime scene."

"Bent County would have other lab reports, right? Yours would be fire. Theirs would be attack."

"I work for Bent County, so we'll work together."

Anna nodded. "Quinn told me Thomas Hart is the detective on the case, and she knows him. Said he's good. Jack hasn't worked *with* him, but I guess knows him in that cop way, and was complimentary. Well, as complimentary as Jack ever is."

Hawk nodded in silent confirmation, which Anna figured was practically like a presidential commendation.

"In fact, Hart brought up an interesting point today." Hawk stopped moving, and Anna could have kept pulling, but there was something about his expression that had her stopping.

"Okay."

"We're looking into your work, but we haven't really asked about your personal life."

She wanted to laugh. Make a joke. It was on the tip of her tongue. And if it had been anyone else, she likely would have teased him about wanting to know about her past lovers.

But someone had tried to kill her, and he looked so serious. And he wanted to *marry* her and be a father to their baby because he hadn't had one.

So, she swallowed down her smart replies. "I haven't..." She felt unreasonably exposed by the admission, even though it hadn't been that long. Even though she *had* been busy. She cleared her throat, trying to push away her discomfort. Because the truth was more important than her ego. "I haven't been with anyone, or seen anyone, since that night at the bar."

His eyes deepened, and that answering flutter started low in her stomach. "It was... Christmas," she managed, though her voice came out strangled. "I was busy."

His mouth quirked up, and the flutters turned into something *far* more dangerous. "And before that?"

She shook her head. "I'd have to look through my calendar to know exact dates, but I'd been focused on proving myself at Fool's Gold, so dating hasn't been high on my list."

"Anything that ended badly? No matter how long ago?"

"I mean, I slashed my high school boyfriend's tires when I found another girl's bra in the back of his precious Mustang, but he's now married to said girl, so..." She shrugged. "Come on. Let's go eat."

Anna led him into the big dining room, where they always tried to have dinner together. And everyone was indeed here today—including Dahlia and Louisa. And Cash's menagerie of dogs.

Pita saw or scented Hawk and scrambled over with an excited yip, though they couldn't have been parted for long. Anna had the strangest sensation that at some point, she'd have a kid…who might just get excited at the sight of their father.

Kid.

Father.

"Anna, are you okay?" Mary asked, looking up from where she'd been placing a big bowl of green bean casserole on the table. "You look pale."

"Fine. Just hungry."

"Well, sit. Eat." She smiled encouragingly at Hawk. "If you have any dietary concerns, just let me know. I'll add it to the spreadsheet."

"I…don't. I'll eat anything."

"Fantastic." Mary bustled off to get the finishing touches on dinner together, and Anna gestured Hawk into a seat, trying to shake off the weird feelings plaguing her. There was a lot of time before this baby was a *real* baby, so a lot of time before she had to figure out what to do with the whole father part.

Her only goal now was to convince Hawk he couldn't possibly want to marry her, so he'd stick to that decision.

Oh, and find out who wanted her dead.

"So, Hawk." Jack stared down the table at him, and Jack looked so much like their long-gone father in that moment,

Anna's heart turned over with a longing so sharp it nearly made her want to cry.

Until Jack said, "Why don't you update us on the investigation?"

Chapter Eight

Hawk felt like he'd been through the weirdest-ass gauntlet he could imagine. He didn't know why he thought he could handle the Hudsons. It was like trying to handle a million yapping prairie dogs with the plague.

He had a headache now, and a weird kind of guilt over quizzing Anna on her past relationships—even though he shouldn't feel guilty, because that was the job. Worse than the guilt was some sort of primal, *absurd* satisfaction that there hadn't been anyone after him.

Like that mattered.

Or the way she'd looked, curled up in her bed, fast asleep. Sweet and vulnerable, while he'd had to breathe through the knowledge someone had tried to kill her. And he was no closer to finding out who.

Now Jack wanted to itemize the investigation for the whole Hudson clan to hear. Uh, no.

"I'm not sure that's appropriate dinner conversation."

"We don't worry too much about appropriate these days," Jack countered easily. "Do you have a list of suspects?"

"Whether I do or don't, I won't be sharing that list."

"Why not?"

"Because involvement by any of you could harm not just the investigation, but the results. You're in law enforcement, Jack. You know as well as I do protocol is just as important as answers. When we find the person behind this, there won't be any loopholes. The case will have to be ironclad so they can spend the rest of their lives in jail, where they belong. I can't risk civilian involvement."

"I'm not a civilian," Jack retorted.

"No, but you're not an unbiased party either."

Jack's mouth firmed, but he didn't keep up the argument.

What Hawk didn't know about the Hudsons, he'd made sure to brush up on today. Even though it wasn't part of the case, per se, he'd thought it smart to understand all the players he would be sharing a roof with.

Jack Hudson was indeed the oldest and had raised his siblings after their parents' disappearance. He'd been in the police academy when it had all happened, and stuck with that, working at Bent County for a time, all the while lobbying the town of Sunrise to start their own department. Once they had, he'd run for sheriff. For eight years, he'd been in the top position at Sunrise, and ran a tight ship.

Which meant he should know Hawk was being honest. He couldn't risk the investigation with a lot of Hudson interference.

Mary, who handled not just playing hostess, but apparently all the administrative and accounting tasks for both the ranch and HSS, expertly steered the topic of conversation away from Hawk and investigations and toward other things, like puppies.

Hawk appreciated the help, but he knew that wouldn't be the end of it. He glanced at Anna. She was whip-smart, so fooling her wasn't going to be easy, but he had to make her feel like she was part of the investigation without that actually being the case.

The list she'd emailed him today had been far more thorough than Quinn Peterson's, even if their conclusions were the same. Sadly, of the top two possibilities they'd both chosen, one had been in a holding cell in Denver the night of the motel fire. The other had been in the hospital.

Ironclad alibis.

There were still other names to check into, and he hadn't gotten into asking her family about threats they might see, because Thomas had said that was on his agenda for tomorrow.

Hawk's focus had to be the fires.

Cash and Palmer cleared the table while Mary and Dahlia brought out dessert and conversation zinged around like a Ping-Pong game with five hundred balls. When Hawk glanced to one side, he caught the little girl, Izzy, staring at him. Chin in her hands with a dreamy smile. "Can you play the drums?" she asked him out of nowhere.

"Uh. No."

She sighed as if this was a great disappointment to her. Hawk didn't know what the hell to do with that, so he kept his eyes on his dessert until he was reasonably sure everyone was finished. He risked a glance up at Palmer, who was whispering something into Louisa's ear that made her blush.

Families were weird. "When you get a chance, Palmer, I want to see the security setup."

Anna elbowed him, harder than necessary. "*I* can show it to you."

"I thought that was Palmer's deal."

"It is, for the most part, but I help, so I know. What exactly is it that you think I do as a private investigator? Google people and pore over their LinkedIn profiles?"

Hawk shrugged easily, because he knew it would irritate her and he wasn't immune to the way she glared at him. "Maybe."

"It's a lot more than that. Especially the cases Fool's Gold takes on. The women who come to us are already close enough to being victims. They don't need more hardship. My investigations have to be just as airtight as yours, to protect those people desperate for help."

She was so…passionate about it. It wasn't that it surprised him, exactly. She was a woman full of…well, passion. Just that he still didn't know what to do with the way she was comfortable with that passion, that emotion, all those feelings. She just laid it all on the line and never once seemed uncomfortable with it.

He turned to Mary, who was clearly in charge of these dinners, no matter what Jack might think down there at the head of the table.

"I feel like I should help with something," he said. "I've been on my own for a while. I can handle just about any chore you throw at me."

Mary smiled kindly at him. "You will, but you get a day to ease in first. I'll add you to the spreadsheet and give you an overview of your duties tomorrow."

"You seem to have a lot of spreadsheets."

"Oh, Hawk." She got up from her seat and took her empty plate and his. "You have *no* idea." Then she headed for the kitchen, and Izzy and Jack were clearing the rest of the table. Because they clearly all had jobs. He supposed it was the only way a family of this size could function *and* run two businesses together.

"Come on," Anna said at his side. "Let's take a look at the security room."

He nodded and followed her out of the dining room. She led him down the hallway and into a smaller room that had probably once been a utility closet or mudroom at one time. Now it was clearly a security hub for HSS.

Anna went through the whole thing. Computers, cameras, monitors. It was surprisingly high-tech and impressive. The whole ranch wasn't under surveillance, because of the sheer size, but the house and the yard had the capability of being completely watched.

"Is this the result of paranoia or experience?" Hawk asked, watching one of the monitors' grainy view of the porch at night.

"Both, I think," Anna returned, unfazed by the word *paranoia*. "We've had a few people not too happy with the cold cases we've uncovered. That's why Cash tends to keep himself separate. Doesn't want anyone targeting Izzy or him, with her mom out of the picture. It also allows us to offer anyone who hires us protection. When Dahlia hired us, she had someone following her, so we put her up here and the cameras helped us catch some of the people involved."

He studied her profile as she fooled with some keyboard. The idea of her being targeted never failed to feel like a lance of pain right in his gut. But the idea she was always out there, investigating things that might come back to haunt her. He really didn't know how to deal with that.

"Any chance this all connects to the family business?"

Anna looked at him and seemed to consider this possibility with the seriousness it deserved. "It's not impossible. We work together, but we take turns being lead. I haven't led any cases since I took the job at Fool's Gold, so, much like the personal angle—it's possible, but seems less likely."

Hawk nodded. That was the same conclusion he'd reached, but it was good to hear it confirmed. Still, he'd ask her brothers, too. And her friends about anyone in her personal life. Or Hart would, since he didn't have a personal connection to the victim.

Hell, this was a mess. She was an entanglement he was now linked to no matter what and that should be scarier than it was. She was hardheaded, stubborn, volatile, unpredictable, obnoxious and abrasive.

Beautiful. Funny... A constant surprise.

She glanced at him as if she sensed him studying her. She turned her body to face him. She looked just as she had that night at the bar. A challenge in her eyes and something... he just didn't know how to characterize. Like she was enchanted, and he just had to reach out to touch.

"You're thinking about me naked, aren't you?"

If only it were that easy. But he hadn't *not* been doing that either, so what the hell? "Yeah, I am."

"Good."

He'd promised himself this whole living under the Hudson roof meant he was going to be hands-off. He'd promised himself no more funny business until she agreed to marry him. Until they'd made some concrete plans about what having this baby meant.

She led him upstairs and made him break every last promise.

ANNA WAS SURE to be up before Hawk the next morning. Part of her yearned to crawl back into bed and have a repeat performance of last night, but she had plans.

She would have preferred to handle this on her own, but she understood the dangers, her limitations here. Even if no one would give her credit for that. Hard to blame them. Historically, she had *not* been good at knowing her limitations.

Still, just because she couldn't go off and do things on her own didn't mean she couldn't *do* things. She eyed Hawk. He was a deep enough sleeper, it seemed, but he was also an investigator, so it would be hard to pull one over on him.

She scooped up the still-dozing puppy, knowing he'd start barking and running around once she opened the door. She snuggled him close so he was quiet, then moved for the door as if she was going to leave the room. Carefully and casually, she hooked her finger through the loop of Hawk's bag and brought it with her. Quietly, she closed the door behind her, then knelt on the ground. She set Pita down on the rug. "Go on downstairs. Someone will let you outside and give you some food."

His tail wagged happily, but he did not follow instructions. Anna sighed. She left the bag by the door but got up and walked toward the stairs. She kept quietly urging Pita to go down the stairs, but he'd only go down a couple, then zoom back up.

Then one ear perked up and with a yip he zoomed down the stairs. Likely he heard or smelled something going on in the kitchen. Thank goodness.

Anna returned to just outside her door and Hawk's bag. She paused, listening for any sounds coming from her room, but there were none, so she unzipped the bag and pawed through Hawk's things.

The first thing she decided to look at was a notebook she'd seen him scribble in when he'd been working on Louisa's family's fire. She opened it and frowned. None of what she saw made sense. It was letters and numbers and symbols in some chaotic order.

She flipped to the next page. The same weird mix of letters and symbols. It was written in sentences, even paragraphs, but there was no way of determining what he'd been writing because the order of letters, numbers and symbols didn't make sense.

"What the hell is this?" she muttered, flipping through all the pages and finding nothing but gobbledygook.

"It's my own personal shorthand to keep nosy, conniving people from reading my notes."

She yelped in surprise, nearly tossing the notebook in the air. She glared over her shoulder at where Hawk stood, casually leaning against the door frame. She wasn't sure how he'd managed to open the door so silently, but he had.

"Hardly *conniving*."

"How do I know you didn't use sex to lull me into an exhausted stupor just so you could sneak through my bag?" he returned.

"Trust me, Hawk, the sex is its own reward."

He chuckled at that and something warm and mushy

moved through her, because he didn't laugh very often, and when he did, it did things to her. And not even like *want to rip his clothes off* things. Warm, soft things.

He held out his hand to help her to her feet. She let him. Even let him pluck the notebook out of her hand. It wasn't like she could read anything in there.

Once she was standing, he didn't let her hand go. Something in his expression had changed and he studied her with a faint frown. "You cry in your sleep, Blondie."

She froze. "What?" She'd expected him to chastise her for going through his stuff. Not…that.

"Last night. You were crying. I thought you were awake, but finally figured out you were fast asleep."

Her heart jabbed hard against her rib cage, and she had to work very hard to keep her breathing even. "I don't…" It wasn't that she didn't believe him. She knew she did. She just hadn't woken up with a wet face and her own sobs echoing in the room since she was a kid. And whatever she'd been doing last night hadn't woken her up, so she was caught totally unaware. She cleared her throat. "Must be a pregnancy thing." She didn't know if he bought that or not, but she gestured past him into her room. "You're like half-naked here. We might want to go back inside."

He didn't immediately react. Still stood there, blocking the door, one hand on hers and one hand holding the notebook. After a long moment where she felt inexplicably like crying into his shoulder, he dropped her hand and grabbed his bag.

She stepped inside her room behind him, though that didn't feel any safer, and had to forcibly refrain from wrapping her arms around herself. Or worse. Him.

Before she could think of anything to say, something wild and unpredictable that would take his mind off...everything, his phone vibrated on the nightstand.

Still just in his boxers, he crossed to it and held it to his ear. "Steele."

She watched as his face changed. It got that blank cop look, which she'd seen on Jack's face enough to recognize as bad news. But he made some affirmative noises, asked a few questions that led her to believe there'd been a fire somewhere he'd have to go investigate on top of her own.

When he clicked End, he slowly set the phone back down. And expressly did not meet her gaze. Which had her nerves start to jitter.

"There was a fire," Anna supplied for him.

"Yes. Another...possible connection to yours." He sighed and met her gaze. "At Fool's Gold Investigations."

"Quinn—"

"She's fine. No one was in the building when the fire broke out. But I need to get down there and look around. Maybe it's unrelated." He made a move to go to his duffel bag, but Anna stood in his path.

"It's not unrelated."

He sighed and rubbed a hand over his face, the first hint he might be affected by this news in any way. "We don't know until I get down there and investigate."

"It's *related*, Hawk."

"That is the likely scenario, but until I have the facts and evidence, I can't tell you that. Or prove it. So get out of my way so I can get to my job."

"You have to let me come with you." He was already shaking his head, but Anna powered on. "I'll stay out of the way, I promise. But I need to talk to Quinn and I need to… Hawk, I need this. They aren't just targeting me now. My truck, sure, but *your* house. Quinn wasn't hurt, but the place I work for her was. I need to…figure out what the hell I could have done to make someone *so* angry they'd go through all this."

"You didn't have to *do* anything for a person to decide to blame their bad decisions on you. Humans are good at shifting the blame." He reached out, and some survival instinct whispered at her to move away. Not to let him touch her like this.

But she stood rooted to the spot while his hand cupped her cheek. "Don't be good at shifting the blame to yourself, Blondie. It doesn't suit you."

The urge to cry was back, or lean into him, and she could not let her walls down. She might never be able to build them back. She had to focus on the issue at hand.

"Let me come with you, Hawk. I'll only hound Palmer into coming with me if you don't. Then you'll have to deal with both of us."

His mouth firmed into a harsh line. "I could have you both arrested."

Anna shrugged. "Hardly the way to get me to marry you. Not to mention, no one at Bent County is going to issue warrants on that, so it'd be a moot point."

"Anna—"

"I won't get in the way. I *promise*."

"I am going to regret this," he muttered, but it was an agreement, no matter how reluctant. He got dressed, and so did she. Weirdly together in her room. Weirdly, it didn't even feel all that weird.

He handed her a leash. "You're on Pita patrol."

"We could leave him here with Cash and the other dogs if you want."

Hawk shook his head. "If he's going to be my dog, he'll need to get used to being around investigations with me."

Why that warmed her, inside and out, she had no idea.

Chapter Nine

Hawk had figured Anna would be a major distraction, but in the end, she wasn't. She kept Pita from getting in the actual crime scene, and she stood with Quinn Peterson and Quinn's boyfriend, talking to them and keeping them from bothering him while he investigated.

The fire at Fool's Gold Private Investigations had been set in the exact same way as the motel fire, so there was no real hope this was an odd coincidence. No, it was arson, and it was about Anna.

Frustration clawed at him, but Hawk pushed it away and focused on his job. Observing, collecting samples, trying to put the pieces together. He had some theories on accelerant he was hoping the lab would be able to verify today. That would give him another avenue of connections to make.

Then the fact that this was another inside job. Like what had happened in Anna's motel room, it was clear there'd been a break-in followed by the fire starting—somewhere farther into the building than any exits or entrances.

Quinn had given him an outline of her security systems, and they *should* have gone off. Should have been able to give them enough video evidence to identify the arsonist.

But, even more concerning than the lacking security at the motel, the security had been taken off-line, with Quinn being none the wiser. She was having her security guy look into it, and he had thought he might be able to find something, but until he did, it was another dead end.

It made Hawk jumpy. Fires were one thing, especially in some remote motel with uninterested employees. But someone who had the ability to bypass security systems and set three fires without being caught over the course of only a few days…

Something was very wrong.

Hawk glanced around, not realizing he was looking for Anna until he found her. She'd moved—he assumed she'd convinced Quinn to move with her, as Quinn was now sitting on a bench and had Pita in her lap. Clearly the other woman was taking some comfort in the dog. The boyfriend was hovering around her, and Hawk figured he'd look into Dunne Thompson too—but his gut feeling told him the guy was clean. Unless he was a hell of an actor, he was just as shocked at the security breach as Quinn was, if not more so.

All to get to Anna. Or scare her. It all connected to Anna and that meant…too many things to count. Particularly since there didn't seem to be any attempt at contacting Anna. No threats, warnings or ransom demands. Just… destruction.

Hawk finished up the necessary tasks, gave the last firemen a few more instructions, then briefly convened with Hart, all the while mentally preparing for the next step.

It was getting close to lunchtime. Anna needed food and rest. He needed to call the lab again, and a million other small tasks that would eventually lead to a suspect. But for now it felt frustratingly slow.

Especially knowing whoever had done this could hack into security systems. Hawk moved over to Anna and gave Quinn a few words of encouragement, told her he'd be in touch. He ushered Anna back to his truck.

"Call your brother," he instructed.

She wrinkled her nose at him. "Why?"

"Because whoever set this fire hacked into Quinn's impressive security. Which means the same could happen at Hudson Ranch. I want him to know to be on the lookout for the same."

He could see by her expression she had a million questions, but she surprised him. Instead of voicing them, she pulled her phone out of her pocket and explained everything he'd said to Palmer while he got Pita settled in the back.

Hawk looked around at their surroundings. Small Wyoming towns weren't usually hotbeds for criminal activity. Someone should have seen something—if not at the motel, then at his house or at the investigation office. Then again, Anna's investigating usually took place in Bent County, which meant that her targets were usually locals. They would know how to sneak around, he supposed. Hide in plain sight even.

But the lack of any threats prior to the murder attempt just didn't sit right. They were missing something. He gave her a sideways glance. Or *he* was missing something.

The fact of the matter was, he might think he had some… strange fundamental understanding of Anna Hudson, even if her family baffled him, but that didn't mean he knew the intricacies of her past.

"Anything you're not telling me, Blondie?"

She turned to look at him, and there was enough confusion on her face that he believed whatever they were missing, they were both missing it.

"What would I be keeping from you?" It bothered him that hurt was laced in her tone.

So he kept his gaze hard on the road in front of him. "I don't know. But I feel like I'm missing this big piece of something. It doesn't add up. A murder attempt out of nowhere, then these two petty scare tactics or warnings or whatever they are. It's backward."

"Maybe, but people sometimes are." She shrugged, and it poked at him she could be so casual about the whole thing.

"That's your grand philosophy as an investigator? Oh well, sometimes people are backward? Sometimes you just *don't* make sense of things?"

"Yeah, it is," she returned. And she didn't get all snarky like he expected, or poke at *his* investigative philosophy. She looked at him with soft eyes and spoke calmly. "Hawk, my parents disappeared into thin air when I was eight. Not only did the whole damn town look for them for way longer than made sense, but also I'd be willing to bet Jack has never actually stopped—though he claims he has. I can almost guarantee every one of us kids spent some time doing our own investigation over the past seventeen years. I know Palmer and I did. Hell, I bet even Mary did, and that's not her thing. My point is some things never make sense. Because the world doesn't have to."

She was right, which was annoying. An arson investigation was less about things like motivation, less about the *reasons*, and more about who started the fire and how. The reason for the initial spark always had answers, and he'd always, always found them.

He couldn't let this case be the first time he didn't find out why. Any other case could be that. Not this one.

He drove out of Wilde, back toward Sunrise, chewing that frustration over. Hart had said he'd be out at the Hudson Ranch around one to ask the family questions. Hawk knew he'd wanted to talk to the family members individually, without Anna around, but Hawk wanted to hear, firsthand, what her family had to say.

He glanced at the clock. He should be able to get to the ranch right in time to walk in on something.

"Did you ever look for your dad?" she asked into the heavy quiet.

He froze, from the inside out. It was an unexpected question, and a painful wound he didn't want to discuss. Ever. With anyone.

But he had this underlying, secondary goal to everything he did with Anna. Because he was determined she marry him before their baby was born. *Because* of all those things he didn't like to talk about.

He didn't think the truth about his life made him sound like a particularly winning prize, but it would at least clarify why he wanted to be fully involved in his child's life. And that was all this was anyway. A surefire way to be a fully committed father.

So why not explain all the ways his hadn't been? "After my mom died, I became a ward of the state. They tried to find close relations, but there were none or they didn't want me. So I bounced around in foster homes till I aged out. When I did, I made it my mission to find my father, even if the system hadn't been able to. I thought I was going into it with my eyes wide open."

"Yeah," she said softly. "Don't we always at eighteen."

He laughed, and it didn't feel as bitter as it once had. Maybe because he wasn't eighteen anymore, and something about the way she said it fully crystallized the fact for him that no one would have been able to convince him not to do it. No one, not even his own mother if she'd lived, would have been able to talk him out of it.

Some lessons you had to learn on your own.

"I found him, felt pretty smug about that, too. I made it clear I didn't need anything from him—not anymore. I just wanted to give him a chance to make up for his screwup. For making it rougher on my mom than it needed to be, for the years of having to be the one to take care of her even though she didn't want me to. For those four years I'd been left with no one. I had it all planned out. I thought I had every scenario worked out in my head. Apologies, excuses, ignorance." Hawk didn't like to relive it, but it was right there. Like a movie playing in his head. "He looked me straight in the eye, said he didn't give a damn about me, or my mom, and never would. No remorse. No excuses. Just flat-out did not care."

Hawk focused on driving, but he felt Anna's gaze on him. She was quiet. Hell, even the puppy in the back was quiet. He'd spent a lot of years trying to treat that one moment like a learning experience: you never could predict the next moment in your life or what a person would do.

At eighteen, he hadn't been prepared for the cold callousness of his own father. All these years later, he understood there were a lot worse things to be. But that didn't ease or heal the hurt.

"You're telling me all this so I'll feel sorry for you and marry you," Anna said softly, surprising him.

Because if Anna wasn't evidence of that *life is unpredictable* lesson, he didn't know what was. She never did or said quite what he expected.

And he didn't hate it when it was her.

In this moment, specifically, because she was right on the money. And there was no point lying about it. "Mostly."

He pulled into the entrance of the Hudson Ranch. All centuries of roots and vast landscapes she belonged to. When he belonged to nothing and no one.

Except the child she carried.

"I can't say it's going to work, but I respect it as a solid tactic."

"Gee, thanks."

She flashed him a smile, and nothing about this woman made sense because in the midst of too many old memories, new problems and pressing danger, he smiled back.

ANNA STEPPED INTO the living room and immediately recoiled at the tension in the room. It was old, ugly and familiar. Even Pita stopped like he could feel it, too.

It was like stepping back in time. Cops in the house. Questions without answers. Worry and fear and no answers.

Except she wasn't a child any longer. In fact, was carrying what would become *her* child. And she knew this was not a future she wanted for her kid. Tension and questions that never got answered.

She looked at the source of it all—Thomas Hart—not

that it was his fault. But he'd obviously been the question asker who had Cash looking furious and Izzy burrowed into his side with two of her puppies on her lap.

Anna had stopped at the threshold because of that wall of tension, but Izzy caught sight of her and jumped up and ran over to her. Anna was surprised by the exuberant greeting. No matter how much Anna enjoyed Izzy and vice versa, they saw each other too much for excited greetings.

"Terrorizing my family, Hart?" Anna said, smoothing a hand over Izzy's braid. It wasn't fair to lay any blame on his shoulders.

But she didn't really care about fair right now.

Hart shared an unreadable look with Hawk, then met Anna's accusatory gaze.

"I'm doing my job and investigating the attempted murder case. Part of that investigation requires me to ask a few questions of the people who know you well, who might be able to give us some leads on someone who might have wanted to kill you."

It was all calm, almost even pleasantly stated. But Anna knew too many cops. How they thought. What they meant. She'd give Hart credit for being able to put a nice little mask on all that.

But *wanted to kill you* was meant to put her in her place.

"Ms. Hudson, I was hoping to question each of your family members alone. It's best if they're not influenced by worrying over your feelings. You're an investigator. You understand."

She hated that he was using that tactic, but she also knew she'd do the same in his shoes. "Yeah, I understand."

"Steele, why don't you—"

"I'm going to be in the room. It's my investigation, too."

Hart's mouth firmed, but he didn't mount an argument.

Which, of course, left room for Cash to stand and mount one. "Izzy's done. You want to go another few rounds with me? Fine. But my daughter is leaving with Anna."

"Mr. Hudson, this isn't an interrogation," Hart said gently. "We're simply trying to—"

"I know what you're trying to do. She's *eleven*. She's done." Cash gave Anna a nod, and though Anna wanted to argue at being ordered around, she also wanted to get Izzy out of this ugly situation Anna had been in more times than she could count.

Anna turned, a hand on Izzy's shoulder, but Izzy hesitated.

"What about my mom?" she whispered up at Anna. But it clearly wasn't enough of a whisper. Anna felt Hawk tense next to her. But Hart didn't hear it, and it didn't appear Cash did either, so Anna just kept moving Izzy toward the kitchen, tugging Pita behind her on his leash.

Leaving the men behind, her heart beating heavy in her chest. She didn't dare look back at Hawk.

She hadn't thought of that little altercation with Chessa around Christmas. It couldn't have anything to do with this, so it just… It hadn't even been a thought.

Hawk would no doubt think she had been purposefully keeping something from him. It shouldn't matter to her if she had or not. Family came first.

Not Hawk Steele.

But she *hadn't* been hiding. She hadn't thought of it as possibly connecting. It couldn't connect.

She tried to tell herself that as she crouched so she could

be eye to eye with Izzy, though it didn't take much crouching these days. The girl was growing like a weed.

"Izzy, that thing with your mom..." Anna didn't know how to explain it. None of this was fair, but she'd been in an unfair situation when she'd been younger than Izzy. She tried to treat Izzy like she would have wanted to be treated then.

"I didn't want to say anything in front of Dad," Izzy said, blue eyes filling with tears. "He gets so upset when I talk about Mom. I know he doesn't want me to see it, but I see it. And I just... The detective asked about people who'd hurt you, and I know Mom hurt you, Aunt Anna. I just..."

"I know." And she hated that Izzy was keeping a secret, but... It would kill Cash. That Chessa had been sneaking around the ranch, trying to find Izzy. That Anna was pretty sure she'd been high on something when she'd almost, *almost* gotten her hands on Izzy. "If I'd thought of..." Anna shook her head. It didn't matter what she'd thought of. "That thing with your mom has nothing to do with this. It was a real smart line of thinking, though. I'm impressed. It didn't even occur to me." Anna tried to smile encouragingly. "But you don't need to worry about that. What we're dealing with isn't about your mom, or her and me fighting."

Which was what adults had said to her for years after her parents had disappeared. *You don't need to worry about that.* Back then, it had made her so mad. Now she understood why the adults in her life had been frustrating. Danger and confusion were no places for a kid.

Before Anna could think of something better to say, Cash stormed out. It was a carefully contained storm, but it was all thunder and lightning nonetheless.

And Anna felt…guilty. Even though this particular situation wasn't her fault. There was that old situation she'd kept from him and…

"Cash—"

"I don't want to hear an apology from you, Anna. This isn't your fault. Someone tried to…" His gaze darted to his daughter. "…hurt you. We need to get to the bottom of it. My frustration over how that cop handled it isn't on you." He moved over to Izzy, ran his hand over her braid. "Or you, sweetheart."

Izzy smiled up at him, but it was wobbly. Anna felt wobbly herself. Because Hawk wasn't going to let this line of questioning go, and it was going to hurt Cash beyond measure.

And it put them no closer to figuring out who wanted her dead.

Chapter Ten

Hawk sat through the rest of the questions with Anna's family. He asked a few of his own. No one said anything of any note. Louisa had noted the tire slashing story from high school Anna had already told him. Mary had mentioned a cold case client who'd asked Anna out and been politely refused a few years back. Palmer had a few names from the rodeo of men Anna had rebuffed, but thought it was a bad thread to tug since none of the men had pressed the issue.

They didn't get a chance to talk with Jack, but Hart said he'd make an appointment at the Sunrise sheriff's office tomorrow morning that Hawk could attend.

Maybe had demanded to attend.

"You're kind of overstepping your bounds, don't you think?" Hart asked, sounding almost casual as he slid his pen and notebook into his pocket.

So Hawk maintained the fake casualness and didn't tense or shoot back the words piling up in his throat. He kept his voice deceptively mild. "My bounds are figuring out who started that fire, same as yours are to figure out who wants her dead."

"Yeah," Hart agreed. It seemed like he was going to voice a "but" but he never did. "I'll see you in the morning."

"Yeah." Hawk didn't offer to walk Hart out. He didn't offer a goodbye. He just turned and left the room.

He needed to find Anna. Because Izzy had said something to her, and Hawk needed to find out what. Needed to understand what secret she was keeping from him.

He couldn't delve into why he was keeping that little piece of information from Hart. It was silly and probably put Anna in extra danger. Hart should share every piece of information there was, just like Hawk. Two sets of eyes, two investigators, were better than one.

But no amount of rational thinking changed Hawk's course of action, because he knew Anna would be hurt by him telling Hart and he just…couldn't.

Anna wasn't in the kitchen with Mary and Izzy. She wasn't in her room, which was empty. It still wasn't quite dinnertime yet, so the Hudson clan was scattered hither and yon doing whatever a cold case investigative business did.

He looked through the whole house and didn't find her. He stepped outside. It was too damn cold for her to be gallivanting out around the ranch. And she was nowhere to be seen in the front.

Just about when his nerves were pulling tight enough to snap, he heard something. More from the back of the house, but still outside. He followed the wraparound porch all the way back to where there was a porch swing.

Anna and Palmer sat on it, chatting and laughing as it swung gently. Anna had a thick coat on—one he was pretty sure was Palmer's—and a blanket tucked around her.

No doubt Palmer was sitting with her because she

shouldn't be alone, and because it was damn cold, but there was also a genuine contentment there. Brother and sister, happily enjoying each other's company.

Because she was always taken care of here—the Hudsons took care of one another. With or without parents. Anna certainly didn't need Hawk's help with anything, and neither would their kid. That was clear.

It was a painful, terrifying thought. One he couldn't sit with because Anna looked over as if sensing him here.

Palmer looked over too, then slid off the swing. "Well. This feels a little too third wheel for me." He walked past Hawk and gave him a little nudge toward Anna.

As if Hawk needed one. He walked over, though he didn't sit. Because Anna's gaze was firmly out on the mountains in the distance. Not him.

Her roots. Her family. This life she had that was perfectly capable—and willing—to do anything for a kid who wasn't even here yet.

"Where's my dog?" he offered, hoping his voice didn't sound as affected as it felt.

"Cash was having a training session with the other puppies, so I figured Pita could use some sibling time. And some work on following orders."

"That he could." Hawk stood there and waited. And waited. Because he could feel the tension coiling into her. Guilt. Finally she visibly swallowed and slowly brought her gaze from the mountains to him.

He'd expected some kind of challenge. A self-righteous determination she was right to keep something from him. Lectures. Maybe he even expected her to use that heat between them to distract him from the topic at hand.

Which might have worked, he hated to admit.

Instead, she looked like she was about to cry. "Hawk, whatever you think you heard, I promise you—it has nothing to do with someone trying to kill me."

He felt twin pangs—anger that she would just make that determination without explaining anything to him, and the desperate need to stop her from looking so heartbreakingly sad.

He decided to hold on to anger, best he could. It felt safer. "Well, how about I be the judge of that, since you didn't want to share it with the police officer investigating the *attempted murder* on you."

"Hawk."

"You said you weren't keeping anything from me."

"And I'm not. This was nothing. It was family stuff. It never *occurred* to me it might connect. I promise." She seemed so desperate for him to believe her. Like it mattered that she kept his trust.

And that it did…mattered to him.

Hell, he was screwed. He took the seat Palmer had vacated, rested his elbows on his knees and looked out at those majestic peaks. He kept his feet firmly planted on the ground, though. No swinging for him. He'd tried to build himself into one of those mountains—strong and immovable. If he looked at her, he was sure he'd crumble.

"This would kill Cash. Just gut him," Anna said quietly. Quiet enough he felt compelled to look and risk that crumble.

"I'm not Cash, Anna. I'm not asking you to tell Cash. I'm asking you to tell *me*. For the investigation. If nothing else, it's another name I can cross off the list."

"Chessa's name wasn't on the list to begin with."

But he knew that name because Hawk had made sure to know *all* the players. "So this is about Cash's ex-wife?"

She blew out a breath and looked away again. "Nothing is about Chessa, because the whole…thing Izzy was talking about happened years ago. It doesn't relate."

"How many years?"

She swallowed, eyes big and swimming with hurt as she expressly did not make eye contact. "Last…year."

Hawk swore and nearly got up off the swing, but Anna grasped his arm.

"She was lurking around the ranch. I happened to be the one who found her. She said she wanted to see Izzy, was trying to get her hands on Izzy. I told her to beat it. She got a little…handsy. But she's just not… It's not like she had a weapon. She was maybe high and tried to punch me. I dodged, gave her a good knock, but—"

"So you got into a physical fight with someone, *less* than a year ago, who was unstable and potentially on drugs, and it didn't occur to you that it might connect?"

She shook her head, and damn it, one of those tears slipped over. "No, it didn't."

The worst part was, he believed her. No matter what kind of fool that made him. "We cannot ignore that kind of possibility. I have to at the very least look into her."

"It doesn't make sense. Why would she want to hurt *me*? She knows any one of us would stop her from getting her hands on Izzy. Cash most of all, so it's not… It wouldn't be personal to me."

"You don't think she'd hurt you to hurt Cash?"

Anna blinked, again as if the thought hadn't occurred

to her. "That… It wouldn't make sense. There are better targets than me. Izzy chief among them."

"You were literally lecturing me a few hours ago on how things didn't make sense and backward things are sometimes just backward."

She sighed, closing her eyes and leaning her head against the swing's back. "Do you have to remember everything?"

"Comes with the territory."

She blew out a breath. "Is there a way to make sure Cash doesn't know Chessa is in the mix?"

"I'll do everything I can."

She turned to him, wrapped her arms around him and squeezed. "Thank you." She pulled back and studied him. "Not sure I would have pegged you for such a good guy, Hawk."

"I think I'll take that as a compliment."

She smiled, her arms still draped over his shoulders. She was so beautiful it made him ache. "This is something, Blondie. I don't know what, but it isn't just because of the kid."

She was quiet for a long moment, studying him with those hazel eyes. He didn't know what she was looking for, what she saw, but she swallowed. "Isn't it?" she asked on a whisper.

"No." No, because it had been like this from the first. And just like the first, he couldn't think from wanting her. So he leaned forward and kissed her. And just like the first time, it was a bolt that made everything else disappear. All that existed in this world was them. The way she tasted like something dark and decadent, but her arms around him felt like sunlight after a long, hard winter.

Someone cleared their throat. Once, maybe twice. It took Hawk a few moments to fully engage with sounds other than the little world of kissing they'd created for themselves.

He managed to move his head away from her and look toward the noise.

Jack Hudson stood there looking like any father of a teenage daughter might in finding said daughter wrapped up in the arms of the town juvenile delinquent.

Too bad they were all adults, and Jack wasn't anyone's father.

"Dinner is ready," he said flatly. "And we have some things to discuss."

"Did you want to grill him on his intentions?" Anna asked, sliding off the swing and throwing the blanket over her shoulder. Hawk followed her over to where Jack stood and figured he might as well start expanding his campaign.

"Please do. I've already told her she should marry me, but she's being stubborn about it."

Jack opened his mouth. Closed it. Then opened and closed it again. All without making a sound.

"Aw, look. You made him speechless," Anna said, grinning as they walked past Jack. "Major points, Hawk."

"Might have to hold you to this point system."

And she laughed. That bawdy, reckless laugh of hers that seemed to crawl inside of him and change everything. And she took his hand, lacing her fingers with his, changing whatever was left.

ANNA FELT ALL warm and fuzzy. She supposed maybe she should feel guilty about that, in the midst of all this ugly stuff, but if there was anything her childhood taught her it was that tragedy and grief went together with joy and love. Good things happened during bad times and vice versa.

As she walked inside, holding hands with Hawk, she put her free hand over her stomach, wondering if the baby growing in there had any idea how much it was loved. Before it was even here. That was a blessing.

Unfortunately, she was definitely not doing a very good job of proving to Hawk she'd make a bad wife, but maybe... Maybe she wouldn't. Maybe...somehow, improbably, they just...worked.

The thought made her nervous, so she pushed it away. Determined to enjoy family dinner, with Hawk by her side.

The warm, fuzzy feeling lasted for all of five minutes. Because that was all it took to have everyone gathered around the table, Pita happily snoozing at Hawk's feet, and Jack taking the lead. Not talking about ranch things or HSS things or even Sunrise things.

"With the lack of movement in the case, Hart wanted the files for all the cold cases Anna's worked on with HSS," Jack said, passing the bowl of rolls over to Grant. "I can't do that, obviously. Much like Fool's Gold, it skirts the boundaries of privacy. However, that's not any reason to let someone keep coming after Anna."

Anna looked down at the food on her plate. She tried to pretend this was any joint HSS case, but how could she just ignore the fact she was at the center of all of it? And her family and Hawk and Hart and probably a million other people were poking through her life, determining who might hate her enough to kill.

It was exhausting.

"Mary's already started organizing the files and will finish after dinner. We'll split them up, go over anything Anna even remotely touched. We'll look through and consider any angry parties. None stick out to me from memory, so this might be a waste of time, but—"

"Nothing is a waste of time in an investigation," Hawk finished for him.

Jack nodded, a change from the disapproval—and then shock—outside.

"Obviously, we're looking for injured parties," Jack continued. "People who feel they might have been wronged, which of course doesn't mean anyone actually *was*." He looked pointedly in her direction, like she needed to hear it.

But she wasn't Mary. She wasn't a blame-yourself-for-the-ridiculousness-of-others type of girl.

"Hawk, do you have anything to add?" Jack asked.

And it was a strange tableau. Loaded plates. Her whole family. Every single head swiveling to look down at Hawk. Except Anna herself.

She could only stare at her brother. Who asked for opinions and input about once an epoch. Now he was asking... Hawk?

"The thing that connects these incidents is Anna and fire. *Anything* that might hint at arson should also be some kind of clue. So even if there isn't a clear case of potential blame, even a hint of fire gets added to the list."

There was a murmur of assent and agreement, a few more comments as they ate. Then slowly the chatter moved toward less serious things. The upcoming springtime calving and Izzy's teacher's latest antics in trying to control the class and even a progress report on Pita's training. It was all very normal and should have lifted her spirits.

But pregnancy exhaustion plagued Anna, as did the idea that they could sit around and act like everything was normal, but it *wasn't*. Because everyone was going to be poring over old files, determining who she might have made angry enough to want her dead.

After dinner, Anna made the excuse that she was tired and left them to it. She didn't want to look at old files. She didn't want to be in the room where all her mistakes were paraded out like a list of facts suitable for an investigation.

She just went up to her room and crawled into bed and tried to fall asleep. But all she did was stare at the wall, feeling weirdly weepy and refusing to cry, while she thought of everyone she'd been not so nice to in her whole damn life.

And now her family was down there, discussing, dissecting and sharing it with Hawk. And it just felt *gross*.

When the door creaked open, she stiffened and closed her eyes without fully thinking the move through. She just…didn't want to face him. Or anyone. She wanted to… Well, if she was being honest with herself, she wanted to wallow in how much she sucked.

Hawk was very careful and quiet. She heard the faint rustle of clothes being changed, but almost nothing else. The bed dipped as he slid into it and she kept her eyes carefully closed, hoping he'd just…go to bed. She felt too soft and vulnerable to talk to anyone, let alone him.

But his arms came around her, and he pulled her close. "All right, Blondie, what's bothering you?"

She didn't know why she liked that nickname. She was sure she should be offended that it relegated her to a body part, but it had become…theirs somehow. And the way he said it, all warm or disapproving or in that sexy growl, it…

meant something. He wasn't a nickname type guy. It made her feel special.

"Oh, Hawk, what could possibly be bothering me?"

He chuckled, resting his chin on her shoulder. She'd noticed he'd been very careful about touching her stomach. He almost never did it, which was a little strange considering he was ready to get married over what was growing there.

But carefully, gingerly, his hands moved over her abdomen and linked there, over the baby they'd created that she was working to grow.

She wanted to cry at that alone.

"Something about dinner, specifically, is bothering you," he said into her ear.

There was something…special about him noticing that. Sure, he was an investigator and maybe it was just an offshoot of that, but for all he didn't know about her, he seemed to…understand pieces of her. She'd had a few serious boyfriends. Well, maybe *serious* wasn't the right word. *Long-term* seemed better suited.

None of them had ever understood her changes in mood. Or tried to. She really couldn't fathom just agreeing to marry Hawk when she only knew bits and pieces about him. Louisa wasn't rushing to marry Palmer when she'd known him practically her whole life.

But they also weren't having a baby, she supposed.

And thinking about all that was better than thinking about what was really bothering her. She knew she could distract Hawk with sex, but she also knew he'd just bring it up again later. It would only be a temporary reprieve.

"Anna," he said, bringing her back to the present.

"I don't know how to explain it, exactly. It's just this

weird… I don't like everyone poking around in everything I've ever done. I get why we have to do it, and when it was my work with Quinn, or even my old boyfriends…that didn't get under my skin. But this is… This is my family trying to determine all the ways someone I've come into contact with might hate me. And it isn't just my life out there. It's about how I've handled cases with our family business." She stumbled over the next words, even though once upon a time she would have announced them loudly, brashly, proudly. She didn't feel very proud right now. "I… I've never been a very nice person."

"Join the club, Anna."

She turned in the circle of his arms, so she could look at him. Or impress upon him that… "But you're a good guy," she said, touching his cheek with her palm.

"And you're a good…gal?"

She snorted.

"Neither of us are perfect, but I think we both have a pretty good sense of right and wrong and wanting to do the right thing. It's why we do the jobs we do." He tucked a strand of hair behind her ear in a soft, loving gesture. "And regardless, even if you were the absolute worst person in the world, I'm pretty sure that family of yours would love you anyway."

Love. She looked at his face, shadowed in the dark, and wondered why that word should stick out. When of course her family loved her. She'd always, *always* been surrounded by love.

He hadn't.

She found herself wanting to be the person who gave

him that. What her family had given her. A soft place to land. Joy. Teamwork.

And yet… She didn't know how to just…accept that. Jump into this whole unknown existence. Particularly when someone was trying to kill her in this one. "You guys didn't find anything, did you?"

"Not tonight, but there are still cases to get through."

He kept holding her there, gently. Because he wanted to protect her from all this ugliness, but she could read him a little too well. The way he tried to shield her. It just wasn't all that different from the ways her family had tried to shield her most of her childhood.

And it *was* born out of care, so she didn't find herself getting angry. Just resigned. She rested her forehead between his shoulder and his jaw. "You think there's going to be another fire, don't you?"

He sighed, the breath ruffling her hair. "It seems unlikely they'd stop."

Motel, her truck, her work. She knew what those kinds of patterns meant. "I don't want it to be here."

"I know."

"You think it will be."

He was quiet for a long time, but he didn't lie to her. He held her tighter. "Yeah, I do."

"So do I."

He tucked her closer into his body, a more comfortable position for sleep. "We've got a lot of security. All we can do tonight is get some rest, so we're ready to face whatever tomorrow brings. We're going to get to the bottom of this. I won't rest until we do."

She knew that was a promise he intended to keep, but

she knew that sometimes…there was no getting to the bottom of it. Sometimes promises were made and not kept.

But she didn't have the heart to tell him that.

Chapter Eleven

Hawk woke up in the dark to the bed shaking and the sound of muffled sobs filling up the room.

Did she do this every night? It damn near tore him in half. "Anna." He gave her a gentle little shake. But she just kept crying. Eyes closed, fast asleep.

It absolutely broke his heart. So he kept giving her gentle little nudges and desperately trying to get through to her. "Anna. Anna. Come on, Blondie. Wake up."

She blinked her eyes open. The dark clearly confused her, but when she turned her head to look at him in the shadows, she seemed to understand.

She lifted her hands to her face and touched the tears there. "Oh."

Just *oh*. Like this was commonplace for her and...well, clearly it was. He didn't think it was just a pregnancy thing, as she'd said before, because she hadn't been pregnant long enough to make *sobbing* in your sleep commonplace.

"Anna."

She shook her head. "It's nothing. Not really. Just happens sometimes."

"Define *sometimes*."

She sighed, exhausted, and he wanted to let her go back to sleep, but…this was like some terrifying unknown he couldn't fix for her. Which felt a little too on the nose considering he also couldn't seem to fix the whole someone-wanting-to-kill-her thing, even when it was his job.

"I'm not sure what causes it. I never remember if it's a dream or… I just wake up and my face is wet and I'm crying. It started after my parents disappeared. I thought I'd grown out of it."

He knew all too well what it felt like to be a child and powerless without your parents. Maybe she'd had a lot more family than he had, but he didn't think it changed it. Sometimes, you just wanted your mother.

And sometimes, she just couldn't be there.

"When did you realize you hadn't?" he asked gently, pulling her close and stroking her hair.

"You said I'd done it the other night."

Stress, clearly. Didn't take a psychologist to figure that out. But it killed him he couldn't take away that anxiety for her.

A knock sounded on the door, and they both swung toward the noise, fighting stances at the ready. Even though a threat wouldn't knock.

"Stay right there," he muttered, sliding out of bed. He opened the door to the hallway light on and Palmer looking grim.

"We've got a situation."

"What kind of situation?" Anna demanded from where she was still sitting in bed.

"You stay put," Palmer said.

"I will not—"

"I don't want her alone," Hawk interrupted, hoping to avoid sibling arguments until he knew what this was. He didn't think it was that fire he was afraid of or there'd be more urgency. "Is Mary up?"

Palmer nodded. "Yeah. I'll walk with Anna down the hall, fill Mary in. Jack is downstairs. He can get you up to speed."

"How about *you* fill *me* in?" Anna demanded of Palmer, coming to stand next to Hawk. Her hair was disheveled, but she'd at least wiped up all trace of tears. Though Palmer did stare at her face for a shade too long.

Hawk pressed a kiss to her temple. "We'll tell you everything, I promise. But right now, you're the target. You stay safe." He placed his hand over her stomach, something he'd been avoiding doing because… Well, for a lot of reasons. Mostly that the idea of a kid jangled up inside of him in a million different knots. He could know he had a responsibility to be a father, know how he wanted that to look.

It didn't mean he knew how to *deal*.

"Your job is to keep you both safe," Hawk said, trying to sound firm instead of strangled.

And he knew he got her there because her expression changed. She nodded and walked with Palmer down the hall while Hawk took the stairs and found Jack.

Jack gestured him into the security room. "Palmer talked to Landon Thompson, the guy who set up Quinn Peterson's security. The computer jargon is over my head, but Palmer thinks there might have been a security breach tonight based on what Landon told him. Know anything about this stuff?"

Hawk surveyed the computers with some irritation. "Not as much as I'd need to."

"Luckily Palmer does," Jack said, and Hawk wished he could find some comfort in that, but he wanted to know what to look for. How to fix this. But all he saw was a maze of monitors and screens and cords.

He did better with facts and names and evidence. The wreckage of fire. Or had, until this impossible case.

"If you married her—" Jack began.

But Hawk was in no mood. "That'd be our business."

"Sure," Jack agreed, far too easily. "Doesn't change the fact that if you hurt her, I'd be forced to kill you and make sure you were a cold case that never got investigated. Married or no."

"Color me unsurprised." Hawk moved his gaze from the monitors to Jack. "Or undeterred."

Jack gave him a nod, like he had tonight at the dinner table. Hawk was hesitant to call it approval, but it wasn't *disapproval.*

"Good."

Hawk found himself oddly…moved by that. He'd long ago learned to live without the approval of anyone. He did what he did for himself, and for the memory of his mother. Nothing and no one else.

But suddenly earning Jack's approval felt important. It would matter to Anna—no matter how much she might try to say it didn't. So it mattered to him.

"Are we threatening him?" Palmer asked, striding into the small room—a room definitely too small for three large men, but they huddled in. Because they had to figure out how to analyze this threat.

"Yeah," Jack replied casually.

"Death or torture?"

"I figured I'd handle death."

"Cool. I'll take torture." Palmer grinned at Hawk. "I'm great at torture."

Hawk understood that it was both a joke and somewhat serious all at the same time. A warning. The Hudsons were a unit, and he was interfering in that unit. But the smile, the teamwork, well, it was a tentative truce and acceptance that they'd work together to keep Anna safe.

And if Hawk always did, they wouldn't have any problems.

"But for now…" Palmer pointed at the computers. "There was a glitch. Just like Landon explained happened in the Fool's Gold security. But I can't get to the source of it or undo it. It's complicated and high-tech. Landon still hadn't gotten to the bottom of it, and I got the feeling he had more skills than I did. The problem is, while we're trying to figure that out, we can't trust what we see up here," he said, pointing to the monitors.

Hawk definitely didn't like the idea they couldn't trust the surveillance. That was the whole point of staying here.

"I have a feeling the next step is another fire," Hawk said, taking in what part of the ranch each monitor showed. "Here. It started with the murder attempt, then it was her truck, then it was her place of work. Home is the next reasonable target. So, if something went wrong with the surveillance equipment tonight specifically, I think we need to look out for the chance of fire tonight. Specifically."

He glanced at the two men, who looked grim and yet unsurprised.

"We'll need to wake up Cash, get Izzy over here. Waking everyone up would be best," Jack said. "All hands on deck."

"It's a big spread. Lots of places to start fires, but it won't be random," Hawk said. The problem was, it all meant something to Anna, it all threatened her or someone she loved, so there were a lot of options. "It'll be somewhere that might hurt. So, yeah. All hands on deck."

And as if he'd spoken it into the ether, a dog began to bark. Pita. Somewhere outside, another one began to howl.

None of the men said anything. They just started running.

ANNA PACED MARY'S ROOM. She couldn't settle because Palmer's explanation of the problem had made her nerves hum. She also couldn't settle because Mary's room was like a shrine to orderliness and cleanliness—and freakishly white. Anna was always afraid she'd mess something up.

And, okay, sometimes she messed something up on purpose. But not tonight. Tonight...

"Anna, you're making me dizzy," Mary said in exasperation. She was sitting at her prim little *white* desk, carefully going through case files.

"I just don't know why I couldn't go down and look at the computers like Palmer."

"Well, you could," Mary said calmly, placing one file neatly on the other, then looking up at Anna. "As I have never once in your entire life known you to follow an order."

Anna scowled, because it was true. Because she *should* just march down there and demand to be involved.

But didn't, because Hawk had put his hand on her stomach, where some baby the size of a peach grew, completely unaware of everything going on around them.

Mary turned in her chair and studied Anna. "I've never seen you like this."

"Well, I've never been pregnant before," Anna grumbled, even knowing that wasn't what Mary meant. Even knowing the way she was acting had to do with Hawk as much as pregnancy.

"So, that's the only explanation for how you are around Hawk?" Mary said, in that careful way that strangers thought meant she was agreeing with them.

She never was.

"And how am I around Hawk?"

Mary took a minute to consider. Then smiled. "Thunderstruck."

Anna recoiled. "I do *not* think so."

"If it makes you feel better, he's equally thunderstruck by you." She turned back to her desk like this was all just normal conversation. And obvious. When surely...

Well, maybe he was a *little* something-struck by her. It shouldn't—she really didn't want it to—but it did make her feel better. The idea of making Hawk Steele thunderstruck, well, it was a powerful feeling and—

She heard the faint yip of a dog. Pita, no doubt. She should go downstairs and—

Then, outside and farther away, the howling of another dog. One of the older dogs that would be over by Cash's cabin. Anna looked over at Mary, who was already on her feet.

"You should stay here," Mary said. "I'll go see—"

Anna crossed and grabbed her sister's arm. "We're going

together. No one goes it alone, right? Did Louisa stay? We should grab her too, if Palmer's downstairs already."

Mary hesitated, but only for a moment before she nodded. "All right. Let's get her."

Louisa was already out in the hall when they stepped out. So were Grant and Dahlia. Grant was carrying two guns.

"We don't know what's going on just yet, but the dogs sense something and the security has been tampered with." He handed one gun to Louisa. "You're coming with me." He looked over at Anna. "You three are staying put."

Anna opened her mouth to argue, rote habit, but Grant shook his head. Still, he handed her the other gun in his hand.

"I know you don't like holding back, but Dahlia hates guns almost as much as Mary does. I know you can handle yourself with one should the need arise, so I'd appreciate it if you stayed back."

Mary and Dahlia might hate guns, but they both knew how to shoot. She scowled at her brother. "You're full of it, Grant Hudson."

His mouth *almost* curved ruefully. "Not completely. It's a solid plan even if you don't like it. We'll send Izzy up when we can. It's possible this is all a…false alarm."

"Don't placate us, Grant," Dahlia said disapprovingly.

He leaned forward and placed a kiss on his girlfriend's cheek. "We'll be back. Keep your phones on you."

Then Grant and Louisa disappeared downstairs, and Anna stood in the hallway with Mary and Dahlia and tried not to feel like some damsel in distress locked in a tower.

"There's plenty we can do," Mary said. "Just because you're used to doing the active work doesn't mean the groundwork isn't just as important. We have case files, and you have some computer expertise."

"Not as much as Palmer."

"Maybe not, but that doesn't mean you couldn't figure it out with time. I'll grab my files, and we'll go down to the surveillance room. It's as safe down there as it is up here."

Anna realized with a little start that she sometimes, inadvertently, underestimated her sister on *this* level. She knew Mary was the heart of how everything ran at both the ranch and HSS. She was the organizer, the analyzer, the details person. And it was easy to forget that because she did it all quietly, in the background. Without ever asking for help, attention or recognition.

Anna nodded, because her sister was right. There was still a lot to be done on this side of things. "Okay, yeah. That's a good plan."

Mary bustled back into her room to collect the files while Anna and Dahlia stood, as if frozen by circumstance.

"It'll be okay," Dahlia offered reassuringly. "Maybe this could even be the end of it," she offered hopefully.

Anna wanted to believe it could be, but it was a big ranch. So many places to hide, so many ways someone could get hurt.

So many ways to disappear.

She swallowed down that ugly thought and forced herself to smile at Dahlia. "Yeah, maybe it'll all be over."

Chapter Twelve

Hawk crept through the dark night, Pita by his side. He'd convinced Jack that a dog was enough of a partner until Cash and one of his dogs could meet up with him once he'd gotten Izzy tucked away in the house.

Which had put him on house duty, while Jack and Grant went to check on the animals together.

So Hawk moved around the house in slowly bigger circles. He listened. He searched for signs of someone. Hawk didn't see or smell signs of any fire, and it ate at him. Because he knew in his bones it was coming...just not exactly where. Or how.

He made another circle around the house. Anna was the target. She'd been the one who'd been hurt and left to die. The following fires being at her work and her truck meant the focus was on her.

But Hawk couldn't ignore the possibility that someone would hurt her family to hurt her. And if Jack or Grant got themselves hurt or worse out there, it would just feel like his fault. Like he'd let her down.

The thought ate him up inside.

He had to stop letting Anna be a distraction. He should

be working night and day on this, not having family dinners and spending the night in her bed actually sleeping and not doing any work. He needed to—

Pita began to growl—something he'd never once heard the puppy do. Hawk crouched, wrapped his arm around the dog. Hawk didn't want him bounding off into the unknown.

He watched the shadows and tried to listen for something. The wind blew softly and cold. There was the odd rustle—but it could have been animal, the line of evergreen trees or even just the wind blowing snow around.

But Pita's growling didn't stop.

Hawk adjusted his grip on his gun. He had a flashlight, but he wasn't going to use it just yet. He also wasn't going to risk his dog.

Pita was vibrating in his arms—Hawk wasn't sure if it was fear or pent-up energy ready to attack. Either way...

"Stay," he said firmly to the dog. If Hawk had brought a leash with him, he would have tied Pita up, but as it was he just had to hope the commands they'd been working on worked. "Stay," he repeated.

Then he moved forward. Into the dark. Toward the sense of noise and shadow. He kept his peripheral vision on the house. Most of the lights were off, but Mary's bedroom was on this side, so a very dim light shone through the curtains there. It gave him enough of a sense that he would be able to see if someone tried to creep toward the house in the otherwise dark yard.

He willed Cash to hurry up because a bad feeling was crawling up his spine. Obviously, things were wrong, but something felt especially off.

Anna telling him sometimes people were backward kept

echoing in his head. Reminding him you couldn't always reason bad choices and soulless people. Patterns didn't always have to make sense to the sane.

He gripped the flashlight and looked back at the dog. Pita was whimpering but staying. "Good dog," Hawk whispered. Cash would take the dog inside once he got here. Get him out of harm's way. So Pita just had to stay put for a few more minutes.

Please only be a few more minutes. The dog was too much of a distraction, a worry.

Hawk crept farther away from the house, trying to put Pita out of his mind. Whoever was after Anna was likely after starting a fire, not hurting a dog.

Hawk stilled and listened, trying to get a sense of what was out here—not worry about Pita and Anna. He'd never felt this torn before. Investigations and danger were easy.

Because he'd had no one and nothing for far too long. Now he had a…family. Weird and complicated and certainly not set in stone, but people and an animal he cared about. Needed to save and protect. Something he hadn't had to worry about since he was fourteen years old.

And look how that turned out.

Hawk shook that thought away. He hadn't been able to save his mother because she'd been *sick*. He'd damn well save Anna from some lunatic who wanted to hurt her. It was his job. Everything he'd built himself into. His very identity. Finding answers and stopping people from doing more harm.

But his heart thundered in his chest, and worry slithered into and scattered his focus. He'd never once had to do his job when he cared this much about the person he was protecting. He'd never dreamed he'd have to.

He heard two things at once—a shuffle, and Pita letting out a pained yelp. Instinct told him to move toward the shuffle sound for his own good, but he couldn't stand the thought of someone hurting Pita, so he turned toward the dog.

Mistake, he realized as pain bloomed out from the base of his skull…and turned his world dark.

"WHAT ABOUT THIS?" Dahlia said, pointing to the file she'd been reading. Anna had dozed off a little, not even getting through one file. She would have thought nerves and worry and frustration would have kept her wired and awake, but apparently not. She could only chalk it up to pregnancy, yet again.

Anna looked down at the keyboard she'd fallen asleep on. She hadn't gotten very far in trying to find the source of the glitch. Some help she was. She swiveled in her chair to try to focus on what Mary and Dahlia had found.

Izzy was curled up in a little nest of blankets in the corner with a puppy, both asleep and snoring lightly. Anna couldn't help but smile at the image they made. And the knowledge she was growing one of those. If everything went the way it should, someday she would have a son or daughter, curled into the corners of the Hudson Ranch… even if danger rained down around them.

She thought of Hawk as a boy, trying to take care of his dying mother. Being left alone. Being told he wasn't wanted by his own father. She wanted this family for him as much as she wanted it for their child.

But now was not the time for these thoughts. Because Hawk was outside, in the dark of night, heading off danger with her brothers and her best friend.

"This HSS client from a few years back," Dahlia was saying to Mary. "He owned a computer company. Wouldn't that mean you know a lot about computers and how to hack into security systems?"

"Maybe," Mary agreed. "This was a client?" Mary asked, frowning as she moved over to Dahlia to look at the file. "Oh, yes. I remember this. A missing wife." She frowned. "But this was when Anna was in the rodeo. I don't think she would have worked any of it."

Both women looked over at her. Dahlia held out the case file for her to read.

Anna studied the information. "No, I didn't work on that case." But there was something familiar about the name of the victim. She tapped the page. "Francine Evans. Why does that sound familiar?" she mused aloud.

"I'm not sure. You might have heard us discuss it. One of the few cases we've ever taken where the missing person was still alive—and had changed her identity on purpose."

"To get away from her husband?" Dahlia asked.

"Sort of. She drained his bank accounts before she took off. He didn't *tell* us that, so it became a whole big complication. When we found her, she acted like she was afraid of her husband. When we told him we'd found her, but refused to tell him any details, he told us about the bank account and was angry we wouldn't help him. Basically, they both did a lot of lying, so in the end, we just pulled out of the whole mess. Told him to have the police handle it."

"So he might be angry with HSS," Dahlia said.

"Yes, but again, Anna wasn't here for that. She didn't work on the case. So why target her?"

"Who was the lead on this case? Cash?" Anna asked, flipping pages. "If I was in the rodeo, Jack was just starting as sheriff, Grant was deployed, Palmer was with me. Cash and you were kind of holding down the fort, though Jack would have helped. And I guess Palmer and I might have stepped in during breaks, but I don't remember this one."

Anna looked back down at the file, and she flipped through it. Cash had indeed been the lead, and there wasn't any piece of this case that was familiar except a vague memory of Cash and Mary relaying the story.

But something about a computer company definitely felt like too much of a coincidence. The husband in this case was Clarence Samuels. He owned CS Computer Systems.

A name that was familiar to Anna for completely different reasons. "The guy I was following for Fool's Gold the day someone first tried to kill me? He was a salesman for CS Computer Systems. The same company this guy owns."

Mary frowned deeply. "Well, that's too close of a coincidence for comfort, isn't it?"

Dahlia nodded.

"But…the salesman. Deputy Hart and Hawk interviewed him. He had an alibi," Mary said. "Airtight. Deputy Hart told me so himself."

Anna nodded, because she'd heard the same from Hawk.

"People lie, though, right?" Dahlia offered.

"That they do," Mary said darkly. "I'm sure Hawk and Deputy Hart will look into it, a possible connection. Dig deeper. This is a good lead. The first good lead we've had." She smiled reassuringly at Anna, but Anna didn't feel reassured, God knew why.

Anna turned back to the computers, determined to figure out the glitch. Determined to *do* something instead of sit here and worry.

But only a few minutes later, they heard the low voices of the men returning. They sounded urgent, and when Jack opened the door and immediately met her gaze, she knew something was…terrible.

"No fire, but we've got a different situation." She swallowed at the bleakness in Jack's dark eyes. "I'm sorry. We can't find Hawk. He's not answering his phone. It looks like…"

"It looks like what?" she said, not sure if it came out as a whisper or a shriek. Because her heart was pounding in her ears.

"There was some blood. Some marks in the snow that made it look like he'd been…" Jack cleared his throat. "Dragged away."

"Then what are you all doing here?" Anna demanded, though she was glad Mary was standing there, holding her up. Because she felt like she might collapse. "We need to find him. We need to—"

"I've called some deputies in. And notified Hart. Palmer is getting a few horses saddled, and Grant and him are going to follow the tracks."

"You will saddle up a horse for me. I don't want to hear

one damn argument," Anna said, forcing herself forward on shaky legs.

But Jack stopped her easily, his hand wrapped around her shoulder gently. "You aren't going, Anna. He wouldn't want you to."

She knew that was true. She *hated* that it was true, and that she really wasn't feeling up to getting on a horse, and probably shouldn't. She hated being held back like this. She needed to...

She looked up at her big brother. She knew he would do anything for her, but he wouldn't let her risk herself under the circumstances. She also knew that because she cared about Hawk, so would Jack.

So she had to trust Jack to take this on, since she couldn't. But that didn't mean she had to just give up and step aside and become the weeping pregnant lady in the corner.

"If I'm not going, *I'm* calling the shots. Palmer stays and helps me with the computer stuff. Maybe we can get something to go off there. Jack, you go with Grant to track Hawk. Your deputies don't need you micromanaging, so Mary will manage them once they get there. Cash can take Louisa and use the dogs to track or whatever he thinks is best. Understood?"

Jack looked at her for a very long time and she was afraid she'd just fall apart, start sobbing and never stop. Imagine every possible terrible outcome of this.

But Jack nodded. "All right, Annie. Understood." Then he cleared his throat. "Just a small...catch to that plan."

"What?"

"Cash is busy right now. He's patching up Pita. The dog's fine, just got a bit of a...gash."

Anna's knees went weak, but Mary and Dahlia held her up until she was steady again. Then she was pushing her way out of the room.

She heard people saying her name, Jack was still holding on to her arm, but she just kept fighting him off. She pushed her way out the back door and saw Cash kneeling next to poor little Pita. He had one of his dog first-aid kits open and was working on Pita while Louisa held a flashlight.

Anna stopped because she didn't want to interrupt what Cash was doing when he looked so intense and Pita was so *still*.

After a few minutes of everyone standing motionless and very quiet, Cash stood. "I stitched him up. He'll be okay." Cash smiled encouragingly up at her. "He will be okay. He just needs some rest."

"Who would hurt a little puppy?" She swallowed, because the answer was terrible no matter what, but whoever it was also had Hawk. A *bleeding* Hawk.

Palmer arrived with the horses, and though they weren't here yet, Anna could hear the sirens of Sunrise PD in the distance. Jack gave out orders—*her* orders, and in a sea of terror and horrible feelings, that was something.

Before Cash and Louisa went to get the search dogs, he reached over to Mary, who was now the one cradling Pita.

"You and Dahlia watch after Izzy?"

"You know we will."

Anna stood in the midst of her family coming together to solve this horrible problem, and she hated that she couldn't wade in there. But Palmer scooped up Pita from Mary, and then took Anna's arm with his free hand.

"Come on. Let's see what we can do with those computers."

And there was nothing else to do but that.

Chapter Thirteen

Hawk came to in a…barn? He opened his eyes and immediately closed them when the world swam. No matter where he was, it sure smelled like horse excrement. And his head ached like…well, like he'd been knocked in the back of the skull with something damn hard.

He worked to even his breathing, to center himself somewhere outside of the radiating pain. He had to stay conscious. He had to get his way out of this. Get back to Anna and make sure Pita was okay.

Had to make sure whoever had hurt Anna and Pita paid. A million times over.

When he opened his eyes for the second time, he was braced for the dizziness. The wave of nausea. The barn was dark, but he could make out shadows. If it was still dark, maybe he hadn't been unconscious for that long. Maybe he was in a barn on the Hudson property.

But when he moved his head a little bit, slowly and carefully to brace himself against the pain and dizziness, he could see the hint of light outside the cracks in the wood around him. Not quite morning, but the hint of new daylight.

Already? That would mean he'd spent far too much time unconscious.

Worse, so much worse than how much time had passed was the realization his hands were tied behind his back and fastened to something. He pulled at the bonds, testing them, but it was plastic or something of the like. Zip ties probably.

It wouldn't make it impossible to get out of here, but it was going to be a process.

"Awake, huh?" He realized now part of the light was the beam of a flashlight around a corner, or something. It bobbed and he realized he was in a kind of stall. So there were walls around him, except for the open door area in front of him.

Hawk squinted in the direction of the voice—female, high-pitched and wholly unbothered at the situation. A bright light flipped on above him and Hawk had to close his eyes against the blast of pain at the shocking change.

When he managed to blink his eyes back open, he assumed the woman standing in front of him was the owner of the voice. He studied her with some confusion. She definitely didn't look strong enough to cart his body around. She was on the shorter side, practically skin and bones with it. She had frizzy auburn hair and wasn't quite dressed for the cold with a long-sleeved T-shirt and some jeans.

But she was also very clearly high, so maybe that explained some things. *Some* things. Not the fact that she looked vaguely familiar. Something about the eyes. Where had he seen those eyes before?

He wanted to demand answers to a hundred questions, but he was with it enough to hold back. To consider. He needed to be smart about this. He wasn't *dead*. So that was something.

If he could get out of these ties, he could easily overpower this woman and escape. She wasn't possibly working alone, but she *was* currently alone. Which meant time was of the essence.

"So, what do you want with me?" he asked, because it was the most direct question that all his other questions stemmed from. If this was about Anna, he wasn't sure how he was being dragged into it. Other than spending some time with her. Or maybe investigating?

The woman looked at her nails as if considering. "Oh, we want lots of things."

We, he noted.

"But we want different things. I'm interested in your bank account." She dropped her hand and studied him. "How much are you willing to pay to get out of this situation?"

"I'm not big on paying off two-bit criminals with drug addictions," he returned, equally as casual as she was being.

Her eyes narrowed, a familiar blue. Why was this woman familiar?

But Hawk figured it was best to keep poking until she exploded. She wasn't strong enough to do any real damage unless she brandished a weapon, and he couldn't see where she'd be hiding one on her.

"I know this isn't really about me," he said.

"If you'd been smart, it *wouldn't* be about you. Never should have gotten involved with Anna Hudson. Or *any* Hudson. A bunch of stuck-up, do-gooder *liars*. It doesn't matter what you do—you're always an outsider there. They never, ever give you a real chance."

Then it dawned on him. He'd seen those eyes in a little girl, who'd sighed dreamily at him over dinner. And he'd not that long ago discussed the possibility of this woman's involvement. "Chessa."

Her eyebrows rose. "How'd you know that?" she asked with more curiosity than malice.

He smiled, because if she was really just interested in money, why not pretend to be friendly? "I know lots of things."

"All right, pretty boy." She flashed a grin. "Don't think you're flirting your way out of this one."

He tried very hard not to pull a face, but it was difficult considering how little *flirting his way out of this one* factored into his plan.

Which was currently rip his bonds off whatever they were tied to and run like hell before whoever Chessa was working for got here.

"So, how much would it take to let me go?" he asked, because that seemed the simplest route to getting what he wanted.

She studied him, frowning. "You just said you don't pay off criminals."

"But you're not a criminal, are you? I checked you out. A few brushes with the law, sure, but you've never done any time for it."

Her chin came up. "Right? Tell that to my uptight ex-husband. I could take care of that brat of ours if I wanted to. But I got to make a living, and don't I deserve to have a little fun after being shackled to that place like some kind of servant?"

Hawk tried to keep his expression bland, but it was hard not to react to the way she spoke of sweet little Izzy. "You're lucky you got out when you did," he managed without sounding angry.

She snorted. "Would be if he'd give me what I was owed. I would have gotten it too if your little girlfriend hadn't gotten in my way. Do you know what kind of money I could get for a cute little girl like...?" She trailed off, blinked, as if realizing she'd said too much. Maybe because Hawk couldn't keep his expression cool or calm.

She was talking about *selling* her child. That wasn't just a bad mother; it was disgusting and inhuman. Hawk didn't speak. He knew it would come out venom. So he breathed, and he tried to dissociate. Tried to approach this like a case.

Not people he'd come to care about.

But it was impossible. He just kept hearing Izzy asking him if he played the drums. Picturing Anna crying in her sleep. Those family dinners that were so overwhelming he wanted to run screaming in the opposite direction...and yet looked forward to. Every night.

"So, what's the plan here?" he asked, working to keep his voice even instead of a vicious growl. "With me?"

Chessa studied him, then shrugged. "I'm not privy to all the plans. Not a criminal, remember? All he cares about is making your baby mama pay."

Over my dead body. "If you get me out of here, we can go straight to the closest ATM. I'll give you everything I've got." He wasn't even lying about it. He didn't care about money. He cared about keeping Anna and Izzy safe.

She scowled, crossed her arms over her chest. "I don't trust you."

"I don't trust you either, but I'll pay."

She considered it. Then without a word she turned on a heel and disappeared behind the corner.

While she was gone, Hawk jerked at the ties around his wrists. He couldn't tell what he was tied to, but he kept pulling in the futile hope that he could break *something*. He didn't even need his hands free. He just needed to be able to run.

Chessa reappeared with a gun in her hand. She didn't point it at him, but he didn't like the idea of her with a gun. She was too unpredictable, and she'd be coming down off that high soon enough.

"I'll take you to the ATM, but any funny business and I shoot you. He finds me, he's going to kill me. So I need the money and time to get the hell out of here. You don't help me get it, you're dead."

"Why don't you tell me who this 'he' is so I can protect you?"

She laughed. "You think I know? All I know is some guy comes up to me at the bar and propositions me. Not in the usual way. Asks if I hate the Hudsons as much as he does. Boy, do I."

She inched closer, the weapon shaking in her hand making Hawk a lot more nervous than he'd like to be. He knew he could take this woman once he was out of the bonds, but the chances of her *accidentally* killing him before he got the opportunity felt a little too probable.

"Who's 'he'?" Hawk asked, watching the gun in her hand even as she pulled out a knife with the other.

"He says to just call him Boss and do what he says. *I* can follow directions and orders, because I'm not holier than thou like all those people you've been hanging around with. You pay me, I'll do whatever."

She crouched next to him, gun pointed right at his chest. She reached around, began to cut his bonds.

"So, he has something against all of them? Or just Anna?" he asked, working hard to stay calm. To not telegraph his intentions, or to worry about the possibility of a bullet going right through his heart.

Chessa shrugged. The plastic snapped and Hawk's hands fell to the ground. She pointed the gun right at his forehead, and hell, he did not like that.

"Get to your feet."

He followed orders. She took a good five steps away, clearly afraid he'd overpower her. And he would, whether she was five steps or five yards. But he wanted a little more information first.

"I'm not sure if he hates all the Hudsons or just knew I did. He's got a bee in his bonnet over Anna, that's for sure."

"Why?"

Chessa rolled her eyes, pocketing the knife. Her hand was shaking harder now, and she was sweating. The gun was still precariously pointed at his face.

She jerked her head toward the corner she'd appeared from. "Walk that way. I'm behind you. One false move, and a bullet goes into your brain. We gotta act fast. Like I said, I'm dead if he finds me before I can run."

Hawk knew he shouldn't ask. It was like tempting fate, but… "Why take the chance?" he asked as he moved forward like she'd told him to.

"His plan is taking too long, and he won't tell me when I'll get my payout. I need money like yesterday."

Translation: she'd run out of ways to get high and cared more about that than anything else.

Hawk would use it. He glanced over his shoulder. She was holding the gun with both hands now.

"I thought this was about revenge on the Hudsons," he said, stepping out of the barn and into the even colder night. There was the hint of daylight on the horizon, but not full morning yet.

"For him, maybe. And sure, I wouldn't have minded seeing Anna taken down a few pegs, but I'd rather take my money and run. They'll have security too tight right now anyway. No chance of getting Izzy. I'll come back for her some other time."

Like hell you will.

"It's too dark to see," he said. Hawk pretended to stumble a little, like he was too dizzy to stay upright. A little to the right, a little to the left.

"Stop that!" she yelled at him.

"I think I'm going to be sick."

"I think I'm going to shoot you and just be done—"

But he was too fast in the dark, too big, and she was too messed up to really have any clue what she was doing. He might have even felt sorry for her, if she hadn't talked about her daughter with such cold, disgusting plans.

He had the gun out of her hands in less than a minute. When she launched herself at him, he easily sidestepped. She tumbled into the snowy ground without any help from him.

He knelt on her back, making quick work of pulling

the knife from her and searching her for any other weapons or anything he could use. He got a flashlight, which would be a help.

But nothing he could use to tie her up with. She was kicking and screaming, but he barely registered any of it, so intent on his plan.

He dragged her back to the barn by the legs, even as she tried to kick them out of his grasp. She wasn't strong enough.

She bucked and tried to roll, but he got her back in the barn. He looked around for something, anything, to hold her, but it was mostly empty. He found a little bit of frayed rope. Not long enough to tie her to anything, but he could maybe tie the door closed.

He let go of her legs, but she just kept thrashing around on the ground. Waste of energy. "I hope your boss is as useless as you are," he said.

She spit at him, but he'd expected that and managed to jump out of the way. None of this would hold her for long, but he'd be long gone by then, and she might be careless, and addled by her drug addiction, but hopefully she knew well enough not to come tearing after him in the cold winter night.

He pulled the barn door closed behind him. He flipped the flashlight on, shoved it in his mouth to hold it as he worked to get the rope through the handle and the small, rusted hook. It was barely long enough to make one little knot, but it might hold for a bit.

She jerked the door, and the rope held. Hawk dropped the flashlight from his mouth to his hand.

"You will *never* get your hands on Izzy," he called

through the door. "I will personally make sure of it for the rest of my damn life."

"They're going to chew you up and spit you out," she screamed, rattling the door. "That's what they do."

He didn't bother to respond. He swung the flashlight around his surroundings.

He had to figure out where the hell he was so he could get back to Anna before the "boss" did. He didn't have a sense of where he was at all. The chance of him picking the wrong direction and getting lost on top of everything else was a little too high.

But Chessa was beating on the door, screaming. He had to put some distance between him and her.

Someone had brought him here—and not just her. So there had to be prints in the snow somewhere. He was no expert at tracking, but it would give him an idea of the right direction. Hopefully.

He walked around the barn, found some tire tracks. Only one set of prints, though. Had she really handled this herself? He shook his head. It didn't matter. It only mattered that he got back to Anna.

He began to follow the tire tracks. Even if it didn't lead him back to the Hudson Ranch, it would lead him to a road, surely.

As long as he didn't freeze to death first, he supposed.

He wasn't sure how long he walked. His head pounded, and he was getting weaker the more he trudged through the hard-packed snow.

The first yip he heard he figured was a coyote or a figment of his imagination. Delirium even. The second yip came with the appearance of a dog.

One of Cash's dogs. Hawk nearly fell to his knees. "Hiya, boy. I don't know your name, but I am sure as hell glad to see you."

A horse appeared through the trees, Louisa the rider. She let out a sharp whistle, then swung off the horse. "Well, you gave us quite a scare," she said. Her voice was easy and calm. She surveyed her surroundings with assessing eyes and didn't let on that she was worried.

"Had me tied up in a barn." He swallowed, afraid he was about to lose his dinner. "Managed to get away. Just one person for now, but there's a boss somewhere."

"You're a resourceful fellow." She came up to him, and even though he was desperately trying to maintain an air of strength, Louisa must have sensed he wasn't up for the fight. She slid her arm around his waist, urging him to lean on her. "Guess you need a ride back, huh?"

Hawk had never felt his knees go weak before, but they just about gave out on him. "Yeah...yeah, I do."

Chapter Fourteen

Anna wanted to take a baseball bat to every last computer and monitor in this worthless security room.

Palmer sighed next to her. "Why don't you take a break, huh? You're running ragged."

"A break? A break? Hawk is out there somewhere and I…" God, when had she become such a crybaby? "He was bleeding." She covered her face in her hands because she just couldn't take this.

What if he died? What if he was already dead? And it would be all because of her. And he wouldn't get to be a father, and he wouldn't get…

"Anna." Palmer squeezed her shoulder, hard enough to get through the haze of terror. "I know how you feel. Better than most."

She knew that was true, even if she wanted to feel like she was the only one in the whole world who understood this horrible, terrible fear.

But Louisa had been taken, too. Not that long ago. Palmer had suffered through this terrible, debilitating fear, and in the end, she'd been okay. Louisa had been okay.

Of course, that had been about Louisa's family, and

though Palmer had been terrified and worried about Louisa, just like Anna had, it wasn't like Louisa had been kidnapped because of *him*. Palmer hadn't felt *guilt* on top of everything else.

It was just taking too long, and so many people she loved were out there in harm's way because...somehow she'd done something so wrong along the way, now everyone was paying for her mistakes.

She sucked in a breath. Okay, she was in a panic spiral. It was dumb to blame herself, she knew, but if she was doing that, she wasn't thinking about Hawk dead, so that was nice.

He couldn't be dead. He couldn't... She pushed away from the computer. She needed to move. This felt all too much like childhood all over again. Being told to wait, to wonder, not to have any say in what went on around her.

All because she was pregnant? All because she was perfectly happy risking her life, but not her baby's. *Hawk's baby.* Their baby. And there was no place to put this fear, this fury. It just churned inside her like acid.

The chime of Palmer's phone made her jump. She whirled to him as he pulled it out, read the text. "They found him," Palmer said, looking up at her and giving her a reassuring smile. "They're bringing him back. No other details. But he's okay and they're bringing him back. So just take a breath, huh?"

She tried, but all the breath had clogged in her lungs. She wanted to feel relief, but there was a frozen band of fear holding her hostage. Until she saw him...

"Come on," Palmer said, taking her arm and pulling her out of the security room and into the dining room. Izzy sat in the corner of the room gently petting Pita, while Mary set up a coffee station.

"Sit down," Mary ordered, and Anna had no doubt she was talking to her, not Palmer. "You should be sleeping."

"How could I possibly sleep?" Anna muttered.

"She'll settle once she sees him," Palmer said reassuringly to Mary.

Mary didn't have anything to say to that as she fussed with an array of sweeteners. Her way of dealing with her nerves. Anna wished she had any kind of constructive way to deal with the feelings battering her.

"How's Pita doing?" Anna asked.

Izzy smiled up at her. "Still groggy but doing much better. Poor guy." She cuddled him to her chest, gently. "How could anyone hurt him, Aunt Anna?"

"I don't know, honey." She was in no space to have positive thoughts about humans as a species when so many seemed bent on hurting good people, innocent animals.

But Hawk was okay. No one would text that to Palmer if it wasn't true. But what if he was seriously hurt? What if—

The door opened. Hawk entered first, but even as she was halfway across the room to him, she could see Louisa was kind of keeping him upright. He was pale—way too pale, but he was on his own two feet. Here. Alive. Pita let out a sharp bark, skittering toward his owner, but Anna got there first. She wrapped her arms around Hawk and cried. She'd be embarrassed about how much and how loudly later. She clung to him like some kind of lunatic, but she didn't care. He was here.

And he held her right back. "I'm all right. I'm all right. Take a breath, Blondie."

But that only made her cry even more. Especially since she could tell he was barely capable of standing, and there was a trail of blood down the back of his jacket. "You need a doctor. You need…"

"We'll get it all taken care of," Louisa said, gently pulling Anna off Hawk. "Jack's grabbing an EMT. Won't be more than a minute or two."

Anna swallowed, trying to get a hold of herself while Palmer and Cash nudged Hawk into a chair. Izzy came over and picked Pita up and deposited the puppy on Hawk's lap.

Hawk smiled at her. "Thanks," he said. "He okay?"

"I stitched him up," Cash said. "Had a little gash, but he'll heal quick. I don't know what kind of sick, twisted person would hurt a puppy."

Anna noted the odd way Hawk looked at Cash, then Izzy, but she didn't know what it meant. Then a parade of people came in. Jack and Grant, followed by a cop and an EMT. The EMT crossed to Hawk, nudging her farther back.

"So what happened?" Jack demanded as the EMT began to check him out. Anna moved to the other side of him so she could hold his hand. She just…had to hold on to him.

"Maybe we could discuss this later," Hawk said through gritted teeth, clearly in pain.

"But—"

Hawk looked at her, those dark blue eyes pleading, when she couldn't have ever imagined Hawk Steele being pleading. "Not here. Not now." He looked to Jack. "Okay?" Then his gaze turned to Izzy, giving the girl an odd look she couldn't read, and suddenly…

She had the horrible suspicion she understood.

"CASH," ANNA MANAGED, though her voice was strangled. "Maybe Izzy should take Pita somewhere with less excitement."

Hawk watched Cash's expression carefully. He didn't think the man knew. *Hoped* he just thought Anna was trying to keep Izzy from getting too involved in a grisly story that didn't involve her.

Izzy crossed over to him and held her hands out for Pita. Hawk wanted to keep the puppy in his lap. Just feel his ribs rise and fall and know that he was okay, but he couldn't say anything he had to say in front of Izzy. Wasn't sure he really wanted to say it in front of Cash either.

Clearly Anna had caught on to his meaning.

He shifted Pita back into Izzy's arms. He managed to smile at the girl, even though the EMT washing out his wound hurt like hell. "Thanks for taking good care of him, Izzy."

She beamed at him, then went with Cash out of the room.

Hawk waited. Let the EMT work. Let silence settle over. He watched Anna, tearstained, watch her brother and niece exit. No doubt making sure they were out of earshot before they discussed anything.

She'd sobbed all over him like he'd come back from the dead. Held on to him so tight he'd nearly passed out from the pain of it. But he hadn't told her she was hurting him because...

She cared about him. A woman like Anna Hudson didn't fall apart over some guy who accidentally knocked her up. Not like that. She was too strong, too bullheaded and determined to appear tough. Crying like that... She cared about him.

Maybe she didn't love him, but it felt like the *possibility* was there. And he... It was just another one of those life lessons. He hadn't wanted love or security—stopped believing in those things after his mother had died.

Then Anna had blown into his life and knocked everything on its axis, and he could only be grateful, because she was everything. And that heart he'd been so sure he'd frozen out throbbed painfully in his chest.

Maybe she didn't love him yet, but she could. Because he sure as hell loved her.

"This might hurt a little," the EMT said.

It did, but so did the dull pain he'd been dealing with since he'd gained consciousness.

"Concussion, no doubt. I'd recommend a trip to the hospital, have some tests run. That's a hell of a bump."

"No," Hawk said.

"Hawk," Anna began, no doubt ready to swoop in and play protector. "You—"

"No. I'm not going to the hospital. I'm fine."

"Don't be stubborn," Anna said, frowning at him. But she never let go of his hand, like she couldn't stand the thought of losing that connection.

God knew he couldn't.

"Rich coming from you, Blondie. Look, when this is all over? I'll see whatever doctors you want, but there is too much danger and too many questions still to answer." He turned to find Jack in the room. "I'll start at the beginning. You want to take notes or do you want to get one of your deputies?"

"I'll take the notes," Jack returned. "I'll record it too,"

he said, pulling his phone out of his uniform pocket. "It'll hold up in court."

Hawk was glad Jack was thinking that far down the line. He couldn't seem to think clearly. Not fully. But he could relate exactly what had happened, and then maybe once his head stopped feeling like it'd been split in two, he'd be able to make sense of it all.

"I wish I had found some answers in all this, but I think I've only found more questions. And more complications. More danger." He blew out a breath. "I was outside, circling the house with Pita like we discussed. Pita growled and I heard something, so I went to investigate, and I told Pita to stay back. Damn dog listened to me, too."

Hawk took a ragged breath because Pita was alive and okay. Anna was here. As long as they were safe, little else mattered. "I heard two different sounds—one in the trees, one closer to Pita. The dog yelped and I knew it was someone hurting Pita. I turned toward the dog, and that was my mistake, what they were likely going for, because something hit me from behind. Hard. When I came to, I was in a barn. How did you guys find me?"

"Followed your…" Louisa trailed off and looked at Anna as if she was reconsidering her words. "Tracks," she finished.

He figured she'd meant to say "blood" but hadn't wanted Anna to get more upset. Hawk nodded, pausing to take a sip of water because he was afraid if he didn't he'd lose the battle with nausea.

"First it was footprints. Then it was tire tracks," Louisa added, for the sake of Jack's recording. "We took the horses to follow those tracks. We found him just west of the property."

"My deputies are treating the barn like a crime scene. It isn't our property, but it is close," Jack said. "What happened in the barn?"

"When I woke up, there was a woman. Short, skinny. No way she acted alone."

He looked away from Jack and toward Anna. She was struggling with this, clearly, but when she spoke it was clear.

"It was Chessa," Anna said flatly.

All the Hudsons in the room had a different negative reaction to that, but Hawk could only watch Anna. He hated that this hurt her even deeper than it already had.

"She's working for someone," Hawk continued to explain. "I'm not sure she cared so much about what they were doing. She just wanted a payout. Clearly she's got a drug problem. I offered her money, and she untied me. Which was how I got away." He turned to look at Jack again. "I gave one of your deputies her description. She's back in that barn."

Jack nodded. "They've got her. She's in the process of being arrested. They'll take her down to the station and we'll question her there."

Hawk moved to stand, had to fight off the dizziness. "I want to be a part of—"

Palmer's hand curled on his shoulder, gently pushed him back down into a sitting position.

"Sorry, pal. You're on bed rest until further notice."

"You can't just—"

"We can. We will. We do," Anna said. "In fact, you

should be in bed right now. You've explained what happened. Now you'll rest."

"Anna, you aren't in charge of me."

"Maybe not, but consider yourself outnumbered." She pointed at Jack, Mary, Palmer and Louisa. "No one gives one little care who you think is in charge. You're not going anywhere except bed. If we all have to carry you up to bed and lock you in."

"Doesn't sound very recuperative," Hawk muttered. But he also didn't know how to argue with the wall of Hudson disapproval. Or how to deal with the strange wave of warmth that swept through him, leaving him feeling even weaker than he had.

"Hart is meeting me down at the station," Jack said. "We'll fill you in on the details for your investigation once you've rested a bit. Hart can handle communicating your injuries with your boss at the county."

"We've got to figure out who she's working for, and fast. Chessa was very clear that her boss is a he, and that his only goal was to hurt Anna *and* any of you. We *have* to find him."

"We will."

"Come on," Palmer said, and suddenly he was being lifted on one side by Palmer, Anna sliding onto the other side.

"I can walk," Hawk muttered.

But no one listened. Mary said she'd bring up some water and cold compresses. Palmer and Anna just kept moving him out of the kitchen and up the stairs.

No one had taken care of him for a very, very long time, and suddenly he had this…pseudo family.

He didn't know what to do with it, except let himself be led around the Hudson house like he had no will of his own.

"He's filthy. He needs a bath," Anna said once they reached the top of the stairs.

"Count me out on that one."

Anna rolled her eyes. "Go grab him some clothes. He's got everything in that ugly duffel bag in my room."

She led Hawk into the bathroom and drew him a bath—which was possibly the weirdest damn moment of his life. But the warm water felt nice, and she kept the lights off so the room was dark.

"No falling asleep," she said. Then she took a washcloth and some soap and started cleaning him up.

"This is weird," he muttered. Because she was giving him a bath, and not in a sexy way he might have preferred if his head didn't currently feel like it had been used as a piñata.

"Well, don't go getting bashed in the head and things won't be weird."

"Hey, you got bashed in the head first. I don't remember giving *you* a bath."

"I'm glad it's a contest," she replied, all prim disgust. "And since it is, I win, because I ended up in the hospital. Where *you* should be."

He heard the worry in her tone, wished he could find a way around it. "I really am fine."

She scoffed. "Hardly."

Hawk closed his eyes, but he couldn't stop himself from making sure... "Pita really okay?"

"Cash isn't a practicing vet, but he has all the training. If he says Pita will be fine, Pita will be fine. If he was worried, he would have taken him to the animal hospital in Hardy."

He sighed, the mention of Cash twisting his gut into knots all over again. "I'm sorry."

"For what?"

"That it was Chessa. They'll have to know. She's..." Hawk swallowed. "She said some awful things, Anna. She doesn't care about Izzy at all." Worse even than his own father's not caring. The way she'd talked about that innocent little girl, her *own* innocent little girl.

"We know it. But they've got Chessa locked up for the time being. So Izzy is safe, and we'll always keep her safe. We always have. It's what we do."

He opened his eyes and looked at her in the dim room as she carefully washed him without getting close to the stitches in the back of his head. "You've got a hell of a family, Blondie."

She lifted her gaze and held his for a long silent moment before she eventually spoke. "I know it. And now you've got them, too."

Chapter Fifteen

She got him dried off and dressed. He didn't even make a joke about being naked, which had her nerves humming. Was he really okay? Should she *make* him go to the hospital?

But she helped him into her bed and arranged everything. She kept the room dark. Rest was the only thing for a concussion. So she crawled into bed with him, even as the sun was starting to shine into her window.

"Tell me if I'm hurting you," she said, resting her head on his shoulder. His arm came around and pulled her closer.

"You?" he said, pressing a kiss to her forehead. "Never."

She wasn't sure how long they lay there. She hoped he was sleeping, but she didn't think he was. There was still a tenseness about him, even if his breathing was even.

Anna knew no matter how tired she was, she wouldn't sleep until he did. Maybe even then she wouldn't, because she wanted to know what Chessa was saying down at the station. She wanted to know if anyone had told Cash yet.

She wanted a million things, but at the end of the day, she wouldn't leave Hawk. He needed rest, and she had to know he was getting it.

"You know, I realized something downstairs," he said, an oddly thoughtful tone to his voice.

She expected him to deliver a joke, or ask about Pita, or something rather bland. Maybe something vague about the investigation. A possible lead.

"I love you."

So instead, she was rendered absolutely speechless. She'd just started to come around to *care* and he was upgrading things to *love*.

"That's a first for me," he continued, just lying there, saying these things. Like it was normal. Like she'd know what to do with it. "Just FYI. Can't promise I'm any good at it."

That cut through a little of her panic. Her heart ached, for a million different reasons even she couldn't untangle. She pressed her palm to his stubbled cheek. "You're very good at it," she said through the lump in her throat. "Hawk, I…" But she didn't know how to *say* things like that. She didn't know how to circumvent the panic coursing through her.

Love. *Love.* She knew all about love. What little she could remember about her parents was love, and her siblings had always been the core of everything loving and good. But how did you *choose* that horrible worry and ache that went along with loving someone and losing someone? How did anyone stand it?

Or did you even have a choice?

"Hawk," she repeated, because she knew she had to say something. Explain in some way that wasn't actually…saying those three substantial and terrifying words.

Even if they were true.

"Don't insult me, Anna. And don't lie to spare my feelings. It isn't you."

She sat up and stared down at him. He was scowling, but his eyes were closed. *Insult* him? *Lie* to him? Of all the…

"You have no idea what I'm trying to say."

"I know what you're trying *not* to say," he returned in that obnoxious law enforcement voice like he was so much smarter than her. Detached and in control of everything.

When no one was in control. Life was a series of… dangerous events and horrible people and fear and worry and…and… He was lying there *concussed*, acting like he had it all figured out.

"BS! You don't know…" She had to get out of bed because she wanted to explode, and there was no staving it off, but she wasn't going to hurt him while she did it. "*You* don't know how to love someone? I have been fighting the world since I was eight years old. And I've had this very enviable cushion in my family, but everything I've done is because losing hurts so much and I want to be the one to control the hurt. I have *never* been so damn afraid as I was tonight. All I could think was you'd be dead, and I wouldn't even have a chance to marry you."

He opened one eye. "So you're going to marry me?"

She stared at him for a full shocked minute. The nerve. "You're *impossible*."

"Yeah, but so are you. Maybe we were made for each other."

She didn't know how he did it, but the anger just leaked out of her. Maybe it was the fact that he looked terrible, or that he was in her bed, or that…he'd said he loved her and then listened to her whole explosion and hadn't exploded himself.

Maybe they *were* made for each other. She wasn't sure she was ready to believe that for certain, but she liked the idea of it, anyway.

She sat back on the bed. She didn't cuddle up to him, but knelt next to him, looking down at him until he opened both eyes.

"I love you," she said, and she'd always considered herself brave, but she was sure uttering those three things was the bravest thing she'd ever done. "But we have a lot to talk about first, before we agree to any...marrying."

He closed his eyes again, on a careless shrug. "Well, that's progress, anyway."

He really was impossible.

"Lie down, Anna," he murmured. "Let's get some sleep."

She didn't appreciate being ordered around, but she saw a flash of how terrible he'd looked when he'd walked in that door. So she lay down. Curled up next to him.

His arms came around her. "Chessa was very clear. Whoever this man is, he wants to hurt you. You have to take that seriously."

She rested her palm on her stomach. "I do." Then she took his hand and laced it with hers and placed their entwined hands on her stomach.

And when he finally fell asleep, so did she.

HAWK WOKE UP a while later with a thundering headache that got worse as he opened his eyes and found the room flooded with light. Anna was no longer beside him, but Pita was curled up where Anna should be.

It eased his frustration a little. As if the puppy sensed him being awake, he wriggled closer and closer until he was curled up in the crook of Hawk's shoulder.

"You're a good dog," he murmured. "But you're never coming along on another investigation, I hope you know. Not until you're bigger and meaner, anyway." He couldn't let himself think about it—that little yelp of pain. How much worse everything could have been.

The bedroom door eased open and Anna stepped in, carrying a tray. "Oh, good. You're awake. Here's breakfast."

He sat up in bed, trying not to wince against the pain. He tried even harder to sound his authoritative self. "I need an update on what's going on with the investigation."

"And I need a mansion in Hawaii to winter in. Doesn't mean I'm getting it."

He scowled at her. "I am the arson investigator on this case, and I'm not going to be shoved out just because of a little head injury."

"Little?" she snorted, shaking her head. "Yours was worse than mine and *I* went to the hospital."

"I'm doing fine, as I'm not pregnant and didn't inhale a roomful of smoke."

She studied him with pursed lips. "You're doing better, but hardly fine." She put the tray on the bed next to him. "You need to eat, hydrate and keep resting."

There was no point arguing with her, or maybe arguing with her just hurt his head. Besides, sometimes it was better not to argue—and just do what needed doing. She couldn't babysit him all day. He'd find a way to get the information he wanted.

But maybe it wouldn't hurt to eat a little first. He started with the toast as Pita tried to climb up on the tray. Anna plucked him off the bed and cradled him in her arms. "You have to eat yours on the floor." She put him down on the ground, then took the bowl off the tray he realized was wet dog food and put it in front of Pita. Then she carefully settled herself on the bed without dislodging the tray.

He ate a little, drank some juice and formulated his plan. Even if he got a little out of her, she wouldn't tell him everything. But a little would give him something to go off of. "The way I see it, you have two choices. Give me an update, or I get one myself in whatever ways I feel necessary."

She laughed and gently ruffled his hair. Like he was a child. He scowled even harder at her.

"I think you underestimate the Hudson machine. You're our prisoner until you're better. Everyone is going to make sure you rest, so whatever you *feel* necessary ain't happening, bud."

"I think you underestimate me."

Anna considered, or maybe she pretended to consider. "You see that puppy right there? The one you didn't want. The one Mary steamrolled you into?"

He didn't bother to respond to that. So maybe he *had* been steamrolled into adopting a dog. And a few other things, but...

"There won't be any you getting your way until you get the all clear from the doctor."

Hawk considered this with the sinking feeling that... she was probably right. There were too many of them. He was outnumbered.

"It's called being taken care of, Hawk. And if you're sticking around, you're going to have to get used to it."

"From your whole family?"

"Yup. We come as a unit. If that scares you off, then that's on you."

"It doesn't scare me off," he muttered. Maybe he didn't *relish* the thought of her whole family "taking care," but he was hardly going to run away with his tail between his legs just because she had some overbearing siblings.

It would take a lot more than that to scare off Hawk Steele.

"Now, if you're a good boy and finish your breakfast, I'll give you an update."

Hawk stared at her and had the uncomfortable realization that if he hadn't been trying to force her to give him information, she probably would have offered that deal in the first place.

So he ate, though he wasn't happy about it. Once he was done, he raised an eyebrow at her and she sighed.

"All right. A deal is a deal. Jack says Chessa isn't talking. He said the running theory is she actually doesn't know anything. She was just a pawn, so we're not much closer than we were on that front."

Unfortunately, that was the impression he got from Chessa as well. "What's the other front?"

"Mary, Dahlia and I found a possible connection and Mary passed that on to Hart last night, so they're looking into it."

"Explain the connection."

She didn't say anything as she got up off the bed. She picked Pita up and put him back on the bed. Then she skirted the bed, came to the other side and leaned over him. She looked him right in the eye. "No."

He could have argued with her, but maybe on this he was finally learning a lesson. "I at least need my phone."

"No screens. You need rest, and that's it."

"I have to call my boss."

"According to Hart, he's informed all the necessary parties that you're out on medical leave until a doctor says otherwise."

"Anna."

"Be a good patient." She leaned over, brushed a kiss over his forehead. "You and Pita." But before she could pull away, he reached for her wrists to keep her there. Maybe he couldn't get through to her about the investigation in this moment, and the investigation *was* the most important thing in this moment, but he wasn't a man who liked losing. He had to win a point somewhere.

"Was I dreaming, or did you agree to marry me last night?"

"You must have been dreaming." She tugged her hands, but he didn't let her go. "I very specifically said we had a lot of things to discuss first."

"First."

"Yes, and *first* comes before *second*, which still wouldn't be an agreement." She kept tugging, but he also knew she was afraid to use her full strength against him since he was injured, which gave him the opportunity to hold on to her and keep her there and face *this*—them—if nothing else.

"Okay, let's start with first. What's the first thing you want to talk about?"

She stopped tugging for a minute, looking at him like she couldn't decide exactly how to feel about any of this. He didn't mind.

She *had* said she loved him, and while he might have been frustrated with her initial hesitation, maybe even a little insecure about it, he'd watched her explode about… *fighting the world* and he'd understood a deeper facet of her.

So he didn't think she was lying, that love was something she'd ever feel comfortable lying about. And she definitely wasn't the kind of woman who convinced herself she was in love with a man to be nice, to be taken care of.

He imagined love was as much a surprise out of left field for her as it was for him.

"I want to live here. Not Bent. Not Sunrise. The ranch." She said it so seriously, like it was some kind of challenge.

"With me?"

She tugged again. He didn't let go.

"No, with Bigfoot, genius."

"That's easy. I don't care where I live." He thought about all her siblings and living permanently under the same roof and tried not to grimace. Maybe not *ideal*, but how could he argue with her wanting to stay here with her family, her roots?

Maybe if he had roots he'd want the same, but he only had himself. "Because I love you, Anna. I don't have ties to my house, to Bent, to anyone. So you want to live here, it means something to you, that's more than all the stuff that doesn't mean anything to me." And their child would grow up a part of all this?

It was no sacrifice. It was a gift.

She frowned at him. "You know, the plan was to make sure you realized I was a bad bet, and you wouldn't *want* to marry me."

It amused him that she'd had a plan. Even if it had been a terrible one. Who wouldn't fall for her? "Major fail, huh?"

"Yeah, major." She heaved out a sigh. "All right, if I tell you about this possible connection in the case, you have to *promise*. No screens for at least twenty-four more hours. You stick to bed. You eat, you rest. You be a good patient."

He held up his hand. "Scout's honor."

"You were never a Boy Scout," she said, eyes narrowed in suspicion.

"On the contrary, I was. For one whole year. Before I got kicked out of my pack for starting a few unauthorized fires at camp, just to see what would melt. And what wouldn't. What can I say? I've always been interested in fire."

She let out a delighted laugh, then settled in next to him. And told him all about the case, curled up with him.

Where she belonged.

Chapter Sixteen

The days passed with no break in the case. Anna was almost relieved, if only because it gave Hawk a chance to recover. As much as she wanted answers, needed to know the people who'd hurt them, in those first few days all she could bring herself to care about was Hawk getting better.

After her harassing, and his boss's insistence, he'd finally gone and gotten checked out by a real doctor. A few days later, he had a clean bill of health to go back to work, and he'd spent the entire day away from the ranch, working.

Anna was shocked and appalled to find herself missing him. What kind of lovesick teenager was she becoming? The closer it got to dinnertime, the less she could concentrate on any task. What if he had some kind of relapse? What if he was hurt? What if…?

What if you got a hold of yourself? she demanded internally.

"Why don't you go set the table?" Mary said pleasantly. The kind of pleasant that was an order, not a request. The kind of pleasant lesser men did not see through.

Anna looked down at the cucumber she was supposed to be slicing and realized she'd chopped it to bits. It wasn't her turn to set the table. Mary just wanted her out from underfoot so she'd stop ruining dinner preparations.

"Yeah, why don't I?" she muttered, then started gathering everything they'd need. She set out plates and glasses, then the silverware, all the way chastising herself.

If she was going to do this whole till-death-do-they-part thing with Hawk, *God*, she had to figure out a way to deal with his job. And he'd have to find a way to deal with hers. They would have to be apart sometimes. They would have to deal with their worry more constructively than she was doing today.

She couldn't feel this way all the time. She'd burst.

But actually witnessing him be injured was like opening up a floodgate of anxiety and worry. How did people do this love thing? It was excruciating.

She heard someone enter the dining room, but focused on her work, focused on harnessing all these terrible new feelings she didn't know what to do with. She didn't want to deal with small talk with one of her siblings or anyone who lived here.

"Hey."

She practically dropped the entire collection of flatware at the sound of Hawk's voice. She had to squeeze on to it to keep from rushing over to him. What was wrong with her? Slowly, she put the forks and knives down and turned to face him, forcing herself to smile casually. "Hi, honey. How was your day?"

He smirked. There was almost an entire room between them and they stood frozen, just staring at each other, all this space between them. Her heart fluttered in her chest.

He was honestly the most attractive man she'd ever laid eyes on. And she loved him.

Loved.

"Annoying," he said. "Hart's as frustrated as we are. The CS Computer Systems is the only real lead, real connection, but everyone's clean. At least as far as we can find. If there's something there, we haven't found it yet."

Anna nodded. That *was* frustrating. Somehow, they had to find a break in this case. So she could go back to having a normal life not worried someone was out to get her. Not wrapped up so much in this man she couldn't *concentrate*.

"And you weren't there," he said, his voice quiet but firm, his blue eyes intense even with the big table between them.

She let out the breath that had gotten clogged in her lungs, all anxiety and stress and *want*. "You weren't here."

She figured they both moved then, since they met somewhere in the middle, but it wasn't a conscious choice. It was like moon to tide, a magnet. His arms banded around her, and she pushed to her toes and pressed her mouth to his.

It hadn't even been twelve hours since she'd seen him, but it felt like centuries, and she just…needed him. Needed this. And it was scary and wonderful all at the same time. To need someone like this. To love someone like this.

To have something like this.

It was like she hadn't seen him in decades, and she didn't know what that was. Just that it *was*. And she didn't want him to stop touching her, kissing her—

"Do you mind?"

She managed to pull her mouth away from Hawk's, look over his shoulder at her brother. Grant's face was all pinched, and he was looking at the ceiling in an embarrassed kind of horror. Poor Grant, who loved his girl-friend, clearly, but *still* didn't engage in much PDA. At least around them.

"Yeah, I do mind," Anna returned. "Why don't you scram?"

Grant scowled at her, and she thought she might have been able to get rid of him, but then Jack entered. His bland expression turned into a scowl.

"You have a *room*," he pointed out.

"What's the fun in a room?" she returned, but Hawk was disentangling himself, setting her away from him. *Coward*, she mouthed at him.

He laughed, but he didn't come anywhere near her as everyone else started appearing, helping Mary set out the dinner. Cash had decided to keep Izzy at their cabin and eat there, as he often did when things got a little dicey.

But Anna also had to wonder if the knowledge Chessa had been involved in all this made him less inclined to be around them. Much like she hadn't loved the idea of her family poking around her past to figure out who was after her, likely Cash didn't like being reminded of what a di-saster his daughter's mother had turned out to be.

But the rest of them congregated around the table, and no one bothered with small talk tonight. They went straight into the case.

"I suppose the only positive is that if the case does go cold, we're experts at that," Palmer said, clearly trying to ease some of the tension in the room.

Jack scowled harder. Hawk set down his fork. It clearly did not have the desired effect.

"I do not plan on letting this investigation go cold. If CS

Computer Systems wasn't the thread we thought it was, we only have to find a new thread. I've got some reports from all the fires. My office is chasing down potential buyers of the accelerants and fire starters used. We should have some names to check out by tomorrow."

"Should have. Check out. These aren't done deals," Louisa pointed out.

"No, they're steps in an investigation. Hart is looking into Chessa. Phone records and the like. It just takes time to get the search warrants and what have you. Tomorrow, we should have a break in the case."

"Or it's all more dead ends," Mary said. She was not usually the voice of doom, so that made Anna's heart sink.

But as she listened to them bandy about shoulds and possibilities and the word *tomorrow* more times than she cared to count, she knew... She just knew what they had to do.

"I think it's actually pretty clear what we need to do," Anna said. She knew no one would like it. Hell, she didn't like it. But it was the only way to end this. "We need to set a trap," Anna announced.

And was shocked beyond belief that Hawk had said the exact same thing in unison.

HAWK TURNED TO look at Anna. She'd said the exact same thing he had. He supposed he shouldn't be surprised. They were both investigators. Both knew how time passing made things more complicated. And she was familiar with cold cases, so she was even clearer on that.

But when she looked at him, so surprised he'd suggested the same thing, he had a very, very bad feeling. "I'm guessing our definition of *trap* is a little different."

The surprise on her face slackened into something a little more Anna-like. Not quite the snarky bravado she'd no doubt get to, but her mouth was on its way to a challenging smirk. "Yeah, I'm guessing it is."

He fought the words that bubbled up. It was no use ordering Anna to do or not to do something, but… "You aren't risking yourself, so I don't know why we'd even bother to discuss whatever you're cooking up."

Anna rolled her eyes and opened her mouth to no doubt argue, but Jack cut her off.

"I'm with Hawk. I'm sure we're all with Hawk. You're not risking yourself." He said it with authority that most people would no doubt mindlessly follow.

Except Anna. Hawk had no doubt Anna would argue until she was blue in the face, but Jack clearly knew this, too.

"Let's hear Hawk's plan. Then we'll come back to your terrible one," Jack said, then smiled blandly at her.

She narrowed her eyes at Jack, which he figured kept Anna's ire geared toward her brother rather than him, which was nice.

"I've caught up on everything today. Talked to everyone. Combed reports. We're at a brick wall, and as far as I can see, the only possible lead through that brick wall is Chessa Scott."

No one said anything. Everyone who'd been listening to him intently looked down at their plates or at the wall or beyond him. He wasn't exactly surprised by the reaction, but he didn't understand why none of them saw this as an opportunity.

"Chessa is our most connected lead. Maybe she didn't

know the guy who hired her, but she's spoken with him. She knows *things* about him. If we lay a kind of trap for Chessa, she can lead us up the ladder."

"I thought Hart was looking into it," Louisa said, frowning.

"He is, but so far he's coming up empty. Chessa knows more. If we get her somewhere she feels safe to spill her guts, she can lead us in the right direction. Whether it's how she got paid or where she met the guy. *Something.* She won't talk to the police, or me, but she might talk to someone she has a connection to."

"She hates us," Mary said, and Hawk was surprised at the sharp note in Mary's usually mild tone. "She wouldn't do anything to help us. I hate to say anyone is all bad or can't be redeemed, but Chessa has been using bitterness as a weapon and an excuse since she was sixteen years old, if not longer. She's not going to help out of the goodness of her heart. In fact, she'd take every opportunity to hurt us—particularly Cash and Izzy, who she blames for the downward spiral of her life."

Hawk glanced at Anna. She was also an "especially" on Chessa's list for having stopped her from getting her hands on Izzy, but Anna was the only one who knew that. "Then we don't appeal to her heart. We appeal to the desire to hurt. To get back at you guys."

"How?"

"We use Cash as the bait. He can handle himself. We'll take precautions so she can't hurt him, but she'll think she can. And in her anger, she might let some more information go, especially since he's not law enforcement and isn't super involved in investigating."

There was a fraught silence, where all the siblings exchanged glances that spoke volumes Hawk couldn't fully read. Clearly there was more history here than he was privy to, and more of that family bond stuff he'd just never fully understand or be a part of.

"He won't go for it," Grant said, and it held weight since Grant never said much.

"Maybe not, but I think it's worth asking. Maybe he'd have an alternate plan along the same lines that he'd be more comfortable with." And maybe he'd just go for it because they *needed* to move forward. Because it was his sister at risk. The Hudsons were supposed to be about protecting one another. How could Cash not step up for this? "We cannot sit around twiddling our thumbs, and we cannot risk you," he said pointedly at Anna.

"But you can risk my brother?" she returned, her voice deceptively mild.

"It wouldn't be a risk for him. Not as much of one. Cash doesn't have your temper, and he's not going to lose his lunch if a smell hits him the wrong way." Hawk looked around the table and could not get a read on anyone's response. "We could do it carefully, safely. It's worth a shot."

Which was how Hawk found himself walking down to Cash's cabin after dinner. Hawk wasn't sure why he'd been elected to go down to Cash's cabin to approach him about the subject alone. Or maybe he knew exactly why.

They'd rather have Cash shellac an outsider than one of their own.

But Hawk could take it. And he could be persuasive. The Hudsons were loyal and protective. Why wouldn't Cash jump at the chance to protect his sister?

Pita trotted beside Hawk, his wound having healed nicely and the dog being back to his eager, puppy ways. Still, Hawk watched his surroundings. The winter sun was falling quickly, and whatever snowmelt had happened today had already iced back over.

Someone was out there…somewhere. And they wanted Anna dead. They'd been quiet for too many days now, and Hawk didn't trust it. The narrow miss with Chessa felt like a wake-up call for everyone involved.

Whatever happened next was going to be *it*, bigger and more dangerous, and Hawk was determined to be the one who came out on top. Whether the Hudsons were comfortable with his methods or not.

A few dogs trotted over to greet Pita as Hawk got closer to the cabin. He walked up onto the porch and knocked on the door, watching Pita bound and prance with the other dogs. But when the door opened, the puppy shot inside before Hawk could get out the order to stay.

Izzy was there to catch him and greet him happily. She snuggled him and laughed when he exuberantly licked her face. Hawk had to work very hard not to think about what Chessa had said about that sweet little girl.

Cash looked Hawk up and down, glanced back into the cabin where Izzy was happily cuddling Pita. "Stay inside with Pita, Izzy. Hawk and I are going to talk outside."

The little girl looked up at both of them with curiosity, but she posed no argument. Hawk had the sinking suspicion that meant she was far sneakier than she let on. But he was focused on Cash and getting through to him. Whatever Izzy found out or didn't was her business and Cash's. Not Hawk's.

Cash closed the door, keeping the two of them outside on the porch. Hawk was huddled in his jacket and felt the frigid evening air biting through. Cash stood there in a threadbare sweatshirt and looked like he was enjoying the tropics.

The Hudson men all looked alike. Big, dark hair and eyes, a kind of restrained cop-like intimidation factor. Though their personalities shone through in the way they acted, moved and spoke, put the four of them together and they were a similar wall of stoicism. Still, Cash was definitely more…fringe than Jack, Grant and Palmer. He lived apart from the main group, focused more on his daughter and his dogs than he did on investigations, and mainly kept his opinions to himself.

Which made it harder to know how to approach him. But Hawk always figured the straightforward way was best. "I need your help."

"I know what you want," Cash returned, leaning against the door as he crossed his arms over his chest. "I'm an investigator, too. Or was. I understand the wall you're at. I understand Chessa's a thread. But I'm staying out of it."

"Out of someone trying to kill your sister?"

Cash didn't even flinch, which surprised Hawk considering how close the Hudsons were. Cash stood there, a foreboding rock of *hell no*. "I've got a kid. Maybe yours isn't real to you yet, but trust me. Once that defenseless baby is on this side of the world, you would do anything, risk anything, to keep them safe. No matter how hard those choices are."

"I'm not asking you to risk Izzy." He'd die for that kid himself, and he didn't even know why.

"No, but you're asking me to risk myself. I know too well what it's like not to have parents. I can't risk that for her."

Hawk's heart twisted, though he tried to harden himself to it. He was an investigator in this instance, not an orphaned kid.

"You're asking me because you don't want Anna to do the risking," Cash continued. "I get that. I respect it and appreciate it, since it means you love her and all. But I can't be the one to step in and do it for her."

"Okay, you don't want to risk yourself. I get it. But we can agree, as two men who love her, that we don't want Anna to risk herself. What do you suggest, then? Because we can't let this case go cold. As a man who has worked on cold cases, you have to know how bad that would be."

Cash simply nodded. And said nothing.

Hawk had to work very hard to tamp down his frustration. "And your ex-wife is part of it."

"Yeah, sounds about right," Cash agreed, and then fell into another long silence.

Hawk shoved his hands into his pockets, both against the biting cold and his threadbare temper. "You have a history with Chessa. If you won't help your sister, you should at least be able to give us some insight. How do we get her to give us information? That's all I'm after, Cash."

Cash studied him coolly, as if he didn't believe him. But Hawk stood there and waited, even as the sun sank behind the mountains and the air got colder and colder.

Finally, Cash sighed. "You want insight? I don't have any. I never understood Chessa. We were kids when we got together, immature teenagers when we got married and had a kid. We weren't ready for anything life threw at us, and she decided to bemoan that fact, and I decided to deal with it—I'd had experience in that, after all. I might have felt sorry for her once, but... She wasn't just a bad mother—she was a dangerous mother. It was a relief when she finally left. I didn't understand her then—I sure as hell don't understand her now. And any connection to Chessa is an avenue into her being more drawn to causing pain and suffering. I can't risk her touching my daughter ever again. Not even to solve this case."

"If we tie her up on this, she's in jail. She's not a danger to you or Izzy."

"And if she slips through the cracks, Izzy becomes a target. My whole family becomes a target. Chessa is driven by anger, spite and the consistent belief she's been wronged. She's an addict, unpredictable at best when she's *not* on something. Forget it when she is. I don't understand anything that drives her, but I understand she's dangerous to everyone I love. So the best thing for all of us is to steer absolutely clear. I don't expect you to take my word on that, but if you ask around, ask Anna herself, you'll find they all agree."

Hawk had nothing to say to that. No smart words, no harsh demands. No easy answers. *This* was why the Hudsons had let him come down here alone, with his head of steam and self-righteousness.

You couldn't risk a kid—couldn't ask a father to risk his or her safety. Maybe he didn't understand all the fatherhood things Cash no doubt did, but he understood this. His kid wasn't even breathing yet, and he...couldn't imagine ever letting his child face any danger.

The problem was, it didn't change the issue at hand. Chessa Scott was their best bet into getting a lead.

Hawk couldn't simply let that go.

Chapter Seventeen

Anna thought about following Hawk down to Cash's cabin. She had no doubt her brother would shut down any and all talk about going through Chessa, but she also knew Hawk wouldn't give up.

And neither would she.

So when he finally came up to bed, she was ready for him. Or she thought she was. She twisted in the window seat where she'd been watching the stars. Hawk entered first. Pita pranced in behind him looking happy.

Hawk looked exhausted. Just worn down to the bone.

"He said no," Anna offered, trying to sound sympathetic without any thread of *we told you so* in her tone.

Hawk sighed. "Yeah. I guess I should have figured you guys knew him better than I did, but I just thought…" He shook his head. "Can't blame him for wanting to protect his daughter."

Anna slid off the window seat. She didn't fully cross to him. She had a feeling if she went over there and slid her arms around his neck like she wanted to, not much talking would get done, and they needed to sort this out.

Because she'd had time to think. Figure out the best

way to get through the brick wall that was Hawk Steele on a mission. But she had to find some…levity. Some of her old bravado. She couldn't treat it so seriously he balked.

But she was having a hard time finding any of her old attitudes when so much felt like it was at stake. "I have a compromise."

His expression hardened and he crossed his arms over his chest as he scowled down at her. "I will not compromise on this."

She had to bite back a dreamy sigh. Even exhausted and clearly irritated with her, he was just so damn attractive. But she had to make her point before she gave in to that.

"You said it yourself—we use her hate. She hates me. I know you want to protect the baby. I get that, but you're not the only one, Hawk. You think I'm carrying around this thing for fun?" She spread her hands over her belly. She thought her pants had been a *little* tight this morning, but it was still early enough sometimes it was hard to believe it was real.

And yet she was thinking about futures and what that looked like with a baby. Worrying over them even though there was nothing to do on the outside except hope they were growing well in there. "He or she is as real to me as Izzy is."

She looked up at him under her lashes, saw the softening. There was no doubt to her that he'd be a good father. Oh, they'd no doubt butt heads on a million choices people had to make when it came to raising kids, but she knew…a safe, healthy, happy child was all he really wanted.

Because he'd lost that safety and happiness when he'd been so young. And so had she. Which made her not want to talk about Chessa or danger. She wanted… "In fact, I was thinking about names," she said.

One eyebrow winged up, and suspicion tinged his tone. "Names, huh?"

"Sure. Eagle if it's a boy. Sparrow if it's a girl."

He rolled his eyes. "Ha. Ha." But his mouth curved in amusement anyway.

She used that. That crack in his armor. That softening. She moved a little closer, reached out and took his hand. Then she placed it over her stomach. Because even with her bird name joke, she *had* been thinking about names. And it *was* serious.

"What was your mom's name?"

He stilled, kept his gaze on his hand on her stomach. She watched, and though not much in his expression or the way he held himself changed, she could *feel* the little war of emotion inside him. "Caroline."

"I like it."

"What about your mom's name?"

"Laura, but… How about this? Girl, we go with Caroline Laura Hudson-Steele. Boy, we go with my dad's name, Dean, and a middle name you think your mom would have liked. What about Hawk? Like a family heirloom. Pass it on down."

He was quiet and very still for a long moment. When he spoke, his voice was rough. "Yeah, that sounds good."

She had to fight a wave of tears. Happy tears, but she didn't want them falling. She wanted to be strong. "It does, doesn't it?"

His blue eyes lifted to hers. A million emotions swirled there, but he kept them carefully controlled. "Anna, I can't... It's too much to lose. I knew that already, but everything Cash said made it...clearer."

"I know." Talking about names made it clearer, too. All the things she *wanted* to do, the way she'd normally act. But things weren't normal anymore. She had to be someone different than she'd once been. "But we can't just... wait it out. We both know that."

Hawk nodded.

"What if the two of us went to the jail? I know Jack won't like it. Hart probably won't either. But we find a way to talk to her there, a way to...get something out of her. Where it's safe. And you'll be with me, okay? We won't tackle anything alone. Chessa is dangerous because she's unpredictable and connected in ways we don't understand, but she isn't loyal to that guy. Jack and Hart aren't getting anywhere because she knows not to trust the cops, *and* she doesn't hate them. Personally. She hates me. Personally. She won't *want* to tell me anything, sure. But if we rile her up, use her anger and her hate, she might slip."

"And if she doesn't?" Hawk asked.

Anna wished she had anything smart to say. Or encouraging. Or anything. But all she had in this moment was the honest truth. "I don't know, but we just keep trying."

HAWK DIDN'T SLEEP WELL. There was too much on his mind. Anna's plan wasn't terrible; it was just unlikely to yield results.

Desperation caused mistakes, and if this was a normal investigation, he'd carefully and methodically be pulling the threads. But nothing felt normal because it all involved the woman he'd fallen in love with.

He watched the light begin to dawn in the window, while Anna slept soundly beside him, Pita down at the foot of the bed.

Terrifying thing, being happy. Knowing how tenuous it all was even without someone wanting Anna dead. All the worse with this cloud hanging over their lives.

And sitting here thinking about it didn't solve that cloud, did it? He slid out of bed, trying not to wake either bedmate, but Pita lifted his head and let out a little whimper. Hawk scooped him up so as not to disturb Anna and grabbed some clothes with his other hand.

He put Pita down in the hallway. "You sit tight," he ordered the dog. He stepped into the bathroom and got dressed. When he came back out, Pita was still sitting there, his little tail wagging. Hawk crouched down and gave the dog a good scratch behind the ears. "You're the best little boy, aren't you?" he murmured at the dog.

"Maybe tied for best."

Hawk looked up to see Anna standing in her bedroom doorway, sleep-disheveled and gorgeous, with that little smirk on her face that tended to make his brain short-circuit.

"Remember how you didn't want a dog?" she asked, tapping her chin. "But Mary walked you right into a corner."

He got to his feet. "Yeah, yeah." He was about to pull her to him when someone's door opened down the hall. A creak, followed by footsteps. A loud yawn.

"Morning," Palmer offered, sliding past them and then to the bathroom.

There were more noises now. The sounds of people chatting, walking. Something clattered downstairs. Her whole family getting ready to start the day. She wanted to live here, and he didn't care where he lived, but damn, he could use a *little* privacy. "When you said you wanted to live here, did you mean in this exact bedroom?"

She smiled. "We each have our own little parcel of land. Palmer's building Louisa a house on his for when they get married. I guess I figured that's what I'd do if I ever found myself ball-and-chained to a man."

"Speaking of that, when are we going to get ball-and-chained? I've got a friend who's a judge. No waiting in Wyoming, you know."

She narrowed her eyes at him—and maybe he'd been expecting that, hoping for that. "There is no big fat rock on my finger, and I am not getting married by a *judge*. There will be a wedding, a white dress, the whole shebang."

"When?"

She all-out scowled now.

"I know you keep thinking you might yet scare me off, Blondie," he said, tapping that scowl. "But I won't shake."

She moved forward, wrapped her arms around his neck and pressed her mouth to his. "Then buy me a rock, Steele." Then she kissed him again.

Until they were interrupted by a disgusted groan. "Your room is *right there*," Palmer said, gesturing at the open door as he passed again, this time to go to the stairs. He muttered darkly under his breath as he disappeared.

But before either of them could say anything else, Jack appeared at the top of the stairs. Considering *his* bedroom was downstairs, and he immediately turned toward their side of the hall, Hawk had a bad feeling.

Anna tensing in his arms added to it. Hawk didn't see

anything different about Jack—all stoic expressions and ramrod postures—but still knew the bad news was coming.

And Jack got right to it as he approached them—not even one comment about their arms around each other. "I just got off the phone with one of my deputies. Someone paid Chessa's bail. She got out early this morning. An hour or two before anyone told me."

"How?" Hawk demanded, at the same time Anna said about the same thing.

"How does that happen, Jack?"

They didn't let each other go precisely, but they turned to face Jack, Hawk's arm around her shoulders, Anna holding on to his side.

Jack shook his head. "I'm on my way to the station to find out. I want you two to stay—"

"I'm coming with," Hawk said, effectively cutting Jack off. He let Anna go and stepped forward. "You, me, Hart, we get to the bottom of this to triangulate our investigations. Grant's here, right?"

"You might be the arson investigator, Steele, but you don't have jurisdiction over me," Jack returned, not answering his question.

"I don't give a rat's ass about jurisdiction. I either go with you or I follow you and bust my way in. It doesn't matter to me. Now, is Grant here? Is Palmer sticking around?" He pointed at Anna behind him, who was being uncharacteristically quiet. "Someone to keep an eye on her."

"Grant and Dahlia are visiting her sister out of town until tonight. Palmer will stick around, and I'll leave it to Mary to update everyone on what's going on. I—"

"What about Cash?" Anna interrupted, without even

chastising him for the "someone to keep an eye on her" comment. "If Chessa is—"

"I already warned him," Jack said, clearly gentling his tone for Anna. "He's decided to stay put at the cabin, locked up tight with the dogs, until she's found."

"Then let's go. Anna, you'll stay here. Never alone. Not until we figure out what's going on," Jack said. Ordered.

Hawk turned to Anna. She mounted no argument, and she didn't even have that look on her face like she was planning something devious or rebellious.

"You're being...not yourself."

She looked up at him, hazel eyes a maze of conflicting emotions. "You'll be with my brother." She looked over Hawk's shoulder to where Jack stood. Held her brother's gaze. "I'd trust him with my life, so I'll trust him with yours."

Hawk pulled her into a quick hug. "Nice guilt trip, Blondie." He kissed her cheek, then looked her in the eye. "Be safe."

She stared at him for a long time. "We split up last time and it didn't work."

"We're not splitting up. I'm with Jack and Hart. You're with Palmer and Mary. No one goes it alone. Deal?"

She looked up at him, and it worried him he couldn't read her expression. But she got up on her toes and brushed her mouth over his. "Deal."

Chapter Eighteen

Anna didn't like feeling shaken, but something about Chessa getting out of jail shattered whatever small amount of peace she'd been able to thread together since Hawk had been hurt.

Anna wished she could believe Chessa would disappear. Take some money and run. But someone had gotten her out of jail, which meant someone was still using her.

Someone. Someone that no one—not herself, when she'd always considered herself an above-average investigator, not her siblings who she'd always viewed as the same, not Hawk—no one could find out who wanted Anna dead.

But Hawk was with Jack. She trusted her brother, *had* to trust him, to keep Hawk out of harm's way. And vice versa.

So she sat at the breakfast table with Mary and Palmer. Grant had stayed at Dahlia's last night since Dahlia had her monthly visit to her sister's. Palmer had insisted Louisa stay with her family until things settled a little.

"So, since you can't stop making out with the guy in our damn hallway, I guess you're going to marry him?" Palmer asked casually, sipping his coffee.

Anna knew he was trying to keep her mind off everything else. She wanted to play along, but she felt wound too tight. Too ready to snap.

"What's the security situation?" she asked.

Palmer sighed, but he didn't put her off. "We've found a solution for the breach, but I don't think we can rely on it the way we usually would. Someone who can create one breach can always create another."

"And no one can find anything incriminating on this CS Computer Systems?"

"You've looked into it just like the rest of us, Anna. If it's a connection, we can't find it. And we can't focus on *one* thing just because it seems more likely, when we're not getting anywhere."

Anna knew all these things. Had probably said these things to frustrated people wanting answers. Now she was on the other side of it, now it was *her* life and… She wanted to go back in time and punch herself in the face. What an awful person she'd been to people in desperate need of answers.

No wonder someone wanted her dead.

"Anna," Palmer said, so sternly he almost sounded like Jack. "It feels different when it's personal. When you're trying to keep people you love safe. That's why we've got people like Hart working on the case, too. You need people who don't have a connection. Who can have that patience we don't have."

"All we can do is keep working," Mary said calmly. "It's what we always do. And it doesn't really matter what we *feel* while we do them, does it? Cold case or new case. You or Louisa or Hawk are victims, or someone we've never met is, we just have to keep connecting the dots. And weathering the storms that crop up while we do."

Anna looked at her sister. She sounded so in control. She always did. Jack, Grant and Mary. Always made it seem like everything was possible. They'd been the backbone after Mom and Dad had disappeared. In the midst of questions that had never been answered, Jack had waded through the financial realities of the ranch, while Cash had taken on the actual labor of it all. Mary had shouldered the administrative tasks to keep the household running, even though she'd only been ten years old, and Grant had driven them to and from school. Checked homework.

All Anna had ever done was be the baby of the family. The one everyone took care of. Even now. What was she doing besides waiting around for someone to solve this case for her?

The landline rang and Mary went to answer it. Her pleasant business smile faded, and she dropped the phone, already running for the back door. "Cash's cabin is on fire. They can't get out."

They all headed toward the door, but Anna and Palmer stopped. Anna looked out the window. She could see the smoke off in the distance. But the fires so far had been warnings. This one wasn't just a warning.

It was likely a trap.

"Mary, don't!" Anna yelled at the same time Palmer did, but Mary had opened the door. She'd only taken a step before a gunshot rang out.

Mary stumbled back as Palmer grabbed her and pulled her out of the doorway. Anna dropped to the ground as another shot rang out, exploding through the window. She crawled over to Mary and Palmer.

"Don't look at it," Palmer ordered, because everyone

knew Mary hated the sight of blood. And her arm was bloody. Just her arm. Just her arm.

Anna repeated that to herself as she ripped Mary's torn sleeve out of the way. Palmer handed her a dish towel and Anna pressed it to where Mary was bleeding.

"Call Jack," Anna said to Palmer.

"You two stay put and call him. I'm going."

Anna grabbed on to Palmer with one hand, while she pressed the bandage to Mary's arm with the other. "You can't go out there alone."

"We can't wait for emergency services to get all the way out here. Cash and Izzy are trapped."

"They're stuck in the house, Anna," Mary said. "You both have to go get them out. I'm okay."

"Not with people shooting," Anna returned. "We have to be smarter than that." And she *was* smarter. She had to stop reacting and actually think. Actually *act*. She took Mary's hand and had her wrap the cloth around her own wound. "Can you hold that there? Keep the pressure?"

Mary swallowed and nodded. She was beyond pale.

"I know you hate blood, so just don't look. Just hold on. Okay?"

Mary nodded, though Anna was concerned it was more of a panic nod than actual understanding. "I'm okay. I'm okay..." she stammered. "Don't worry about me. Get Cash and Izzy."

Anna turned to Palmer and looked at his gun. Cash had guns locked up in his cabin, and hopefully had been smart enough to grab one. They had some back in the security room, but it would take too long to get them. They needed to act now.

"Give me the gun," she ordered Palmer.

He hesitated, but only for a second. She unlocked the safety, positioned herself next to the window. She had a hole to shoot through, and a good view of the field between the big house and Cash's cabin where the smoke was coming from. She couldn't find the gunman. Yet. But she would.

"I'll cover you," Anna said to Palmer, though her gaze never left the area around the fire, searching for a shooter. "If there's more than two gunmen, you come right back. If there's one or two, I'll take them out, and you get to Cash and Izzy." She moved her gaze from outside to Palmer. "Got it?"

He gave a short nod. Then Anna looked out the window, pointed the gun in the most likely direction of one shooter and pulled the trigger just as Palmer took off toward the smoke.

HAWK DROVE HIS own truck and followed Jack to the Sunrise jail where Chessa had been held. Pita sat happily in the passenger seat, watching the snowy world go by. Hawk parked next to Jack when he pulled to a stop in front of the small building that housed the sheriff's department.

Hawk got out and grabbed Pita's leash, letting the dog jump out on his own. The puppy didn't do his usual sniffing around. He followed Jack as if he knew this was all serious business.

Hawk didn't have to be a mind reader or a psychologist to know that Jack Hudson's mood was foul. It radiated off the man as he strode inside the building—even before he started barking out orders to his staff.

It was interesting to watch the deputies and administrative assistants jump to do exactly what he said. No shared looks of irritation or hesitation. If Jack was a hard-ass, he was at least a respected hard-ass here.

Hawk had to appreciate it. He tried to allow the quick, helpful reactions to give him some hope that they could figure out what had happened with Chessa.

A young woman in a police uniform strode up to them. "Ferguson is the one who took care of it. He's over at City Hall right now. Should I go get him?"

"Yeah. Make sure he brings a copy of the receipt or the ID."

The woman nodded, then strode past, though she did flash the puppy a little smile as she did.

Jack looked at an elderly woman behind a big desk. "When Brink gets back with Ferguson, have them come to my office. In the meantime, make sure Kinsey sends the video surveillance directly to my email. No one else. Understood?"

"Yes, sir," she said, then handed Hawk a dog treat. "Always keep these on hand for our four-legged helpers."

Hawk thanked the woman, then tossed Pita the treat. Jack jerked a chin at Hawk, as if to say *follow me*, but they both stopped short when Hart marched in. Hawk had never seen the detective look quite so angry.

"How does this happen?" Hart demanded of Jack. "She was my one lead."

"She was *our* one lead on the attack on my *sister's* life, so spare me your outrage," Jack returned. "We're questioning the officer who took the bond. We won't all fit, but let's head back to my office."

Jack led them back into a tiny room, barely the size of

a closet. He strode inside, set his keys and hat down on the desk. A cat figure-eighted around one of the legs of the chair.

Hawk and Hart exchanged glances. Even one of them would be a tight fit, so they both wordlessly agreed to hover in the doorway.

"Maybe this isn't a disaster," Hawk suggested. "Maybe it could be a lead. She had a decent-sized bond. Whoever paid her way has means. It's got to be our guy, or she wouldn't have needed the payout in the first place."

"Maybe it is, but I doubt it. At best, he sent an intermediary. At worst, Chessa's dead and *all* our leads are gone."

Hawk looked from Jack to Hart. "That your read?"

"Look, we've got a guy willing to kill Anna. I don't know why he'd worry about killing anyone else, and if he thinks Chessa has information? It adds up. Maybe. Certainly a possibility we can't rule out."

Hawk didn't say anything. If whoever had bailed Chessa out was the man who'd been trying to kill Anna, who'd bashed him over the head and hurt Pita in the process, he was certainly capable of killing Chessa to make sure she didn't talk.

But Chessa hadn't been talking. There'd been no name. No connection. Bailing her out to use her again seemed far more likely in Hawk's mind, which meant he was going to view this as a lead.

It had to be a lead.

Eventually, the female officer returned with a young man who looked pale and nervous. Hawk watched him carefully.

"Tell us about last night."

"Sir?"

"Chessa Scott. Someone bailed her out. I want to know how it went down."

"Oh, uh." The kid—Ferguson—looked around at Hart, then Hawk, then at the female officer. Brink, Jack had called her. "Um. Well, he came in. Said he wanted to pay Chessa Scott's bail."

"Did you take his ID?"

The man—*boy*—blinked. "What?"

"Did you take the damn ID, Ferguson?"

"Y-yes, sir. I followed the protocol."

"And?"

"I don't… I'd have to go look at the records."

Jack rubbed his hands over his face. Hawk wondered if the man would have an aneurysm right there, but the female officer from before held out a binder. "Here's the book."

"Ferguson, find me the receipt and tell me anything else you remember."

Ferguson nodded, taking the binder with shaky hands. Hawk exchanged a look with Hart as if to say *who hired this guy?*

Ferguson cleared his throat. "He didn't say much. When I let Ms. Scott go, she said he was her boyfriend, then kind of laughed a bunch."

"Did he argue with her? Act like he was?" Jack demanded.

With shaking hands, Ferguson pulled out a piece of paper. He handed it to Jack. "Neither. He just kind of dragged her out of here. He had the money. Everything was on the up-and-up. I didn't do anything wrong." The kid looked around wildly. "I followed directions and—"

Jack silenced him with a sharp look as he took the receipt. But that look chilled considerably as he looked down at the receipt. Hawk's nerves began to hum.

"Hawk? Go back to the ranch," Jack said, his voice cold and detached as he handed the receipt to Hart.

"What? Why?" Hawk demanded, thinking he was being shuttled off for some obnoxious Hudson protection reason that he'd never begin to understand.

Then he saw the cold fury on Jack's face as Jack grabbed his keys and slid his hat back on his head. "It was one of my ranch hands."

Chapter Nineteen

As Palmer ran, Anna shot. She caught a glimpse of one shooter and focused all her fire there. After a few shots, she was almost certain he was the only gunman. But she was having a hard time getting the right angle to take him out.

Which left Palmer way too out in the open as gunfire echoed through the otherwise calm Wyoming winter morning.

Anna wanted to look at Mary and make sure she was doing okay, but she couldn't take her eyes off her target. She couldn't stop focusing her shooting toward the person who might shoot Palmer.

Then she caught it. The little flash. The gunman moving just enough into range she pulled the trigger and watched as the man jerked. She didn't even hear the explosion of the gunshot. It didn't matter. Nothing mattered except that she'd hit him.

"I got the shooter. I'm going after Palmer."

"Anna—"

"Stay put. Wait for help," Anna called over her shoulder. She didn't know if Mary would listen—probably only if she wasn't capable of walking. But Anna had to get over to where all that smoke plumed in the bright blue sky.

She wasn't foolish enough not to be careful. She eyed her surroundings, the horizon, as she jogged toward the cabin, toward Palmer. She kept the gun in her hand. She'd shoot anyone who got in her way.

She didn't see signs of anyone else. It would be reckless for one gunman to think he could take on all the Hudsons living here, but maybe he'd assumed the fire would panic them.

Or maybe there's more coming.

Maybe, but she had to focus on Cash and Izzy in this moment. She reached Palmer just as he'd made it to the window Cash had clearly broken from the inside. Cash was working from the inside, Palmer from the outside to pull Izzy out. Once Palmer had her, he passed her to Anna so he could help Cash.

The girl was getting far too big for Anna to carry, and Izzy was coughing up a storm. So Anna half carried, half dragged her away from the burning house.

"Daddy," Izzy croaked.

"He's coming, sweetie. You're both okay." Anna surveyed the landscape. Mary was scurrying across the yard, towel still clamped to her arm. She came up to Izzy and wrapped her arm around the girl. "Come on. Let's get you into the house."

Izzy was crying now. "Daddy. I want Daddy."

"He's coming," Anna assured her as Palmer helped Cash away from the house. Cash's face was streaked with sweat and smoke, and he was coughing, too. He wasn't limping, but he seemed to need Palmer's support to walk.

Anna looked around. Where the hell was help? She needed someone to track down the shooter she'd shot in case he hadn't been shot that badly and came back.

Mary was cradling Izzy, but she pushed away from Mary—causing Mary to gasp in pain—as Cash approached. Izzy threw her arms around her father.

"I'm okay," Cash rasped. "You need to get inside, sweets."

"The fire trucks and ambulance should be here any minute. Any minute," Mary said, repeating it over and over again, like that would make it so as they trudged toward the house.

But the shooter was still out there. Everyone here was safe from the fire, though needing medical attention. Anna watched their surroundings as they clambered onto the back porch.

They could barricade themselves inside, but it would be another loose end, another question mark. Anna had to find the gunman and make sure he was down and identified. That he couldn't come back. That this *ended*.

She pulled Palmer aside. "I've got to make sure he's down."

"Not alone, Anna."

"He's alone. I've got a gun and I'm not shot like he is. Keep an eye on these three. They're hurt and they'll need someone to flag down the EMTs." Someone to stay, and Anna wasn't any good at comforting.

Besides, this was *her* fight.

So she didn't bother to argue with Palmer. She took off. She couldn't let the guy get away. She hadn't seen him enough to ID him. They needed a lead. They needed to find out who was terrorizing them. All because of her.

She ran toward the spot where he'd been when she shot him and was gratified he hadn't gone far. There was a trail of blood in the snow, and then a man crawling away. Slowly. Haltingly.

But Anna recognized this man. It made her steps falter. "Tripp?"

The man looked back over his shoulder at her. Then his eyes widened at the gun in her hand. He stumbled a bit, so he fell on his back, and she could see she'd shot him in the stomach. He was bleeding badly.

Tripp. One of their ranch hands. She didn't want to believe it of him—she'd herded cattle with him, she'd *joked* with him just last Christmas when they'd passed out the Christmas presents. He'd been a trusted member of their team.

And he'd done *this*? She pointed the gun at him. Right between the eyes, anger and shame making a dangerous storm within her. Because how *dare* he?

What the hell might she have done to make him want to kill her? "What do you have to say for yourself?" she asked. Her voice shook, but her hands on the gun didn't.

Tripp's eyes were wide and wild. He held up his hands in a kind of surrender as he kicked his legs against the ground like he could scoot away. Blood oozed from his torn shirt. "I…"

But then she heard a gun cock, right behind her. The cold press of steel to her temple.

"Don't move," the low voice ordered.

Anna did as she was told. She held herself very still. Using only peripheral vision, she looked around and tried to spot any of her family members.

But she'd fallen into a trap, hadn't she? She'd been foolish enough, angry enough, to leave herself vulnerable. Always her downfall.

"You know the worst part of this whole thing?" she said,
imbuing her voice with all the old casual bravado she didn't
even remotely feel.

"That you're going to end up dead?"

"No, that I don't even know *why*. I don't know who the
hell you are, pal. So whatever number I did on you, I don't
remember. I don't know which one of us that makes more
pathetic. Maybe both."

"You think this is about you?" The man laughed, his
breath hot on her neck. "You would. You're all a bunch of
selfish, self-absorbed criminals. And you're all going to
pay. You had to make it more difficult. You had to make
me angrier. Now it won't just be blame they're heaping on
themselves. They're all going to watch you die."

HAWK SLAMMED ON his brakes as he approached the Hudson house, one hand on the wheel, one arm around Pita.

He saw it in the distance: smoke. Fire. Not at the main
house. *Hell.* Cash's cabin.

There was no way his car would make it over the drifts
of snow, so he got out and he ran. Pita must have jumped
out of the driver's side behind him because the dog was
right next to him, racing toward the danger. There was no
time to tell him to stop.

Hawk's chest constricted as he got close. Fire consumed
the cabin. If anyone was in there... No, surely—

He saw tracks leading to and from it. Clearly people had

run back and forth. As he got closer, he could see the front window had been broken. They'd gotten out.

But someone had barricaded the door shut. Hawk tried to ice away the cold fury that swept over him. He had to think clearly. Carefully.

They'd gotten out, which meant everyone would be back at the main house. So Hawk ran for the house, where the tracks led, Pita still by his side. The back door was open, and Mary, Cash and Izzy were just inside in various states of disarray.

But no Anna.

Mary was holding something to her arm, and Izzy was coughing. Cash stood there abnormally still, like he was hurt but was trying not to let on. Hawk didn't see Palmer or Anna, so they had to be together. Which was good. He could relax.

He could not relax.

"Where's help?" Cash demanded when Hawk jogged up the porch stairs, Pita wriggling past him to go lick Izzy's face where she sat on the floor, leaning against Cash's leg.

"When did you call it in?" Hawk asked, because they hadn't gotten word of it at the police department.

"Too long ago," Mary said. "They should be here."

But he knew how time could stretch out and seem longer when everything was terrible. "We must have left before the call came through. Jack just found out it was one of your ranch hands who bailed out Chessa, so he sent me out here."

"One of the…" Mary trailed off, looked at Cash. His face was covered in grime, but as far as Hawk could tell, his expression didn't change from one of grim acceptance.

"What happened to you?" Hawk demanded, seeing the trail of blood seeping out from under the towel Mary held on her arm.

"Shot."

"Shot?" It was dumb to repeat what she'd said, but he was honestly so shocked he didn't know how to comprehend the word. Mary, of all people, being shot, when there was a fire raging, did not compute.

If there had been shooting...

"The fire was first," Mary said, as if reciting math facts. She didn't look at Hawk or Cash now. She stared at a wall. "Cash called the house because they couldn't get out. I ran out, foolishly, and someone shot at us."

Hawk's body went cold. Not just a fire. A whole damn setup. "Where's Anna?"

"She took out the gunman," Cash said, in a similarly detached voice as Mary. "Which allowed Palmer to help get Izzy and me out the window. Then Anna didn't think the gunman was dead, so she was going to find him. Palmer went after her. She's not alone, and the person they're after is hurt. They should be fine."

Well, that was some kind of relief, but he wouldn't be able to fully relax until he saw her. Because *should be* fine didn't necessarily mean much in this whole mess of a case.

They all heard the sirens then and, as if a unit, turned toward the sound. The trio here were too injured, too worn down. Hawk wanted to find Anna, but... She was with Palmer. They could handle it. "I'll grab the EMTs, tell them you're in here."

Cash nodded. Hawk looked down at the dog. "Stay," he

ordered. Pita wagged his tail in Izzy's lap. Then Hawk took off toward the emergency vehicles.

As he approached, Jack was already leading the fray.

"Call came through my radio when I was on my way, but they caught up quick," Jack said as Hawk approached. "Everyone's all right?"

"More or less," Hawk returned. He gestured at the ambulance crew. "Follow me."

As he led the EMTs, Hawk relayed what Mary had said to Jack, noting the hitch in Jack's step even as nothing showed on his face. But as the house came into view, Hawk stopped and turned to Jack.

"I'm going to track down Anna and Palmer. I don't like them being out there on their own."

"No, I don't either. But you need someone with you. Best to travel in pairs."

"I'll catch up with them and then we'll be a trio. I think they'd all be glad to have you in there," Hawk said, nodding toward the house.

Jack turned behind them. "Hart?" Jack barked, and waved the detective over.

Jack was ordering him about before he'd even fully come to a stop.

"Go with Hawk here," Jack said. "There was a gunman on the property. Anna and Palmer might have taken care of him, but let's make sure."

Hawk saw a flicker of irritation cross Hart's face—since Jack was neither his boss nor his superior officer, and not even that many years older, if any, no doubt—but he didn't argue. He nodded. "All right."

Hawk might have felt some sympathy for the man on

getting caught up in something where everyone wanted to be in charge, but he was too intent on finding Anna to care about much else.

"Everyone seems to think there was only one gunman, and Anna took him out, but I haven't seen a gunman, Anna *or* Palmer since I got here."

Hart nodded as they walked across the snowy ground. There were secondary tracks leading away from both house and cabin, and Hawk figured those were the best to follow. If someone had shot Mary going out the back door, it made more sense it was in this direction rather than closer to the front of the property, where emergency personnel now swarmed.

Behind a tree, triangulated to have a good view of the back door *and* the cabin that was on fire, the tracks—Anna's smaller prints, and then no doubt Palmer's larger ones obscuring some as if he came in after her—led to a little pile of snow, as if the gunman had built up a snow cover for himself. Behind the snow, streaks of blood were garish against the white.

The blood led, dripping and smearing, around the fence line. Almost like it was making a big circle around the house—toward the front. The cars maybe? Was the gunman trying to get to an escape vehicle and Anna and Palmer had followed at a distance?

Hawk scanned the horizon, but he saw no one. He glanced at Hart, who'd drawn his weapon as he surveyed the landscape around them.

"We better follow it," Hawk said, focusing on that step, rather than what might lie beyond it. Clearly the shooter was hurt, so wherever Anna and Palmer had disappeared, it was no doubt just tracking the guy. That was all they were doing. To ensure he didn't get away.

It had to be.

Chapter Twenty

Anna was led in a wide circle around her home, the gun
constantly pressed to her head. The man she'd shot, their
own damn ranch hand, limped and crawled and moaned
behind them, but he followed.

"The fire trucks will park more toward the cabin. We
should be able to get in the mudroom door without anyone
seeing us," Tripp said.

Anna tried to whip her head around to glare at him, but
the man with the gun to her head had wrapped his hands
into her hair and painfully kept her looking straight ahead.

Anger, fury, outrage swamped her, even with the gun
pressed to her head, but she tried to breathe past it. *Think.*
They wanted to go into the house? What the hell was this
guy after?

"We want to make sure the sheriff has joined us," the
gunman said. "So we'll wait for the sirens."

But he still pushed her forward, until they were in the
little line of evergreen trees her great-grandmother had
planted before she was born. It gave them cover from anyone who might look out from the house.

She could make a run for it, and she would have if she

wasn't pregnant. She would have risked getting shot for getting away.

But she couldn't risk her baby.

So she had to be smart—instead of smart-mouthed and impetuous, which was what usually got her through a dangerous situation.

They wanted Jack—that was what he meant by waiting for the sheriff. Because this wasn't about her. But then, why was she the target? It didn't make any sense. She tried to think of what the man said. That they'd all pay. That they'd watch her die.

It had to be about Hudson Sibling Solutions, then. There was no other explanation. "So, what, we didn't solve your cold case and now you want us dead? Way to go. That's a rational response."

Okay, maybe she'd always use her smart mouth whether *that* was smart or not.

"You're sure a mouthy one. Makes me feel less badly about choosing you. I thought about the uppity secretary. Figured she'd be the easiest target, but I want her to pay, too. You're the only one who wasn't involved, so you get to be the victim. Aren't you lucky?"

Anna let out a low whistle. "Have you considered therapy, bud? Because this is beyond messed up. It's not even rational revenge. Have you thought about meditation? Getting a puppy? Maybe solving whatever cold case yourself instead of blaming everyone else?"

"Would you shut her up?" the man demanded of Tripp.

"No one can shut her up," Tripp muttered darkly.

She smirked at Tripp, who was looking like he might pass out at any minute. He was pressing his hand to his gunshot wound, but he'd had no help. The guy holding a gun to her head hadn't even offered him some compression for the wound.

"If you die, Tripp, I won't waste one ounce of guilt on being the one who killed you. Traitorous bastard."

The man pressed the gun harder into her head, making Anna's heart flutter—though she told herself he wanted to kill her in front of everyone, which meant she had time to escape. She had time to figure her way out of this.

She had to keep telling herself that. She couldn't just die here. She couldn't. There was too much to live for.

"You won't be alive to feel guilt," the gunman said, shaking her roughly as if that would get her to stop talking.

But sirens sounded in the distance, and that did the trick. Help was on the way. She only had to make it until those sirens got here. Then if she ran, there'd be people to help. She couldn't risk her baby, but if help was nearby...

The gunman pushed her forward so hard, she nearly fell. Which would have given her the opportunity to fight without the gun pressed to her temple, but he caught her by the arm at the last second, gun still pointed right at her head.

She wanted to swear, or fight, but she forced herself to remain still. To be pushed forward toward the side door. She had to be careful, more careful than she'd ever been. For her family and her baby.

Something thudded to the ground. Both the gunman and Anna looked back. Tripp had collapsed into a heap in the snow.

The man looked down at Tripp with some disgust. Then simply shrugged. "Don't need him anymore anyway." With no warning, he reared back and kicked the mudroom door.

It splintered, gave, but didn't fully open. Anna thought about running. He still had the gun pointed at her, but with the second kick, his attention would be focused on the door.

But her family was inside. She might be the target, the one he wanted to kill to hurt them, but he was clearly unhinged enough to kill anyone. And Izzy was in there. What if he decided she was a better target?

Anna's blood ran cold at the thought, so she stayed put while he finished kicking the door open. He gestured her inside with the gun. "Take me to that fancy room where you lie to people and tell them you'll find their lost loved ones. Where you take their money and lie and lie and lie."

Anna sucked in a breath. He wanted her to take him to the living room. Where they tried to make clients feel at home, taken care of. Because they knew the emotional toll of a cold case, of having *no* answers and still having that sliver of hope that answers might be out there.

He had to be a former client, but why hadn't his case stuck out to them? He wasn't Clarence Samuels—the case she'd been away in the rodeo for. He wasn't the man she'd been following when she'd been attacked.

It had to go back further than that. Not just a case she hadn't been involved in, a case before she'd been involved. Jack had started HSS when she'd only been fifteen. She hadn't been allowed to help then.

It had to be a case that far back. She wished she had any way to get that information to Jack. To Hawk. To *anyone*. But she could only walk this man through her family's home and pray they figured this out before something went terribly wrong.

She stepped into the living room. Where she'd watched

cartoons on Saturday mornings before her parents had disappeared. Where she'd gotten into a rage of a fight with Jack over wanting to go to the rodeo, and Palmer had stepped in and smoothed things over. Where she, Mary and Louisa had giggled over boys and first times. Where she'd cried in relief when Grant had come home from deployment. Where she'd walked baby Izzy in circles while Cash slept on the couch because sometimes only Aunt Anna had the right touch to get her to sleep.

Which made her think of her own baby. She didn't bring her hands to her stomach, though she wanted to. *I will do anything to protect you.* It was the only vow she knew how to make.

"No one's here," she offered to the gunman.

"You don't say," the gunman replied. "Yell for them."

Anna hesitated, which earned her a painful jab of the gun into her temple again. She winced.

"Jack?" She tried to sound…different as she called for her brother. Anything to give him a hint all was not right. Afraid, but not hurt. Shaky but not so shaky he'd come running without thinking. "Can you come into the living room? Please?" she added, because *please* wasn't in her normal arsenal.

Please read into that.

She was relieved when no thunder of footsteps started. Instead, Jack slowly entered the living room from the dining room, gun drawn.

But he stopped on a dime when he caught sight of her with a gun pressed to her head. Cash and Mary had appeared behind him, Cash with a gun of his own, Mary and Izzy holding on to each other.

"Drop the guns," the gunman ordered

Jack stilled, that cop look immediately taking over his face. Cash shoved Izzy behind Mary and Mary paled even more than she already had. But Palmer didn't appear. Where was Palmer?

"Now. Or I pull the trigger."

Jack and Cash carefully crouched, placing their guns on the ground, their gazes never leaving the gun on Anna's head.

"Kick them over here."

They did as they were told. So that they stood in a kind of standoff, the family couch between them. No one spoke. They just did what the gunman said, and Anna couldn't meet their gazes. She might break apart.

She had to find a way to get out of this situation, without dying. Without anyone she loved getting hurt.

"Hello," the gunman said, suddenly pleasant. "Remember me?"

No one said anything. Anna saw similar looks of confusion on everyone's face—except Mary.

"You're Darrin Monroe," Mary said calmly. She had her hands clasped behind her, on Izzy's shoulders as if to make sure she was always a shield.

Anna didn't recognize the name, but she could tell Jack did.

"You were one of our first cases," Jack said grimly.

"Yes, and you *failed* me. I want you all here. All of you. For every minute you're not all here, I'll make her death that much more gruesome," he said, shoving the gun hard against Anna's skull as if to prove the point. "Grant and Palmer are missing. I want them here."

"Grant is out of town. I can call Palmer, if you'd like," Mary said calmly, as if she was talking to any client they took on. Offering coffee or a place to stay.

"Yes," Darrin said. "Get Palmer here. We can do this without the other one. He wasn't part of it anyway."

"I thought I was the only one not a part of it?" Anna couldn't help but say to her captor. "Wait, I get it. You're afraid the ex-soldier could kick your ass, but the young woman wasn't a threat to you?"

"That's right. And I was correct, wasn't I?"

Well, unfortunately, she didn't have anything to say to *that*.

"We didn't fail you, Mr. Monroe," Cash said. "We found your son."

"Dead. You found him *dead*. And you were meant to find your sister dead, and never know how or why, but she just couldn't die. So now you'll watch her die. All of you. I want Palmer here, *now*."

HAWK AND HART followed the trail of blood around to the other side of the house. The man shot had clearly hidden here behind the trees for a while because there was a bigger pile of blood. Hawk peered through the trees.

Then he saw a man's body crumpled next to a broken-in door. Fear and worry twined inside him, but he pointed at the body without saying anything. Hart nodded and they moved forward as a unit, both with guns drawn. They arrived at the crumpled body and Hart crouched next to it, checking the man's pulse.

Hart looked up. "Not dead, but nearly."

"Take him to the ambulance."

Hart stood, disapproval waving off him. "Something bad is going on, Steele. You shouldn't go in there alone."

"I'm not," he said, gesturing at the broken open door. "Palmer's right there." Palmer didn't look back at them, his attention on whatever was going on inside the house. Hawk could only hope like hell Anna was safe somewhere beyond what he could see.

"I'm not taking him," Hart muttered. "I'm calling for an EMT. I'll stay here with the body, but I'm coming in after you once he's gone."

Hawk nodded, then stepped inside the mudroom. Palmer spared him only the flicker of a glance and put a finger to his lips in a *be quiet* gesture. Hawk moved forward silently to where Palmer stood. As far as he could tell, there was nothing to see but the long empty hallway.

Once Hawk was close enough, Palmer spoke in a low whisper. "He's got Anna."

Hawk didn't hear the rest of it at first. His head was a buzzing mass of static and panic. But he didn't move. He didn't yell and break things like he immediately wanted to. He breathed and pushed the thought of Anna and their baby as far out of his mind as he could.

"Who has Anna?" Hawk asked, quietly. Calmly. Maybe.

"Some guy. He popped up out of nowhere. I don't know who the hell he is, but he said he wanted to kill her in front of all the siblings to make us Hudsons pay. I followed at a distance. He doesn't know I'm here, but there hasn't been a chance to safely jump in. He's keeping that gun pointed right at her head."

Hawk had to work very hard to filter through all that information and not picture Anna with a gun to her head.

Not think about the very real possibility Anna would say something rash and smart that would make him laugh like a loon.

And get her killed.

Palmer pulled his phone from his pocket. He showed Hawk the screen. "Mary is calling me."

"Go outside and take it. Don't tell her we're out here. Just get all the information you can from her."

Palmer nodded and then hurried outside. Hawk stayed where he was and listened to what was going on in the house. He could hear the low murmur of voices far off, but nothing more. He began to creep forward. Down the hall, as quietly as he could. He forced himself to be slow, methodical, even as he was desperate to run in guns blazing.

But that could get everyone killed, and the only thing that mattered was getting Anna out of this alive.

Alive, alive, alive. He repeated it to himself as he moved with slow, methodical purpose. A mantra. Speaking to any spiritual *whatever* his mother had believed in that would listen.

When Palmer rejoined him, Hawk had only moved maybe a quarter of the way down the hall.

"He's working alone, as far as anyone can tell," Palmer whispered. "Biggest hurdle is he hasn't stopped pointing the gun at Anna's head the whole time. He wants me to come in there. Once we're all there, he's going to kill Anna."

No. Hawk wasn't about to let that happen. He needed a plan and quick.

"Go around the house," he said to Palmer in a low whisper. "Go in from the dining room, but don't go into the living room. You step in, he could just pull that trigger, so you need to be quiet and stay out of sight. I'm going to make noise here. See if I can draw him out."

Palmer nodded.

"Shoot him. The minute I get him clear of Anna, you shoot. Even if I'm in the way."

"Hawk—"

"I mean it. She's number one. I'm collateral damage."

"You think she'd see it that way?"

They didn't have time for this argument, even whispered. "If she's alive, I don't give a damn how she sees it. Now go."

Palmer seemed to consider this and then nodded. "Give me three minutes to get around to that side of the house. Then I'll be ready for whatever happens."

It was Hawk's turn to nod. He watched Palmer go, started the countdown and crept closer to the living room, gun drawn and ready.

He'd save Anna and his baby no matter what it took.

Chapter Twenty-One

Anna was not good at waiting under any circumstances, but the whole gun-to-her-head thing was not making it any easier to keep her mouth shut and just *wait*.

Jack and Cash seemed like they could wait forever. Stoic walls of disapproval, though Anna knew them well enough to see the fury and worry simmering underneath. Mary had that bland expression on her face, but her eyes gave her away. Worry and terror. And Anna could hear Izzy crying behind Mary, though clearly the girl was trying to hold it together.

Anna's heart ached. This was too much for all of them, but definitely more than too much for an eleven-year-old.

The man with the gun, Darrin, was silent and patient. Way more patient than Anna. "Are we really just going to stand here all day waiting for my brother to show up?"

"I could knock you out again, and *then* kill you. Would you prefer that?" Darrin asked mildly.

Anna didn't bother to respond. She just sighed heavily and shifted on her feet. They were killing her. She was hungry, tired and thirsty. She wanted to cry and she wanted to rage.

She really wanted to punch this Darrin guy right in the face. She considered the angles. If she got an elbow up quickly enough, would it dislodge the gun or at least angle it away from her head?

The problem was, any stray bullet could hit any of the people she loved who were all across from them. Was there a way to angle her elbow backward so the gun went that way?

She considered all this, even though she'd considered it a million times. There had to be a way because she didn't think Palmer was coming. He was somewhere on the property, and obviously Mary had told the gunman he was coming, but Palmer had to know what had happened. He'd been outside with her. He'd likely followed her.

If he showed up, she'd be dead and they all knew it. So he very much shouldn't come. Gruesome death or no.

She didn't allow herself to think about Hawk. Maybe he was out there with Palmer. Maybe he was out at his office in Bent, completely unaware what was happening. It didn't matter where he was, as long as he was safe.

"This is taking too long," Darrin said. "I want him here. Now."

"We haven't invented teleportation, bud," Anna muttered.

He yanked her hair so hard she saw stars. Then he kicked out her legs so she fell to her knees. Hard enough she let out a pained hiss, barely managing to suppress a yelp.

"I've had enough of you," he said, shaking the hand that was fisted in her hair as she knelt there trying not to sob in pain.

Jack and Cash had moved forward, but that only prompted

Darrin to shove the gun at the back of her head now. "I will shoot you all. I will kill every last one of you. I'd prefer it to end in emotional agony, but if it's your deaths, it'll be your deaths. You took my son away from me."

"Your son ran away from you," Jack returned. Coldly. "For whatever reasons, we had nothing to do with that or his death. We are sorry for your loss. We know—"

"Shut up!" Darrin screamed.

Anna tried not to wince at all the pain coursing through her. The bite of metal, the burning pain of him yanking her head around by the hair. She just had to breathe and be calm. She just had to survive.

She *had* to.

There was no way she could get away from Darrin's grasp right now, but she wasn't that far away from the guns her brothers had kicked over. She couldn't reach for one, but if she could get her leg out from under her without Darrin paying her any attention, maybe she could pull one toward her.

She shifted her weight, whimpering in pain. She *was* in pain, but the whimpering was put on.

"Stop squirming," Darrin ordered, pulling her hair again.

Her gasp of pain was real this time. "I can't sit on my knees like this," Anna said, wriggling even though it hurt like hell. But she managed to get into a seated position, her legs spread out in front of her. Darrin still had a grip on her hair and a gun pointed at her head.

She couldn't tell where Darrin was looking, but if it was at her siblings, maybe she could move her leg enough to get the gun.

She looked over at Jack and Cash. Their gazes were

firmly on Darrin. No doubt watching her would be too hard on them. And they were looking for ways to eliminate the threat.

But Mary was watching her. Anna tried to use her eyes to get a message across. She looked at Mary. Then the gun. Then Darrin. Over and over again.

"Mr. Monroe," Mary said in that prim hostess voice of hers. Clearly trying to hold Darrin's attention so Anna could try to reach the gun. "I know you're upset and rightfully so. You lost a son. You want someone to blame."

"*You* are to blame! If you'd found him sooner, he would have been alive."

Anna wished she knew anything about this case, but when Jack had first started HSS, Anna had been so infuriated he was keeping her out of it that she'd refused to have *anything* to do with it. Fifteen wasn't an easy age for anyone, let alone a girl who'd lost both parents and was being raised by her grumpy older brother.

"Your son made his choices, Mr. Monroe. That isn't on us," Jack said firmly. Maybe a little coldly. Even though Anna knew Jack took every failure too much to heart.

She inched her foot closer to the gun. Darrin's grip on her hair kept her from being able to move much farther. She wouldn't be able to get either gun to herself, but she could kick out. Maybe hit one of them. Maybe send it back toward her brothers.

But she'd have to time it perfectly. Have to somehow get Darrin to stop pointing his gun at her head, even if he still held on to her hair. Would that be enough time?

It would have to be. "You know, I don't think Palmer's coming," Anna announced. Her brothers whipped their gazes to her, as if she was insane. And, well, maybe they weren't wrong. But she just kept talking.

If there was anything she was good at, it was talking herself into problems her brothers solved. Right? Why not lean into it?

"He shows up, he knows you'll kill me. So why would he come? You thought that one through, Darrin?"

He jerked her hair again, and she winced at the pain that shot through her body. But she didn't stop. She couldn't stop. She needed just a few seconds where that gun wasn't pointed at her head.

"Honestly, this plan is just ridiculous. You should have kept trying to kill me when I was alone. Needing an audience has just dragged everything out. For every second we stand around here *waiting*, there's another cop figuring it out. They could be surrounding the house by now."

"Jesus, Anna," Cash muttered.

"I don't care about cops. I don't care if they catch me. I care about your suffering."

"I'm not suffering. I'm just bored," Anna returned, heaving out a sigh that allowed her to move her foot that much closer to the gun without Darrin looking down. "Aren't you bored, Darrin? Let's get this show on the road."

"Shut up. Just…shut up," he yelled, shaking her harder and harder until she had to shut up or she'd just scream in pain.

"Just let her go," Jack said in that authoritarian cop voice. "HSS is my creation. Your son was my responsibility. If you found our results lacking, you're mad at me. You're blaming me. Focus your anger on *me*."

Anna groaned. Loudly. "Oh my God, Jack. Why do you

always have to be the martyr? Do you really think you're *that* important?"

Jack straightened, frowned at her. "It's my responsibility. HSS was created because of *me*."

Anna didn't know if Jack was playing along or if this was a real argument, but it didn't really matter. "Mr. Oldest Brother always thinking everything is his responsibility. Well, we're adults, too, you know? HSS is *all* of ours."

"You weren't even involved in this case, Anna. You were fifteen years old. Let her go, Mr. Monroe."

"Yeah, do what Jack says. He thinks everyone has to," Anna said, sounding as aggrieved as she possibly could.

"I cannot believe you're arguing at a time like this," Mary scolded—and Anna knew for sure *she* was playing along. Since Darrin couldn't see Anna's face from where he stood behind her, Anna grinned at Mary.

"And I can't believe you're making it all about you, Anna," Cash added. He wasn't smiling at her; in fact, he was frowning with all that fatherly disapproval he used on Izzy. But she knew it wasn't disapproval over what he was actually saying, but that this was her ploy. "Typical baby-of-the-family behavior."

"Shut up!" Darrin screamed, clearly losing whatever tenuous grasp on control he had, thanks to the sibling bickering. Who knew that would someday come in handy? "Fine! That's what you want. I'll just kill her. I'll just kill all of you!" But Darrin made a small mistake in the anger and frustration Anna had led him to. He lifted the gun from Anna's head and pointed it at Jack. "And you'll be the only survivor to grieve."

But the gun not being pointed at her anymore meant that everyone else could move. She was held by her hair, but she managed to kick out, which sent a gun skittering toward Jack.

Jack caught the gun, but before he could pick it up off the ground, a gunshot rang out. And all hell broke loose.

HAWK WATCHED AS Anna baited the man. He wasn't sure which feeling was more prevalent: one of frustration that she was *baiting* the man with the gun to her head, or one of awe that it was working.

Only Anna Hudson would come up with this ploy, for good or for ill.

Darrin was getting more and more angry, and while that made the chances of Darrin shooting Anna all the more possible, it was also making his arms shake. So if he pulled the trigger, it might not be aimed perfectly at Anna's head.

Then the siblings all joined in. At first Hawk was so angry that they weren't taking this seriously, he almost stepped into the fray. But when he caught Anna's profile grinning at Mary he realized this was some kind of…trick.

What the hell was wrong with the Hudsons? And why did he want to laugh in the midst of all this? That they would use the most unbelievable of arguments to distract a gunman. It was *insane*.

But it was working. Darrin was getting more and more red-faced and shaky. Hawk couldn't let this go on. He had to act. He was about to make a noise, just so Darrin would whirl on him, but Darrin started screaming. Palmer appeared behind his brothers, but it was clear he couldn't get off a good shot that didn't risk Anna.

So it was up to Hawk.

Everything happened too fast as Darrin pointed his gun at Jack. Hawk seized the moment. He had to. He pulled the trigger and shot. Then swore because he'd been so worried about hitting Anna, he'd missed Darrin entirely. The bullet crashed through the damn window.

But it shocked the gunman enough to let go of Anna and whirl, which allowed Hawk to get off another shot that landed.

Unfortunately, so did Darrin.

The explosion of pain was a surprise. Hawk knew all about pain, but he'd never been shot and he didn't know what this felt like. He tried to stay upright, tried to make sure he saw what happened to Darrin, to make sure Anna got away.

He saw the front door splinter open, cops rushing in.

Then his body couldn't seem to hold him up any longer. Worse than the blow to the head. Worse than that one time someone had tried to run him over with their car. Worse than everything he could think of—physically, anyway.

It was just overwhelming. A black cloud of horribleness and he couldn't seem to move. Or was he moving? Was he writhing in pain or as still as a corpse?

Was he a corpse?

He could only lie there and stare at the ceiling, wondering if he was still alive. He knew there was a commotion, but he couldn't seem to hear it. Couldn't seem to get his mouth to work. Was this death?

He'd watched his mother slip away. It wasn't like this.

She'd made horrible breathing noises. Muttered about going home. She'd slipped away.

He felt like he was being ripped in half. No homecoming. Just blackness.

Then he saw Anna crouch over him. She was yelling at people. Crying. Everything about her looked wild and desperate.

But she was alive, and wasn't that all that mattered? He couldn't care less what happened to him, as long as she was okay. He wanted to reach for her, tell her it was all okay. Maybe he did. He wasn't sure.

She disappeared for a few seconds as strangers knelt over him. He was almost certain they were EMTs, and that they were working on him. Maybe they'd bring him back to life, since he was most assuredly dead.

Because it couldn't be *good* that he didn't feel anything they were doing to him. Then he was moving. Or being moved? None of it quite made sense, but Anna was back in his vision. Tears streaming down her face. She really was just the prettiest thing, but he didn't want her crying over him. How on earth had he gotten so lucky?

Probably just another tally in the whole being-dead column. Hawk Steele hadn't had luck a day in his life...except that he'd had the best mother. And then Anna.

Finally something pierced the hazy world that surrounded him, a sharp bolt of pain. And then Anna's voice.

"Don't you *dare* die on me, you absolute jerk." Anna, sharp and demanding, just like she should be.

"Love you too, Blondie," he said, or tried to. He didn't feel fully within his body, but he kept his gaze on Anna's hazel eyes as long as he could.

She was okay and that was all that mattered. Her and the baby. Okay. Taken care of.

Who needed him, anyway?

Chapter Twenty-Two

Anna was held back as the medics rolled Hawk away on a stretcher. She fought anyone who tried to hold her back, but there were too many people. Every person she managed to shove away, a new person came in to grab her.

Until she was finally met with the brick wall that was Grant. He looked right at her with dark eyes. Their father's eyes. "Stop," he said. Forcefully. Sharply. When everyone else had been pleading.

And she didn't know what else to do, so she stopped. Looked up at him and he pulled her into a tight hug, when out of all of them, Grant was the least likely to hug *anyone*. She'd barely even seen him hold Dahlia's hand.

But he held her there and all that spiraling panic stilled into just…straight-up fear. But Grant held her tight and spoke calmly and low in her ear.

"There is no point going in the ambulance. He'll have to go straight into the ER. Dahlia and I will drive you to the hospital so you can wait more comfortably."

"But—"

"No buts." He shifted her so he had his arm around her shoulders and started propelling her forward.

"But Pita…"

"Cash is handling the dogs. The EMTs cleared him and Izzy to stay home and take it easy, and they stitched Mary up. Just a scratch—she doesn't even need to go in. Palmer and Louisa are going to stay here with them and keep an eye on things." Grant just kept leading her to his truck, where Dahlia stood waiting for them.

They ushered her into the back of the truck, and Dahlia climbed in next to her. She held Anna's hand the entire interminable ride to the hospital. They led her to the waiting room and didn't let her talk to anyone. They kept her in a bubble, in a cocoon.

But none of it mattered until someone told her…

Dahlia continued to hold Anna's hand, though she realized now it was less about comforting her and more about keeping her still while Grant talked to various hospital employees.

When Grant returned, it was with a doctor. Anna scowled at them both, but she didn't fight off the doctor as the woman checked her out. She sat still and miserable and let the woman examine her scalp and ask droning questions about how she felt.

Like my entire heart was ripped out, thanks a lot.

Eventually the doctor left. Anna didn't even bother to ask what the consensus was. She wasn't leaving this seat until someone was ready to let her see Hawk.

After a considerable amount of time, hours, days, she didn't know, someone came to stand in front of her. She could tell by the shoes it wasn't a doctor, so she didn't look up at first. She really didn't want to deal with anyone. No doubt her family or a cop, but she just…wanted to be alone in her own horrible thoughts to wallow in fear and awful things. In the bubble, in the cocoon where she could live in denial. Forever.

But when she forced herself to look up, it was Jack standing there. He looked rough. As rough as back when Mom and Dad had first disappeared. When he'd been left in charge of five kids and a mystery they still hadn't solved.

How did he stand it?

Without saying a word, Grant got up and let Jack take his seat. So Jack sat next to her, looked right at her, and there was a softness, a vulnerability there in his gaze she wasn't sure he'd ever allowed her to see before. "I'm sorry," he said, his voice rough.

At first she assumed it was just the thing to be said. *Sorry the man you love might be dead because you're such a horrible person.* But she realized this was Jack and that was a guilty "I'm sorry."

She stared at him. "You... You aren't honestly blaming yourself."

He took a sharp breath in. "I created HSS because I needed to *do* something. I should have considered that it might eventually put us in danger. And it has, over and over again, but never like this. You became a target because of a choice *I* made."

She stared at him for a good minute. Then she shook her head. "Jack, you are an honest-to-God fool."

He got that pinched look on his face she often brought out in him, but even if he didn't mean to, he made her realize something very important. "The only person's fault this is is the man who couldn't handle his son's death. And I can't imagine. Don't want to." Her hand rested on her belly, almost like a reflex. Like she could protect the little bundle of cells in there. "But his grief isn't our fault. His break with reality isn't our fault. His violence isn't our fault. Deep down, I hope you know that."

He didn't say anything to that, but that was how she knew he was trying to take it on board. That he wasn't arguing with her.

"I love you, and I've never thanked you for everything you've done for us. I've only ever given you a hard time. It's all I've ever been any good at."

"Well, I guess that saved our lives today, Annie."

She opened her mouth to argue, but then she just kind of…laughed. Maybe it had. But Hawk was still… She swallowed. Hard. "I don't know how to lose him, Jack. I barely had him."

Jack nodded, then took her hand. "He isn't gone yet."

A few minutes later a nurse came over. "Are any of you family of Hawk Steele?"

Anna stood. "I'm his fiancée." Because they were getting married. They were going to raise this baby together. And have more. Yes, they'd have more and be happy and build a house at the Hudson Ranch and…and… Everything would be okay.

It had to be.

HAWK FIGURED THIS strange black floaty area he was in had to be death. Hell, maybe. He probably deserved it. There was blackness and no pain and no escape. Just this weird nothing.

And then he heard something that was pain. Because he hadn't heard it in years.

His mother's voice. *Hawk.*

He tried to see through the black. See her face. Find her. His heart scrambled and none of it made sense, except his yearning to hear it again. To see her again. "Mom."

But it was just her voice, whispering around him. *Go on home, baby.*

"I don't have a home."

Sure you do.

And then it was gone. Her voice. Any sense he'd had of her in this black world of nothingness. But then he heard… Anna's voice. Felt something squeeze his hand, and he knew it was her.

His home.

He blinked his eyes open and was met with hazel ones. The ones he'd met across the smoky barroom and felt something. Immediately. The moment their gazes had locked.

He opened his mouth, but whatever came out wasn't words.

"Shh. Give yourself time," she said, brushing a kiss across his hand in hers. Things went black. Then she was there again. He was in and out. Then he dozed off. Then he woke up.

He wasn't sure how long it took, but eventually he was awake and with it enough to remember what had happened, to understand where he was and how to talk again.

He supposed he hadn't *really* heard his mother's voice. It had been a dream or something. But he also knew of all the spiritual things his mother had believed, him hearing her voice would have been one of them.

He turned his head. Anna was still there, though she'd dozed off in the chair she'd pulled next to his bed. She was holding his hand limply. She was pale and no doubt needed a good meal and some good sleep.

"Blondie."

She jumped straight to alertness at impressive speed. "You're awake. You're talking."

"Yeah. I guess I'm going to live, huh?"

She leaned forward, studying every inch of him. "That's what they say. I guess the only worry now is infection." And clearly she *was* worried, because she just sat there staring at him, holding his hand like it was her only lifeline.

And if he wasn't mistaken, guilt lurking deep in those hazel eyes.

"You know as well as I do, someone was going to get shot in that scenario. I'd rather it be me than you. A hundred times over."

She swallowed. "Doesn't mean I have to like it," she croaked.

He could tell she was close to tears, but he didn't want that. He wanted this to be…positive. Moving toward happy. "Besides, now you owe me one. You can pay me back. In the bedroom. Once I'm up for that sort of thing again. So, like, tomorrow."

She rolled her eyes. "In your dreams."

He tried to pull her hand up to his mouth but couldn't quite make it. He sighed. "What about this Darrin guy?"

"Arrested. Hart isn't sure he'll be considered fit to stand trial. But he'll get help if he isn't, so that's something. Tripp, the ranch hand, he's in a coma, I guess. Chessa's…missing. No one's sure if she's dead or alive. They'll keep looking for her, though."

Hawk nodded but felt tired again. Worn to the bone, and

like he'd doze off again. "You should go home. Get some real rest."

"Like I could rest with you in here. I'm not going anywhere for the duration. So, you want me to rest, you're going to have to recover fast."

He didn't know whether he was amused or resigned, he was so tired. "I'll see what I can do."

"Hawk."

His eyes had closed on him, but he managed to open them again and look at her. She was very grim and serious.

"The minute you can stand for more than five minutes at a time, we're going down to the courthouse and getting married."

"Thought you wanted a real wedding."

"I don't care anymore. I just want to be married."

He saw all the pain and worry in her eyes. And he wanted to give her everything. Because she'd given him everything. Love, a family. Home. "I'm going to have to insist on a white dress. Your family. And a honeymoon."

"I'll do whatever you want," she said, so solemnly. So seriously.

He looked at her and laughed. Maybe it was the painkillers. Maybe it was just knowing her. "No, you won't. And thank God for that."

Her mouth curved. "Well, I'll try for a little while, anyway."

"Okay, maybe we should take a bet on how long that lasts." Pain was slithering through the cloud of weird exhaustion, and he tried to find a comfortable position.

She snorted, but then she stood and leaned over him. She brushed his hair off his forehead, in a move that poignantly reminded him of his mother. And he remembered the blackness.

"I heard my mom's voice," he heard himself say, though he hadn't thought he'd meant to tell her that. Surely it sounded way too out there.

Anna stilled and tears filled her eyes. "What did she say?"

"She told me to go home."

"Not, like, heavenly home, I hope."

"No." He looked up at her. Anna had changed the course of his life. And thank God, because whatever came next with her—marriage, kids, a *life*—it was better than anything he'd planned or hoped for. "No, I think she meant you."

A tear fell over onto her cheek, then dripped down onto his. Anna wiped it away, then leaned down and pressed her mouth to his. "I love you," she murmured.

"I love you, too."

And when they got married a few weeks later, she wore a white dress and Pita wore a bow tie. All her family was there, and they did it at the ranch, rather than a courthouse. Izzy was the flower girl, and there were quite a few canine guests.

And as they repeated their "I dos," a hawk swooped down and perched on the eaves of the house, as if looking down at them. Anna squeezed his hand and grinned at him, because as much as he resisted all the woo-woo stuff his mother had loved, Anna had leaned into it, and was now constantly talking to him about spirit guides and ghosts and all that other nonsense.

Which didn't feel so much like nonsense in the moment.

So, with what felt like his mother watching, he promised himself to Anna and his baby.

Because Hawk Steele considered himself a man who rolled with the punches—and Anna Hudson, now Anna Hudson-Steele, and their baby-to-be was the best sucker punch he'd ever get.

* * * * *

MILLS & BOON MODERN IS
HAVING A MAKEOVER!

The same great stories you love,
a stylish new look!

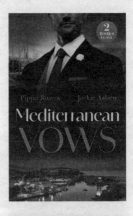

Look out for our brand new look
COMING JUNE 2024

MILLS & BOON

COMING SOON!

We really hope you enjoyed reading this book.
If you're looking for more romance
be sure to head to the shops when
new books are available on

Thursday 6th
June

To see which titles are coming soon, please visit
millsandboon.co.uk/nextmonth

afterglow BOOKS

Afterglow Books are trend-led, trope-filled books with diverse, authentic and relatable characters and a wide array of voices and representations.

Experience real world trials and tribulations, all the tropes you could possibly want (think small-town settings, fake relationships, grumpy vs sunshine, enemies to lovers).

All with a generous dose of spice in every story!

OUT NOW

Two stories published every month.

To discover more visit:

Afterglowbooks.co.uk

LET'S TALK
Romance

For exclusive extracts, competitions and special offers, find us online:

f MillsandBoon

X @MillsandBoon

◉ @MillsandBoonUK

♪ @MillsandBoonUK

Get in touch on 01413 063 232